"mesmerizing"

THE AUTOBIOGRAPHY
OF BUSTER KEATON

Alan Ramón Clinton

The
AUTOBIOGRAPHY
of
BUSTER KEATON

ALAN CLINTON

ACKNOWLEDGEMENTS

The author gives a tip of his pork pie hat to the following people and institutions who gave him aid and/or inspiration in the production of this book:

Atlas Press, Stephanie Bass, Donna Clinton, James Clinton, Posin' Hair fo' Chinos, Columbia University Press, Matt Culp, Dorsch Gallery, Doubleday and Co., Angela Flury, Charlie Franco, Eden Grey, John Paul Hand, Harvard University Press, Kelly Huddleston, Queen Lear, Walter K. Lew, Mary Muffle-Holds, O Miami Poetry Festival, Penguin Books, Quadron, Robert B. Ray, Trent Reznor, Trevor Richardson, Pauline Réage, David A. Ross, Fly-On Shit-On, Dina Smith, Demanda Trailer, Michael Uebel, University of Michigan Press, Samuel Weiser

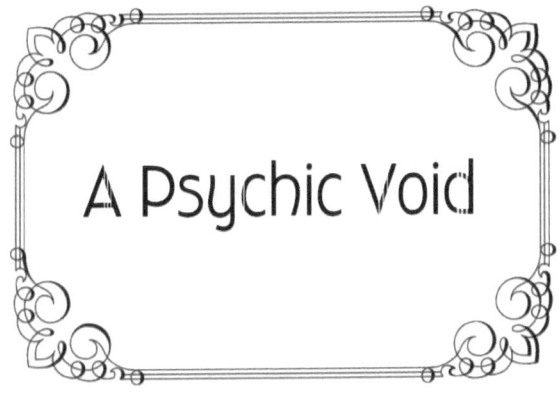

A Psychic Void

My girlfriend of the time told one of her students that she was dating someone who reminded her of Buster Keaton. Then she told me about the incident, perhaps thinking I would find it amusing. In actuality, it opened up a gigantic void inside, something akin to an air bubble (I am certain that Lacan has a diagram of this in one of his seminars). Although I didn't admit it to her at the time, I had never actually seen a Buster Keaton film. In fact, I wasn't sure if I had ever seen Buster Keaton himself. I had heard the name several times of course - descriptions and allusions - and these instances always evoked the image of a hobo in a tattered top hat, thick-lipped and unshaven. Whenever this image came, I was pretty sure it was just something my psyche had thrown together, but even though I knew it was wrong, I couldn't stop the image from coming. What is even more bizarre, this image had the effect of so absorbing my attention that whenever someone began to talk about Keaton it sounded like someone talking underwater. I would actually get that underwater seasick feeling you get when people are talking about something you feel like you should know but don't - and it's way too late to admit your ignorance. "I'll inform myself later," you tell yourself, but you never do.

So when my girlfriend mentioned the incident, I had no way of knowing if she was referring merely to a shared physical appearance, or to something more significant about our lives. Although I put it off for some time, perversely allowing the void to become larger, I eventually went in search of my doppelgänger. We did look a lot alike: the lazy eyelids, the prominent nose, the questionable posture. As I investigated further, his life slowly became an obsession. I found that we had much more in common than mere appearances, that he could serve as something of a guru to me. I know this probably doesn't reflect very well on my own ego integrity, that I would so quickly jettison *my* self-image to create parallels with Keaton, to start asking of Buster the "What would Jesus do?" question, but I've done a lot of other stupid things in the past - perhaps none of this magnitude. "Besides," I told myself, "Cultural Studies (my chosen field) has suggested that the integrated ego is overrated, that overly clinging to it may even be a symptom of fascist personality traits."

Perhaps, if I was diligent enough, I could even develop homoerotic feelings for him, which my colleagues could one day analyze, maybe publish papers on.

As you can tell, I'm pretty good at looking on the bright side of things, which other people call "making excuses." A girlfriend tells me to exercise; I reply that "self-improvement is a slippery slope." If a psychic void opens up in my life, I figure it is the academic's equivalent to a mid-life crisis. Except rather than being embarrassing, you can play it off Antonin Artaud style: "Someone who does not know depression, who has never felt the soul encroached upon by the body, invaded by its weakness, is incapable of perceiving any truth about the nature of man." Take that you well adjusted freaks. Nevertheless, if I was really going to become a doppelgänger of Buster Keaton, I'd have to convince the well adjusted freaks who pay me that I was doing something related to Cultural Studies. That shouldn't be hard, since such a field should, if one takes its name seriously (and believe me we do), apply to almost everything. It was Thanksgiving break, and I spent it breaking up with my girlfriend so that I could watch all the films of Buster Keaton - at least the ones that he wrote and directed, when he really became Buster - because I respected her acumen about people so much I knew she must know something about me that I didn't. Plus I had to come up with a 'thesis' that was sufficiently obscure enough to get me some time off.

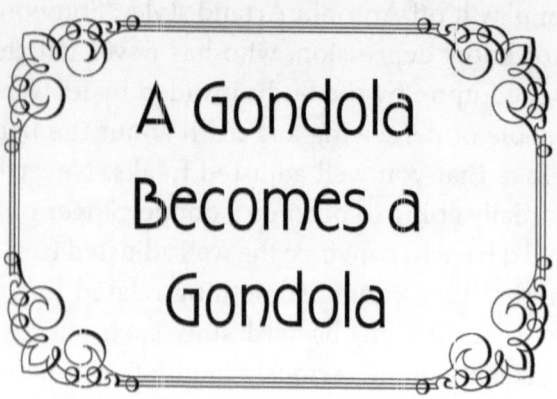

A Gondola Becomes a Gondola

Over break, which I spent with my parents, I made the breakthrough I needed. Since there's only a week of classes after Thanksgiving, I figured I could just email my students the final assignment and the administration my proposal - which would undoubtedly be accepted - for a paid leave of absence the next semester to study the life and work of Keaton. I needed to make it to Niles, California, where I falsely assumed Buster started, and I needed to make it fast.

The breakthrough came when I watched a film called *The Balloonatic* (1923, Joseph M. Schenck), in which Buster becomes the navigator of a hot air balloon when someone accidentally cuts the ropes while he is pasting a "Good Luck!" pennant on it. Making the best of an unforeseen situation Buster tries to cook some dinner, burning out the bottom of the balloon's gondola which necessitates hanging on for dear life to the gondola's sides from below. However what was left, in fact, according to Aristotelian categories, could not be rightly called a gondola because it does not possess all the requisite characteristics for the gondola category,

namely, a bottom. At first I thought a rhetorical analysis of Keaton's films might prove a suitable means of escaping my university duties, but luckily I avoided this stale approach to my inner void and to Buster himself by watching the rest of the film.

You see, later in the movie, after crashing the balloon in the wilderness and winning the love of a lady hunter, the last scene of the movie shows Buster and his now lady hunter lover paddling a canoe merrily down the river whose current is heading towards a waterfall the existence of which neither one of them seems to be aware of - perhaps this could lead to a gender studies project on marriage relationships as reflected in comedy. Then I remembered my old professor, with whom I still argue in my dreams, who said the following, "The extraordinary contagiousness of cultural studies lies precisely in its generalizing power and finds its representative in Roland Barthes' *S/Z*, which uses one Balzac novella (and a minor one at that) to make an argument about narrative in general. Having seen that approach in action, cultural studies scholars have ignored its lesson and insisted on using it as a model for case-by-case analyses. But if you understand Barthes' points about storytelling, you do not need to see them worked out with a hundred other examples." Although I was always one of his worst students, even I could do better than reduce Buster into a semiotic whipping post. Because if that was all Buster was worth, then that would be all that I was worth. I would fill my psychic void alright, but with shit. I hoped and prayed that we were both worth more than that, and continued to watch the movie.

Suddenly, instead of the two of them crashing over the waterfall, you see the boat floating in mid-air! Buster has reattached the hot-air balloon, sans gondola, to the canoe they are in, thus restoring a 'gondola' to the balloon that disappeared earlier in the film! In other words, the movie is not just a comedic short, but a magical ritual in which one thing, the gondola, is converted into a canoe and back into itself again. A gondola is converted into a gondola. A transformation that, due to its utter uselessness on the level of language (if you told someone that you had magically transformed a gondola into a gondola, they would think you were crazy) is far more fantastic than anything recorded in Ovid's *Metamorphosis*. I remembered a book I read in graduate school, when one of my advisors was wisely advising me not to write a dissertation on Poetics, Tarotics and Magick, penned by a certain Karl Abel. In *On the Antithetical Meaning of Primal Words*, Abel argued - I had remembered the words to this very day - that "Man was not in fact able to acquire his oldest and simplest concepts except as contraries to their contraries, and only learnt by degrees to separate the two sides of an antithesis and think of one without conscious comparison to the other." Since I was never able, for instance, to think of a guitar without automatically having the image of a ukulele enter my head, I felt as if my professor, via Abel, was not so subtly implying that I had not yet surpassed the primitive state of human progress. Needless to say, this quote, this subtle implication, this slap in the face set me back for months on my own dissertation, and still haunts me today whenever I wake up and try and do things, which for me is like trying to shuffle cards in the rain. As the cards get more and more soaked, shuffling them begins to resemble working with plaster rather than the crisp coitus that one remembers from our parents' basement casinos. All the things I have to do are made of cards while it's raining outside - indoors too - except somehow it's not raining for everyone else when they shuffle their cards. And when I have to make decisions, I'm looking at a deck of tarot cards while everyone else is playing a basic game of five-card draw. And since the cards are wet, the tarot cards look as if Salvador Dali had painted them. Seeing this I have to go to the nearest Salvador Dali museum and purchase the tarot deck that he actually painted so I can compare them, as they get wet as well, with the ones that he didn't paint that have been wet for longer. All these wet cards, psychologically speaking, put me at a distinct disadvantage when attempting to stay competitive in the global marketplace.

And then I remember going camping with my dad when I was a kid, a teenager, and a primitive adult. We went camping because it was cheap and easier to hide from the police when you were out in the woods. Every single time, without fail, as I would hopelessly try to help him set up the tent, he would say (unless it was actually raining), "Now remember, this would be a lot more difficult if it was raining." Except for me it always was raining, always has been, and probably always will. It's okay, don't worry, being bad at life doesn't mean you can't enjoy it. I'm not Bob Dylan with the rain falling down on my shoes, paying dues, etc. It's just that I've learned to enjoy, when others are not present to do things for me, the bad version of things. And though difficulties do present themselves, the bad version of things is usually a lot more fun than the good version - assuming no injuries are involved.

The
Magic Linguist

Then suddenly it hit me. Someone who made such brilliant comedies that not only were funny but were endless explorations of man's haplessness with respect to modern spatiality - something I could definitely identify with - must also be hiding secret, yet deathly important messages in his films. Intuiting that very few people read books on linguistics, Buster of course realized that he could hypnotize people with his theories via the cinematic medium, and that they would learn the truth without knowing they knew it. The truth would be inside them, which is all that matters.

Here is what Keaton showed me, though suffice it to say I did not put it in quite these terms to the Cultural Studies department. In addition to providing entertainment and existential meanings for those who are into that kind of thing, Keaton was secretly refuting the theories of Karl Abel, showing that primitive magic was indeed superior to the "two sides of the antithesis," that the purpose of magic was precisely that of turning a gondola into a gondola. After all, his father was a performer as well, who was good friends with Houdini, suggesting not only a magical kinship but a magical lineage that went back, who knows how long? It was Houdini, after all, who, when he saw toddling Keaton fall down a flight of stairs immediately expressed, not concern, but instead proclaimed, "That was a real Buster!" It was as if Houdini himself had sensed Keaton's powers and, knowing that the child would be unhurt by the fall, proclaimed the word that Buster would become. A 'buster' would become a Buster and that is exactly what happened. I would set out to prove that all of Keaton's films were re-enactments of this magical act which, just as with every other true ritual, grows in power each time it is performed. My professor's admonishment about repetition applied only to non-sacred interpretations. I would of course begin when Keaton became completely his own writer/director, escaping the influence of Fatty Arbuckle who was undoubtedly not fully aware of the Keaton family's magical tradition, and in addition to proving a thesis I was becoming more and more convinced of, I decided to live like Keaton as much as possible to understand what the master could teach me.

I know it's making me start to sound like one of those guru junkies we all love to hate, the ones out in California, especially in the Bay area, chock-full of those people whose philosophy is the exact opposite of "Self improvement is a slippery slope." And, as we all know, except the junkies of course, the reason not to improve yourself is so obvious it is almost embarrassing to have to spell it out: but basically, once you improve one thing, you will inevitably find something else that needs improvement, and this can be, as you will understand, very addictive. So, guru junkies are, at first glance, sort of like the hillbillies I grew up with. They work their full time jobs but instead of coming home, drinking moonshine, hunting, and watching TV, they spend all their spare hours following various leaders, all of whom are granted a 'spiritual' value, although it is not quite clear to me how so many things can be spiritual - and it wouldn't be clear to you if you heard some of the things the gurus and their junkies espouse - or why some of the gurus don't just cancel each other out, spiritually at least. But then again, I'm not a guru junkie, so I wouldn't understand the nuances of guru addiction.

But on the other hand, if guru junkies are the sluts of spirituality, maybe they bear other resemblances to the rest of us. To follow in the footsteps of Buster was to risk, a very slight risk in my estimation, that the devotion I felt toward him might transfer to others and put me on the guru junkie circuit. It was definitely a risk worth taking. Plus, I was already starting to learn from Buster that you really can't control who you fall in love with, and if I was going to be spending much time in Niles (once known as the Hollywood of Northern California) and the surrounding area, a guru junkie romance was a mathematical probability. Then I'd have to learn their ways because one thing you always want to do is make your woman flutter her eyes at you - always and every day as if for the first time at the end of a Keaton film.

One Week
for Liftoff

In *One Week* (1920, Metro), Keaton's first movie that he produced himself, a newlywed couple receives the gift of a new house from their uncle. Only it's one of those new 'portable' houses that come in a box which you have to build on your own. If the uncle had known Buster in the least, he would have known that such a gift could only result in a Frank Gehry house *avant la lettre*. A house that when the first major storm comes, is a house spinning on its axis leaving Keaton nothing to do but try to push it back in place, which of course results in him hanging on for dear life as it spins round and round, which is what life, if it were a house, does to all of us who aren't good at hiding it. So what do we do when we move the house from the wrong address to the right address, transporting it on train tracks and, when we see a train coming, manage to move it over to the other set of tracks just in time - for a train coming the other way to demolish it? We stick a "For Sale" sign in the rubble, and spin around with our bride to walk away to a new life, only to spin around once more to attach the directions for the next couple who must, in order to be happy, magically transform spinning into spinning.

It was sort of lucky that I had cancelled all of my classes the previous week, which my students have a habit of skipping anyway. Teaching at a private school, which I had never attended in my student days, I learned a lot of things. For instance, private school students have absolutely no problem telling you that your classes are boring. It stings the first twenty or thirty times, even making you nostalgic for the time when you believed a graduate degree, no matter how pointless the subject, would get you far in life. That one day you would have students who were as interested in the subjects you taught as you were when, at a tender young age, you thought "The Love Song of J. Alfred Prufrock" had everything to say about life as you lived it. But something, probably something like pornography or easy access to consumer items preceded by the letter "I," as in "me," "mine," not yours, changed all that. So like I said it stings the first forty or fifty times you find out your classes are boring but then you eventually get used to it and, through a medicine regimen that 'abilifies' you, things start to smooth out. You cancel a lot more classes, cool with the fact that they are indeed boring and pointless, and understand that students, when given vacation, follow the Tao of "the existence of this vacation has inconvenienced my travel plans so much that I must take even more vacation either before or after (sometimes both) than my private university has allowed." You have never, after all, been one to interfere with those who are "on the path," as they call it.

As far as "getting far in life goes," I had traveled

far in distance, but not in any other way. All the way from Tennessee to Boston (Wellesley) I had traveled with books of portable boredom. Interestingly, Buster Keaton's *College* (1927, United Artists) specifically takes place in California where I was headed, a strange detail to put at the start of the film because there are colleges everywhere, and of all of Keaton's films, one about college would seemingly be the most portable in terms of illusions of mise-en-scène. The only thing the film's "location" allows for is for things to begin with a rainy day, no, make that a hurricane rain, that Buster and his mother suffer on their way to high school graduation - a wry joke at the expense of "Sunny California" and perhaps a signal that for Buster, making films had nothing to do with the glamour of Hollywood and everything about passing along the "arcane knowledge" we used to associate with college but which in Buster's case had to do with the alchemical goal of making a working love catapult - the mechanism I would soon discover was Buster's secret weapon - and its relation to refuting Karl Abel's *On the Primal Meaning of Antithetical Words* by causing things to transform themselves into themselves.

So even though my university frowns upon the practice, I was glad I cancelled that whole week of classes for the reasons stated above *and* because it gave me plenty of time to watch the films before announcing my trip to Niles, CA during Thanksgiving dinner itself, that meal when all great things are announced.

Troubles On the Home Front

The other thing was, after I had obtained Buster's films, it was great to have 'work' to be doing that required nothing but me sitting in my room and not moving. This is not only because I am fairly lazy, not to mention uncoordinated which makes moving in general quite dangerous, but also since I find my family pretty intimidating, especially my father. He had done a stretch many years ago and then, back when it was still possible to do this with a criminal record - thanks to our need to defeat the Soviet Union - he had gone to school and gotten a job as a chemical engineer helping make sure the nuclear plant wouldn't explode while it enriched enough uranium to ensure that Mutually Assured Destruction would prevent World War III. "I'm a one issue voter," my dad used to say, "and that issue is survival." And while I did not doubt his integrity or desire to keep our family safe, the way he looked right through me whenever he said this did not fill me with warm fuzzy feelings.

As I watched Buster's films, I began to feel like *he* was more like my father, at least taxonomically speaking, than my genetic father. Dad, thinking it was better to be safe than sorry, wanted to teach me how to break rocks in prison, just in case. While one would think that there's not much technique involved in this, other than brute force, I could never get the hang of it. He would bring rocks home from work specifically for the purpose of showing me how to break them. Unfortunately, he could only sneak one rock a day from the nuclear plant without arousing suspicion. I don't want to put all the blame on my dad, but I think that he was actually too good at breaking rocks - if this can be believed - to adequately teach someone else how to do it. Out of concern for my safety he would make me stand fifty feet away from the rock at a point where I could barely see the rock in the first place, then, as he thanked the Lord for the rock He had provided, the hammer came down and the rock was gone, just like that. As the dust cleared, I could see my father pulling what must have been fragments of rock from his bleeding face. But before I could ask for a more detailed explanation about how he did it, he would have already excused himself to the washroom in order to properly cleanse his wounds.

So, because I wanted to please him, I would find some rocks of my own around the neighborhood and try to figure out how to break them. When watching *Convict 13* (1920, Metro Pictures), I had the strangest feeling that my ex-girlfriend had intimated even more than she let on, like she knew that Buster and I were living parallel, if not overlapping, lives. In the film, just like my dad, Buster was caught in prison and forced to break rocks. But he was doing it exactly like I had as a kid. We were both too gentle. We did not treat the rocks

as rocks, but instead as if we were looking for some kind
of circuitry inside. While I can't speak for Mr. Keaton, I
actually *was* searching for something inside the rocks. I
was searching for the reason why, even though I made
extremely high grades at school, I couldn't learn to do
something as simple as break rocks in prison. Every
single time, things would end up the same for both of us.
We tossed the hammer down in frustration and, with the
uncanny precision only the truly inept possess, it would
recoil from the rock and knock us right on the head,
putting our lights out until the next day.

But then, as I contemplated the film, what I will now
refer to as *The Refutation* kicked in. Buster was not trying
to break rocks in prison, but stones, and the reason neither
one of us was ever any good at it was that when we looked
into the depths of the rock, we saw our own stone faces,
and the instincts of self-preservation kept us from trying
very hard, even though we looked like we were studying
the rocks carefully in order to find the point of greatest
vulnerability. Stone converted into stone.

Once, while he was teaching me how to survive
a nuclear war, I asked my father where he had learned
to break rocks so well. Rather than looking perturbed
at my interruption of his current exposition, he proudly
announced that he had learned to break rocks from
reading a book. He explained that one can learn to do
almost anything from reading a book, even how to play
ping pong. He could not remember the name of the book,
which he had read in college, a time when he seemed to
do most of his reading. There was no way of locating the
book. To this day neither Buster nor I are very good at
breaking rocks.

Scarecrow Notes

In reality, there is really no one to blame for my inability to break rocks in prison or encountering all existence as if it is continually raining on my Salvador Dali tarot cards. If only things happened as easily as Buster once imagined it, longingly, in *The Scarecrow* (1920, Metro Pictures). In love with the farmer's daughter, Buster bends down to tie his shoes, and his beloved thinks he is proposing to her and says yes. Buster would never have had the courage to actually propose, so it is fortunate that his "tying the knot" is transformed into "tying the knot." To confess your love, to place yourself on the love catapult so that you can fall in love and proclaim it to the world no matter where you land, is, if done in complete earnest, the most difficult and noble thing a human being can do. Buster has taught me that most important lesson in a way no other guru could ever hope to.

After that, getting hitched on a motorcycle whilst fleeing the farmer and your rival is really nothing at all.

But I was just a kid back then, and while Buster

dressed up like a scarecrow in order to escape his beloved's angry father, I just stood there like one, watching but uncomprehending. Why was I able to understand so many things, but never anything my father tried to show me? The more I think about it, there were many things I didn't understand, where no one was showing anything. Whenever I did understand something, it always came as a fragmented message, written in haste, shoved through a hole in the wall, just like Buster Keaton's *Neighbors (1920, Metro Pictures)*, where there are many holes and messages but little communication between lovers. That film makes me feel as if I should sometimes have tried out the profession of inventor rather than writer. I have so many unsuccessful love poems under my belt that I once made a collection of them and titled it *Unsuccessful Love Poems*. But I could never find a publisher, so the whole affair achieved nothing but the sting of love being unrequited twice over.

And it's not like I didn't try, with both the actual objects of my affection and all the literary houses I thought were worthy of my efforts. Even though I had vowed in high school to never write a single poem again, due to a bad experience with censorship from the school newspaper, I was able to get around my injunction by secretly referring to them as "love-acquiring devices." And since I wanted my "devices" to be up to date, I read the *Norton Anthology of Postmodern Poetry* backwards and forwards (which seemed like a fairly postmodern thing to do, according to the editor's introduction), producing poems in all the styles, using all the up-to-date techniques, and employing all theoretical points of view I felt held some promise. I wrote love poems in prose, poems with only one word per line, poems with the words spread randomly across the page or even curving around in spirals. I varied the size of font, both from poem to poem and within individual poems. Right justification, left justification, dashes, ellipses, centered. I moved back and forth from Objectivism to Imagism, Constructivism to Vorticism. Surrealist and Cubist poetry. I wrote some of Ron Silliman's "new sentences," employed parataxis, catachresis, and at least once an anacoluthon. I wrote Conceptual poetry, Language poetry, New York School—I think, that one was a bit more difficult to figure out but I used a lot of dedications and mentioned several abstract expressionist painters, how much they made me enjoy walking down the street—speaking of which I also wrote concrete poetry, cowboy poetry, Nuyorican, feminist, speculative, mixed media, hybrid genre, straight narrative, digressive narrative, speculative narrative. I was deconstructive at times, using phrases like "windows to the soul" ironically. I employed formalisms of all stripes, both new and nude. I was hysterical on purpose in order to trick my victims into knowing what I was talking about.

Short lyric, epistolary poems, apostrophic poems to lovers imagined as dead in the future, linear vs. rhizomatic, Zaum—or poems made not of words but the approximated sounds of love. Marxist, existentialist, extended sequences with roman numerals—the kind where at poetry readings the poets insist on reading the Roman numerals, as if that somehow gives anyone an Apollonian heads up. I wrote slam poems of both types, the rapid fire virtuoso kind and the slower ones following the tradition of wisdom where you interject "you see" a lot to maintain a sense of contact and communal experience with your audience, so that they are suitably edified.

Situationist poems, Warholesque poems which merely transcribed the traffic reports as a simulation of my pining love. Poems of abjection, introjection, *and* incorporation. Third and fourth order puns. Anticipatory *and* retrospective plagiarism. Doppler-like oscillations between Classical and Baroque styles.

Despite such monkish study and Herculean practice, it seems like I never really found my voice, or in McLuhanesque terms, the right sender-receiver combination with a proper balance of pure noise and redundancy to result in a love-procuring device that was successful in either personal or literary terms.

And my poems were erudite to boot. With allusions I also worked like a photographer, who takes a thousand pictures in hopes of finding that one immortal negative. Shakespeare, Pyramis and Thisbe, Spinoza both young and old. Rumi for the madness of love. César Chávez I linked not only to love as committed and populist, but to Dionysus, god of wine and revelry. Love was like Pandora's Box, a dialectical box of course. Hieroglyphs, both Egyptian and Aztec, found their places. Freud, Lacan, Buddha, John Dee, Monet's lilies. New wave cinema, geomancy from Feng Shui to Ikebana. Herbert Spencer, St. Theresa's ecstasy, what Wagner may have thought about the Audubon Society. The militant wing of the Audubon and their wildcat strikes during the construction of the Autobahn. The secret relationships between Priapic cults, the history of capital punishment, and Italian architecture. Hermetic statehood, Orphic films

about Korean boys who mistreat their grandmothers. The catacombs of Paris, the discourse networks of 1900 and 2000, anthropologists I admired *and* the ones I thought were full of shit—usually avatars of my rivals in love and the degraded nature of their sentiments as compared to mine. With Descartes, Pascal, Sade and Masoch, capitalism and schizophrenia, the history of cybernetics and *The Garden of Earthly of Delights* at my disposal, I viewed my efforts as a one way road to what I most sincerely wanted, literary fame and/or a sustainable version of *amour fou*.

But alas, when my love devices were not simply ignored, they were met with stark fear, moral outrage, or tepid form letters. While I've long since burned the poems themselves, I have saved my most (and only) complementary rejection letter, for what reasons a therapist could probably tell me if I could afford one:

Dear Sir,

You don't make it easy for the reader to enter, that's for sure. It's not saying what you may think it's saying at the top, or for that matter, the bottom, assuming we can even speak of such things given the tome sitting before me.

Here's what I want to say to you—caveat being of course that mine is one voice only, with a large helping, always, of subjectivity—there are some wonderful passages in here. But you front load the manuscript, first, with three quotes (two of them lengthy—and geez, could you set the bar a little higher?) and then with some impenetrable opening pieces.

Something about the point of view and the writing itself made me flip to the end and read backwards from there. Perhaps it is because you sent me a 500 page manuscript of *unsuccessful* love poems? I like some passages, but in general, what in the world were you thinking? I mean, with all those attempts, wouldn't you think that you could produce at least one successful love poem? Even a few? The bourgeoisie were extremely impressed by the fact that Picasso could actually draw, and this raised his stock immensely. Perhaps you could start off with some successful love poems, however you are defining success (I assume some sort of reciprocation or consummation is involved), just to let the reader know you are intentionally writing unsuccessful poems rather than merely displaying a lack of literary skill.

So, why don't you give that a shot. Until then, for my press at least, you don't quite have a publishable book here.

P.S. If and when you resend anything to me, please only send me successful love poems. As I'm assuming, given the fact that these are *all*, to a poem, unsuccessful, that will allow me a much quicker read through. Send me, say, 20-30 pages of what you deem successful love poems, and if I agree that they are successful, then we can talk about selecting a few of the more interesting unsuccessful love poems so we could think about having a more balanced, perhaps even dialectical, approach to what is, we must both agree, a dying subgenre (love poetry) of a dying genre (poetry).

As potentially encouraging as that offer may have been, I somehow knew that I would never be able to produce the 20-30 pages of "good" poems the publisher was asking for. And maybe she was right. For fuck's sake, maybe I had taken Pierre Reverdy's suggestion about the distance between images too much to heart, so that there was no connection whatsoever between one line I wrote and the next. "The more the relationship," Reverdy proposes, "between the two juxtaposed realities is distant and true, the stronger the image will be—the greater its emotional power and poetic reality." Or perhaps I merely misinterpreted what he said. At any rate, rather than taking the publisher up on her offer, I merely gave up poetry (for the second time) even if I had to continue publishing the occasional Cultural Studies article in order to remain employed at the institution where my students were bored by me, and my colleagues hated me.

Maybe I should have been an inventor. . . In *Neighbors,* which is of course a love story, the magical transformation of a flyswatter into a flyswatter has nothing whatsoever to do with the main plot. At one point, when Buster is being escorted by the police, as he always must be, he and the policeman, with absolutely no reason from the standpoint of narrative causality, pass by the back of a baseball stadium where Babe Ruth just happens to be at bat. They both agree to pause and watch the ultimate "fly-swatter" (this is my term, not used in the film). Several minutes later, we learn that Keaton is an inventor, and we watch him test out a giant fly-swatter (this time named as such) in his backyard. Since this invention is likewise narratively unimportant (the invention is never mentioned again, does not help Buster win his love or make him better marriage material through a patent), the magical nature of transforming a word from itself to itself is all the more important, as if this film was meant to show us, due to the "tangential" nature of the transformation (swatting a fly with a revolving two-by-four as in the film), the true nature of what Keaton was attempting. Since the film is about feuding neighbors, it can also be read in terms of Abel's antithetical meanings which are really closer than one might think, and this signal to understand Keaton's ritual would thus result in neighbors being turned into neighbors, a double transformation within a mere 17 minutes! In *Neighbors* we have both the meta-cinematic explanation and the intra-cinematic exposition of Keaton's method, which is also always about love, since to turn a gondola into a gondola is really to show how the opposing meanings of words, of anything, are really deeply connected, married to each other. Perhaps this is why it is so easy (in terms of time elapsed) to get married in Keaton's films.

But regardless of my decisions with respect to writing love poems, I, like everyone else, am stuck with writing, with messages. One such message from way back in the day was a drawing of a vagina that a friend made me for my birthday. As the closest I had ever come to seeing a girl's privates involved an agreement with my friend Hope to take turns showing each other our butts, the note made me recognize what a true friend I really had. He even had the presence of mind not to give me the card at my birthday party, but to slip it to me through one of the rust holes in my father's Chevy II Nova, one of the holes my father had not, as yet, covered over with wood paneling. When my father was watching the road especially closely, I took a peek at what I knew, based upon its means of delivery, must be both extremely important and taboo. Of course, at the time I didn't know the word 'taboo,' but every kid grows up forming his identity in between the spaces of the taboos that life presents him. Yet, here I was being delivered one of my very own, in secret! I felt both a sense of utter fear and paradoxically, what academic types call "agency," as I opened the folded piece of paper. Even though I had never seen one, I knew based upon the formless shape with spikes jutting out in every direction that I was looking at a pussy. It also helped that my friend had labeled the diagram. He had given me secret knowledge, forbidden by the gods, for my birthday. He had given me a pussy. I buried it deep in my pocket, where it immediately began burning a hole, hoping my jeans would last until the end of the wilderness survival weekend when I could put the pussy where it belonged - underneath my mattress.

The whole weekend, but especially at night when I lay underneath the two feet of leaves that would keep the rain out of my shelter, I thought of that pussy, tried to remember what it looked like, knowing what danger my friend had put me in and yet thanking him secretly for it. I also thought how it was a strange coincidence that two feet of leaves was guaranteed to keep out rain just as two feet of concrete was guaranteed to stop gamma rays in a nuclear war. How thick was my mattress?

I thought about the pussy as we pulled roots from the ground and cooked them on a fire made by friction, as we ate insects and slugs, as I listened to my father say, "This would be a lot more difficult if it were raining." Although at the time I couldn't wait for the weekend to end, in retrospect I feel as if my inability to look at the pussy bequeathed to me granted it a certain mythical significance, so that it seemed to permeate all of nature, lurking everywhere, whispering to me in echoes, much like the Great Spirit must have spoken to the Indians. I was like a shaman who had left the village to find knowledge, and who could only return when that knowledge was granted, the only difference being that the knowledge I sought would be granted *after* I returned from the wilderness, which I eventually did.

I studied the pussy carefully, every single day, until one day it was gone and a sick feeling entered the pit of my stomach. The gods had found it and I would be tied to a rock and pecked at for eons by voracious birds. Later that day I found out that my mother had discovered it while making my bed. She didn't recognize what it was but knew, based upon its location, that it must be illicit. She gave it to my father for decoding, who immediately recognized that I was trying to learn how to break rocks in prison by drawing force diagrams. He admitted to me, for the first time ever, that he had lied; that he hadn't learned how to break rocks in prison by reading a book, and that I definitely would never learn by drawing my own sketches. He vowed, not knowing I had my own supply, to try to sneak more than one rock per day from the nuclear plant so he could have more practice demonstrating the process to me. I had no idea how to react to this at the time. Later, people would supply me with the term 'family romance'.

Prison Dies Hard /
Getting to the
Airport On Time

The week off also allowed me to realize that it wasn't mere exhaustion that caused me to not recognize my home. Working at Wellesley, where the rich, luscious female students are always telling you how boring your classes are, makes you want to seek some affirmation. And since my flight was early, I made my usual decision to stay up all night at a strip club where, as long as my money lasted, I was sought after by the type of women Buster is always falling for – that is if they were slutty and seemingly eager for full-friction dances. I'd become sort of a strip club aficionado after one of my Cultural Studies acquaintances started bringing me to some and introducing me to the dancers. He had developed a theory of strip clubs so stupid that it, at least from my point of view, was like Edgar Allan Poe's "Purloined Letter" of fake theories. By claiming that such establishments were actually centers for the expression of male masochism, he actually got the Psychology Department to pay *him* to go to strip clubs. Not having external funding myself, I cooked up excuses in my mind for attending on a slightly less frequent basis such as, "You'll sleep through your alarm and lose hundreds of dollars on your plane ticket if you stay at home, so you'd better go somewhere and spend a few bills and just head straight to the airport afterwards. If you go to a casino, you'll just lose several hundred dollars and feel like a fool on the way to the airport. But at a strip club, those dollars will procure the delightful sensual attentions of naked women about the age of your students but who seem extremely interested in everything you say, and who will 'give' you dances where you just sit back and enjoy." So I never got the masochism thesis, which from the quite non-masochistic look on my colleague's boob-filled face always seemed like a pretext anyway - but as long as he was churning out articles, Wellesley was happy.

My favorite club was a place called The Play House, which was known for a certain laissez-faire attitude with respect to what customers and dancers decided to do. I loved that and the feeling that, after a couple double vodkas, all the women seemed, in a sort of Doppler effect, alternately unique in their own beauty and yet exactly the same. An all-nighter there, I realized later, usually ended up much like Buster Keaton's film *The Playhouse* (1921, First National Pictures Incorporated). Just as the Bible, which my father discovered in prison and, like the main character in *Slingblade* (1996, Miramax Film Company), "thought he understood a good deal of," is apparently so complicated that only those truly devoted can piece together a doctrine that could otherwise easily be misrepresented (difficulty thus preventing a difficulty), *The Playhouse* is so full of Keaton doubles (one of whom happens to be in love with twins) that

one is easily distracted from *The Refutation* in this film
- a barber is turned into a barber. When Buster, who
performs all kinds of duties at the playhouse, filling in
for whomever is absent (including the indispensable
monkey required of all vaudeville acts), discovers the
lead actor has caught his beard on fire while smoking
a cigar backstage, he springs into action. Able to read
but completely lacking in common sense, he sees an axe
behind a glass sign saying "In Case of Fire." So Buster
busts the glass and takes out the axe, first knocking out
the actor with its flat end, then shaving off the burning
beard with the axe, becoming in effect a makeshift
barber. The excessive violence in this scene by Keaton
standards would clue one in to the fact that this might
be the site of a transformation. Indeed, someone who
performs as much work as Buster does around the
playhouse surely would have more common sense about
how to put out a fire. So the true acolyte recognizes
where the initial site of transformation occurs. But how
does Buster, who then goes on to put out various other
"fires" to keep the show running, once again become a
barber? It is apparent at this point that, for some reason,
Keaton was worrying that the magic he had discovered
was perhaps becoming too powerful, because one has to
have some pretty arcane knowledge to find him become
a barber once again. Near the finale of the show, there is a
war scene involving, strangely enough, Zouave soldiers.
Now, a dilettante might think the Zouaves were chosen
because, this being a vaudeville show, they had the most
flamboyant war costumes - in most cases this would be
true. But Keaton specified Zouaves because they were
recruited from the Berber tribe in North Africa and,

as is often the case when it comes to colonialism, they did not name themselves. Rather, they were named so as to sound like Barbarians, noteworthy for nothing but fighting and wearing thick beards. Since the 'Berbers' or Zouaves had all quit that day, Buster had to recruit some construction workers (and himself) to do the Zouave or 'Berber' scene. And that, my friend, is how Buster transformed himself from a barber into a barber.

It would seem I have used *The Playhouse* to allegorize the sort of hijinks that go on at The Play House, in the name of general modesty and of protecting the identities and actions of the wonderful women who work there. So be it, Buster himself I'm sure would show similar discretion. Besides, this allows me to both advertise the revelry that goes on at the latter establishment while continuing the Great Work that goes on in the name of elucidating Keaton's brilliance.

The one downside about this method of getting to early flights on time is that a usually onerous task, getting through airport security, comes to seem a task requiring skills of an almost acrobatic nature. Still inebriated, one experiences the winding airport lines as slightly more like walking a tightrope through the labyrinth imprisoning Dedalus and Icarus with the deadly Minotaur. Putting your personal items in the correct bins comes to seem slightly more like performing a juggling act with knives, burning torches, and other items the TSA frowns upon. Almost inevitably, Oedipally, and like this time too, I end up walking to my gate in my socks, leaving my shoes to who knows what kind of fate - undoubtedly trembling in some windowless room being x-rayed and dissected for incendiary materials. I always realize too late I've abandoned my own shoes, and always say a prayer that they will, perhaps, be intact enough for some friendly TSA employee to walk home in a pair of Eccos, or Doc Martins, or whatever other pair of shoes I've purchased between one early flight and the next.

Then if you're lucky, you can slide into a window seat (I never select my seats, believing I can shed some karma by not doing so) and sleep through those early morning hours, the plastic siding of the plane greeting you like satin. But this wasn't going to be one of those days I sensed, slightly less inebriated, slightly more irritable, for I would have to fly first through Dallas before making my way home. And one of those crazy thoughts entered my head, interior monologue style: "I better not find a cowboy hat in the overhead bin." It was even worse. When I got to my seat in Dallas, I realized that I would be sitting between Larry Hagman's doppelgänger and a Bayer aspirin salesman. "Maybe I can score a sample off him," I thought, having forgotten my own head shrinking pills. Then I looked up at the bin and saw a Brooks Brother's jacket meant to look like something more fancy, spread out like a Persian rug, and Larry Hagman sitting there smugly wearing not just a white shirt, but a vest to boot. I pulled the big and tall jacket out of the bin and loudly proclaimed, "Who's wearing a suit!" Several people raised their hands and then Hagman reached for it. "Put it under your seat!" I ordered. Under the polyester Arabian carpet sat a backpack so tiny it might have been able to hold a 12-pack of condoms and an I-Pad, at most. Never had I seen such small items take up so much space - Euclid must have been rolling over in his grave. "Is this yours too Hagman?" He stood up and grabbed it, pressing his bulk against my Busterian frame: "What do you think you're doing?"

"Well JR, I'm telling you to put your shit under your empty seat, while you look like you're trying to start something. These bins aren't oil spouts you can just claim like some redneck Sheik." He sat down and did what he was told, and I sat in between Hagman and Bayer. Bayer turns to me and goes, "Where in the world are you coming from." "Well Bayer," I replied, "I'm coming from the real world where people put their shit under their seat like they are told by the flight attendants. But if you want to be an ass, next time I suggest you pay for first class." I sat in between them and closed my eyes as the flight crew begged over the intercom for people to put as many of their items as possible under the seat. Then a plot twist. I had mixed up my seat assignment with the gate assignment, and someone else needed to take my seat. I got up and walked back to my actual seat and someone with a Samuel Clemens moustache and a Dear Abby personality weighed in: "I bet you feel like an ass now." "Excuse me, are you talking to me." "Yes I am, and I think what you did back there was totally uncalled for and I don't appreciate your language. And you must really feel like an ass now." "Well in fact," I said, "I do not feel 'like an ass' because the principle still applies, don't put tiny shit up in the bins where people need to put actual luggage. I fucking hate Texas!" "Well I'm not from Texas, how do you feel about that." "I also hate people who think like Texas so why don't you go fuck off." He did, and I went to my 'actual' seat and slept like a baby. That is, except for the guilt dream I had where Woody Harrelson walked up to me on the street and said, "Boy, I don't know where you're from, but you'd better learn the cowboy way." Turns out I'm not as much of an ass as I pretend to be, at least when I'm unconscious.

So with all the previous night's carousing and my diplomatic relations with Dallas, Texans, one could predict that home might not feel like home due to my exhausted delirium. But in fact, as I soon realized, home really was different yet again. It was another episode of my dad instituting a prison flashback, different every time, in the house's organization and coming up with new instantiations of his hybrid genius - that always impossible to anticipate Cold War, survivalist, mad scientist imagination had once again transformed reality. And then there were in-laws.

The Unrecognizable House

For one thing, in his spare time my dad had been studying evolution and neuroscience, claiming that, given enough time he could prove both areas of knowledge had absolutely no basis in fact at all. A state he referred to as, "Nooooo Body!" As repetitious as he could be when he was in the midst of such inspirations, I never understood my dad's explanations of these things. But they were fascinating, and while others usually seemed extremely bored or confused by his proclamations, I reveled in his penchant for metaphor and descriptive flourishes like, "Just imagine the entire state of Tennessee covered in six feet of electrons, and there is only one red electron. What do you think the chances are you'd be able to find the red electron in one try?" That's when I would usually drift off from the line of argument and just imagine trying to make my way down the street pushing electrons back and forth which had somehow enlarged themselves to ping-pong ball size, which made the fantasy more tangible to me.

So while my dad's discussions were, for him,

explanations, to me they were excuses for excursions to *The Frozen North* (1922, Joseph M. Schenk), in a manner of speaking. In this film, the Parisian subway leads all the way to the northern edge of Quebec. Someone familiar with Buster's other work will be surprised to see him, once he arrives, attempting to rob a bar with a cardboard cut-out sign of a gunslinger – this despite the fact that he owns an 'actual' gun. Something we find out when he shoots his wife whom he sees cavorting with another man. Only, Buster soon realizes he has gone to the wrong house where his 'actual' wife is waiting with open arms. And yet, within moments, something falls off of the wall and hits her on the head, killing her instantly. The police arrive to check about the other murder, which Buster seems to have already forgotten about, because he is worried about his current dead wife, as if he himself had 'willed' her dead. He turns on the gramophone and dances with her fresh corpse so that when the Mountie looks in all appears copacetic. Seemingly out of control, Buster immediately searches out another woman, and doesn't seem to care that she is already married. He's so obsessed about obtaining her 'hand' that he follows the couple to their vacation cabin, makes improvisational snowshoes to get around, steals another man's ice-fished fish to sustain himself, and pursues the woman relentlessly until he is finally shot by his 'actual' wife who it turns out was not dead but merely knocked out. With this relaxation of Buster's normally impeccable morality, the interchangeable nature of real and represented objects, and spatial/temporal transitions that are not absurd in the normal Keaton fashion but merely discontinuous, we should not be surprised to find him, at the end of the film, asleep in a Parisian theatre with his hand lying in the 'frozen' mop bucket. The Parisian subway has been transformed into the Viennese subway, Freud's unconscious. Although this is a relatively simple transformation on the level of language, it signals Keaton's familiarity with Surrealism's fascination with the unconscious and its relation to cinematic space. It also describes the strange journeys my dad's lectures allow me to take while listening to them in a sort of trance state.

The only thing holding dad back from completing his proofs were all the animals that came to the house because, despite his somewhat intimidating demeanor, he and my mother were such loving people. Instead of refuting evolution and neuroscience as he was born to do, he had to change litter boxes and piss-mats several times a day, as he could not abide the odor of these things. He had to do this because the commercial propaganda about litter boxes and piss-mats hiding the odor of animal refuse is a complete lie. There is a dog that he takes on walks in the dark morning before sunrise, because its feces are so large he has to be extremely careful to find places for the dog to hide its productions. I can't blame my dad for this breach of suburban decorum, which can sometimes cause neighbors to raise their fury to Old West levels. Being a former criminal, both skilled in subterfuge and instilled with a strong desire – despite nostalgic breaks – not to go back to jail, he has found a way to handle the dog's copious productions. And, until the neighbors combine Old West fury with CSI technology, I think he's pretty safe.

But as I previously noted, it is obvious that on some

level he misses jail from time to time, for the previous incarnation of the house (which was so transformed I have no memory of it) had now been converted into the sort of place that Frank Lloyd Wright had nightmares about. Every room has to be sealed at all times. In fact there are so many new doors that my parents have had to build more rooms to accommodate all the new doors that are required to be sealed at all times. And they can only be opened when one desires to pass from one threshold to the next. Several of the thresholds even have obstacles in the floor, like miniature hurdles, that you have to step over after opening the doors. When I questioned my dad on the new state of things, he dismissed my theory about him missing prison by explaining how the new system of doors had been designed to keep each of the animals in separate rooms because they were always fighting one another over the tuna supply which they did not realize was endless. Then my dad opened all the cabinets in the kitchen and showed me a veritable warehouse of tuna cans with enough mercury to poison everyone on the Pequod. No, my dad said, he had done everything in his power to maintain a sense of morality and stay out of prison, trying to do at least one good deed a week, to account for the dog poop left hidden around the neighborhood. For example, last week he and my mom had invited a black family from church to have Sunday dinner with them. Before I could ask how exactly that constituted a good deed, my grandmother, who had recently moved in with us with all her furniture which she apparently had irrevocable emotional attachments to, making our house even more like a miniature version of an Egyptian crypt - or an expanded version of an Iron Maiden - asked if the black family smelled funny. Feeling extremely fearful for what happens next, I said, "No, Granny, it's the Cave Indians who smell funny," which seemed to defuse the situation as no one in the house knew any Cave Indians. My brother, who was also visiting when I arrived, had recently married a Jewish sexologist, and together they were writing a book on Jewish sexual positions inspired by the Old Testament. Their favorite position was called the Ted Bundy, in which the woman lay on her back and pretended to be dead while the man fornicated with her with all his energies, screaming that she did not look dead enough for his sexual satisfaction. Apparently the brilliance of the Ted Bundy was that it constituted a veritable reinvention of the missionary position in a way so radically Old Testament and misogynistic that it resembled the ancient art of alchemy, converting lead into gold. Plus they had a special attachment to the position as they had conceived their baby (still in the oven) during the Ted Bundy. They did not know if it was a boy or a girl, but either way they were going to name the child Violent Mandala hoping the child would be both deadly and peace loving, sort of like Jekyll and Hyde if Jekyl were King David and Hyde were the Dalai Lama. To me it sounded about as sound a plan as the boy Johnny Cash knew whom their parents named Sue. All in all it sounded like a pretty good naming plan.

Unfortunately I could not be proud of my brother and his wife's breakthroughs in a Hebrew version of the Kama Sutra. My brother and I had always been natural enemies, as if he was a horse and I was a horse door keeping him out of the pasture, or I was the horse and he was the horse door. It had always been that way, one brother's triumph the equivalent of another's degradation. One of us was always in a place of confinement and humiliation. In *Our Hospitality* (1923, Metro Pictures), you'll see the nature of this dynamic, thanks to the actual presence of a horse door. A horse door opens horizontally in two sections so that one half can be opened to feed an animal within such as a horse. It is a common door to have in a barn, but not as one's front door. Thus, when Buster enters through it (and he is the only one in the film to do so), he is effectively transformed into a horse, as technically only a horse would use a horse door. When he travels down to Rockville to claim his inheritance, only to find out that his family has a longstanding feud with a 'neigh'boring family, he attempts to escape the pistol toting brothers (who happen to be natural allies) by dressing up as a woman. When his costume is found out, he jumps on a horse and attempts to escape, brothers and father right behind him. They think they have Buster cornered when they see the dress and umbrella he has been using as a disguise, but just when they are about to shoot him in the back (they think), a horse turns around and we discover that Buster has doffed his outfit and pinned it on the back of the horse itself. It has the strange appearance of a door opening, or closing, on its hinges (because of the way a horse turns, where space formerly was, there is now a horse) so that we might say of this horse that it is a horse door. And not only has a horse door been transformed into a horse door, we could also say that a horse (Buster using the horse door in New York) has been transformed into a horse (the horse wearing Buster's women's clothes). I suppose we could reverse this and say that, via the medium of a horse, a

Buster Keaton has become a Buster Keaton.

Sadly, this triple-crown *Refutation* was not likely to have its equivalent in the relationship between my brother and me.

Nevertheless I said in all earnestness that I hoped Violent Mandala was a boy so that I could attend the bris, since I'd never seen one and they sounded really cool. I had even, upon hearing of the pregnancy, composed a song I hoped I could perform at the ceremony called "Welcome to the Bris": "Welcome to the bris, we've got fun and games, we're gonna cut your foreskin off before you have a name." Then out of nowhere my dad intoned in a way I had never heard before: "I'm warning you, there is most definitely a right way and a wrong way to perform a circumcision!" When we pressed my dad for details, he backed off, saying it wasn't proper dinner table conversation. We were all so disturbed by the tension surrounding his outburst that we begged him to tell us some of his old stories of fending off sexual assaults, through lightning fast Hentai style circumcisions, when he was in prison. These stories always made us laugh when we were kids because not only was my dad an expert at fending off sexual assaults, he also narrated each episode with his entire body, practically acting it out as if he were part Southern Baptist preacher and part Samurai, which I guess in some way he was.

In other words, I had entered not my own childhood home but the sort of place where, among other things devils, skeletons, antique mirrors, and fat women could fall on me at any time. People I didn't recognize could jump out of a closet and challenge me to wrestling matches, either fully clothed or in my underwear, MMA or WWF version. In *The Haunted House* (1921, Metro Pictures), Buster is knocked out cold when capturing a group of counterfeiters hiding in a haunted house, which makes him dream he is descending into hell to meet the devil. When he wakes up, he is lying in the lovely arms of the beautiful daughter of the grateful bank president. Knowing Buster's love for women, I know that this common equation of women with the devil (the devil thus being transformed into the devil) has nothing to do with misogyny. It's just that Buster is warning people like me who can and will eventually marry almost anyone (as we soon shall see) - heroin addicts, 500 pounders with borderline personality disorder, policemen in bowel movement ceremonies, transsexual butlers who later accuse you of sexual harassment, countless Indians, belly dancers who force you to wear a spiked dog collar -that at least some of those unions will have unfortunate outcomes, and in the 1920s the only way you could represent this on film was in the context of a heterosexual marriage. But what would eventually happen, at least in terms of my unrecognizable house's effects upon my psyche, was already happening. And this is the house in which, at Thanksgiving dinner, I announced my plans to travel to Niles, CA and study the ways of Buster Keaton.

After the Announcement

I should have guessed that no one would really have much reaction to my plan. My family had decided years ago that I had basically thrown my life away by choosing a career in 'The Humanities' since "Hey, once you've figured out survival, what else is there to worry about on that front?" But, they had always tolerated my decision and to them, the whole Buster Keaton thing was just another hallway in the Bedlam I had entered years before. My dad did have some survival advice, of course, strange as it was. He had decided from reading about all the guru junkies in California that the only reasonable back-up plan if my funding didn't go through - even though it was an utter certainty - was to try to get a job reading Salvador Dali painted tarot cards. I protested that I had no direct knowledge of the tarot (as I've noted metaphorically when describing how I experience reality) which puts me at a distinct disadvantage when attempting to stay competitive in the global marketplace, but my dad explained I could just read a book on it and have a basic working knowledge. I wasn't surprised that my dad had forgotten the topic of my life's research, which is so common to parents whose children work in 'The Humanities' that it could almost be considered a scientific law. Yet, I couldn't protest, since he had learned how to play ping-pong that way, and he always beat me. Maybe with all those years of theorizing about Poetics, Tarotics, and Magick, I had indeed developed an affinity which would translate into an ability to use the cards themselves.

But although my parents didn't object to my 'life choices,' they were never very much help either. Having decided to ditch my flight back to Boston, which was in the complete opposite direction of California, I needed some form of transportation to get me there. I had spent all that month's pay at the strip club, and even if I could admit that to my parents, it wouldn't have mattered. If I had become penniless by donating my entire salary to UNICEF, they would still have no interest in funding my endeavors in 'The Humanities.'

Maddeningly, my parents' yard was the vehicular equivalent of the Egyptian crypt inside of their house, only turned inside out. Walking inside or outside their front or back door, if front and back still applied, was like navigating a Mobius strip or one of those M.C. Escher paintings where you can walk upstairs and downstairs at the same time. The yard was almost completely filled with used Toyota Camrys, and my father would not part with a single one to assist me in my journey. His explanation was something to the effect that these used cars represented a safety net. If one Camry broke down, they could save money by just insuring another one. Or rather than going to a Toyota mechanic and waiting on an ancient part to arrive, he could often take one working part from a non-working car and get a mildly afflicted car running by merely trading out the parts. The system's success, which struck me as something akin to an organ donation farm, relied on the multitude of used Toyota Camrys carefully picked out of the newspaper classifieds whenever my family obtained a little extra money. Dad said that his records of which cars performed at which level, including a full listing of each car's working and non-working parts, which he kept on white slips of paper he would shuffle back and forth across his work desk as if he were playing solitaire, would completely fall apart if a single car were removed, because what he had in his yard was not a dozen Toyota Camrys but, in reality, something far greater, a sort of single, transcendent Camry that consisted of the virtual relationships between each of the dozen shells littering the yard. Using mathematics that had aided him in his dismantling of the twin sciences of evolution and neuroscience, he estimated that if he were able to eventually obtain 19 Toyota Camrys, something which he referred to as "the singularity" would occur and the Toyotas would, in such close proximity given the size of our yard, begin to actually develop their own methods of communication and exchange of parts, thus becoming something altogether different than a Toyota Camry, rather an inorganic life system which would cease to be a tool and, to my mind if not his, refuse to propel human beings at all.

"Plus," dad added, "If I gave you one, you would just drive that car as far as you could and abandon it out west, perhaps on the docks at night, sadly agreeing that it would have been best if this Camry had remained behind with its comrades." As fascinated as I was by this 'singularity' my father spoke of, I was also disappointed that someone who had always been so generous in helping me with respect to survival situations before, whether it happened to be a nuclear war, getting lost in the wilderness, or breaking rocks in prison, suddenly felt that I was so unimportant to him - even if it was for 'The Humanities.' Like I was a jacket that Buster had placed over a puddle and my dad was a beautiful woman who simply walked around both the jacket and the puddle. Was I no longer his son?

The Saphead (1920, Metro Pictures)

While others were busy watching football games, having arguments, and beating on their loved ones as most people do after Thanksgiving dinner, I wandered around my old neighbourhood believing my own anti-hype, thinking there would be no way to make it to California and that I was just a saphead who couldn't live up to his father's unstated yet quite obvious expectations. I stopped by all the old haunts, places where I should have gotten laid but didn't, backs of schools where I shouldn't have gotten beat up but did, haunted by names of humiliations like the curvaceous Jennifer Hand-"Job" (as she was known to us junior high kids) who lived down the street and stood looking at me quizzically while my parents tried to spread to her and her family the messages they felt were so important, the grace of the Lord Jesus Christ, surviving nuclear war which would require the whole neighbourhood to pitch in for a communal shelter, and of course surviving in the wilderness - a bonus message of sorts.

Maybe there were only points of connection

between Buster and me, like being haunted by names to the extent that we could never be sure whether they were echoing through sound waves or cycling internally in our brain waves. But what if it was nothing more than that? One day when Buster was on the stock exchange, he kept hearing the name "Henrietta" shouted again and again. The only thing Buster could do to stop it was shout "I take it!" until the voices died out. It was a variation on Nietzsche who said that the only way to survive life was to say yes to it all, to claim one's fate as if one had authored it oneself. Yet, this was, for Nietzsche, an internal change of disposition that bore no illusions about one's ability to actually change the phenomenal world. In this respect, I credit Buster for choosing to suffer a more specific malady that he could control. Yet as I meditate on his success in suffering a curable malady, I am unable to duplicate it. For while I too have been haunted by names, names that sounded like flight, that sounded like mules, that sounded like Indian goddesses, like piles of stones, I never wanted them to stop. In fact, I wanted to live with them forever. But, as if the stock exchange were a stage-which-is-all-the-world, whenever I wanted to fall into their soft fields, they instantly stopped. Now I can't remember any of the names I held so dear, only their junior high variations. Perhaps Buster and I were leading parallel, if not overlapping, lives, but what good would that do me now? He made his own way to a much deserved stardom, while I merely continued to be haunted by the absence of names dissolved into pure sound.

But the more I continued to feel sorry for myself, the more my thoughts returned to Buster, and then back to myself, merry-go-round style. For us both, the haunted quality of names seemed to apply to all texts. One time, alone and in a new city, Buster stole a newspaper from someone riding a merry-go-round. Perhaps he should have known that a merry-go-round is no place to steal a newspaper, just like I should have known that trying to fill that psychic void, the one opened up by a single comment from my now ex-girlfriend, could only end up like this. As I tried to situate the paper, no matter how I folded it, it kept getting larger and larger until it was practically the size of a tent. I fell asleep inside and woke up in the mountains with my family - my younger brother, my mother and dad, and me. It was dark outside, with nothing but the sounds of black bears running around trying to get the food everyone hung from wires that park rangers had stuck between trees just out of their reach. Fortunately, we were in an area where the grizzly and brown bears had become extinct, because those kinds of bears will forget hanging food and head straight for people. You should only go in such areas if you have a bell and a high caliber rifle. In this case, though, it was the people I had to worry about. We were camped next to several. One couple in particular concerned me because even though 'the wife' hadn't done anything wrong 'the husband' had spanked her very loudly on the buttocks - right in front of the whole campground. And even though there were several other people around, it seemed like I was the only person who noticed it and, just as I have vowed in life to never be the first person to mention a pussy, I let this incident go unacknowledged even though I feared what it portended. Once, when I was younger and my family had a lot of company in the living room, I saw a group of boys pick up all the guns I had left in the front yard after a battle and fly down the street. As the conversation in the living room continued, which I think had something to do with the Lord Jesus Christ, a sick feeling emerged in my stomach. It is my earliest memory of guilt or the internalization of shame. I don't know which. Since we were Protestants, I had from the earliest shadows of consciousness intuited that there was nothing anyone could do about guilt. It lives inside of you and grows like Kudzu, forever. That knowledge, in addition to the fear of interrupting important adult conversation, in addition to the feeling that once older boys turned a corner they were gone forever, that telling my father about the stolen guns would result in nothing but getting in trouble for leaving the guns unguarded in the front yard, kept me silent and planted the mustard seed of guilt which, as Jesus noted in a parable and I have since experienced personally, can move mountains.

Back in the mountains, as I stared up into the ceiling of the tent amidst all the commotion outside, the waterproof yet breathable nylon veil was illuminated and covered with scripture. I was having something that I now know Catholics refer to as a "saintly illumination." The married couple next to us, the one where the wife got spanked in public for no reason, was having sexual intercourse! Although I still didn't know what a pussy looked like, I now knew that it was called a vagina and that husbands inserted their penis inside. Although my parents had, in their description, mentioned nothing about sexual intercourse having any element of sound connected with it, these sounds spoke to me like the burning bush spoke to Moses. I lay there in what philosophers call "fear and trembling," hoping that, as with the undeserved spanking earlier, I was the only one who heard. As the sounds continued it appeared I might be safe.

But a surprise was in store, both for me and those older boys who stole the guns. After the company left my parents decided to take my brother and me on an evening walk. Amazingly, in a set of tactics I found hard to believe for older boys, they had commenced their battle *just* two blocks away. As we walked in their direction, the sick feeling of guilt rising up into a disorienting vertigo, my father asked, "Aren't those your guns?" There was no way I could deny it, but could my father, even though he had broken rocks in prison, beat up that many older boys? He swaggered over to them in a way that reminded me of how sheriffs walked down the street in cowboy movies. By that point the older boys had stopped their battle and given him their full attention. "Dad, are those people being eaten by bears?" my brother whispered with a mortal fear that was matched only by my psychological terror. "Oh no son, black bears aren't interested in eating people, otherwise we wouldn't have gone camping here. Married couples just make noises like that sometimes." My father then put his hands together and made a sort of flapping motion - the older boys immediately dropped my guns and ran for their lives. Of course, the law of simultaneity prevents us from suggesting, in *Battling Butler* (1926, MGM), that a Butler has transformed into a Butler, since three co-exist: Alfred Butler (Keaton), Battling Butler (the boxing champion), and Buster's actual butler, whom he cannot travel without. However, since Buster must pretend to become Battling Butler to win the lovely woman he discovers on a butler-assisted camping trip, one could say that at *that* point a Butler has become a Butler, especially since Buster must pretend to become Battling Butler, enter the ring, and give her 'the ring.' Luckily, during his three week ordeal of training, Buster's beloved decides she does not like fighters anyway, a survival method the Greeks referred to as a "god in a machine," the machine referring in this case to the beloved's brain changing her heart, at least about fighting. So in a bout of cinematic magic only Keaton could have prepared, a ring is transformed into a ring and then ceases to be one type of ring while remaining the other, most important ring of all, the wedding ring. In a similarly magical "*deus ex machina*," my father's gesture in combination with his response to my bear-fearing brother, has made it clear to me that just as Keaton is the master of refuting the linguistic theories of Karl Abel and (as we shall see) the construction of the life-propelling love catapult, my father is, at times, not only the master of breaking rocks in prison, but of all sound, word and gesture. I myself, of course, remain a Saphead.

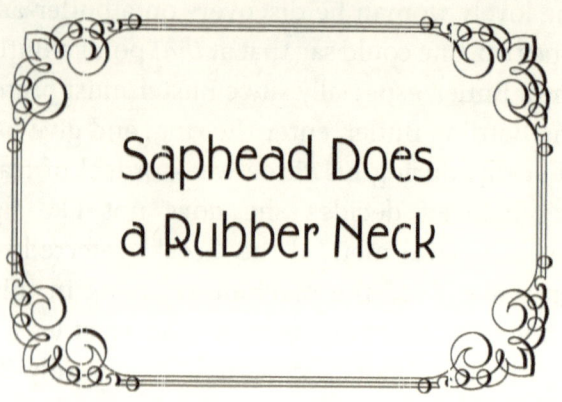

Saphead Does
a Rubber Neck

As one would suspect, as shoulder pads crashed and family members argued and beat one another in what for everyone else was a happy Thanksgiving afternoon, I began to contemplate suicide. All our real problems begin in our adult lives. This, as Pip said in *Great Expectations*, is where all our troubles began. I was the one who had left my home to build my house on 'The Humanities,' but spend money at strip clubs and elsewhere like an oil baron. I had, from time to time, tried to repair my house since you can never obtain a new 'house of life.' But as one might imagine, things went about as well as they did for Buster in *One Week*: poking larger holes in a leaking roof, sawing myself off planks I'd used to support myself, entire panels falling, and second-story doorways that led to drop-offs. Even though my first real home was not given to me by an uncle as a wedding present and I didn't have to build it myself, the first place I really lived alone in was similarly mass produced - or so I thought. I didn't notice that when I signed the lease my new home was located smack between a graveyard and an old factory which, because part of it had been torn away, had second and even third story doors which led to drop-offs. I tried to console myself about these drop-offs with maxims I was starting to learn in graduate school such as, "The productions of the bourgeoisie are ruins even before they have crumbled," but they were powerless against the larger forces that seemed to be at work. You see, doorways that lead to drop-offs, as Buster must have realized while building his house, are, even more than Freud looking at his reflection, emblems of the uncanny. We begin to recognize them everywhere even as we know that we will never recognize the ones that pertain to us.

Luckily most of us who consider suicide never actually do it. We either talk ourselves out of it like Hamlet did, worrying that killing oneself is just like falling through a trap door from a bad situation to an even worse one, or we try to cheer ourselves up like Buster in *Hard Luck* (1921, Metro Pictures). If only I was as resourceful as the man who turned an armadillo into an armadillo. I mean, who but a suicidal Buster would think to join an armadillo hunting club in order to cheer himself up. Granted they all get lost on the hunt and end up at another kind of club, but he is still alive and this club has a swimming pool. After Buster dispenses with some of those ruffians who are always terrorizing country club patrons, he decides to take a dip in the well-earned pool, starting of course from the high dive. He misses the pool entirely and falls into a hole nearby, and this is where I know Buster transforms into an armadillo, because otherwise there would have been no way to survive this mistake and return several years later with a Chinese wife and two kids. This latter "gag" on digging holes to

China is not so much a silly way to end a movie as an intentional confirmation of Hamlet's theory that indeed, for better or for worse, we do "perchance to dream once we go to sleep," whether it happens by accident or taking too many sleeping pills. There is always another side; every hole really is drop-off leading somewhere, a trap door to another floor. But why take the chance? Granted, Buster seemed to have adapted to his new realm with aplomb, even joy, but who's to say we would be as adroit as him?

And the more I began to think about that, the more I bummed out on being a saphead like Buster in *Saphead*, the more I realized just how much genius and wonder was out there just waiting to be discovered. One can be easily fooled by the transformation of something into itself, and since *The Saphead* was Keaton's first feature length film, it was important for him to demonstrate the actual procedure involved in his refutation of Karl Abel's *On the Antithetical Meaning of Primal Words*, his 'methodology' if you like. For something to transform at all, a temporal transformation must first take place. Time, even the smallest amount, must pass for a gondola to become a gondola. To demonstrate this elementary yet all important concept, Keaton bases his film on Buster's confusion between a mine named 'The Henrietta' and a dancer named "Henrietta." This confusion momentarily leads Buster to become estranged from his beloved Agnes. But, since both Henrietta's exist at the same time, no transformation has taken place, not by any cosmology imaginable (and by 1920, when the film was made, Keaton would have been well aware of the temporal theories of both Henri Bergson and Albert Einstein, neither of which refute the notion that time must pass for a thing to be transformed into itself).

A seeming continuity error at the very end of the film will reward the true Keaton adept to this secret of the transformation. Once Buster's innocence has been discovered and he and Agnes are married (off-screen), we suddenly see a calendar on the wall. It is a bizarre moment because *voila*, there it is, seemingly non-diegetic, as no one of Buster's standing (in the movie) would own such a kitschy calendar with its arrow-toting cupid on top holding an hour glass as well. Seeing as this object does not exist in the world of the film and it is not necessary to know that it is September 1920, we must read this moment symbolically. Here is the strange thing that happens to the already strange calendar. We see "Tuesday September 27" transform into "Tuesday September 28." That is, Tuesday has transformed into Tuesday. Just to make sure we do not read this as a continuity error but as the fundamental theorem of time required for a thing to transform into itself, we see that a year has passed since the previous scene (before the calendar scene) in which Buster has reconciled with his father, because the very next shot shows Buster standing outside of a door. A doctor comes out and holds two fingers up, indicating that Buster and Agnes have had twins. This Tuesday is definitely a transformed 'Two's day,' as there is no better image of a thing transforming into itself than a baby (or two) crossing the vaginal threshold to become a baby, an image which, due to cinematic decorum, we must conjure up in our own minds. And if we do so, we recognize yet another transformation, the original 'Saphead,' Buster's profligate character created because he read a book on how to attract women which said the modern woman likes bad boys, becomes the sap-covered head of a baby that has not yet had the placenta and other bodily fluids wiped off before being presented to the beautiful mother's arms.

This pun on 'two' is furthered by the fact that Buster Keaton himself was born on Oct. 4, giving him the same astrological sign as the twins born to him in the film. That is, Libra, the twin scales. Thus, we can see this film as a major 'coming out' for the initiated because of the astrological connection; that is, the 'birth' of Keaton's refutation of Abel's *On the Antithetical Meaning of Primal Words* bears an auto-referential element in the invocation of his birth sign. Note that the "goal for Libra is to witness the importance of cooperation and harmony in human life," and is this not the 'theme,' more or less, for the uninitiated viewers of his films? As with any sacred text or set of sacred texts, there is a message for the masses - seeking balance in Keaton's case, and there is a message for the initiated, in our case the revelation that things can be transformed into themselves. It's just that, in order to emphasize this obvious theme, Keaton must enter a cinematic world in which precisely everything is off-balance, but what we witness is Buster's indefatigable attempts to restore balance to this off-kilter world, however maladroit those attempts might seem.

It is also worth noting that Libra is the only sign on the zodiac to be represented by an inanimate object, which coincides with Keaton's onscreen persona as described by Keaton in his other autobiography, *My Wonderful World of Slapstick*, that is the autobiography of Keaton I am not writing, even if Keaton's cinematic destiny, at least with respect to physiognomy, was not necessarily to his liking: "Down through the years my face has been called a sour puss, a dead pan, a frozen face, The Great Stone Face, and, believe it or not, 'a tragic mask.' On the other hand that kindly critic, the late James Agee, described my face as ranking 'almost with Lincoln's as an early American archetype, it was haunting, handsome, almost beautiful.' I can't imagine what the great rail splitter's reaction would have been to this, though I sure was pleased."

Other than James Agee, who seems to have a strange fetish for inanimate faces - his suggestion that both Lincoln and Keaton are beautiful sidesteps the fact that both had stone visages - people recognized and loved what Buster himself could not love, his own face. But what should be inspirational to us all is that despite Buster's self-loathing, it did not keep him from falling in love and getting married every single day of his life, which we all do if we are open to it. Buster, as in his films, took what he had, his destiny, and turned it to his own ends. For Libra is an air sign, and if you can imagine a giant Libra, constructed so that a man could fit in it, and weighted the scales properly, and that man, standing on one end of the scales, arranged for a large object to fall on the other end, isn't it uncanny how much this would resemble, to the point of actually being functional, a catapult, Libra becoming an 'in the air sign'?

I am certain that this film represents an authentic revelation, a fact reinforced by Keaton because by changing the 27 to a 28, making it Tuesday September 28 but not changing the Tuesday, he reminds us even today that in 1920, September 28 did indeed fall on a Tuesday.

Catapult of Love

I practically skipped home, avoiding ledges, speeding cars, sleeping pills, razor blades, and all the poisonous plants and berries my father had pointed out to me on our weekly "missionary walks." I was newly dedicated to not only pursue my love of 'The Humanities' but a love of humanity that, if it did not avoid lust altogether, would at least transcend it. I knew that this would involve falling in love, getting married every single day of my life - though I still wasn't quite sure what that meant - and finding out all I could about love's secret mechanism, the love catapult.

I walked home avoiding suicide and considering Buster Keaton's *Three Ages* (1923, Metro Pictures). No doubt, I must be somewhat enamored of Buster due to *his* fascination by multiple lives. It is the repetition that occurs over the ages. Who else would even have the idea - much less the genius and fortitude to carry it out - of exploring the similarities in love rituals from the Stone Age, ancient Rome, and the modern world of speed and greed? In its explicit attempt to show that "love is an unchanging axis" by demonstrating its constancy over three periods of time, *Three Ages* anticipates the essay film of the *Nouvelle Vague* by 40 years. And what did Buster discover about love in this exhaustive quest? That true love, at least attaining it, will always at some point require a catapult. We often speak of falling in love, but from where do we fall? Just as Marx and Engels noted about labor, "No production [of love] is possible without an instrument of production, even if this instrument is simply the hand," and, "It is not possible without past, accumulated labor, even if this labor is only the skill acquired by repeated practice and concentrated in the hand of a savage," no one can fall in love without at first building and then being thrown into the air by a catapult. Of course, everyone already knows this on a deep, genetic level. Otherwise, the human race would never have propagated itself. As I look back at my own feeble attempts at falling in love and getting others to fall in love with me, I see, as with second sight, that a catapult was always involved, one of my own making. The problem, however, is that I never knew I was making a catapult at the time, I just thought I was trying to get someone to fall in love with me. But now, knowing that I have to build one, I can do so deliberately, not leaving things to chance. I just hope that building catapults is easier than breaking rocks in prison. Based upon his studies, Buster seems to think that it is.

As previously suggested, Keaton does not 'invent' the love catapult in this film, for it has always existed, but like Prometheus, Keaton *reveals* it to us. Interestingly, though a catapult sends you hurtling through the air, its etymology emphasizes the downward part of the journey, as 'cata' means 'downward' in Greek, thus revealing that, as a device for 'falling' in love, the love catapult is perhaps not only a redundant phrase; it is also as much a metaphysical concept as it is an ingenious device. In the beginning was the love catapult, a Platonic form, while its mechanical instantiation, used for love, warfare, whatever, is merely a supplement. The catapult was always about falling in love, and love has always been a process of catapulting. No doubt, those who performed the Rites of Eleusis in ancient Greece were privy to this knowledge, but somewhere along the line it got lost, and its secret was only revealed again when Keaton transforms a catapult into a catapult, that is the Platonic form of falling in love into an actual device throwing him into the air and into the arms of his Stone Age Siren. We know that Keaton must have had this in mind, for when he and his beloved enter their cave, he is obviously alluding to Plato's eponymous parable.

Confession time. I was so excited by these Busterian revelations, seeming to just fall from the sky, that I found myself next to the lake where I had first confessed my love to a girl. It was the hardest thing I had ever done, and I actually felt relieved when she very politely noted that, since I was attending a state school and majoring in 'The Humanities,' we were not a good match. Cuz what would I have done if she felt the same way? I had absolutely no idea. This was way before I had seen *Sherlock Jr.* (1924, Metro Pictures) and realized that, if necessary, I could have learned to romance her by watching movies, even copying what the leading man does in real time. It also never occurred to me because I was only allowed to watch films about Vietnam, nuclear wars, and battles in space - romance, and the carnality that comes with it, was a strictly forbidden genre. But it doesn't really matter, because F. said no to me anyway and in addition to the film's not so subtle instructions on how to commit romance via peripheral vision, its main subtext (in addition to *The Refutation*) is that love is nothing but false bottoms upon false bottoms.

While the film's opening intertitle reads, "Don't try to do two things at once and expect justice from both" (in my case confessing love and acting upon it as well), even so, the basis of comedy is doing the wrong thing. So Buster is immediately caught by the viewer in the act of attempting to learn how to be a detective (from reading a book, interestingly enough) and work in a movie theater at the same time. And as Keaton must have realized this would become his most famous film, packing "within its modest 45 minutes enough comic material for several ordinary features," he brilliantly (both in the form and content of *The Refutation*), alludes to the fact that Abel's theory starts from a false supposition about the primitive nature of indigenous cultures and their need for "antithetical magic." In doing so, Keaton converts a false bottom into a false bottom.

When Buster is escaping the real crooks, as it is always a case of Buster being mistaken for them, he jumps into an open brief case which his detective's assistant Gillette is holding while disguised as a street vendor. Since it has a false bottom, Buster is able to elude his pursuers long enough to lock them into a barn which has a "false wall" that is really a revolving door Buster has entered. When the men discover it, they push their way in, but since it is a revolving door Buster swings out this door on the other side, allowing him to escape. Indeed, if we side with the atomic theories of Lucretius, which deny the concept of up and down as we know it, then this false wall could also be classified as a false bottom.

Nevertheless, there is one more false bottom, and that would be the chassis of the gangsters' car which Buster has stolen and which separates from the top when Buster slams on the breaks, *catapulting* Buster and his beloved into a lake, where the true top of the car with the false bottom floats long enough for them to make it across due to Buster's ingenuity in propping up the convertible's *tonneau* cover, thus causing it to behave as a sail.

Ok, there is at least one more false bottom in the film that is also a true bottom. Buster has found himself, without support, on the handle bars of a motorcycle which a policeman had been driving until he fell off. Unbeknownst to Keaton, who thinks the policeman is still driving (yet another false bottom, there are so many now I can barely count and no doubt closer viewings of the film would reveal even more), he has been steering the motorcycle true with his own true bottom. At one point, he is jetting across a bridge that has not been finished. Luckily, two trucks pass one another at the very moment Buster rides across. All this, of course, is out of Buster's field of vision due to the speed at which the motorcycle is moving and also due to his odd position on the motorcycle, bottom on the handlebars. So, from Buster's perspective, what looks like a complete bridge with a true bottom is really an unfinished bridge with a false bottom (false in that Buster thinks the bridge has a bottom). But when the trucks pass at the exact moment his motorcycle crosses, the bridge suddenly has a true 'functional' bottom which is also a false bottom since it is only a bottom temporarily squeezed together by the hands of fate.

But suffice it to say that in my state of elation over the love catapult I was not in my right state of mind, and rather than thinking back upon the sorrows the lake of my first love once produced, I must have tried to build a love catapult right then and there. Apparently this is not so easy to do, especially when one half of the brain is standing in front of the movie screen and the other is in the movie itself. Like Horace Walpole, in his frenzied excitement after dreaming the plot to the world's first Gothic novel, *The Castle of Otranto*, I threw myself into the task, possessed, not even stopping to sleep. Just as with Walpole's experience writing the novel, I was heartened by the knowledge that rather than trying to remember how my father broke rocks in prison I was working from pure inspiration - so much so that the catapult seemed to be building itself. I knew that true love was just over the next fortification. But alas, although my experience started out as enchanting as Walpole's creative process, it ended as strangely as Walpole's castle of elephants urinating acid from the sky, cracking the helmets of warrior giants and making saints explode in puffs of acrid mist.

Truth be told, as I navigated the catapult's tunnels, vaults, grottoes, and catacombs, I lost consciousness at some point. When I woke up I was standing next to the lake, the catapult nowhere to be found. There was nothing around but an open sailor's chest filled with fake penises which I was throwing one by one into the water as far as I could. As I was throwing the penises into the lake, I observed each unique flight through the air and Icarus crash into the water - I have no idea why - like Edweard Muybridge without his cameras and tripwires. After I had thrown the last fake penis, I stood watching the once again tranquil water for a bit. Until I remembered that in the event of a terrorist attack poisonous clouds of gas would tend to linger over larger bodies of water. I sprinted as fast as I could until I felt I was a safe distance away, and then, probably from all the activity of building the missing catapult and tossing the fake penises into the river, realized how hungry I was.

I didn't really know where I'd run to, but I saw a restaurant that seemed quite popular as it had a large number of people lined up at the window. Even though the wait would be excruciating I had the strangest feeling that the kind of hunger I had inside could only be satisfied by what lay at the end. Call it a gut feeling, as Buster might say. At first I thought it had to be the delirium of fatigue and hunger, but after a while it seemed as if the slow moving line was not moving at all. I kept looking toward the front, and sure enough people were receiving loaves of bread they seemed to relish like those who are starving. So I kept my faith and good spirits up and stood in line rigid as a statue. Suddenly, I felt arms around me and, too weak to resist, found myself being carried into the shop next door to the restaurant. I had no idea what sort of deviltry awaited me until I recognized the two men who were directly in front of me in the original line. They seemed to be in as bad a shape as I was as they put forth no resistance to the diabolical pervert who began removing their clothes. Tie, jacket, shirt, cummerbund; I watched in fear and fascination unable to move. Pants.

They weren't wearing underwear.

Then I realized what I had been doing - in a state the French have described as *automatisme ambulatoire* - rather than building a love catapult. I had been breaking into all the department stores in town and stealing the fake penises off of all the mannequins I could find, somehow managing to carry a giant sailor's chest under my arm and not get caught by the police. But someone must have seen me, like in *The Goat* (1921, Metro Pictures) where a man is turned into a man. Of course this would only be possible if Buster were first standing so still in a bread line he was mistaken for a mannequin, just like me. Was I a real cigar store Indian, or merely modeling the clothes of one? I couldn't wait around for my situation to turn into some humanist masterpiece. Still hungry and delirious, I foresaw only three possible outcomes - my first love passing me by on the street only to turn and say, "You're an illusion to me now," or being restored to manhood via mistaken identity, "Dead Shot Dan," a man but not the right man, or worst of all, a department store worker on her lunch break screaming at the police and calling me out as the real me, "Penis in the Hand." That final nightmare gave me the strength to flee, hiding in trains and under hospital beds, until I was able to make it to the next town.

On The Run

In my new fugitive state, I was forced to learn about Buster in a more haphazard manner - through life experience, and through memories of the films I'd watched in what now seemed not like my parents' 'unrecognizable house,' but like an agoraphobe's last stop on the road to nowhere. I wandered for weeks with nary a samurai sword or bullwhip knocking leaves off of the trees overhead, nary a barefooted soul tossing his red socks out into the street and then, at the risk of his life, retrieving them in order to do it again. I walked for miles, I stole food and the occasional bicycle, I rode the rails when America's infrastructure allowed, and I lived "on the road" and let me tell you Kerouac's novel may be autobiographical but it is not in the least bit realistic. "Down in Denver all I did was die" does not begin to capture the sort of loneliness you face on the run. I felt like I was disappearing and probably would have if I had not kept Buster Keaton's *The Blacksmith* (1922, Comique Film Co.), where a dark horse is transformed into a dark horse is transformed into a dark horse, close to my blackening heart.

As a blacksmith's assistant, Buster, like me, is a dark horse for a man. Hopeless with a hammer and nails, he seems to be unable to do anything except cook eggs on the smithy. When his boss gets arrested, however, Buster is forced to hold the fort himself, in particular fixing a Rolls Royce and putting new shoes on a beautiful woman's beautiful white horse. The damsel leaving to return later, Buster characteristically tries to do two things at once, that is fix the car and shoe the horse. The inevitable happens, of course, which is that Buster ends up squirting oil all over the horse as it stands next to him, turning the white horse into a dark horse - or at least one side of it. When the woman returns, Buster is able to keep things copacetic by casually helping her onto the horse while only showing its unmarred, pearly side.b Given that Buster is a dark horse as a man, he is also a dark horse as a husband, particularly the husband of a woman whose white horse he has besmirched with the blackest of the earth's blood. But, as we all know, a true dark horse always ends up winning in the end. When one of the woman's friends notices the black side of the horse, she screams so loudly that the horse is spooked and starts taking her terrified owner on the ride of her life. Buster, who is running away from the newly sprung boss who is angry at him for accidentally destroying the Rolls Royce that came in for a simple tire change, sees the horse and lovely rider barreling toward him and dives into a nearby bale in hopes of escaping. The woman obviously has the same instinct, as she dives off the horse as it passes that very hay bale. Like all women of that era, she has fainted in mid flight,c only to wake up in a bale of hay in Buster's arms. Assuming that the blacksmith's assistant who had earlier that day shoed her horse has now saved her life, she decides that he is the man for her. They get up and, running for their love, hop on a passing train to elope. A dark horse has been transformed into a dark horse which in turn has transformed into a dark horse (as trains were known as iron horses by the Native Americans).

1.   Doing two things at once, we might note, while stupid in most cases, is exactly what a pun does, which is only further evidence that the pun as a form of magic runs throughout Keaton's psyche in even deeper ways than previously imagined.

2.   The similarities between this incident and the story of the Yoruba trickster Eshu's two-colored hat, one side painted white and the other side painted black, specifically designed to get friends to quarrel over what they have seen - one having seen him passing in one direction and the other passing in the opposite direction - are too obvious to be mere coincidence. Although this allusion to the trickster, whose main purpose, according to Lewis Hyde, is to point out to us foolish humans the ambiguous and unreliable nature of semiotic 'sign systems', is no doubt lost on the casual viewer, it was definitely not lost on Keaton the director, whose encyclopaedic knowledge of both history and prehistory was revealed one year later in *Three Ages*, which we've already discussed.

3.   In addition to being obsessed with clairvoyants, psychiatrists of the late Victorian and early

Modernist eras were confounded as to whether fainting caused women to fall or falling caused women to faint. Indeed, the infamous quarrels between Freud and his student Jung on this matter undoubtedly, despite the complacent critical consensus concerning their castration debates, were the main thing that led to their acerbic parting of ways. The debates became so labyrinthine and nuanced that Jung eventually evaded the subject (and attempted to get laid with that old 'I'm a feminist' trick) by developing a theory that everyone has both male and female characteristics and is thus equally susceptible to fainting. Freud, for his part, noted that by the 1930s women fainted a lot less than they used to and speculated on how shifts in civilization might account for this.

It was during these dark days, hiding from the cold like a beached whale among some subway station punks, that something strange happened. Amongst my new "family," news of Buster was being bantered about so carelessly that I was like a guest at another family's Thanksgiving who, overwhelmed at the rate and intricacy with which the food is passed around the table, forgets to take any for oneself. On the run, there was very little talk of Buster, much less his prescient warning that, at any given point in time, one may get married by accident. This is not a warning about protecting yourself against taking marriage vows, which is impossible, but something more along the ontological lines delineated by the author of Ecclesiastes who informs us of the world we must live in whether we like it or not. When one of the beached punks, a needle hanging out of his arm like a fake penis, whispered, "We get married almost every day of our lives," I recognized by the very reverence with which he uttered the words that they must have somehow been channeled from Buster's own mouth. In fact, I lay back with my eyes closed and imagined them coming from his mouth like a bubble in a cartoon and my entire world transformed retroactively. I realized that since skipping town I'd been married at least forty or fifty times.

This gave me the courage to marry two men whose lodgings had seemed too good to be true, as they were offering them to me for the little money I had earned working as a barker in the local shooting gallery, mysteriously finding a skill I never knew I had. No matter what the target was, I simply couldn't miss, which not only impressed my bosses but whomever passed by our booth! I actually had some traveling money for once, which is a good thing to have when you are on the run, and even better when you're ready to open up your heart and settle down. I married them both at once and moved in that very evening.

As a five hundred pound sufferer of borderline personality disorder who was too large to wipe his own ass, Ted was not the ideal mate. Fortunately there was a Rosencrantz to his Guildenstern, Todd, who was living with us and did not seem to mind taking on the ass wiping duties. I never asked Todd about the alacrity with which he assumed this particular job, although in retrospect I probably should have. It seemed, for a while, a happy threesome, with one spouse wiping my other spouse's ass, and me enjoying nothing but conjugal bliss in between 'movements.'

Toilet Training

Even though I was somewhat disgusted by Ted, and one of his shits precipitated the episode which led to our break-up, it was ultimately his borderline paranoid personality disorder that made it impossible to continue living with him. As might be expected of a five hundred pound borderline paranoid spouse who never left his home - one day he moved something through his bowels prodigious enough to stop up the toilet. Although Todd had, quite lovingly I might add, made Ted's ass as clean as a five-hundred pound man's ass can be made to be, he seemed to have no idea how to unstop the toilet whose contents floated dangerously near the edge of the bowl. This discontinuity in Todd's fecal résumé was odd enough, but what was even odder was the fact that a five hundred pound man who took such prodigious shits should not have equipped his home with an industrial strength plunger. In fact, amongst all the radio equipment for keeping tabs on the outside world and packaged food which Ted scuttled to on his wheelchair at night, not even the most modest of rubber plunging devices was to be found. Knowing that I myself would have to take a dump sooner or later, and having grown fond of no longer having to find clandestine locations in the city's streets and alleys, sometimes getting married to a police officer in the very middle of a bowel movement, I set out in search of a plunger that King Arthur would be proud of. I went to a hardware store, and then a drug store. No luck. Next morning on my second grocery trip that weekend for my five hundred pound borderline paranoid spouse, I checked the grocery store for a plunger. Again no luck. I started to get paranoid thinking that the local plumbers' union had made some shady deal to prevent plungers from being sold around town. In fact, the first thing I noticed about the town was its plethora of plumbing companies and beauty salons - way more than its heads of hair or population of five hundred pound borderline paranoid spouses would justify. The controlled constipation techniques I'd learned on the road from a kind guru junkie who'd moved east from California - reducing food intake, going easy on the fiber - have a limited life-span for the most experienced of yogis, much less me.

I remember it was a Sunday morning when the shit finally hit, partly because I was getting ready to skip church as usual, but mostly because a post-controlled constipation urge, at least your first, will sear itself indelibly on your bowels' memory. Practicing my stance and my gait, which is sort of like a mix between a cowboy after a long ride and a ballerina trying to keep her thighs together, and then praying to my bowels that my lower intestines (which are not referred to by doctors as "the second brain" for nothing) would restrain themselves even when they caught site of the oasis, I made the mile long walk to the health club I had just joined primarily in order to have a place to take a shit - given that I was living in a city where your best bet on a public place to go is to ask the nearest homeless person for a good alley. Those last steps, when you're already in the facility, are always the hardest - that's when the second brain really goes into overdrive, but when I finally made it to the stall it was one to savor, one for the "three ages." And, as it was the industrial strength type of toilet they install seemingly everywhere except in people's houses, I decided to savor it. "Can I get a courtesy flush!?" some roided out bruiser shouted. "Request denied motherfucker!"

Then since I was already at the gym, I worked out, cowboy boots and all. Feeling pumped, I came back home, took a shower, and prepared myself some of the food I had purchased over the last two days. Now mind you, I had personally gone out and shopped for this food, and I had a hankering for some fiber as you might imagine. There was so much on Ted's shopping list that, not owning a car, I had to go both Friday *and* Saturday morning and the grand total was around two hundred dollars, of which the five hundred pound borderline paranoid spouse had contributed a hundred. As soon as I opened the fridge, he asked, "What are you eating?" I told him what I was eating. "That food has to last me all month," he said. "Love," I told him, "you gave me a hundred bucks. I spent two hundred bucks on food. So don't give me shit about eating food that is half mine." He then started quizzing me on how much I'd spent, demanding to look at the receipts. I told him that I would look to see if I could find them but for him to leave me the hell alone so I could eat my food in peace. I came out of our room a couple of hours later and placed both receipts on his desk. He asked me what it was, and I told him it was the receipts for the two hundred bucks of food. He then went into demon mode, calling me a "prurient, inbred Southern piece of shit," and a "bitch." Shaking (or is it jiggling?) with rage, he screamed, "Get out of my house." I told him to take his fucking medication and walked out the front door, slamming it behind me. "Fine," I said to myself, "I need to find out more about Buster Keaton anyway." I came back the next morning at 6:30 to go to sleep. He was awake lying next to me, saw me, but I didn't say a word to him. Same treatment when I woke up. Same thing the next day. On my way back from hanging with the subway punks, whose company I enjoyed due to our mutual love for tripped out banter whilst in a prone position, I stopped into a plumbing company to inquire about their services as our toilet was still stopped up. As the secretary took the information, I asked to use the bathroom, knowing what I'd find inside. I heard the phone ring and the secretary answered it. It was time to make my exit. I burst through the bathroom door, then race-walked out the front door, carrying the plunger on my shoulder like a lumberjack would rest a long-handled axe. When I had turned a sufficient number of corners and slowed to a more normal pace a journalist of some kind suddenly appeared and took my picture. I guess he thought the sight of the plunging lumberjack in a town devoid of civilian plungers was newsworthy enough to warrant a photo, but if I were him, I would have considered how easily I could have taken off his head with one deft swing. Lucky for him, I didn't want to have to use a bloody plunger on the five-hundred pound borderline paranoid spouse's toilet and decided to let things slide. In retrospect I should have recognized the photo as a bad omen.

As soon as I walked through the door, which was held open for me by the apartment manager, I heard her utter the word "thirty-six," our apartment number. As I walked up the stairs I saw someone following me. "Excuse me, excuse me sir. Hey, you on the steps…" "Do I know you?" "I'm the owner of this building." That answer came right as I was standing in front of our apartment and unlocking the door. As the door swung open, he asked me, "Do you live here?" Now, I was too tired from my theft and getaway to remember the five hundred pound borderline paranoid spouse's total ban on revealing that I lived there - apparently some local statute against polygamy. I was always supposed to say, "I'm helping Mr. Kennedy." But being so tired I was confronted with the dilemma of "yes" or "no." I said "yes" because it seemed like, holding a plunger in the manner that I was, that "no" would not be very convincing. So I said "yes," and he paused to say "Okay" and asked if I had gotten the package that was on top of the mailboxes. The door was open this whole time, and the five hundred pound borderline paranoid spouse, who never leaves the common living area, heard it all. He said to my Todd, "Okay, I want him out of here right now," urging Todd to physically throw me out as he threatened to change the locks. I got right in front of the five hundred pound borderline paranoid spouse's face to tell him off. He threatened to call the police, and I said, "When they get here who do you think they're going to take away? The guy with an entire pharmacy of anti-psychotic medication who knowingly committed Section 8 fraud for polygamous purposes, or the fugitive who married him?" They might throw us both out, actually, but I tried to play it cool as if I had the advantage. As I walked into my room, I saw a note on a trash can that read in cursive letters too graceful for fatty's fingers, "Dude, let's have a talk." Todd had gone outside to smoke. I followed a few minutes later under the pretense of taking out some garbage. Todd said to me, "Dude, I've been 'thrown out' twenty times since I've lived here. I've been saving up some money, and I'm out of here first of the month." Todd knelt down before me and asked, "Would you do me the honor of divorcing Ted and becoming my one and only husband?" Under the circumstances there seemed no way I could refuse, and the look in Todd's eyes made me realize I didn't want to refuse. As soon as I said yes, in addition to that love rush a bride gets when she says yes to her husband-to-be, it felt like a great weight, around five hundred pounds in fact, had been lifted off my shoulders.

Domestic Bliss

After the papers came back from Reno, sealing our twin divorce from Ted, the five-hundred pound borderline schizophrenic seemed resigned to his fate. He watched mutely as we moved our things out of the apartment and into a van. Since we had to keep going up and down stairs so much, on every trip Ted took the opportunity to ask me for "one last hero" at the corner store. I'd go get the hero after putting our boxes in and bring it up to Ted, and then by the next trip down he'd be finished with it and ask for "just one more," just one more for "old times' sake." I wasn't sure whose old times Ted was referring to, but the nine hero sandwiches I purchased for him while Todd and I moved out seemed well worth the price of the five hundred pounder's relative silence.

The first few weeks with Todd were like a dream. With my stolen plunger I got a job as a plumber and began to make some serious money. Meanwhile, Todd showed me how to pick up girls around town and how to secretly, with strings attached to dollar bills, trip people with whom I was angry and send them flying across the street right through a store window. But little did I know that Todd's body, well-toned from positioning Ted's body in order to wipe his ass, was planning to fall off a wagon I hadn't seen him riding. I'd always wondered how he always had so much money when I was the one with the full-time job. I don't know how many times I came home to chocolates or flowers or a fifth of Irish whiskey and a prostitute so we could enjoy an evening of three-way lovemaking, which we both missed from time to time. I'd protest of course, telling Todd not to waste his money on me like that and he'd tell me not to worry my pretty little head about that kind of stuff, and that I was worth every penny he'd spent and more.

But apparently, not doing heroin does wonders for the bank account. And Todd had been negotiating with the monkey on the sly. Indeed, if I'd known it was so lucrative I probably would have ditched the whole plumbing thing and not done heroin myself.

One night we were walking down the street and I saw the most beautiful pink-haired girl of all time. I knew we were meant to be together because she had made a pair of handcuffs into a belt, the most objective of correlatives I had ever seen. And yet I had nothing to say to her. How could I become her prisoner? "Hey, we're looking for a little pink poodle that's gotten off its leash," said Todd. "You haven't seen it have you?" The handcuff girl started laughing at this allusion to her beauty and said no she hadn't seen it. Like some sort of Neanderthal, I sputtered out in a creepy monotone, "I like your belt." "Well sailor," she growled while scratching my chin with her razor-sharp pink claws, "it might be your lucky day, because as it just so happens . . . my belt likes you back."

Maybe it was my imagination but I thought I saw a twinge of jealousy in Todd's face as the handcuff girl led me away to a weekend that would be more difficult to escape than I ever imagined. But what could either Todd or I do about it? He was the one who'd taught me everything, which I learned as well as I had learned to break rocks in prison, not very. Somehow he was the one who knew that an imaginary poodle was the key to handcuff girl's belt. He always knew, but looked a little shaky as she and I walked together down the street - like a Shaolin master whose student hadn't given him proper respect.

It was obvious that, despite the number of times I had already been married, I still had more to learn about the ways of love. To be quite frank, I probably had little agency when it came to staying with Todd or going with handcuff girl, or for that matter how long I would be in her basement apartment, or what I would do there. First O (which I soon found out was what I was supposed to call her) had me remove my clothes, but instead of reciprocating, she went into another room and brought out a tuxedo, which she ordered me to put on. It fit me pretty well, which made me believe she either happened to like people my size or had several versions in her closet. Then she handed me a sheet of paper, which she referred to as a "release form," and asked me to read aloud and then sign. The "release form" was both titillating and slightly scary:

> Keep me rather in this cage, and feed me sparingly, if you dare. Anything that brings me closer to illness and the edge of death makes me

more faithful. It is only when you make me suffer that I feel safe and secure. You should never have agreed to be a god for me if you were afraid to assume the duties of a god, and we all know they are not as tender as all that.

Signed,

Then, just as soon as I'd put my tuxedo on, O ordered me to remove the pants, including my underwear so that all I was wearing was the jacket, the shirt, the cummerbund and a bow tie to top it off. O had chosen the 'Tail' style as the tuxedo coat with fabric hanging down the lower back for a classy look. The 'Cutaway' style coat would have been embarrassing with my bare butt cheeks showing. The tie was a fairly standard small black bow that could be found at almost any clothing store. The cummerbund, I was told, was perhaps the most important part of the tuxedo. It was a broad, black sash that wraps around the waist. These are worn in a very specific way, and the technique of tying was originally intended to allow the wearer to quickly insert a ticket stub when attending an elegant show. It has grown to be an integrated part of the tuxedo image, and now is considered to be an essential part even if its original functionality is largely obsolete.

After I was fully half-dressed O led me down into a dark basement room. As my eyes adjusted to the darkness, I noticed, with excitement, that O had stripped down to just her pink handcuff belt and black satin undergarments. It was then that I realized that she was not alone, but also had an accomplice fully-dressed in a period piece, breasts pushed up, costume-ball gown. Her 'friend's' face was hidden behind a mask like we were in some low rent version of *Eyes Wide Shut* (1999, Warner Bros.). Shuddering at what I thought I might have gotten myself into I was ordered to sit upon a throne-like chair where at O's command Emma, as she was called, removed, in a very slow and delicious manner, my cummerbund and unbuttoned by shirt exposing my stomach. Emma then removed O's handcuff belt, and handcuffed me to the throne-chair. Then O took out a zip lock bag of makeup and made a clown face on my bare chest. Painted in a 'Heavy Metal Glitter' pink eye-shadow my nipples were the big droopy eyes of the clown. My sternum bore an outlandish clown nose painted in what I could only, in all honesty, call a 'Megawatt Smile Red' while my stomach, as the clown's puckered mouth, was done up in a 'Sushi Flower' pink. I was not allowed to speak as the two women made me up whilst they pinched and poked various parts of my body like school-girls rough-housing on the playground. All in all, I can't say that I didn't enjoy my entrée to whatever my 'Master' had in mind. I almost imagined myself in the 'make-up' chair getting ready for my close-up.

However, things escalated quickly, when over the next several hours the dildos, and not the cameras, came out, breaking my reverie, and not a single one of my holes was spared. Even things I had never really thought of as holes, such as armpits, were ravaged without remorse. Feeding off my submission to their poking and prodding, the two women gagged me when they wanted to hear me moan, ungagged me when they wanted to hear screams, and tickled me when they wanted to make me giggle and laugh. In addition, there was the usual whipping, flogging, lashings and other indescribable (because I couldn't be sure exactly what was being done to me, nor what exactly to call it) tortures. At O's command Emma would whip, or flog or lash, me mercilessly while O laughed, literally tickled pink. The fact that the smudged pink clown face on my chest was beaten beyond recognition might have had something to do with that. When Emma grew too tired to continue, O would literally take the reins for a bit. After being unshackled from the throne-chair, the torture continued in various devices which the women had either purchased or constructed themselves. Each time I was placed in a new torture device, I tried to remember all the medieval diagrams my strip-club attending, masochist theory wielding colleague from Wellesley used to show me both during and after our outings. "She'd look good in this one, don't you think?" he would ask, "Or, how about this one?" I tried, throughout the machinic phase of my ordeal, to isomorphically connect my body to the machines my colleague had sketched with amazing precision on those cocktail napkins and remember whether those who entered particular ones generally lived or died. I do know that he was adamant about some being truly deadly, whereas others were merely constructed for 'fun.' But I was either just not a very good spatial thinker or, because of all the torture, too battered and disoriented to come to any recollection one way or the other. Maybe it was just the simple fact that I had never studied his napkin drawings or their codex forms back at his office with the thought that I might, one day, have practical use for them – though I did marvel at how similar they were to catapults.

After this ordeal, the two women took me to an old claw-toothed tub filled with warm water where they finally stripped me naked, sensuously sponged my body and cleansed my wounds. After consuming a gourmand's meal prepared by a third woman who had been hidden in the kitchen the whole time, we all retired to a king-sized bedroom and had a very tender, dare I say loving, foursome. The pain and the pleasure of the whole experience was almost more than I could handle. Thankfully I dreamed of Buster and for a brief moment I could imagine what it must have been like for him to return from an especially dangerous day of filming, only to be treated like a god among men by his adoring female fans. Even he must have had patches of makeup stubbornly remaining after a hard day's work.

Little did I know that I was merely being groomed for the next evening, a party in which I was the main attraction. A night produced by random words generated by the guests and turned into a violent sexual fantasy thanks to the story-telling powers of O. That night, each invited masked guest (only O never bothered to wear a mask) picked a word at random according to the method of the Surrealist game which came to be known as "The Exquisite Corpse," due to the first sentence produced by the method: "The exquisite corpse will drink the new wine." The same sentence structure was used at O's "Mouth Wide Open" party, with each guest suggesting a word from the part of speech - a noun, a verb, an adjective, and so on - that they had been assigned. Without knowledge of what words had been picked by the other guests, they combined to write the "high concept" version of my script with the following sentence: "The whalebone servant fended off the electric eels." From this sentence, O devised a story that the entire crew was to act out.

The guests were apparently, in a scenario that sounded somewhat foreign and somewhat familiar to my literary memories, meant to act out the role of an African tribe who, while out sailing, discovered a sinking ship flying a French flag. O of course cast herself as the Queen of the tribe, who, upon saving me, a female servant headed for the Americas in search of a better life, decides that I would best be rehabilitated by continuing my existence as if I had made it to the Americas and was forced to continue my indentured servitude. In this way, the patrons mystified in the orgy scene of *Eyes Wide Shut* would be revealed in *Mouths Wide Open* (2013, Undisclosed Basement Productions) as nothing but prudes with money, who could only get it up by "fucking with their masks on." On the other hand, the logic itself, like that pushed forward by certain colleagues of mine, was starting to seem a bit tortured in its own right. It seemed to me they wanted to have their cake (me) and eat it too (also me) by exposing the hidden cultural message of Kubrick's film: once a servant, always a servant – no matter the individual aspirations, thereby reinforcing their own class existence. So, after a period of bed-rest and forced fed yams, cooked many delicious ways by the hidden chef, to fatten me up to a delectable level, I was given a hoop skirt and whale-bone corset to wear to my debut feast.

Amazing costumes aside, it was, for all intents and purposes, a fairly elaborate story, composed *ex tempore* by O and loudly proclaimed to the guests who cheered at every explanatory detail, raising their goblets that unfortunately seemed more Viking than African in nature, likely a result of their limited prop supply. Continuing, O declared that, unlike the already discomfiting corsets worn by indentured women of the era, the African tribeswomen had actually worn corsets made entirely of whale bones which would pierce into their flesh and cause, depending upon how much they writhed in pain, various levels of bleeding ranging from the ornate cascade to the emergency-room gusher. However, like the wrong goblets, from what I could guess, I was not wearing anything with real whalebone in it, but merely one of Emma's cheap plastic corsets with some carefully placed bobby pins – but the intended effect was real enough to me, and hopefully for the 'audience' as well. Everything that evening was the most bizarre negotiation between exigency and truth to realism, so much so that the means by which O actually pulled it off were almost enough to keep my mind off the pain, both immediate and ongoing, literary and actual, from time to time.

It goes without saying that O, as Queen of the Tribe and quite cosmopolitan given the time period and geography she had chosen as mise en scène, had figured that although I declared myself an indentured servant lost at sea, trying to make my way to safety in America, that really was a euphemism for me being a sex slave (which I was in reality, having signed my 'release'), and that in order to maintain the space-time continuum that this particular African tribe required in her story, there was no reason I should not be subject to sex slavery for the enjoyment of all the participants. And, as this tribe of masked wealthy patrons to her 'secret sex party' had no seven year contract with me, they could leave me abandoned and alone as soon as they were tired of me, or basically when they found another sinking ship out on the ocean full of fresh slave meat. The event would almost be a cautionary tale, with their violence reminding me, over a period of mere days, what I had signed up for, however unknowingly, in my trip to the Americas. Seen in that light, being a sex slave was apparently a win-win situation.

I can't over-emphasize the amount of pre-festivity exposition that O went into so that every aspect of my impending torture would have a sense of narrative cause and effect, if not "realism" in the traditional sense. For instance, as I stood there in my hoop skirt and Emma's cheap plastic corset, there was quite a lengthy debate as to whether the group should try to procure actual electric eels to flail me with, which apparently were available in Chinatown, though it would be a significant use of time and money to obtain them, or whether a suitable substitute might be found. In the end, it was decided that, as with the Viking goblets, "regular" belts would be used, and that the cook from last night would make electric eel sound effects by caressing a light bulb with a sufficiently grounded wire after every stroke. Regardless, as people have said at least since the first Christians were thrown to the lions, "let the games begin." I was taken into the 'party' hall, which I had not yet seen, and lashed to a four wheeled device which, moving back and forth along a set of tracks, seemed like a rough device for tracking shots in early cinema. The cook sat in the corner with her light bulbs and grounded wires whilst the guests sat around the "camera cart" as if it were a mansion's dining table, holding belts of various length, width, substance, and bejewelment. O and Emma sat at the 'head' and 'foot' of the table, respectively, and pushed the hand cart / tracking device back and forth from one end of the group to the other, allowing each passerby to attack me with their "electric eel" from a premium vantage point. Apparently the device was sufficiently greased so that O and Emma could set me rolling with a minimum of physical effort, although they switched out with the guests so that they too could whip me while other guests kept me rolling. Indeed, things proceeded like a game of musical chairs, so each guest was able to enjoy whipping me from every possible angle. Only the cook maintained her position throughout, apparently she was the electrician of the house as well. As promised in the stochastic sentence created by the group, I was allowed to "fend off" these strikes, although with my legs and my arms tied in such a way so that I had only a Tyrannosaurus Rex range of motion with my arms, that element of the narrative was weighted heavily against me.

Then, just when I thought I couldn't take another blow, I was untied and brought back to the dining table, then placed upon it with my hoop skirt like I was giant dessert cake. As I lay there on the dining table, like the night before, which I should have suspected given the fact that I was an indentured sex slave, the dildos were once again brought out, only more this time since more people were involved, and absolutely no hole was spared including holes I had never really considered holes such as the backs of my knees and the clavicles in my neck.

Sometime during the proceedings, I was either

able to escape or allowed to think I had escaped because of a turn of events in O's story, most likely the latter. Someone having forgotten to cuff or tie me to the dining room table, I simply stood up, tore my cheap plastic corset from my waist, ripped through my hoop skirt and bellowed "My penis needs to breathe – wearing all this whalebone clothing is intolerable, no wonder the tuxedo remains king." I then launched myself past the befuddled cast and, grabbing the various parts of my tuxedo, sprinted out of the basement. From below I could hear O yelling that I was in breach of my sex slave contract and that she wasn't going to "play" with me anymore.

Walking through the subway, I realized that from my Cultural Studies viewpoint of erogenous tolerance I couldn't really cast aspersions upon the sexual proclivities of O and her crew, but based upon the soreness to all those holes that were not spared, even the ones that weren't really holes, in addition to the 'electric eel' beatings, "play" wouldn't personally be my thing in the future. And besides I'd already been away from Todd for almost 48 hours and I really missed him. I was also worried. Would he be furious with me? Would he be worried sick? All I knew was that I wanted to see him again as soon as possible and that after he had heard the story of O, he would no doubt soothe both my mental and physical wounds in a way only he knew how to do.

Though the haze of the weekend was still very much present, something - let's say a giant clock face high above the street corner - told me it was Monday morning and I was late for my plumbing work. But where was I? The subway system, whose extent was vaster than I'd ever imagined, so cavernous on a rainy

Monday morning, was in no hurry coming or going, forcing me to wait on the platforms for what seemed like hours. Furthermore, every single motorized walkway and escalator was still as death forcing me to run up and down the stairs, my tuxedo tails flapping behind me. Navigation in such a situation is quite a bit of guesswork. Would the friendly little subway rats direct me to the left, to the right, or straight down if I could ask them the way? If I took the one working elevator down, how far down would it take me? So when I finally got to the plumbing company late in the afternoon, the combination of lateness and my absurd tuxedo dress was too much for them to take. "Who the hell are you?" my boss said to the man in a tuxedo with a plunger over his shoulder. I tried to explain that I was their trusty plumber, but I was sacked of course, my plunger stripped from me like medals from a disgraced soldier. When I finally got home, literally dragging my tail between my legs, the door to Todd's personal bedroom (which he insisted on) was closed. No sound came out but an occasional congested cough. Todd must be sick with missing me, I thought, and so I went to the cookie jar where I left all our serious money so I could get him some cough medicine and get something to eat at a restaurant that didn't cater to penis-less mannequins. However, when I opened it, every single bit of the cookie-jar money was gone, and it was then I realized seeking a soul mate who was willing to wipe the ass of five hundred pound borderline paranoid individuals was probably not, on paper, the best of picks. But as we all know, we don't fall in love based on algorithms.

Junk Sickness

Todd had cleaned me out and I didn't know why. He'd always been so flush and generous since we'd become a relatively exclusive duo, I didn't know what to think. He was a free spirit both sexually and in the way he could turn the most mundane situations into an epic goof. I thought he'd wanted me to go out with the pink-haired girl, O, that somehow he had some inner sense that I would learn something for us both by flying solo. I thought about these things as I made the hardest, longest walk of my life down to the police station. And it wasn't just because of my dad's archetypal fear of the law, or my fear that my face might be posted on their 'Most Wanted' board for stealing fake penises. I felt quite helpless, knowing it was a choice between his existence and my existence. Todd or me, there is no us. Yoda logic could sometimes rival that of the Stoics in its concise ruthlessness. And here I was turning to the people I hated most because they were the only ones who could help me make the choice to go on living - alone.

I gave the officer the history of my case, which seemed pretty open and shut to me, but my emotions must have made my sell sound a little shaky. "Hold on there a minute," he said, "This is not an open and shut case."

I really couldn't believe it. I was sure that the tuxedo I was wearing, as torn-up as it was at the sex party, would provide incontrovertible proof of my honesty and standing in society, and I told the officer as much. But he just replied that we couldn't just go and arrest Todd until we heard his side of the story. Listen, I said, it's just like Buster Keaton's *The High Sign* (1921, Metro Pictures). I was hired by this woman to protect her father from The Blinking Buzzards, and though I'm a poor marksman I was able to social engineer the Blinking Buzzards to hire me to kill the father. This allowed me to get close enough to the Buzzards to infiltrate the gang without any real fighting skills. Blinking (the slow motion blink required to accurately fire a rifle, or pretend to be doing so) is transformed into a Blinking (Buzzard). Only, this time the woman had pink hair and a pair of handcuffs for a belt and had hired me to protect an indentured servant her tribe had discovered in a sinking French ship off the coast of Africa. Meanwhile, Todd was the Blinking Buzzard who infiltrated the cookie jar full of money while I was out all weekend doing a good deed, in fact several of them related to the whole indentured servant situation.

I thought that by putting things in terms of one of Buster's greatest crime dramas that my story would appeal more to the police officer class, but then I was thrown a curve ball. "Perhaps this is much more insidious," the officer countered, "like Buster Keaton's

Cops (1922, Comique Film Co.), which just so happens to be the master's first foray into the question of existential philosophy, Professor, or Butler, or whatever you think you are in that get-up. Surely you know the one, where having been told by the Mayor's daughter (aka the pink-haired beauty in your case) that she won't marry him until he becomes a successful businessman, Buster sets out to become just this. Jean Paul Sartre, whom Buster anticipated by many years, would call this inauthentic behavior since, rather than creating his own reality, he accepts the reality given to him by others. What Buster takes as essence is really nothing but existence. But even without knowledge of existentialism (it is clear that Keaton but not the character he plays is aware of its philosophical implications), one can be quite successful. In the hustle and bustle of urban ambulation, Buster bumps into a guy with a fat wallet, maybe this Todd fellow you're accusing. It happens more often than you would at first think in a big city and we'd all be fools to not constantly be in that Buddhist state of mindfulness which will allow you to find wallets full of money on the ground. Then let's say you're suddenly flush with enough of Todd's capital - yeah with Todd's dough - to buy a horse and wagon to carry furniture for those moving from one abode to the next - what in Buster's time was called an 'expressman.' Of course, neither you nor Buster realizes you're not an 'expressman,' thinking that you own the furniture. When he's disabused of this mistake and hounded by us cops, Buster must use all his wit and resources to evade them, transforming himself from one 'expressman' to another type of 'expressman,' one who is actually on the run. But you, genius, you just walk right into the precinct here hoping someone will listen to your heartbreak stories.

"But in the end you both end up losers, yeah, rebuffed by the mayor's daughter one last time - or the pink-haired beauty if she even exists, rosy-palms - cuz both of you are employing a tactical rather than a strategic approach to the global economy, with you both again transformed back into an 'expressman,' that is, in the sense of being "expressly man," existence without essence. Yeah, this is one of the rare films in which Buster does not get the girl, and if you knew your Keaton you'd have taken this as a warning that only by behaving authentically can we truly lay claim to being successful existentialists. Only successful existentialists will get the girl, according to Keaton and, much later, Sartre."

In a town where even the subway punks whispered tales of Buster, I guess I shouldn't have been surprised to be matched, film for film, by folks who could put cinema to forensic - and apparently philosophical - use. The worst part was that in a court of law the most elaborate explanation always wins, and this cop definitely had me outmatched today, having lost my wits to being an indentured servant, then sacked by the plumbing company, not to mention the hunger, penury, and sense of betrayal. I felt my world starting to slip away, more Camus than Sartre style. Luckily "the big guy," Detective Duffy, was brought in to settle the matter before I took a real existential beating.

Tall, bald, shades, leather jacket, and string goatee-style beard, Duffy got one whiff of my story and said, "OK, let's do this the old school way. We'll go there right now and see what Mr. Sanginario has to say for himself." In the meantime, they ran his name and got quite the list. Todd had been so sick sounding when I left that I assumed he was 'coming down' with something and would be in bed all day. But when we got there he was gone. Detective Duffy had no problem searching through all his stuff for drugs and a picture of him, and to see if he was hiding under the bed or in the closet. He found nothing of note, but said the burned top of his light bulb looked suspicious, like he'd been using it to cook on. I agreed it was odd as we had a nice kitchenette, at least by the standards of the sort of apartment we had landed. Todd even did most of the cooking, with brio, and he always made full use of that kitchen, not some kind of wilderness survival hijinks in his room. I thanked Detective Duffy and he said that they'd start assembling a case. I told him that Todd had a driver's license, so Duffy figured he'd just run that for a photograph.

I went back into my half of the house to sulk, knowing that even someone as formidable-looking as Detective Duffy didn't have much to go on. He said the evidence was purely circumstantial, which in layman's terms meant that I hadn't caught Todd with his hands in the cookie jar. But even if I had done that, it would have been a he said he said situation, with the relatively anonymous nature of legal tender making it hard to prove ownership. If you could prove ownership, that's apparently 9/10ths of the law, but in a jury trial, you need a unanimous verdict.

Over the next few hours I thought about ways to prove what I knew was true. Eventually Todd came home and shut his door. During the next few hours he came out a few times but my door was closed. He left a note in the bathroom saying, "Dude, we haven't touched base in a while." The note, for some reason, gave me new resolve. Maybe the peremptory baseball metaphor - or was it a paintball metaphor – was just enough to allow my bad-ass, Texan hating instincts to overcome the first real domestic bliss I'd felt in some time, perhaps ever.

I shaved and showered, readying myself for some schooling the next morning. Woke up at ten til six, put on my tuxedo, grabbed a screwdriver just in case, and ambushed Todd in his room. I told him that he had to get his things and leave in fifteen minutes. That I had already contacted the police. That they came yesterday and his best bet was to not be seen anywhere near 46 Vinal Ave. because a) I can't have his ass there anymore and b) the police were on their way as soon as they had an arrest warrant. Todd began sobbing what I later learned was the addict's sob, the one that almost gets to you and almost got to me even and especially when you recognize it for what it is - total hopelessness. He even, between gasps, offered to start wiping my ass like he had done for Ted. I was tempted for a moment, but luckily remembered that I actually enjoy wiping my ass. He calmed down a little, half asleep and strung out, asked if the cops were going to tackle him when he walked outside. "No, if they were here I would have already let them in." He had nowhere to go. I answered, "Sure you do - out the door and down the street."

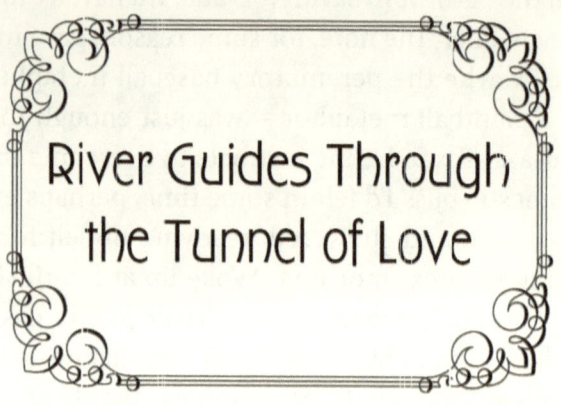

River Guides Through the Tunnel of Love

Despite the difficulty of playing tough, which only desperation and my knowledge of *film noir* allowed me to do, telling Todd to walk on down the hall was one of the toughest things I'd ever done. I'm still not quite sure how I pulled it off, but I think my ability to turn the situation around is a classic case of what Buster Keaton calls "Turning A Train Into A Raft." You see, despite the promises that conductors may make, a train may be derailed at any time. You may suddenly find yourself rolling down the road instead of train tracks or, even worse, sinking to the bottom of a river. In the latter case you must act quickly. First you have to climb out of the window and run along the top of the train to the train engine. Then, using whatever tools you can find, you have to detach the engine from the rest of the train. Whatever you do, don't worry about the other passengers. They'll figure something out. Your job is merely to choose the flattest piece of wood before it's tossed into the engine's furnace and paddle to the riverbank like your life depends on it, because it does. However, it is important to remember that turning a train into a raft is only a stopgap measure. Even with you paddling as if your life depends on it, the train engine will soon sink to the bottom, or it will be carried over the edge of a waterfall.

So I was riding high for a few days on my ability to turn a train into a raft, but emotionally speaking, I felt like my shot at domestic bliss had turned out more like *The Electric House* (1922, Buster Keaton Productions, Inc.). When Buster and those nearby him (Ted, Todd, and me?) drop their diplomas at a 'State' university graduation ceremony, they accidently switch them, allowing Keaton to switch careers and obtain a lucrative gig as an electrical engineer or a "dealer in switches." When the real electrical engineer finds out what happens, he sneaks to the mansion which, after having read *Electricity Made Easy*, Buster has converted into a wonderland of gadgetry - that is until the 'real' electrical engineer sneaks into the switchboard room during a party and switches all the cords so that books punch guests, dishes in an automatic dishwasher become weapons of mass destruction, and Buster switches to Sisyphus as he attempts to walk up the electric stairs which have been switched to move down rather than up. Finally, after momentarily thinking the house is haunted, Keaton figures out what is really going on and electrocutes the engineer behind the switchboard with a bucket of water. The 'real' electrical engineer, who somehow has survived the electrocution, is disgraced and given the bum's rush, as is Buster for his fraudulent endeavours. Yet, rather than merely leaving the premises, Buster ties a rock around his neck and dives into the pool, which has a giant lever (switch) that can cause the pool to be filled and drained in a matter of seconds. The young lady of the house takes pity on poor Buster and pushes the lever to undrain the pool just in time. Then the father comes along and switches it back to suicide mode. He leaves and the girl switches it back, only to find that Buster has fallen down the rather large drain hole which has made the insta-pool possible. He is swept down a rather lengthy culvert, at the end of which he finds his 'companion', the real electrical engineer, sitting there. It seems they have both switched from promising young men to bums at the end of a drainpipe, a sorry 'state' indeed.

Washed up as I was emotionally, and thinking Todd must be in an equivalent 'state' just like the 'real' engineer (or was he the fake one?), I did what seemed natural. I wandered around town for a few weeks drowning my sorrows at all the holes in the wall I could find. I figured I had been in enough trouble with the law already, so I stuck with houses of medium repute. Even though I knew of no nearby rivers, one time I chanced upon a river guide, with curves that were nothing like any river I'd ever seen, drinking right next to me. Feeling as if my train-turned-into-a-raft had already gone over the falls I asked her, for future reference, what she would do or has done in similar situations. It didn't hurt that I found her extremely attractive, gorgeous even, like some water nymph you'd encounter in a gigantic river gorge - and this despite her broken leg and two dislocated shoulders. "If I had three arms, I would have dislocated that third shoulder too!" she joked while her laughter gave off a sort of bizarre mermaid vibe. For some reason, all her injuries (she was living off of disability - like Ted minus 380 pounds) made me regard her not as a bad river guide, but as someone who had truly given everything for her job. Plus she was the only river guide I'd come across, and when there's only one fortune-teller in the room, you don't make her try to guess your birthday. So when I asked her what she would do or what would happen when a raft, whether or not it had originally been a train, plunged over a waterfall, this is what she had to say: "A couple of things can happen. One of the common occurrences is that the guide, usually sitting in the back of the raft, or what you call a 'train-raft', will end up sailing up and out over all the other customers. She will literally get catapulted over the customers as the 'train-raft' drops over the waterfall. Then when the raft hits the bottom of the waterfall it can crumple together so that it folds up a bit like a taco shell but springs back out quickly. Of course everyone gets thrown against each other and one of the biggest sources of injury is a result of people smashing into the T-grip end of the paddle, which I have seen cause many a black eye and broken tooth."

Did you notice, as I did, that this former river guide, whom I will refer to as R.G. for purposes of discretion - if anyone asks me what R.G. stands for I will say "Rhonda Henderson" - mentioned the possibility of the train turned into a raft "catapulting" the guide? Could this, in fact, be the elusive love catapult I had been searching for? A working model or a sly declaration of love for me on Rhonda's part? I know that for my part the one possibility I refuse to consider is a reference to a catapult being simply coincidence. For as I continued to drink on my stool, I suddenly tipped over, almost diving straight into Rhonda's lap. I don't know, perhaps a catapulting action may have been involved and I should not have resisted, for when I said, "Whew, we almost avoided a disaster there," Rhonda replied mysteriously, "I've never thought of my lap as a disaster."

My catapulting and her comment made me think that I had a real shot with Rhonda - that she really did think of her *mons venus* as a Vesuvius fly trap with my name on it. Using all the money I had accumulated from not doing heroin, I pacified her with pint after pint of Irish lager to stave off her boredom - until I could be sure she was hooked, that Rhonda had fully understood my ideas about Buster and love more generally and we saw things eye to broken eye-socket. Things seemed to be going pretty good. Unlike that time from my youth, now I had seen how you can trap a girl in a projection booth, or in this case on a teetering bar stool. First I tried to excite her with tales of love's danger, not the gross ones with plungers, but the idea that we have no real idea what to do when it comes to love. I presented her with an image of unrelenting, *film noir* style honesty and toughness. "Love is not a matter of destiny or even desire that builds its own catapults," I said to Rhonda with narrowing eyes, "but of contingent projection booths on the mountainside. Yet, my dear, what can we do? Pour coffee through a funnel in hopes of not spilling it? No, we must pour ourselves through the funnel, with or without a love catapult." I thought this last image would appeal to her past as a river-rafting guide even though I hadn't explained to her the theory of the love catapult.

And just when I thought I had her by her broken wrist, Rhonda asked the obvious, "What in the world is a love catapult?" Caught between an unrelenting horniness and that evangelical desire to talk about Buster with anyone who would listen, I soldiered on, explaining how falling in love is not merely a metaphor, that you actually have to be thrown up in the air first, which is where the love catapult comes in.

"Although natural love catapults exist everywhere," I continued, "they often exist in veiled form, and since I leave nothing to chance I've chosen as my life's work to intuit, through meditation on Keaton's films, the lost art of building a working love catapult of my own. The only problem is that as a human being I'm pretty inept, so even if I do learn the ancient secrets of its construction, my chances of constructing a functional love catapult are slim. Nevertheless, what choice do I have, wanting to fall in love and knowing that, if others knew that I knew the secret, they would no doubt attempt to steal the catapult for themselves under the pretense of helping me construct it, as true love is, each and every time, a completely new experience, and thus a love catapult can only be used once. In fact, I believe that we probably walk by love catapults on a daily basis, but not only do they exist in veiled form, even if we did encounter one it would likely be one that has already been used by someone else and thus has undergone reverse alchemy into an everyday object. This would account for the difficulties people experience in trying to fall in love. So I continue on, meditating, occasionally taking apprentice work in blacksmith shops or plumbing companies in the hopes of becoming less inept, so that when I do find the secret blueprints I will be sufficiently not inept enough to complete my life's work."

"Reverse alchemy?" Rhonda asked.

Grabbing Rhonda's broken wrist and using it to punch myself in the eye, I sufficiently punished myself for using the term "reverse alchemy" without first explaining the philosophy, especially with respect to Buster, of the alchemical principle of the "chemical wedding" as they call it in darker circles. All I had to do was explain *My Wife's Relations* (1922, Comique Film Co.) and we would really see each other black eye to broken eye socket.

"*My Wife's Relations*" I explained, "embodies Keaton's philosophy of 'the instantaneous and continual transformation of things into themselves,' which is a corollary to his conclusions two years earlier in *Saphead* that 'for something to transform at all, a temporal transformation must first take place.' Basically, and without contradicting either Einstein or Bergson, Keaton realized that he needed to emphasize that, although things do require time to transform, this should not lead us to think that such transformations are rare or to forget that even in something 'instantaneous,' an 'instant' has still occurred. It is obviously an alchemical principal derived from those ancient experiments involving the conversion of base matter into higher states through complex chemical processes. Wanting to keep 'the occult' occult, in the film Buster disguises the alchemist's laboratory as a candy store. Buster is thus working as a *confectioner*, making a gigantic roll of taffy on his taffy rolling machine, which is inauspiciously located right next to the door of the confectioner's shop. This is of course a sign, the shop itself being an unfortunate confection. One could say the same of Buster himself, which is part of his charm, particularly if we view him in light of the following definition. Confection: 'something, as a garment or decorative object, that is very delicate, elaborate, or luxurious and usually non-utilitarian.' In Buster's case we could say 'always non-utilitarian,' and as someone who anticipated Heidegger's notion of *Dasein* or 'being thrown' into the world, Buster is always alluding to his own status as an object in motion or at rest, but at the very least always a 'being there' rather than a 'being here.' So, when Buster hears the postman enter the shop to deliver the mail, he of course goes to greet him, four foot taffy roll and all, which results in a temporary confection of the postman, Keaton, and the bundle of letters which, having fallen out of the bag, are now stuck everywhere. Confection: 'compounding, preparing, or making something.' The postman escapes but not without the taffy roll confection resulting in the tossing of a window breaking object into a woman's window. This woman then chases Buster down and takes him to court for the 'offense.' Unfortunately, the Polish speaking judge is expecting two Poles about to get married and assumes that this woman and Buster are the couple. They are confected in marriage, and as this is not an age where one takes marriage lightly, she brings Buster home to meet her family. Meeting one's in-laws, pretending to like them, is always an act of confection in the sense of 'something made up or confected; a [dubious] concoction.' Sample sentence: 'He said the charges were a confection of the police.' Indeed, Buster would not have survived one day with his in-laws if one of the letters confected to him in the postman incident were not a letter informing its recipient of the inheritance of a large sum of money. Then the in-laws are all 'sweet' on Buster, but of course only because they think he has a lot of money. When the whole family moves from the alley to the avenue into a luxurious and outrageous apartment where they continue their old ways, in a strange confection, making homemade liquor in the kitchen with the vat placed right in the center as if it were an idol to be worshiped, the in-laws finally figure out that Buster is not the intended recipient of the inheritance letter, even if, thanks to confection, he was the actual recipient. They propose to kill him and then leave the premises and Buster barely escapes, at one point rolling himself up in a carpet as if he were the pale cream filling of a canoli. The last scene shows Buster on a train to Reno to get a divorce, but the look on his face tells us that this is a temporary solution, as the corollary of the 'instantaneous and continuous transformation of things into themselves' is the 'instantaneous and continuous subjection to confection.' The latter would be the Buddhist equivalent of Samsara, or the suffering of this world, while the former would be the state of enlightenment. It is the difference between a true alchemist and a mere confectioner, which is all the difference in the world."

I ended my explanation with a loud thump on the bar, startling Rhonda from a deep sleep. I must have used too much of my non-heroin money wetting Rhonda's lips because this was one of the most impassioned and fascinating explanations of anything I had ever given - the subject matter no doubt bringing out the orator in me. Shit, even my students at Wellesley would have called it "not boring." Rhonda just stared around the bar with glazed eyes as if she didn't recognize a single thing, and then asked the barkeep to get her a cab home. He seemed to know what was up.

On the Inconstancy of Man

I walked out of the bar alone thinking the obvious… what anyone in my situation would be thinking. Is romantic love all there is to life? Aren't we neglecting much of what is out there in dwelling upon it to such an extent? Not if we consider love to be an allegory of the larger things we can achieve in life. In other words we rely upon the tiniest things such as love to teach us about the most expansive ones. Call it the rigor of reduction. Take Buster's attempt to build a sailboat that could make it under even the lowest hanging bridges. What good would it have done him to stare at those bridges all day long? Their arches looming over his imagination. Instead he asked an even more forbidding, if tinier, question. How does a ship get inside of a bottle? That gave him the idea for a sailboat whose deck could be raised and lowered with a single rope attached to a pulley. In a similar sense, once while touring Westminster Abbey, I stared at an ant making its aimless pilgrimage for over an hour. This made me realize that once I got to Dublin I should attempt to see two prostitutes within a twenty-four hour period.

Growing quickly bored of the memory of Dublinesque prostitute feats, I turned instead to the question of the choice between domestic peace and adventure. Is it possible for us to have both? In *The Boat* (1921, Comique Film Inc.), Buster, his wife, and their two kids find out how a hose is turned into a hose. Having built a boat named the *Damfino* inside his house, presumably to prevent thieves from stealing it, Keaton is finally ready to launch it for a family outing. Although the most famous "pun" in this film is the boat's name and the phrase, "Damn if I know," Keaton's magic is not about joking around, but to teach us. A wife wearing black hose is perhaps not a real wife, but instead just a little tramp. So already one is suspicious of the combination of domestic bliss and family adventure Keaton has set up for us. Launching the boat results in the accidental knocking down of the family house and sinking of the family car, all of which is to be expected in pure comedic terms, but when Buster attempts to nail a picture to the wall of his boat, thus making it homier, he springs a leak. Spinning around and around in the rat race of his mind where he thought he could have it all, he gets disoriented, thinking he's really back home again where he could deal with a leaky roof by letting it drain out of the floor. But of course, this floor leads straight to the ocean, so when Buster drills a hole in the bottom of his house/boat, water comes shooting up into the cabin like a hose turned on full blast. But of course, it is not just *like* a hose. The little circle he has carved in the wood, combined with the immense water pressure, functions as an actual hose. A hose has become a hose. We know this is the primary magic word (and its corresponding cautionary tale) because, when the family crash lands on a deserted island, the very last scene shows them walking up the beach. And if you look closely, you can see the wife's black hose has slipped down just a little, to reveal a tiny bit of her calf, thus drawing our attention to the hose which has been transformed into a hose and once again into a hose and the corresponding lessons we learn from this.

Wavering drunkenly through the dark city streets, I realized that all my attempts at distracting myself were leading to anecdotes about boats - or in other words my desire, now an impossible dream, to kiss Rhonda the disabled river guide. Only reason, not pipe dreams about storybook romances, would fish me out of this funk. In order to rid myself of the desire to find or build a working love catapult, I braved the chill night air with thoughts of a much more mundane yet historically verifiable love device, the kissing booth. Whither the kissing booth, many have asked? I happened to be one of the few people who knew the answer to this question.

Most are unaware of the origins of the kissing booth, where one pays a certain fee to kiss someone, usually beautiful, usually a woman, in post-Enlightenment Germany. With the dispersion, more or less spectacular (see France in 1789), of wealth from a few prominent, unproductive royal families to the bourgeoisie of modern capitalism, the need to find new means of funding state projects led to the production of objects (such as the kissing booth) which, through the lens of time, appear simultaneously strange and apropos. In the case of Germany, it was these very forces, as well as others, that led to its invention (by Humboldt no less) as a means to raise money for the birth of the modern university.

The kissing booth of the late eighteenth and early nineteenth centuries is, on its face, a bizarre object looking back towards the past, forward to the future, and outward to the historical *Zeitgeist*. Although it may at first seem counterintuitive that scholars would be the ones who would invent and promote the kissing booth, further inquiry will show that its birth from their Zeus-like wigs was inevitable. First, we must not forget that the kissing booth, whatever else we may think of it, is a form of prostitution. And, while prostitution has been derided for centuries by various clergies and governments, it has continued to be a vibrant part of economies across the world, including Europe. In cultures which we might anachronistically call libertine, such as ancient Greece and Rome, it would never occur to anyone to defend prostitution as such - it was as accepted a fact of life as other natural bodily functions, and thought of regulation would only be practical in nature, such as one would not question the need to urinate but might consider the best means of its disposal from populated areas. Indeed, prostitution was so prevalent and so cheap that, if anything, one was more hard pressed to defend, in practical terms, the act of masturbation - which Diogenes famously did by stating, "If only I could cure my hunger by rubbing my belly."

With the rise of Christianity, prostitution did not abate, but it was not a topic of debate, as church leaders set the tone by arguing against it in Latin (against which the people were defenseless) and publicly flogging all those caught in the act of prostitution, but mostly the prostitutes themselves. This caused prostitution to "go underground," resulting in the rise of what we now refer to as "pimps" or "procurers" as well as a subsequent rise in the prices prostitutes had to charge to cover the expenses involved with hiding the crime and suffering its punishments (both by clergy and clients, among whom there was quite a bit of overlap, as one might well imagine). For centuries, including the dark ages but also the so-called "Renaissance," prostitutes had many users but few defenders.

Indeed, only with the rise of the modern intellectual (as opposed to medieval scholar) could we ever imagine people mounting arguments in favor of prostitution, not so much because intellectuals had undergone what we now refer to as "The Enlightenment," but because the modern intellectual invented the art of "creating an analytical justification for everything one does." Such arguments brought prostitution back into the light, granting it some legitimacy, even at times caché, but as with most intellectual movements, the results were a watered-down version of the original topic of argument.

So, emboldened by their enlightened view of prostitution and their practical need to finance the modern university, these intellectuals came up with the kissing booth. And, the continued flowering of the German university attests, even today, to the brilliance of its invention. There was a ready population of women - most of the original inhabitants of the booths came from the prostitute class, although as it gained in prestige, the kissing booth would occasionally be graced by adventurous middle-class women and even, on special occasions, by ballerinas and opera stars - ready to enter the booth, and the male population seemed more than eager to finance its operation. This latter fact also bears examination.

As with kissing booths of the 1950s in America, the 19th-century German kissing booth offered a cheaper and more respectable form of prostitution. Indeed, whereas 'straight' prostitution bore the stigmata of personal guilt and illegality, clients of the kissing booth could get a 'taste' of the goods and still feel vindicated because they were promoting the greatness of Germany by 'donating' their money towards the education of its brightest members. Sure, the progenitors of the booth could have simply asked for donations, but they had enough foresight to make kissing booths the *only* means of donation, thus liberating clients from any guilt that they were merely purchasing a service whose 'surplus labor-value' happened to go to the university. That said, it was the service aspect of the booths themselves that granted a low overhead, thus maximizing the margin on 'donations.' And the kissing booths 'manned' by prostitutes, which were the most common and most popular, truly did give clients a taste. For, just as contemporary strip clubs come with possibilities of 'private-dances,' 'champagne rooms,' and even more, the unpaid inhabitants of the booths made most of their money via the services offered "behind the booth" as they say.

This leads us to the booths themselves, of course, which were instrumental to the appeal of the services provided in them. With the woman standing behind a wooden construction, as if she were a prisoner of the booth, she evoked the nostalgia of the stocks and guillotines which were quickly falling out of fashion legally but which still retained an allure in the public imagination. This in turn led to the development of specialty booths which could be decorated with an imaginary guillotine above the woman's head, a noose, or carved simulacra of gallows. And we must not forget the 'confessional-style' kissing booth in which the patron sat down in a chair himself, paid his donation, and was treated to a sideways kiss from a beautiful pair of lips and eyes suddenly appearing from the sliding grate behind which would normally sit a scaly old priest (at least in Catholic countries).

Nevertheless, there is yet another mystery to the booths and indeed to the prevalence of prostitution in Germany (as well as the rest of Europe). After all, the many wars that had been fought had created a massive excess of women in relation to men (who had died in the wars). One would think that the readily available supply of women as opposed to men would discourage prostitution, as the remaining men would have the "pick of the litter," as one might say. Of course, a closer look would reveal what any semiotician of kissing booths should realize: a) the desire for prostitution bears no relationship to the availability of 'virtuous' women; b) the massive presence of 'unmanned men,' amputees and such from the wars, left the percentage of men who felt attractive as such to women far less than one might think (indeed, those who are interested in searching archives will find many kissing booth sketches from the period showing armless, legless men waiting in long lines on crutches, held in makeshift gurneys by their fellows, or simply dragging themselves to the booths like pilgrims on their way to Mecca); c) the lack of marriageable men resulted in a large widow and unmarried female cohort who were newly detached, left to make their own way in the contemporary capitalist economy - and those women who could avoid the limb-lopping, fire-catching factories by entering the booths did so with little or no hesitation.

As the universities broke ground and started charging tuition, as the 'viable' male population gradually increased between the old European wars and the Great Wars of the twentieth-century, the popularity of kissing booths began to die out in Germany and in the other parts of Europe to which they had spread. A burgeoning 'class' of professional police became hip to the kissing booths as gateways to much more nefarious sexual activities. Soon, the kissing booths which dotted almost every major European city like smallpox were dismantled, used for wood-burning stoves or revolutionary barricades, with only a few surviving here and there in gypsy camps which moved from place to place holding 'carnivals.' And even these booths were plagued by their reputation for being the playgrounds of pickpockets, as one's pockets are never more unprotected than when leaning over a booth to gaze into the eyes of an exotic 'gypsy-woman' and graze her lips with yours.

The reemergence of kissing booths in the post WWII United States at first glance seems almost as unlikely, if not more so, than does its original emergence in post-Enlightenment Germany. The few scholars who have addressed the subject have, unfortunately, been of the postmodern persuasion, suggesting that the society of the spectacle as embodied in the ubiquitous image of the sailor who rape-kissed the nurse on V-Day in Times

Square was a simulacrum giving birth, somehow, to the thousands of kissing booths of the 1950s. But if we look to more historical conditions, we see almost the same variables at play as in post-Enlightenment Germany: 1) a massive drop in the 'viable' male population; 2) the lack of a 'female gaze' to make anyone think twice about the connections between prostitution and women 'volunteering' to stand behind a booth and be kissed by scores of strange men; 3) the need to fund a new University system, this time one that could educate the scientists and engineers who would help defeat the Soviet Union; 4) a relative rise in the female population who was newly independent and looking for ways to survive on their own in a capitalist economy that no longer allowed them to work in the war factories.

Yes, looking back, the spectacle of men of all stripes standing in line and paying to kiss a girl standing behind a booth seems almost impossible to visualize in our contemporary post-feminist landscape. And when we do visualize it, it is impossible to do so without feeling a bodily and collective cringe of national embarrassment, regardless of one's political persuasions.

Compared to its tenure in Germany, fortunately, the United States flowering of the kissing booth was a relatively short-lived affair. We can partially credit this to the 'great-divide' between feminists and sexists where the intellectual justifications were not made on behalf of kissing booths, prostitution, and the like, but against them. Other factors, such as the crisis of masculinity causing 'embarrassment' in males "having to pay for it," a greater awareness of germs, and the subtle ideology of America wanting to appear wealthy but not decadent no doubt also played a factor (see the great Kitchen Debates between Khrushchev and Nixon). Mainly, however, I think we need to credit the United States' quick kissing booth demise to: 1) the post-war economic boom, giving men more disposable income to engage in 'actual' prostitution; 2) the McCarthyist insinuation that kissing scores of men for the purposes of 'charity' smacked of communist ideology; 3) the Francophilic transformation of the original kissing booth, at least on the part of clients, into a 'French-kissing booth,' requiring much more overhead as men became more aggressive, 'thriftily' wanting 'more' for their money, which in turn required the invention of 'the bouncer' to 'bounce' unruly men and precipitated many ugly scenes in town squares.

Two things happened when the kissing booths disappeared from American towns. The new 'bouncer class' migrated to taverns around the country in order to enact 'crowd control,' an industry term learned from the para-military groups which roamed the country to stop the violent anti-war and anti-segregation protestors. This made the old fashioned 'bar-fight,' where a single patron's anger would result in the gleeful entry of every patron present until not a single person, bottle, or piece of furniture was left standing, a thing of the past, of television lore. This is a good example of what we might call the ancillary benefits of historical problems. For, while we may long for the days of yore when the bar fight was a more populist, if more brutal, affair, in the long run the proto-fascist demeanor of bouncers and their counterparts in the American police force, at times bringing us to the very limits of our Zen defense mechanisms, is perhaps a small price to pay in eliminating the hordes of crying widows at weekend bar funerals, and the fights at the funerals leading to more crying widows.

In the meantime, with feminist intellectuals winning the arguments with respect to prostitution, the profession went back underground as in the pre-Enlightenment days. Yet, just as with the post-Enlightenment German intellectuals, the post-60s feminist intellectuals overstated the terms of their victory. They won the war of words in the ivory towers, breaking the glass ceilings of Harvard and the like where hiring a so called "entertainer" for the weekly faculty meeting very quickly became déclassé, but those same professors still visited prostitutes all the way from Cambridge Avenue to Times Square. In those days, times were booming, with prostitutes serving all walks of life.

The real attrition of the prostitution industry came in the 1980s, and it had less to do with the rise of feminism than the decimation of the middle class. With the scientifically knowledgeable engineers becoming largely an import, in combination with the deindustrialization of the U.S. labor force and attacks on unions, the wages of the former middle class not only stagnated, but steadily decreased in real terms over the next thirty years. Your hard-working engineer was no longer the head of a nuclear family and the client of a nice middle-class prostitute; he was supporting an extended, non-Western family and more interested in praying than playing. Likewise, the demise of the automobile and steel industries forced your average tough worker from welding steel to serving happy meals. If he was able to see a prostitute at all, it was no longer the local pub's sweet Sally, but a crack-addicted tragedy down the alley, though possibly still named Sally, as in "Alley Sally". Prostitution itself, like the rest of the economy, has suffered the demise of the middle class. And, as is the case in pre-war America and third-world countries to this very day, such an economic divide results in the proliferation of two types of prostitutes - those who fuck the very poor and those who fuck the very rich.

Still, unlike kissing booths, prostitutes have always retained a certain cultural fascination. Their sacred quality is alluded to in the smash hit film *Pretty Woman* (1990, Touchstone Pictures), starring Richard Gere and Julia Roberts, in which Roberts is instructed by her more experienced prostitute roommate to "never kiss a client on the lips." This, because, apparently, doing so could cause the prostitute and/or the client to "fall in love" (catapulted), a situation which is not only unlikely given Gere's fear of heights (and hence love catapults), but which allegedly can never work because they come from different social and economic classes. Indeed, this film has little to teach us about love as compared to Keaton's films where people from different social classes are catapulted into one another all the time. Regardless, perhaps this taboo against kissing, inasmuch as it can be regarded as a truism, explains the brief and intermittent lightning flashes that kissing booths make in the long steady rains of history. Only in times of great national need may the prostitute risk, even unconsciously, 'the kiss'; this fact perhaps is the transparent yet bulletproof Pope-mobile which necessarily surrounds the kissing booth at most historical moments.

And yet, the rich always get what they want, and what they want is to be the exception ensured by their economic rule. They want what Julia Roberts initially denied, and then gave, Richard Gere. Whatever you think of the aesthetic value of *Pretty Woman*, its influence on American and world culture is undeniable and, perhaps, incalculable. We can say with certainty that Pretty Woman is responsible for that privilege demanded by the rich and now provided by the prostitute, which has been termed the G.F.E. or "Girlfriend Experience," the most famous recipient of which is former Attorney General of New York, Eliot Spitzer, who patronized a young woman by the name of Ashley Dupré at the Emperors Club VIP. There are many ways we can characterize the G.F.E. - the Better Business Bureau might call it false advertising. The Cultural Studies scholar would call it the evisceration of reality's richness and subsequent reduction to a few impoverished signs, or false consciousness, as the service known as the "Girlfriend Experience" is nothing more than the offer to kiss the client on the mouth and allow him to not wear a condom during sex. The idea of the girlfriend experience being reduced to these acts is not only abhorrent from a feminist perspective, but completely unrelated to the experience of having a girlfriend. Indeed, we have always had, at least since the Marquis de Sade, the girlfriend experience widely available in the sex industry, and that experience is provided by the dominatrix. Although this too is an unfair reduction of what real girlfriends actually are and do, almost no one would deny that, in the world of prostitution, going to see a dominatrix is far closer to the experience of having a girlfriend (for any length of time) than the so-called girlfriend experience. As proof I offer up the following challenge. Find a single ad - digital, print, or otherwise - where a dominatrix offers the "Girlfriend Experience" as an "addition" to her normal services. This is obviously not because the two experiences are antithetical to one another, but identical. For a dominatrix to advertise the G.F.E. would simply be redundant and, in all fairness, we could say the same for a male sadist prostitute promising, in addition, the "Boyfriend Experience," or the B.F.E. Advertisements are paid for by the word, and you'll never see an ad reading, "Used Car Salesmen, and for an extra fee, he will sell you used cars."

No doubt it was an ingenious pimp or prostitute who first advertised the G.F.E., just as there is no doubt that rich married men are the only ones who would pine for the girlfriend experience. Perhaps they are merely naïve, or perhaps what they want is not an intensified, "exciting" relationship, but a calmer one, having themselves lived through, as I have, the W.F.E, or the "Wife Experience."

Whither the kissing booth? When will the next kissing booth appear? For surely as long as we have nation states, the kissing booth haunts them, reaching over them like a specter. Unfortunately, I am a mere Cultural Studies scholar and not a prophet, so I will not hazard a guess as to when, but when the next one does appear, I will explain it then.

On The Inconstancy of Man (The Next Day)

I woke up alone in my apartment the next day in my normal state: depressed and horny. If I had learned one thing from my break-up with Todd, it's that certain things can cause lots of laughs from one viewpoint and still not be what we call "comedic." People mistakenly think that *The General* (1926, United Artists), for instance, like Keaton's other work, is a comedy. But it is not. A superficial definition of comedy would define it in Aristotelian terms (a story that ends in marriage) or perhaps in Comtean terms by assigning a certain number of jokes or laughs (successful jokes), but with Keaton, we must consider the definition of comedy in terms of how and what he transforms into itself. Being a serious man deep down, Keaton would never make a "comedy" about The Great War of Northern Aggression. Rather, we must note the extreme number of things that are transformed into themselves in this picture, but in very fragmented or narratively undeveloped ways, almost as if, through these brief transformations, Keaton wanted to simulate the severed limbs that might litter a Civil War battlefield. I'll give a necessarily incomplete list here:

1.   A confederate (Buster) becomes a confederate when he is turned down for military service, by
disguising himself as a Union soldier and rescuing
the captured Annabelle Lee, which, along with other
feats of heroism, allows him to receive the honor of
becoming Lieutenant in the Confederate Army. This
string of confederacies is the most sustained set of
things transforming themselves into themselves in
the movie, thereby suggesting the agonizing, seemingly endless nature of this four year war between
the states. All other transformations, compared to
this, are mere casualties.

2.   Riding the grill of a train with a crosstie on his
chest, Keaton transforms a cross into a cross.

3.   While Buster hides under the table of the Union
cabin, the table cloth is burned by the cigar of one of
the brass, thus creating a small hole. When Buster
hears the captured Annabelle's voice, he turns the
small hole (peephole) into a peephole by staring
through it to confirm it is her.

4.   When the Damn Yankees are fighting from the river, Buster shoots a cannonball at a nearby dam, turning
them into 'dam' Yankees floating down the river.

5.   After he's made a Lieutenant, or someone in lieu
of tenancy, Buster has nowhere private to kiss Annabelle, and is in lieu of tenancy as he keeps getting his
kiss interrupted by the need to salute everyone who
passes by.

6.   The burned bridge that Annabelle creates when

THE AUTOBIOGRAPHY OF BUSTER KEATON

she thinks that Buster has deserted the confederate cause is mended when Buster sets a bridge on fire that the causes the union train to collapse into the river.

We notice that, in addition to these stump-like transformations meant as an homage to the many stumps created by the war (stumps outside the film, in history, transformed into stumps inside the film?) that one object which, in a comedy, would be irresistible to transform into itself due to its absurd appearance and pun-fertile name, a railroad handcar, is never transformed into itself. Rather, it forlornly remains itself, just as the stain of the Civil War will and must remain unredeemed, untransformed.

Thinking about it, I realized that no matter how bummed out and horny I was, it was pretty uncool to compare my situation to something as horrible as the civil war. It was as uncouth and in bad taste as using a term such as "mild diarrhea." And just as it takes a truly depraved person such as myself to compare his personal heartaches to the ravages of war, only the most decadent of cultures would ever have the temerity to inflict a term such as "mild diarrhea" upon its populace. My first thought upon hearing this term while watching television at my parents' house was, I imagine, similar to that of many Cultural Studies scholars: "Can any form of diarrhea be classified as 'mild'? Isn't the very nature of diarrhea itself a state that, from an anal perspective, can only be considered catastrophic? To use the term 'mild diarrhea' seems as bizarre as to speak of 'mild suicidal tendencies' or 'mild torture.'"

Of course, it is only an accident of history that

diarrhea refers mainly to fecal issues, as if fecal diarrhea were the 'literal' denotation with all other references being supplementary, metaphorical and thus parasitic upon literal diarrhea. Indeed, adding a third level of metaphorical remove, it would seem that excessive use of such metaphors, at least from a contemporary perspective, would constitute a diarrhea of diarrhea. But in truth, the word flows directly from a Greek term meaning "to flow through." There is no modifier in the etymology at all (in the Greek, the flow is not burdened with a sense of whether or not it is excessive in any way), which was only added later, perhaps for onomatopoetic reasons. What else would drive famed poet and dramatist Alexander Pope, as ill-tempered as he could be, to wish the following fate (in 1703) upon one of his lady friends: "seems but upon the whole to wait for *the next cold day to throw her into a diarrhea,* that must, if it return, carry her off." I do not mean to suggest that catastrophic anal events do not occur - indeed the bile in Pope's letter leaves us with no doubt, despite the contextual ambiguity preventing us from ascertaining if he wanted this poor damsel to be thrown into her own state of anal distress or the product of someone else's, that there was nothing "mild" about his curse. It's just that we are stuck with 'diarrhea' for now and, apparently, a set of vague adjectives designating its alleged nature.

Indeed, speaking of catastrophic anal events, I allegedly, as an infant brought to Mexico by my parents - who were on an evangelical mission - almost died (a "mild death"?) from a parasite to which the body reacts with what would most likely be designated as "severe" or "critical" diarrhea. And, no one in any culture would disagree with the need to martial all of that particular culture's resources to prevent anyone from falling at the hands of a life-threatening anal condition. It is the notion of non-mortal gradations of diarrhea which, even as the very notion repulses us on some deep moral level, interests us here.

Diarrhea and its gradations could send more sober minds into fits of aporia, even a "mild panic," if they truly thought a phenomenology, much less an ontology, of this "condition" were a necessary task. Would one start ex nihilo, with no feces, and proceed from there? Or might one take a more Platonic approach, assuming feces of ideal consistency from which all other feces are degradations, either moving to the side of mild to more severe constipation or in the opposite direction from mild to more severe diarrhea. Perhaps someone of the Heideggerian inspired, deconstructionist school might suggest that we are flung into a world of fecal events of varying natures. A strict Heideggerian (one who suffers from Heideggerhea?) would suggest that it is one's duty to proceed from this state in search of a truly authentic doodie, whereas a deconstructionist would say that each piece of feces only takes meaning in relation to its difference from other feces, that each bowel movement is a unique event unto itself which can be removed, at any time, from its so-called original context.

What should be clear is that feces is as subject to philosophical discourse as any other topos, thus granting it a certain dignity that most people would like to ignore. Indeed, we can only conclude that the exclusion of feces from philosophical discussion is the result of a collective social decision, and that the result is the rather sloppy set of terminologies that have been used, mostly by pharmaceutical companies, to attribute certain characteristics to various forms of diarrhea. Since such slippery terms as "mild" and "severe" are used as if they are merely being thrown against the wall to see what sticks, we must determine who is doing the throwing and whose wall is receiving that which does or does not remain.

Provided with a terminology so impoverished, at least on the face of things, determinations such as "mild," "moderate," and "severe" diarrhea are left in the hands of the shitter himself - it is the shitter's response which matters here, in more ways than one. Indeed, I would say that more important than diarrhea itself is its modifier, particularly the modifier "mild." I joked earlier about "mild torture" and "mild suicidal tendencies," but people do consider whether they suffer from things such as "mild depression" or "mild arthritis." Whereas such things used to be known, respectively, as "sadness" and "pain," if they were considered at all, the word "mild" transforms them into potential gateways to pathologies of greater and greater severity, leaving one to wonder where and when someone should build a wall against the oncoming siege. Likewise, before the introduction of the term "mild" to diarrhea, feces occupied a very small portion of most human imaginations. While this might have been good for humanity, it was not good for capitalism, which thrives on the "colon"-ization of all aspects of life, treating not only the earth and its more tangible resources, but all nameable human experiences as potential markets. Whereas people were once able to "be sad," "suffer pain," and "have bowel movements" without giving these things much consideration, now they must be constantly monitored by the consumer as a potential 'mild' condition that may need to be treated (with a commode-ity, naturally) before it becomes more severe. Once upon a time, bowel movements used to be part of the normal digestive cycle and thereby integrated into the larger contexts of nature's abundance, but now every single shit one takes amounts to an existential crisis: "Was my feces close enough to a Platonic norm, or is it a 'mild' yet still important deviation requiring the purchase of a regulating product?" As any hypochondriac will tell you, the more you think about your body, the greater chance you will find an illness. Likewise, the more you think about your feces, which for most people is now not only "every single time" but something more pointed, a lonely, individualistic judgment call about how someone else, some panoptic regulator who inaudibly mumbles his "scatechisms," would judge your feces, the more likely you are to detect a 'mild' deviation which you would be a fool not to stanch with a quick trip to the safest place one can be during a fecal siege - the drug store.

No, there would be nothing 'mild' about today. I resolved right then and there to get out of bed before noon and do whatever it took to find some love, if not 'the' love. I would be every bit as persistent as Buster Keaton in *Seven Chances* (1925, Buster Keaton Productions, Inc.). As persistent as Buster, his company about to go bankrupt, who receives an inheritance letter giving him 7 million dollars if he gets married by 7 pm on his twentieth birthday. As one might suspect, that birthday would be today. Luckily, Buster has wanted to tell his 'girlfriend' for over a year that he loves her, and this contract gives him the excuse. While Buster practices his proposal tactics in the garden, the girl who had no idea she was the object of his affections overhears him and is won over, but when she asks why they must be married that day, he tells her about the inheritance and is rebuffed, as she thinks Buster has only asked her for the money. Hopefully this would not happen to me, because the rest of the film/day proves quite exhausting to Buster. First, Buster's business partner tries to 'help' him find a wife, and after being rejected by all seven women he knows, he walks the streets in dejection until he sees what appears to be a burlesque show and, since he's already "proposed to everything in skirts, including a Scotsman," he decides to propose to the star. Only, when Buster comes back with his head smashed through his hat and a black eye, a closer look at the poster reveals that he has proposed to the famous female impersonator Julian Eltinge, a real historical figure. The Scotsman is a false female impersonator, because while he wears a kilt he is not trying to pretend to be a woman, while Eltinge is a true female impersonator, though apparently more homophobic than the Scotsman. Time is running out, and Buster's partner runs an ad on the front page of the afternoon paper explaining everything and telling women which church to meet at. Now, these women are true women, but could really be classified as female impersonators because the only true female in the film is the one Buster loves. When Buster, exhausted from all his proposals, wakes up from a nap in the church to a congregation full of potential brides and finds out that his true love has had a change of heart, he attempts his escape and is chased through the streets like Frankenstein by the villagers, only of course Buster's escape involves a love catapult in the form of a crane and many more flips and far more boulder dodging than Mary Shelley's monster had to endure. Buster makes it to the house, where the parson has been driven, just in time, and marries his bride, though everyone gets to kiss her before he does, including the Great Dane. All told, we have one false female impersonator (the Scotsman) transformed into one true female impersonator (Julian Eltinge) transformed into hundreds of true/false female impersonators (the brides to be who are not true women because there is only one true woman for Buster.)

Seven Chances
(Doppelgänger Version)

It would be tough, as I had only my own desire to drive me, but I was determined. Despite lacking the 'survival' aspects driving Buster to marry his own true love that day, I vowed to channel the sheer energy Buster mustered in the final boulder-chase scene, and if necessary suffer the humiliations of a dog getting to kiss your bride before you do, in order to get laid. I was also banking on the possibility that, just as younger siblings learn much faster by having the older one to imitate, the example of the doppelgänger would translate into the success of his reproduction.

If the day was going to go correctly, I knew that I would have to prepare a kit. A friend of mine once informed me about the history of 'toy kits' which really took off in the 1950s. As she states, until the 1950s, making things "had hitherto, or historically, been a non-leisure activity." However, the "task of making something became a leisure activity especially for men who increasingly worked in suits and ties rather than in overalls. To satisfy (and exploit) their need to use their hands (also a masculine activity) they bought kits." Well, as perhaps one of the most uncoordinated men in the world, I definitely fit that description. So a kit it would be. But what would I put in it?

After the age of the kit had begun, there was no stopping it. I thought back to Thanksgiving at home, which already seemed like years ago, when I had hatched my plan to follow in Buster Keaton's footsteps. It was my year to cook the turkey, a family tradition of passing the cluck which I was surprised, given my last attempt, had not been altered. Fortunately, although we were rednecks, I was allowed to buy a turkey at the grocery store, and was pleased to find that they no longer sold turkeys at the grocery store, but turkey kits.

All kits come with instructions which, while you would think this would "break the frame" of making something by hand, actually adds to your sense of accomplishment as the decoding process helps to supplement the emptiness one feels at having been left out of the "actual process" of doing the thing. Everyone now feels this on some deep inner level. Even Ted Nugent. Did he carve arrowheads out of flint and construct the bow he shot his Thanksgiving turkey with? I think not. Hence, on some deep level I think he feels empty and unmanly in a more immediate way than those of us who have moved further up the feeding supply chain, which might explain his radical politics and crazed demeanor when it comes to guns. The hysteria with which he denounces leftwing enemies of America and cheerleads the NRA is really, unconsciously, the cry of a deep embarrassment that he only kills animals with guns or compound bows rather than his bare hands.

Anyway, normally I wouldn't be caught near an unprepared turkey, even one that came in a turkey kit, except it's not only impossible to escape one of our family traditions, it was hard to refuse an "invitation" to help prepare food on the only day of the year (if you're not Jewish) when you don't have to decide what to eat that day.

In case you were misled beforehand that you were cooking a turkey rather than assembling a kit, you will be disabused of this notion once you open the package and realize that what you have is a slippery egg shaped object with a hole on either end. One of the holes is the turkey's neck, which inside has a plastic bag of innards which most of us discard. The directions say, locate the neck of the turkey and remove the plastic bag from inside. Okay, there I sat with a spherical object and the ambiguous directions that kits are infamous for. Like some sort of Aztec paleontologist I held the bird in the air and examined it. I both studied and imagined (in my mind's eye, of course) which of the slippery egg's protuberances were legs and which were wings, and once I had located the wings, I had to figure out which direction they would point when flapping, which required me to "re-feather" them in my head. About fifteen minutes later, I was able to "make heads and tails of it," as they say, and the mysterious thing about kits is that, if you are alone or with someone equally inept, there is no 'discovery' that makes you feel foolish, that "how could I have not seen it" feeling. Conversely, one always has a visceral feeling of conquest, which is undoubtedly why kits of all kinds are so popular. What I am trying to suggest here is that a kit is not so much an item as an existential category unto itself. For when I went on YouTube to figure out how to 'carve' a turkey, something any fool with a big knife should be able to do instinctively, what was I doing besides watching a virtual kit? And, after opening that kit, or what one might call a "para-kit" to the original kit which was the turkey itself, I did a fairly reasonable job of carving up that bird if I do say so myself - that is if one acknowledges the inevitable gap, when it comes to doing things with one's hands, between mental knowledge and physical execution.

When I think of cooking and carving turkeys I'm reminded of sadomasochistic sex, of which I apparently had the dimmest knowledge about before my residency in that pink-haired pervert O's lair. The similarity between these two activities relates not only to their social nature, but in how much trouble one goes through in order to make each one happen. That's why people only cook turkeys on special occasions and why, if I had to make an educated guess, sadomasochists don't really have sex all that often. It's just too much trouble. You can have sex all the time or you can have sadomasochistic sex occasionally, or I guess the other possibility is that sadomasochists (like carnivores, turkey eaters) could have regular sex most of the time and sadomasochistic sex on special occasions like anniversaries and three-day weekends. Of course, sadomasochism comes with kits (sold in sex-shops and lingerie stores) as well which can make it easier to perform, especially if you are more turned on by the gear itself as opposed to the actual pain, mind-games, rape scenarios, and the Eagle Scout knowledge of knot-tying that comes with straight S&M.

Speaking of sadism, I think that contemporary

philosophy is barking up the wrong tree when it comes to the concept of the gift and all the complications it produces. The problem is that they assume, in that counterintuitive move that is *de rigueur* amongst philosophers of all stripes, that all gifts are equally bad. As if a gift were a letter in the alphabet whose only source of meaning was its difference from all the other letters. Let me tell you, there are some gifts that are worse than others, and the worst gift of all is to bestow a model (the glue and plastic kind) on someone who does not have the patience to build models. Those who give models to people without knowledge of whether they like building models are committing the worst kind of blackmail. They're basically saying, "Here, spend the next several hours/days/weeks doing something you may or may not like and next time I come to visit, I'll have proof one way or the other as to whether you properly acknowledged my gift." I mean, if someone gives you an article of clothing you don't like, you just wear it around them occasionally without too much pain (unless it is a sadist who gifted you a tight-fitting leather collar) and then take it off. Even with a puzzle, when the person comes over you can say, "Hey, let's do it right now," thus calling their bluff. But a model, my friend, is a one person job on a long one-way street filled with traffic going the other way.

But then, I guess, there are people who genuinely enjoy models and it would be a shame for them to never receive one as a gift. The only model I ever completed - because it was fairly simple and corresponded to my favorite television show, was 'The General Lee,' a car (or more precisely 'the car') from *The Dukes of Hazzard*. Looking back, I think what fascinated me more than anything else on the car was that it had the number "01" on the side and this was never explained on the show, and the zero sitting (redundantly?) in front of the 1 held a certain, shall we say, fascination that we could call the child's equivalent to the Kabala. That is why I waited until every part of my General Lee had been constructed before I solemnly placed the sacred decal on the door. I was reminded of that moment when I had the more visceral sense of triumph with the turkey kit. If one could, in a kit of some kind, combine that visceral, chthonic moment with the more esoteric mysticism of the "01" on The General Lee, I would proclaim that person a shaman.

Thinking about these things as I prepared my love kit, I threw in a decent length of rope, a hammer, a couple of knives, a collage I had been working on during my spare time, money I had saved from not doing heroin, a guitar, a couple of wrenches, a pair of shades, a baseball cap with the planet Venus on the front, some women's clothes, a "wife-beater," a George Thoroughgood CD, and of course my now quite rumpled, if still elegant, tuxedo from my weekend with O. On the way down the street I picked up a couple of forties so that I could get really sloshed, headed down to the local coffee shop, and pretended to be a famous artist.

I entered the coffee shop filled with eighty ounces of beer, dropped my kit (which was in a burlap sack) with a jingle-jangle on the ground, and looked for woman who had what I needed, namely those long eyelashes and wavy curls that had recently, to my delight, come back into fashion. It wasn't long until she appeared, looking across the room for a "famous artist" to come sauntering her way. I promptly pulled the collage from my love kit, which was double-sided and designed just for such an occasion. I started making collages back in college, when I realized how easy they were to make, and found out that women were drawn to creative men. "I have been making this collage for weeks," I lied, "knowing that you existed and it would be only a matter of time before you would enter my life."

My love looked at me a little nervously, but took the 9x12 collage in her hand and began to examine it.

"What does this say?" she asked.

"I don't know my darling, as I don't speak German."

"What does this say then?"

"I must confess, my love, that I don't speak French."

"Then why don't you put any English on the 'collage' as you call it."

"As an appreciator of the arts, you must know that it is meant to evoke a certain atmosphere. Besides, I was only testing you, as each of these passages I cannot only translate, but explain their poetic value in relation to the larger context."

"Really, how about this one then."

"I will read it first in French, so that you can get a feel for how it sounds in the mother tongue. It is a poem I made using the methods of Guillaume Apollinaire, who first pioneered the idea that poetry is everywhere - it need not come from the depths of the soul, but from stray conversation, newspapers, and magazines. This one I constructed from a newspaper while visiting the Louvre in Paris. I call it 'Der Zweifler.' It is of course a love poem, as I made this entire collage in the hopes of winning *your* love, even though I only just met you."

"Well then, Romeo, let us hear 'Der Zweifler.'"

"Der Zweifler...

Immer win unz
Die Antwart off een Frag geefunden shine
Lost eye-ner unz ander Wand die Shnure dear allten
Off-jerrol chin Leanwand, so dab, sigh, herabfeel und
Sickbar Man off dear bank, dear sire."

"And what does it mean, love?"

"Dare's Wife Lair

Immerse when once
Die ant wart! Off! Enough rage! Fun then shine!
Lost eye near us and dare wand! Die sneer dare all ten,
Off Gerald's chin, lean wand, so dab, sigh, hear a field, and
Such barman off dare bank, dare
Sigher."

"I must confess, very little of it makes sense, and what does seems more angry than loving in nature. Are you quite sure you have composed a love poem?"

"It is a love poem from the great Symbolist-Romantic school of poetry; it is about the rage every lover feels when confronted with the fact that he cannot fully express the sublime nature of his love."

"And what is an 'ant wart.'"

"Ah, I thought that might come up. Ant wart is a French idiomatic expression for venereal disease, although in the context of the poem it is symbolic of anything that might have a corrupting influence on the purity of love."

"Although some pimp's hat is covering part of the 'poem,' are you sure it isn't really composed in German and doesn't actually translate to:

The Doubter

Always when one of us
Appeared to have found the answer to a question
One of us loosened the rope
of a rolled up Chinese screen on the wall, so that it fell down
and revealed the man on the bench, who
doubted so very much."

"Quite sure, my little ant wart. But enough of this one island in the archipelago I have made in your honor. Gaze upon the rest of the images which translate love in any language. Remember, the collage is double-sided."

I gazed at my beauty's fluttering eyelids as they roamed over the masterpiece, both sides of it, over a tiny Van Gogh sketch of Manchester, over a conehead facing away from the spectator, over the pimp with one woman in each arm, over Hitler reaching for a million Euros behind him (I didn't know what many of these images were but my love to be was quite informative), over a dusty little ragamuffin carrying a ladder around (a disaster waiting to happen if there ever was one), over a mugshot of someone named Podpis Majitele, over a woman sneezing into a kerchief, over mirror headed magistrates and pasty faced rock gods, over the winding stairs of Chinese castles, over the curvaceous form of someone with a woman's body and a monkey's head, over nose crushing gnomes and bicyclists wearing camouflage, over one of Cezanne's paintings from his mystic period (or did I paste that third eye there, it had been a few weeks and more than a few drinks), over socialites dressed as peacocks and men dangling cocks, over bare-breasted women surrounded by floating bottles of perfume, over a lion named Friedrich Schiller and a woman luxuriating in the embrace of a swan. My collage was a multidimensional equation that added up to one thing: seduction.

The Butler

I walked back to my apartment with my complete love kit, including the collage, sans Siren. I was mad at myself. Rather than attempting to seduce at least seven women to get one, the sort of work ethic Buster maintains, I had merely given this *barista fatale* seven incoherent explanations regarding my artwork's lasting significance and why this should cause her to fall in love with me. Apparently because she worked there, she didn't feel comfortable merely telling me to get lost, but she made sure to let me know that her shift was about to start and that she had to concentrate. It wasn't that I don't know how difficult preparing coffee can be, don't even get me started on my trials with coffee kits, it's just that I was amazed that I was not only completely unable to seduce her, but even get her number in the fifteen minutes of brilliance and charisma I had expended upon her. I could see it in her eyes, which in fifteen minutes had turned from a state of curiosity and amusement to the eyes of one of my Wellesley girls after an entire hour's worth of lecturing. I knew she despised me, and

I barely had enough energy to adjust my rabbit ears to see if there was any professional wrestling on TV. Alas, it was a weekday (I had long lost track) afternoon and it was a choice between "talk" shows, in which the fake throwing of Thanksgiving dinner at one's licentious in-laws was such a poor imitation of wrestling that it only made me more depressed, and a soap opera on the Spanish station which on a brighter day I might have used for masturbatory purposes. I left the *telenovela* on as background noise and eventually was able to tug one off between bouts of tears elicited by thinking about what was certainly Keaton's bleakest film, exploring the dark side of existentialism (Camus as opposed to Sartre, or was it the other way around), *The Love Nest* (1923, Buster Keaton Productions, Inc.). To emphasize that life is a meaningless, painful voyage with nothing to guide us but chance, Buster is dumped by his fiancé. There is no reason given, as in other films where Buster's lovelessness can at least be attributed to his inability to be competitive in the global marketplace. It just happens. Buster tries to take control over his existence by sending his ex-fiancé a letter saying he won't marry her now that she has cancelled the engagement, but we can only read this absurd missive as a general assertion that all language is, as certain medieval philosophers believed, merely nominalism, a meaningless stand-in for universals we have no real access to. Heartbroken, Buster sets out in a small boat called *The Cupid* to wander aimlessly through the world. It would seem that we cannot escape the human condition of loneliness and the desire for love, which is also, as the nominalists would say, even crueler since this entrapment in love is nothing but to be trapped in the prison house of language, a hermeneutic swirl down the toilet of life. This is further emphasized when Buster encounters a whaling ship called *The Love Nest* whose lifeboat is called *The Little Love Nest*. The captain of the ship, who cruelly throws his men overboard for the smallest of mistakes, obviously recalls Melville's avatar of pointless obsessions, Captain Ahab, as well as "the hand of fate" that makes each human life disposable and interchangeable, as Buster replaces the man who has most recently been thrown overboard. And then, the pun that is the thing itself becoming itself. A whale arrives and the captain calls, "All hands on deck!," and Buster, being a nominalist, gets on his hands and knees in order to actually put his hands on the deck of the ship. It would be worth noting that this is also the position one assumes when life fucks you in the ass. It's like the opposite of the love catapult in that while one deliberately constructs a love catapult, which can only be used once, one always assumes the position for life to fuck you in the ass, and one always does it by accident. You would think it would be easy to not get on your hands and knees, "hands on deck," and avoid life fucking you in the ass, but it's not. It's like giving birth; you forget how painful it was the last time and all of a sudden you're on your hands and knees again, only seconds away from another ass fucking. Either that or life will distract you or trick you into assuming the position, because in reality (check the *Kama Sutra*) there are many positions in which one can be fucked in the ass, and that's just with actual ass fucking. With metaphorical ass fucking, and all of life at your disposal, the number of positions in which one can be fucked in the ass is mindboggling. So, when Buster shoots a hole in *The Love Nest* and then, while waiting in *The Little Love Nest* for the larger boat to sink, lays his hands on a deck of cards to play solitaire to bide his time ("hands on a deck" becoming "hands on a deck"), as confident as he seems at that moment, undoubtedly life has already come up with a really good way to fuck him in the ass. This is emphasized when Buster's boat ends up bumping into a gigantic placard (like a billboard) in the middle of the ocean - and Buster can't avoid being fucked in the ass by meaningless chance because he only sees the billboard *"a tergo"* as Freud would say. The front of these billboards all have numbers on them, making them look like gigantic playing cards, but they are really test targets for the Navy. Standing innocently on "card 3," it is only a matter of time before Buster, who is now resting his ass on the top of the billboard, gets hit by a Navy cannon and shot up into the stratosphere. The last scene, which in another context might seem like a cheap plot device but in this case takes on a grand philosophical significance, has Buster waking up from a dream, never having left the dock because he forgot to untie his boat and took a nap. No, the implication is that, in the prison-house of love and language, we walk around nowhere in circles, and life is just an illusion in which we keep getting fucked in the ass. Of course, the illusory nature does not keep the ass fucking from seeming real, since as part of the illusion we are as real as it gets, and let me tell you, life generally doesn't use lubricant. This is such a dark reading of existentialism that it is unclear whether it represents Keaton's actual beliefs (and whatever Keaton believes, I must believe, since I am writing his autobiography) or merely his attempts to extend a philosophical system to its uttermost limits. Let us hope it is the latter. In the meantime, watch your ass, though it won't do any good!

Between tuggin' one off, and thinking about Buster's ass, using my "*bi*-tasking" abilities, which are my own inept version of what others call multitasking, I noticed that most of the *telenovelas* on the Spanish channel took place in large mansions. Apparently, in Mexico that is where all the really cool stuff goes down. I also noticed that all these mansions were filled with maids – and man were they bursting at the seams - and butlers. The maids were generally at the mercy of the men of the house, whereas the butlers tended to have more insidious roles, generating the evil required of a *telenovela* (besides the more banal evil of sexual harassment). It made me think that, if life was going to fuck me in the ass, I should at least use my non-heroin using money to give a certain dignity to my surroundings, and servants were definitely the way to go.

What I needed, and what I'd unconsciously put off admitting until now, was a butler. I definitely preferred a butler since, if I was going to have a servant, I wanted one who would fight the power, and the maids in the *telenovelas* didn't seem very interested in doing that. Still, I was even nervous about having a butler, as it always seemed like one aspect of Buster's philosophy that struck me like a weakness, an unnecessary prop for some flaw in his character. Perhaps the most glaring example of the stupidity endemic to Buster's own butler owning characters occurs in *The Navigator* (1924, Metro-Goldwyn Pictures). Rollo Treadway (aka Buster Keaton) is introduced as a dissolute young man of privilege or as the film puts it, "every family tree must have its sap." Buster just wakes up one day and decides he wants to get married and books tickets to Honolulu for the honeymoon. Only thing is he hasn't asked the woman across the street, who of course refuses him. Buster takes a long walk back across the street to get over his heartbreak (he had previously been driven across the street) and decides to go on the honeymoon alone. So while she is the Queen, he is the Jack rather than the King, a fact confirmed later - Buster's beloved and Buster himself accidentally stowing away on the wrong ship, *The Navigator*, that has been intentionally set adrift to prevent it from tipping the balance in a war between two small countries - after Buster tries to shuffle a deck of cards melting from the rain (his existential reality being my metaphor of existence). The only two cards visible to the eye before they completely melt are a Queen and a Jack, side by side. Even after Buster saves his beloved, using a swordfish as a sword to fight another swordfish, and fending off cannibals just long enough for a submarine to happen along and save them, perhaps he is a King for a moment when kissed by his beloved. This would be the teleologically necessary moment for the transformation to take place as there must be a transitional state between a thing being itself and then being transformed into itself. Then and only then can he become a Jack again as her kiss causes him to fall backwards onto the submarine's alignment jack and send it (and them) spinning round and round like the contents of a washing machine.

Given the above you can understand why, before studying the *telenovelas*, I was somewhat hesitant about getting a butler. But now I realize that if this is a flaw in Buster's character, it must be one in mine as well. These character flaws however cannot be permitted to stop us from achieving what we need to in life. Buster and I may be bad at doing things, but that is nothing more than a product of our accidental encounters with the external world. At our innermost cores we are good even if we live in a fallen world.

So the very next day I put out an ad and was soon auditioning butlers, and here, if I may be permitted to retract several previous mistakes, is where my troubles *really* began. Although all of Buster's butlers have always been men, I thought to myself, "Hey, we live in the modern age, why can't I have a female butler?" It didn't hurt that the first person to audition was a drop-dead gorgeous woman with icy blue eyes who dressed and spoke like a butler should. After telling me about her previous experiences as a butler, I knew she was the one.

"In my previous position," she said, "I was the butler for a 'Mr. Benson' who although he owned a house wanted me to be in charge of his aquarium. More than anything else, Mr. Benson loved his penguins. At first I thought this was a good sign. If a man loves penguins so much, and penguins look like butlers, then he'll obviously treat me well. And at first this seemed true. Mr. Benson made sure I had the best of everything and he didn't treat me like a butler at all. Rather than always ordering me around he would offer me drinks and ask me if I 'needed anything' or if I 'was quite comfortable.'"

As she spoke I was struck, as if with twin bolts of lightning, by her combination of humility and ignorance. Did she not realize that Mr. Benson was merely acting as any gentleman would when in the presence of such a beautiful lady? My heart went out to her. I wondered what previous trials in life had made her feel as if ordinary gallantry were some sort of special treatment. I began to fantasize about "unhappy virtue's tears." Had her parents been thrown into bankruptcy causing them both to commit suicide? Had an evil sister taunted her for her too tender feelings? Had she been abused, pinched, tickled and bitten by old men with erectile dysfunction? Perhaps she had been unfairly accused of stealing diamonds and sent to prison and then broke out with a group of hardened lady thieves who took her out into the woods to be ravaged by their boyfriends. And when she refused, was she forced to act as bait for unsuspecting travelers whom the thieves and their boyfriends took captive and held for ransom, one of whom she helped escape. And in thanks he took that thing from her which young girls hold most precious and dear. After which she stumbled upon two men, a beautiful priest and an ugly layman, engaging in the most unspeakable acts, who subsequently tied her up with her own clothes. Deciding to spare her, they untied her and forced her, in return for her life, to take care of their aunt, during which time she fell in love with the priest, even though he had threatened her life, and forced her to listen to arguments which shook her faith to the core such as, "What is religion if it cannot prevent the tyranny of the strong over the weak, or the rich over the poor, or those who are in power over those who are not in power?" Perhaps this very same man, so beautiful on the outside and so rotten on the inside, had attempted to persuade her to help him kill his very own aunt, but her virtue forced her to reveal everything to the aunt, even going so far as testing the bottle of poison on one of the aunt's dogs, which broke the girl's heart because she so loved animals. And when the priest found out about her breach of confidence, he took her to the very same tree where she had first witnessed those unnatural acts and forced her to watch them once again as he performed them with relish upon his ugly lover, and then left her in the woods to her own devices. After which she found a doctor who cured her wounds and offered her a position as companion to his own daughter, with whom she became fast friends, only to learn that this same doctor was planning on flaying his very kin alive in order to study the processes of circulation in the name of science. Unable to save her dearest friend, she found herself in the woods once again, and after many days of wandering she found a monastery where she was able to confess her sins, particularly the most gruesome and obscene ones. Unwittingly this made her eligible for a most elite order of retainers whom the monks joyously flogged, raped, and abused day and night, and her tears only made them more violent as they dug their nails into her breasts and tore at her hair, but not too much. Now a godly young woman, the final straw came when one of the monks ejaculated upon communion wafers she had been forced to use as tampons during her monthly curse. Blasphemy being the mother of invention, she devised an ingenious plan for escape from her labyrinthine prison, and upon its consummation, she wandered through the night weeping for the innocent girls she had left behind at the monastery. No sooner had she found an empty bed to cleanse her defiled dreams upon than two men awoke her and shoved her into a giant burlap sack. She was taken to a castle to become the governess of a woman whose husband was a blood-letter, perhaps because he had a small penis. The sight of the dripping blood and the small penis filling her with anguish beyond measure, she convinced the Marquise to write a rhetorically effective treatise balancing ethos, pathos, and logos which she would then, being an expert at this point in scaling walls, publish as a broadside in order to awaken the populace to the menace of blood-letters who imprison their wives in castles. Despite the eloquence of the treatise and her tireless efforts at the broadside's distribution, *Kairos* was not on her side, the winged deity having made a permanent home in other media. Nevertheless the broadside did fall into the hands of a man whom she no longer recognized, who later sent her a note claiming he had once done her wrong and wished to make amends. Not wishing to stand between any man and the expiation of his sins, she went forthwith straight into the clutches of the man who had taken that thing which is most precious to young girls, who was now a professional dealer in such things, and offered her a position in finding young girls who still had this thing which was most precious to young girls. Of course refusing the offer and, in the manner of the Apostle Paul, wiping the dust off her feet, she left town. It was then, perhaps, that she ran across a young man being robbed by two other men, whose wounds she nursed until he was strong enough to take her to his particular castle, one that specialized not in blood-letting but in slave labor, including all the naked buttock whipping necessary for such an enterprise. And when she tried to work upon the man's conscience by reminding him of the good she had done for him when he was being robbed and severely beaten, he confused her by stating that she only did so because her own conscience had compelled her to do so, and so she was really only serving her own needs, not his. All the while he enjoyed strangling the slaves while he ravaged them, and after ravaging them, forcing them to run the presses of his counterfeiting operation. Only a lapse in the young man's judgment, the foolhardy plan for one more score, the big one, ensured her escape, once again, from certain death. It was only after he had lowered her several times into a pit of rotting bodies belonging to slaves of whom he had grown tired that the castle was raided by authorities. And only by telling her story to an honest magistrate was she able to gain her freedom - for a short time. Because it wasn't long before she bumped into one of her old jailbreak lady friends at a café who told her that a man in the corner had his eye on her, and that if she would take him for a stroll out in the country she would be richly rewarded by half the take of his house which they would be robbing during that time. She did as she was told, but warned her admirer to make sure his servant guarded his house as they went on a picnic prepared by the jailbreak friends, which just happened to include a poisoned bottle of wine. While picnicking he was so thankful that she had warned her about the robbery that he offered to marry her on the spot, but after a spot of poisoned wine he began coughing and was quickly dead. The only man who had truly loved her had only been able to do so for a few minutes. A misfortune she pondered as she walked the boulevard that evening, only to be kidnapped by a man whose pleasures with women only reached their peak after they had been decapitated. Fortunately the man was very old and thus he fell asleep after an especially prodigious and wine-soaked dinner, allowing her, once again, to escape without harm. As one might imagine, it wasn't long before a newspaper reporter caught wind of her story, and she was awarded the title secretly coveted by a mister Aleister Crowley, "The Most Unfortunate Girl in the World." This newfound fame led to her position as the nanny of a beautiful young child whose mother traveled from town to town giving seminars on the perfect child care regime, one that just happened to coincide with the age and needs of her growing child. Over time they came to be popularly known across the countryside as the "Postpartum Seminars." One night, the hotel they were staying in caught fire. The mother, grabbing what was most important to her, her lecture notes, made it out just in time. The girl made it out as well, only to realize the child was still inside. Since it was her job, she went back inside the burning, crumbling labyrinth and saved the beautiful young child from the flames of death, only to trip on a disintegrating drawbridge on the way out and, her reflexes betraying her moral soul, tossed her charge into a mountain of burning ashes. With her career as a nanny ruined, the most obvious career transition was to train as a butler. Which is naturally how I met her.

This long tale of imagined woe, which I was certain was not far afield of her actual circumstances, only added to the young woman's appeal as a potential butler. The rest of the interview only confirmed these initial impressions. She showed me the scars on her otherwise flawless body where penguins had attacked her even as she was cleaning up their feces, then assured me that this had nothing to do with any tendency towards coprophagia on their part, as in dogs and apes, but merely from boredom (here I might add my own theory - a taste for the delectable flesh of beautiful women). Notwithstanding the daily dangers of her job, she grew to love the penguins almost as much as Mr. Benson, who taught her all about their history and how to mimic their calls (which, as one might imagine, resulted in even more scars). So imagine her surprise when she discovered that men who were refined enough to hire butlers were only slightly more refined than men who lived in monasteries and castles. True, Mr. Benson didn't flog her, rape her, or threaten to cut off her head, but he nevertheless broke the sacred vows of marriage by asking her to become his mistress in exchange for which he would train her in the dark arts of law. Little did Mr. Benson know that while he spent time alone with his penguins or dining with his wife she had perused enough of his library to know that what he was proposing was known as sexual harassment and that furthermore she had no interest in pursuing the dark arts of law. When she presented her case to Mr. Benson, he tearfully gave her a generous severance and two of his favorite penguins who had, by the way, grown quite attached to her.

I assured this young lady, my potential butler, that she had nothing to fear from me. Not only was I not married, but I had no special skills or talents other than those rather distasteful abilities secured as a former plumber, with which to barter for her virtue. Which in my eyes was eternally renewed by the way in which she faced the trials of existence and, of course, by her angelic beauty. Certainly her penguins could come along with us. And of course she could go to bed every night at 8:00 p.m. if she so desired. I desired this young lady's services so badly that I refrained from explaining to her that, according to Buster's theory, she had probably already been married to Mr. Benson when he made his scandalous proposal.

For a while our new arrangement worked swimmingly. The young lady performed her services as a butler with admirable dexterity and, as our agreement stipulated, I had a month to find a new job as a plumber (my non-heroin using money starting to run out) before presenting her with the first installment of her yearly allowance. But alas her virtues catapulted me into such a trance of love it seems (because I remember nothing of this and can only refer to depositions the result of which left me utterly penniless and deeply in debt with my creditors) I one night entered her room after 8:00 p.m. She had, I think on purpose, left it open for me. "I have been a devotee of the pussy since the tender age of seven years," I allegedly said, "and wish to examine yours as if I were a gynecologist from a Marquis de Sade novel." She was apparently (and I do remember this, though I have since without success attempted to forget the image) naked and horrified that I had entered her room without permission at such a late hour, revealing her darkest secret, that in the evening her spiked vagina turned into an enormous penis with gigantic testicles that hung all the way to the floor. In short, every night after 8:00 pm she transformed, much like in the legends of Melusina, into a hermaphrodite with elephantitis.

It really seems impossible that I would say such grotesque and childish things to my butler, and wondered if my main crime hadn't been the discovery of her genital secrets. I do know that I apologized profusely the next morning for my indiscretion with regard to her living quarters, and she seemed mollified enough to stay on. I not only agreed to recompense her for my violation but made it my personal mission to make her feel less self-conscious about what had happened. I made it a point not only to have her "surprise" me while I was naked most every day, but to purchase some devices I heard spoken of while trapped in O's lair. Apparently, all of her male guests wore weights around their testicles so as to extend them lower and lower, much like the braces placed around the necks of certain African women in order to achieve a similar effect, except with an upward gravitational force in the latter case. So I went to a local sex shop and bought their entire shelf of testicle weights so that by extending the hang of my scrotum, my butler might be less self-conscious about the size of her testes. With this twin-testicular attack, I seemed to be making some progress so that my butler's nervous laughter at our initial run-ins gradually came to be replaced by what I took to be sly, knowing grins between us. So imagine my complete surprise and horror when two weeks later I was not served dinner one evening, but a sexual harassment suit. And she gave me the papers under a silver platter and everything! I was so humiliated. It is true, the saying that "no good deed goes unpunished," but until you've actually experienced this truism in real life, you have no idea what the Spanish word "embarazada" really means. Those two weeks I thought we had been establishing a rapprochement; she had merely been building a case.

Escape by Lepidoptery

In order to escape my creditors and the sexual harassment police I had to flee to the forest. I was utterly depressed. I felt as if this lady-man and her lawyers had found me praying in a church and grabbed me by the neck, tossed me onto an ornately carved throne where only the priest should sit while giving communion, slapped me back and forth, disrobed me and pissed on my clothes, pissed in my mouth and up my nostrils, took the sacred chalice and smashed it across my skull, jacked me off until they drained my balls into that chalice, strapped my hands and legs apart with a belt, jumped up and down on my stomach like it was a hotel bed, strangled me, tore one of my eyes out and shoved it deep up into my ass. I hunted and fished as best I could, not knowing where I found my will to live. I made a birch bark canoe and snaked down a nearby river. The water was black and glistening and reminded me of my days as a plumber, which seemed so simple now compared to my current delirium. I tried to appreciate the beauty of the forest but the very trees looked like graffiti in three dimensions. Sometimes I lost the will to paddle and the wind twisted and drifted me silently downstream. I don't think I'd ever felt so far away from everything, the city skyline, the thousands of square glowing windows. To motivate myself I imagined police boats, full of sexual harassment officers, speeding after me waving their writs and warrants, which would usually get me paddling again. Once, I'll admit, I forgot my sorrows and really got caught up in the thrill and excitement of being chased and completely lost track of my actual surroundings, the result being that I almost drowned in rapids but was saved by a beautiful woman in a mysterious veil. She saved me and broke my heart, saying she was not interested in me per se but in refugees more generally, that she had others to rescue. Though she slipped away like some sort of Indian, I tried to follow her anyway, as I howled at the moon and bashed my head with rocks. Though she never responded, I talked endlessly to her into the night. I followed shadows everywhere, of men, women. I got married endlessly to the local Indians in exchange for whatever food I was able to find, but didn't love any of them. I frankly don't know how much longer I could have gone on, because at some point one's subterranean will-to-die overcomes one's best intentions - one forgets that someone like Buster Keaton ever lived, forgets one's own face. One forgets - and then you have to get your lights punched out because *only* then can Buster arrive with a stretcher and put you in the ambulance that always takes you to a higher state.

Or perhaps we should say a higher state, and then a lower, and then a higher, one's head bobbing as it inevitably will when chasing butterflies, as in Buster

Keaton's *The Paleface* (1921, Comique Film Co.). Although my lights had not literally been punched out, I was suffering from similar symptoms due to hunger. I wasn't actually at a low point, more of a swaying this way and that point due to hunger and thirst, when that film reminded me that nature can always be enjoyed, in any state, through lepidoptery.

As any lepidopterist knows, the joy of collecting butterflies has several dimensions. First, there is the challenge of catching these creatures that move so erratically that even a butterfly net makes the process, at times, seem like shuffling cards in the rain that are melting even as you shuffle. Secondly, there is the strangeness of the butterfly itself - are there two creatures more different than the whimsically inclined, infinitely varied, tragically ephemeral butterfly and the stone-faced lepidopterist who hunts them down with a resolve we imagine must be equivalent to the bards of old who spent their entire lives composing epic poems for posterity? Finally, there is the uncanny transition from the free and yet tragically mortal state of the butterfly and its transposition, through the care of the lepidopterist, into a state of immortality where the lepidopterist's act of mounting the butterfly behind glass is equivalent to the Grecian Urn Keats writes so eloquently about. And yet, if there were a utopia behind this utopia, for the butterfly, it would undoubtedly be that vertiginous moment of being caught in the net itself, caressed by its delicate fabric. I'm almost certain that at that moment the butterfly must sense that it is trapped in a state of love, overwhelmed as Leda was by the swan. It is the very definition of love which, of course, is the most important thing Buster has tried to teach us, always trying out a new parable. The dream would be to be permanently ravaged by the swan, to be eternally in that state. As in *Paleface*, when Buster has saved an Indian tribe from having its land stolen by oil barons, we know that he has transformed this ideal butterfly net (originally just an actual butterfly net) into a metaphorical butterfly net when, joining the tribe and taking a squaw as his bride, their nuptual kiss lasts for two years - two years of being simultaneously a butterfly and a lepidopterist in a strange romance that is yet sanctioned by the gods. And so it became clear to me that this butterfly net, once transformed into itself, is what we all must aspire to.

I devised a makeshift butterfly net by taking off my tuxedo pants and belt (luckily I had dispatched of O's cummerbund) and, using some sap from a tree, glued (or sapped) the bottoms of the pants legs together. I found a stick of suitable length and curvature to hook through two of the belt loops so that, when butterflies came by, I could swing my pants through the air. I was actually quite pleased with myself, as I had never seen a double-tubed butterfly net before and it also seemed, in my opinion, that using my pants for the net part of the net allowed me to double my chances of catching a butterfly with every swing.

I spent the next several days in my underwear, desperately trying to catch a butterfly, but the forest seemed utterly devoid of them, so I tried using the pants to hunt squirrels. I figured if I ate one immediately after killing it, it would be sort of like hillbilly sushi. I sat still as a stone in front of a fallen tree I had littered with acorns, so that the squirrel would just barrel down the trunk in one direction while I swung in the opposite one. And when a squirrel came by that was so wild it had no reason to fear the smell of humans, it did exactly what I expected it to. My pants swooshed through the air and that squirrel went right to the bottom of the right cuff, trapped in sap. I was just about to tie my pants off when I looked in and, in what I suppose must have been a sudden reversion to civilized reflexes I screamed, "Shit, I've got a fucking squirrel in my pants!" By the time I was able to regain my killer instinct, the squirrel had made its way out the waist and headed for the thicket, no doubt warning the entire forest about the kidnapper in his underwear trying to get squirrels in his pants. I felt like a pervert. An extremely hungry pervert.

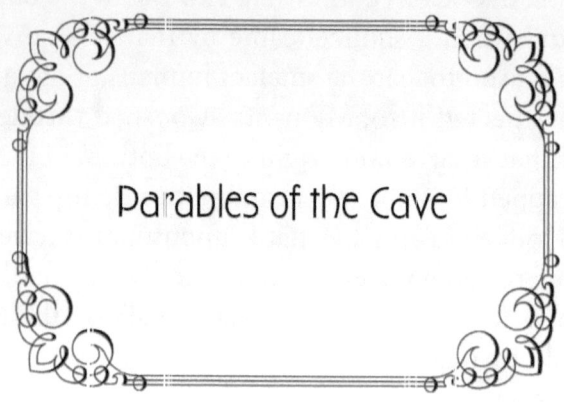

Parables of the Cave

Dejected, I went down to the creek to eat some of those reeds I'd seen deer munching on, thinking that, at worst, they would only give me a bad case of the runs, and if I was lucky, only a "mild" case of diarrhea. It was then, like all great tricksters from folklore, that Buster came by with the metaphorical stretcher and ambulance and took me to a literally lower state. Along the side of the creek, what I had several times mistaken for a round shadow was in fact the entrance to a cave. Perhaps I needed to make one of those entrances into the underworld required of all epic heroes, but then remembered I wasn't an epic hero. I didn't *need* to make any sort of entrance. Still, I had nowhere else to go, so I considered it regardless.

Normally I would have avoided entering a cave due to Plato's warnings about these places - warnings I could never quite remember and the parts I did remember made me feel like I was in a battle with superheroes both gay and straight. The superheroes always denied their status one way or the other, beating me to a pulp, all the while disavowing that they had any will-to-mastery, so much so that they offered up scathing critiques of themselves, how they were so poorly paid but did not deserve anything better because all they had going for them were cans of pepper spray which could be picked up anywhere, that they constantly felt bedeviled by stuttering and anorexia, that they sometimes felt like using their powers against little girls and cute animals, and that most of the time they were lost in dreams of total fullness which, as we all know, can never be obtained when we see nothing but shadows on the cave walls. More than anything else they just dreamed of being normal humans with better career opportunities, but the only escapes from their narcissus narcosis they could dream up involved breaking up into multiplicities that would undo their subjectivity. They wished they could become engineers because that would always get them hired, but they couldn't face the rigorous hours of study and the tinkering with hydraulic devices to fire eggs across endless, barren classrooms that were largely devoid of female visions of beauty. Instead, they went through their days with flattened affects, only affected by their environment, if at all, in incidental and unremarkable ways. Were they wasps, orchids, or proto-fascists? These were the thoughts that occupied them most of the time.

But since I had never actually encountered one of these superheroes, I had no idea if they actually existed or if I had only imagined them. Despite all these red flags, since a childhood friend of mine had once told me that he often found old copies of Playboy in caves and in my own loneliness I had also recently checked for copies of Playboy hidden in double-sealed plastic bags under rocks in streams - to no avail - I decided to chance the cave, regardless of Plato's warnings. I had only planned on going into the darkness a little ways since I figured that people would hide copies of Playboy near the entrance to a cave, so as to allow for some light in order to see the forbidden pages, but things did not work out that way. The first thing I saw was a skull on a ledge and it seemed to be singing to me, rather howling like a ghost or evil spirit. I backed against the wall into a burning torch that was hanging there, catching my shirt on fire. I ran like a madman, in the wrong direction down into the depths of the cave, shirt and back burning, as the ghostly howling became a whole opera of ghosts. I wished I had a gun, a cabbage head, anything. What would I have thrown a cabbage head at? I wished I were in a haunted house, because there the ghosts are always real people. I wished my mom was with me, who once punched a guy playing a ghost in the stomach and made him apologize for scaring me so badly even though we had actually paid money to enter the house in order to be scared. I wished I were sitting in Spiderman's lap. I wished I were anywhere else, in the mountains, a gambling ring, the last stop on the subway, the frozen north. I wished I were breaking rocks in prison just like Buster had taught me.

As often happens in such situations, I passed out, and the dank cavern floor put out the fire on what was left of my shirt. The place I woke up, which I felt must have been in the deep recesses of the cave, was at least lit, even if torches were kind of scary, with their shadows and whatnot, and the way they cast my own shadow everywhere. I became fascinated with my own shadow, hoping my profile wasn't as bad as it looked,

but it probably was and thus made me feel even more alienated from Buster Keaton. As I lay there, I began contemplating all the reasons I was bad marriage material, and by marriage material I mean a real marriage, not the existential, ghostly kind that Keaton has told us happens every day of our lives, not that he doesn't address the former. In *Daydreams* (1922 Buster Keaton Productions, Inc.), when Buster asks the hand of his beloved if he can marry her, he is confronted by the quintessential father's question, "Can you support her?" Buster vows to go to the city and "perform great deeds" and the father says, "I will lend you my revolver." In a rare, and thus deliberate, continuity error, Buster is not given the revolver but instead becomes one when he is fleeing from the police (Buster + city = fleeing from the police) and hides in a ship's propeller, which resembles the inside of a revolver as it is being loaded, in addition to being a revolver unto itself. Like a bullet swinging around the bullet chambers in some weird Vietnamese roulette game, or like a hamster in a cage, Buster runs inside the propeller, trying to keep up, but is ultimately thrown into the water and caught by a fisherman who mails him back to his beloved's house. It is then that the father opens a drawer and hands Buster the ungiven revolver to shoot himself. Fortunately he misses, being inept, and is merely tossed out the window into the garden.

Anyway, here is the personal and admittedly offhand bad marriage material that occurred to me at the time:

1. Ugliness (and here I must note that although

there are certain physical resemblances between Keaton and I, mine are more like caricatures of that leading man), including my pronounced hunch and the profile, both of which I was reminded of in the shadows on the cave wall.

2. Poverty (caused by the sexual harassment lawsuit filed against me by my former butler), unemployment, and a lack of an inheritance from rich parents. Although Keaton rightfully points out that such an inheritance often results in dissolute individuals generally lacking in character, it is also true that such character flaws are easily cured by life struggles and the right woman – sort of a reverse Horatio Alger tale. Whereas without the inheritance, one is left relying on the good fortune of being near someone with such an inheritance who is treating a woman badly who will, if she is grateful enough to you for extricating her from the situation or simply letting her know - assuming she doesn't know - what a scoundrel her rich boyfriend is, afterwards walk with you down the empty streets with nothing between you but the love you share. Such a positive reaction from the woman is far more likely to occur if you remind people of Charlie Chaplin, which I don't, and I think for good reason. I feel that Keaton, at least on this level, is more of a realist than Chaplin.

3. Inability to obtain plastic surgery (to correct #1). This is due to the fact that I am now running from my creditors, which leads right back to #2,

plus I am not sure if there is a surgery that cures a hunch. I have never heard of Quasimodoplasty. Although it is fair to say that there are a lot of things I am not aware of and I have not been keeping up with the latest in plastic surgery.

4. Ineptness. For instance, I am unable to break rocks in or out of prison, fix household items, garden or landscape, maintain an automobile, cook well or even prepare food in a way that most people would classify as cooking - burning rabbits or fish over an open flame or preparing "hillbilly sushi," assuming I could catch it, does not constitute a romantic date for most women. It was once suggested to me that I could tour with a circus troupe as "The Most Inept Man in the World." SEE HIM FAIL MISERABLY ATTEMPTING TO COMPLETE THE SIMPLEST HOUSEHOLD TASKS! I actually have no doubt that I could probably make a decent living doing this. But even if I made good money what self-respecting woman would want to be married to someone whose claim to fame was being the most inept man in the world? Surely whispers of all kinds would circulate constantly, particularly as to whether such ineptness carried itself back into the bedroom. It's the reason executioners in the Middle Ages always wore black hoods. No doubt they were well paid - upholding the laws of the kingdom and the absolute sovereignty of the local lord - but on a first date at the mead hall, when the woman asked what the executioner did for a living, well, that

would be a little too creepy for her to associate herself with - no matter how much he made. I'd imagine that the executioners of the Middle Ages are the equivalent of today's plumbers, in that strange disparity between income and social status. The modern day equivalent of this would be someone finding out that the flame beginning to burn in his long term heart is a stripper. Because that disappointed suitor would be well aware that, despite protestations from the stripper and strip clubs more generally, all strippers, at the very least, jerk guys off as an unofficial part of their job.

5. A history of chronic depression in both myself and in the rest of my family which has shown a surprising resistance to everything but, what I like to refer to as, "double-barrel" therapy.

6. Lack of a car. Although technically there are no roads in caves or the forest I was hiding out in, I still held out hope that one day I might find myself back in a place where cars were central to courting rituals. But even if I did make it back, even if I were able to assume another identity that would shake my creditors - increasingly hard to do in this electronic age of total economic surveillance - see #s 4 and 5 for reasons as to why it would be difficult to obtain funds for a street car named Desiree.

7. Inability to lower my standards. Surely, one might say, having been married to a five hundred pound borderline paranoid individual who did not own

a plunger though he shat vociferously, I could surely just marry someone uglier, and even worse off, than me. But the exact opposite has been the case, since, as my sense of identification with Buster has increased to the point where I feel that if I were a body he would be my soul, and if I were a soul he would be my flesh, I have gradually come to realize that I can only imagine falling in love with such wavy-haired sirens as Buster fell in love with in his films.

8. I was lost in a cave.

Who would ever have thought that the cave itself, as an atmosphere, a mood in all its Heideggerian inclusiveness, would end up becoming one of the great loves of my life, so much so that it ceased to feel like a cave and more like a world unto itself. Its ceiling became a blue sky and the shadows on its walls were palm trees blowing in the wind. Who could have guessed that upon rising to my knees and then precariously to my feet I would find the following inscription on the wall, evidence that the Indians there were not only not savage but were in fact the most enlightened apostles of Buster Keaton I had ever seen:

> It seems to us that a portrait, even if it dates only from the previous year, is always a mockery. It is never more than a species of cadaver and constitutes, of itself alone, by the very fact of its existence, a bewitchment. To drag one's old portraits along in one's wake is to become, as it were, a serpent entangled in its old skins.

Better, as often as one can, to change one's name, appearance, occupations, wife, ideas, and friends. That is no doubt the only course that permits us, without shame, to tolerate the sight of a photograph showing us as a child, unless we possess - like the Buster Keaton of the films - an inviolable sangfroid such that, stiffened like a stake by the sword of humor and, never laughing, we become an axis about which the nonsensical trivialities of shifting events gravitate.

The inscription seemed to offer two options - as if there were only two - but that they were inevitably the same. Always and only Buster Keaton, the one whose expression never changes as the *Dasein* swirls about him. Who never changes even as he, in his many films, tries every walk of life, as we all do. And like Buster, we have no choice. We don't direct the films. They direct us.

Inhabitants!

I was soon to discover that there were three Indians who lived in the cave. The leader was Chief He Who Deserted the Chiefs. He was once a great warrior but had retired to this cave to study the teachings of Buster Keaton, which was difficult given that, like myself, he had never seen a single Buster Keaton film when he embarked on this journey. Indeed, unlike me, due to the lack of cinemas in the forest, he had *still* never seen one of Keaton's films. Chief He Who Deserted the Chiefs explained that it was unnecessary because, since Keaton embodied in his actions and relation toward life all the universals, then one could study Keaton by carefully exploring all aspects of the forest, wherever one felt a connection to him, the drops of water in a pond, the fractal patterns in trees, the social rituals of wolves. The more he attuned himself to Keaton, the more he felt that a single fish splashing in the river contained an image of all rivers, a truth he referred to as the *River Otter Samadhi.* This truth had led him to leave the meandering animal trails the other Indians used and to find himself increasingly walking in an ever-expanding labyrinth of square patterns, spontaneously coming up with shamanistic mantras like, "Buster Keaton is the embodiment of Enlightenment in the form of Samsara." Buster knew the truth, Chief He Who Deserted the Chiefs explained to me, that most people wasted years seeking Enlightenment when they did not realize that Samsara and Enlightenment are the same.

Despite this latter piece of wisdom, I learned that the engraving Chief He Who Deserted the Chiefs referred to as the *Buster Samadhi Of Flow And Stasis* (B.S.O.F.A.S.S. for short) which the Chief heard in a dream and believed was dictated to him by Buster himself, had actually taken two years to complete. This was due primarily to the incompetence of his companions, Brave Humble Birth and Squaw Who Shits A Lot, who in addition to their respective genealogical and physical maladies had absolutely no understanding of the fact that it was not the content of the words themselves, profound as they were, that would produce Enlightenment but the choice of wall, the spacing of each word, indeed each letter, in relation to one another and to the space of the wall itself. Did I mention that the shape of the B.S.O.F.A.S.S., the shape that produced the Enlightenment, was identical to the eccentric square labyrinth that Chief He Who Deserted the Chiefs had begun walking in the forest that one day, and led to the cave we were now all living in? As for my fears of caves, Chief He Who Deserted the Chiefs said that my fears were mercurial, abusive, and narcissistic and that especially my fear of self-effacing superheroes both gay and straight was an emanation of my fear of life itself, as Buster Keaton was the living refutation of Plato's sophistry.

Brave Humble Birth was so named, Chief He Who Deserted the Chiefs told me, because he was not a real Indian at all, but belonged to a race of people who were destined to lose everything, including and especially their fiancés, and that this was because they, being of such humble origins, could not even imagine the possibility of having wives and thus on the eve of every wedding they snuck out of their tribe and left for good, spreading misery and bad luck wherever they went. They were bewitched; catching their feet in their own traps, casting disastrous spells in the rain, for magic energy was their only redeeming virtue. Chief He Who Deserted the Chiefs felt, nevertheless, that he could harness Brave Humble Birth's cursed magic and use it to further reveal the eternal mysteries of the B.S.O.F.A.S.S.

At one point Brave Humble Birth took me aside and categorically denied this genealogy. He acknowledged the fact that certain members of his tribe did leave their fiancés on the eve of their weddings and that he in fact was one of those members. However, only shamans of his tribe performed this rite as the final moment of training in their abandonment to the ways of magic. Did I notice those howling ghost voices when I first entered the cave? That was all Brave Humble Birth's work, or as he was actually called by his own people - Brother New Home. All shamans were named in honor of their itinerant ways because for all their magic power they never used it in their own tribe but felt the duty to spread it throughout the world wherever their wanderings might lead them. Indeed the powers of his own tribe also derived from the teachings of Buster Keaton, which rather than coming from some random relation to the forest or its denizens were contained in the *Sacred Summaries of Buster Keaton's Films* (S.S. for short), which Chief He Who Deserted the Chiefs had recently stolen from him and hidden in the depths of the cave. When Brother New Home confronted him he was flabbergasted by Chief He Who Deserted the Chiefs' response: "I'm horning in on your books! You never read them anyway! When the *Sacred Summaries* stood on the cave shelf for over a year, I just wanted them for a bit of fun! I can have my way with any sacred book I wants! If I'm to blame at all, it's for not lecturing you, for two hours at minimum, for leaving such sacred books just lying around for anyone to take." Brother New Home's commentary on this, for my ears only: "As if, a relative newcomer to the cave, I could have hidden these books from that self-serving troglodyte by trade." Chief He Who Deserted Chiefs continued: "You have totally brought this upon yourself with your bad book judgment! Because, Humble Birth, it's like you wanted to have these books stolen, just like all the other the other members of your tribe, who are always running away from their fiancés and sacred books! You're a walking runaway train shot out of a cannon Humble Birth. Buster Keaton himself will come by your house, and you'll miss out because you've run away from *it*, from *your* house, two years before he even got there because you Lover Leavers just can't get your shit together with your most prized possessions. But now I've exposed your negligence, ripped it open and glaring like a pool of blood on the snow - Gangsta style! I don't care what you think, cuz I'm the Book Man Muthafucka,

I open 'em all, I read 'em all, and I keep them safe from people like you who can't be trusted with a single new Keaton revelation etched on a cave wall, much less his entire *Sacred Summaries* - Deal with it!"

"So what you're telling me," I said, "is that Chief He Who Deserted the Chiefs is not to be trusted. Rather than a high priest of Keaton, he is more like a five hundred pound borderline paranoid spouse, or someone who wipes the ass of such a spouse, or a penguin pecked female butler?"

"Something like that," Brother New Home said. "And that B.S.O.F.A.S.S., that's the killer. It's like he'd forgotten that it came straight from the Sacred Summaries, because even in his tirade to me he held on to that old notion that he'd dreamed the thing. It is a beautiful engraving, and I was happy to help him place the passage on the wall of our home, along with Squaw Who Shits A Lot, but if you spend much time here you'll find the *Samadhi* written in several parts of the cave with almost indiscernible variations. Chief He Who Deserted the Chiefs had the crazy idea that the precise arrangement of the *Samadhi* would do more than instruct us in our life's journey. He actually thought that some form of magic would result, not the great magic that comes from meditation on the *Sacred Summaries* themselves (which is why I didn't mind redoing the *Samadhi* over and over), but something you can see, something so intense it would be like a blade flying from the hilt of Buster's own grasp and sailing right through your heart.

It was hard for me to decide who to believe, Chief He Who Deserted the Chiefs or Brother New Home, since both of their stories were so perfectly coherent

as to defy believability. What was beyond dispute was
the incredible beauty of Squaw Who Shits A Lot, who
floated out of the cavern's darkness like savory smoke
from a black table cloth. Her small face was a glowing
cameo that slowly grew to an exquisite illumination as
she came right up to my face and asked, "Do you have any
assignments for me? Any magic you need me to perform,
for although I have diarrhea, I am a master of several
magic arts. I can construct fetishes that act at a distance,
compose music that bewitches any ear in its reach,
combine the past and the future in a single word, and
produce fairly decent knockoffs of several Impressionist
painters." I was so stunned by the physical wonder of
Squaw Who Shits A Lot, and by her numerous magic
powers, that there was no way I could come up with an
assignment for her - her gracious proposal had the effect
of knocking me off whatever train I was standing on, that
I thought I owned, and I could only watch it helplessly
turn the corner as Chief He Who Deserted the Chiefs
whisked her down an unknown passage, claiming it was
time for one of her 'sessions'.

There was, however, one evening (at least I think
it was evening), that the four of us spent together to
commemorate the date of Keaton's death. Having lost all
sense of space and time I could only trust Chief He Who
Deserted the Chiefs and welcome the fact that the elusive
Squaw Who Shits A Lot joined us. Indeed she was the
matron of festivities, Chief He Who Deserted the Chiefs
taking a rare occasion to cede the floor to someone else's
talents, who could know why? Squaw Who Shits A Lot
began the evening by singing the B.S.O.F.A.S.S. in her
melodious voice, and then produced a specially designed

peace pipe which she encouraged us all to partake of. With this we seemed to melt together warmly in the remembrance of Keaton in his bodily form, but soon time passed in a very strange way. Rather than the cinematic movement I was used to, I began to see only individual frames. I had no idea how much time had passed between one frame and another but I felt that the gaps were long and uneven. It seemed like I was responding to questions that I did not even remember hearing, or that had been posed many hours before so that my response would not even be recognized as such. At one point I recall asking Squaw Who Shits A Lot about the cause of her malady, and how it was she had avoided her affliction this entire evening. Rather than receiving an answer (but who could tell?), she gave us all accordion-like instruments made of wet birch and told us to play and recite whatever elements of Buster emanated through us. As we did this, saying things like "Love laughs at locksmiths," she walked around and touched all of our facial blemishes (there were many) so that we all felt beautiful and loved. I could have sworn that she blew softly on one of my warts, making it fly off my face and float down a corridor as if it were merely a butterfly that had landed there. Oh what would we not have done for her that night, having each received, from her first movements, eyeglasses made of swirling candy? We all dressed in one another's clothes - including hers - pretending to be one another. We pretended to be monkeys. I told her that I wished I were a pile of dust she could sweep down a bottomless hole. She said that I was only drowning in a giant aquarium and that she would bail me out slowly with a teacup, and when I was about to die, sing a note that would sound like Buster coming out of the silent era, making my heart beat so fast it would shatter the glass cage and rush me into the beauty of the world.

How long after this was I in my right state of mind? The first thing I wanted to do, after marrying Squaw Who Shits A Lot, was ask Chief He Who Deserted the Chiefs what exactly had happened to us all during the commemoration, and how Squaw Who Shits A Lot had obtained such powers. Fortunately the first person I ran into was Brother New Home. I asked him where Chief He Who Deserted the Chiefs might be, and Brother New Home replied, "Dude, you'd better stay away from Chief He Who Deserted the Chiefs for a while, if not for good. He's convinced you entered an 'intense nature psychosis' during our commemoration, and he is furious."

Brother New Home had never addressed me as "Dude" before, which brought back both fond and bitter memories of my husband Todd. I also remember that whenever Todd had addressed me as such, something disastrous was eminent.

"What is an 'intense nature psychosis'? Can one survive it?"

"I pretty sure that it's just something he invented, like all that stuff about seeing Buster in fractal leaf patterns, but you did do some pretty strange stuff that night. At one point, you were intently playing with tiny sticks, as if you were trying to make something that moved back and forth. You were hunched over so I couldn't tell quite what it was, but it was pretty weird, and you spent hours on it, only lifting your eyes to say things as enigmatic, if not as poetic, as the *Samadhi*."

As soon as Brother New Home mentioned the sticks, which had totally escaped both consciousness and memory, I realized that I had been attempting to construct a miniature love catapult for me and the Squaw, but I kept it to myself.

I said, "You have to tell me exactly what Chief He Who Deserted the Chiefs said about me."

Brother New Home looked at me as if he were about to break my heart - I knew the look - and prefaced his remarks by saying that the evening was strange for him as well, so that he couldn't attest to the veracity of the Chief's statements, especially given all the craziness with the Sacred Summaries. Regardless, when I heard what Chief He Who Deserted the Chiefs had said about me, I felt like a parade that an anarchist had tossed a bomb right in the middle of, killing no one, but breaking almost enough fire hydrants to spew the number of tears I wished to cry.

"Well," Brother New Home said, "the first thing he did was call you a 'Honkey Jackass.' When I pressed him to define what he meant by this strange neologism, this is what he said."

Brother New Home assumed the posture and manner of Chief He Who Deserted the Chiefs which, I now recognized, was eerily similar to that of Buster Keaton despite his admission that he had never actually seen one of his films, and said, speaking in the Chief's voice: "I'm still too pissed to talk productively about it. But couldn't you sense his ingratitude after I had treated him to an extravagant feast and performance by Squaw Who Shits A Lot? It's a true sign of nature psychosis, whose symptoms are characterized by a totally narcissistic hipsterism and arrogance, and then later, unbelievable impertinence. Don't you remember the endless insults, at least five hours of them, calling me "Chief He Who Fled the Chiefs" in front of Squaw Who Shits A Lot while constantly flattering her, as if he thought he could have some chance of making her interested in him? But I'll be catapulted into a regiment of palefaces if he thinks he's going to steal my wallet, and while I'm trying to get it back, slip me an empty wallet while stealing my cab, making sure I can't chase him by, not daring to punch me with his own fist, hitting me with a boxing glove he has attached to a spring-loaded device normally used for signaling traffic. Two weeks before our frickin wedding as if he were the one the commemoration was for."

"Wait, Chief He Who Deserted the Chiefs is being married to Squaw Who Shits A Lot?" I cried, trying to disguise the effects of the sinking feeling of my drowning heart, doing my best to adopt, as the Samadhi puts it, that "inviolable sangfroid" that would cause my face to "stiffen like a stake."

"Oh, he didn't tell you? Typical. Yes the date has been set ever since we finished the Samadhi. But dude, with his sense of entitlement and the paucity of doable chicks in this cave, you might have put two and two together."

Yes, I might have put two and two together, if I weren't so similar Keaton himself, as the girlfriend I had dumped what seemed so many months ago was kind enough to point out.

Then Brother New Home continued the tale of the tirade in the manner of Chief He Who Deserted the Chiefs: "And after all the hours I had spent with him as a new arrival to the cave, explaining to him the true nature of how to understand Keaton - fractals aren't easy - when I could have been with Squaw Who Shits A Lot, and he doesn't even have enough sense to justify all the time I spent with him. All night, he UNRELENTLESSLY horned in on it. Appalled, I just sat there playing dumb and hoping this nightmare of a gnome would just vanish - but he didn't! Also, because every time I said something, he jumped down my throat trying to deconstruct it in his really boring droning croaking ways - you know his voice. AND THEN HE ASKED ME WHY I WAS SO COMPETITIVE!! I must say it puts in a different functional light his constant flattering of us all (such as last night, complementing Squaw Shits A Lot for having a deeper kinship to Keaton than me) and his interest in her magic, which I am beginning to see is just a cover of 'irrationalism' for whenever he wants to act like a jerk. And the recurrent stumble I've had with him is his condescension toward my fractal method of studying Keaton - which he pretends to admire but I can see the disdain in those lazy eyes of his - I can tell he secretly believes that the best way to know Keaton is to watch his films, an inexplicable strain of positivism given his obsession with Squaw Who Shits A Lot's magic. How can someone be more enamored of her than me? Or at least make more of a show of it? He talked incessantly to and of her. That's fine, being enamored is delightful, but what I didn't enjoy was all those strange things projected on me, like I was being 'competitive' (when all I remember doing was lying down and smoking most of the time). That I am an 'angry Indian man,' 'paranoid,' filled with 'phobias' about the palefaces (of which he forgets he is a 'honkey jackass' member). Hearing our ceremony and attacking *us* - and you know that before I deserted the Chiefs I was imprisoned several times by the palefaces and developed a feel for it almost as strong as my telepathic bond with Buster."

With His Tux Between His Legs (Redux)

I sat there, as I've mentioned, feeling like a parade that an anarchist had tossed a bomb right in the middle of, killing no one, but breaking almost enough fire hydrants to spew the number of tears I wished to cry. It seemed a long time before I could speak again, recover myself, almost as if I had to wait until the next year and become the parade again. When I did, I told Brother New Home that I couldn't confirm or deny most of Chief He Who Deserted the Chief's accusations. In fact I couldn't understand what most of them meant. It was true that I was enamored of Squaw Who Shits A Lot, and that if I hadn't bumped into him first, I was heading straight to her - as straight as I could head, given the labyrinthine nature of the cave and what I perceived as her somewhat reclusive ways - to ask if she would marry me.

"Well," Brother New Home responded, "you're going to have to get over her somehow because there's no way that you are going to marry her. As they say in your culture, you might as well try to pack a vase in a suitcase without smashing it, or as they say in mine, you might as well try to speak to a horse over the telephone. But don't worry, if you decide to leave the cave, as it appears you must, after standing in the presence of the *Buster Samadhi Of Flow And Stasis,* amorous women and men will chase you by automobile, train, horse, bicycle, roller skates, wrecking ball, boat, and if you manage to escape them all, you'll be so exhausted that you'll fall asleep in a church pew and wake up next to the woman or man of your dreams."

The day I left the cave, Chief He Who Deserted the Chiefs wasn't quite as encouraging as Brother New Home was: "Maybe you'll inherit a lot of money from an uncle, or invest in apples in the stock market and quintuple your money, and then *maybe* you'll be able to find a woman almost as pale and lazy-eye-lidded as you are, with as bad a posture, who *might* have the stomach to marry her mirror image!"

As I headed out of the cave and into the wide forest, I realized that I had nowhere to go but back to my parents' home. After having learned the Keaton *Samadhi*, now was a good time for the prodigal son to return. I thought it would take forever to find a way out of the wilderness of America, but apparently I had been mostly (in addition to my time in the cave) wandering around in circles and in what is known as a "pocket wilderness" and, like in the M. Night Shyamalan film about people who thought they were trapped in the nineteenth century, I was actually quite close to a local highway and my first of several hitchhiking endeavors. Getting out of the woods was the easy part, getting back through the strange ways of the United States was, as usual, what took so long. Nevertheless, I made it back as quickly as I could, stopping only to mistakenly propose to a mannequin, get married to a belly dancer (actually, she referred to it as a 'collaring ceremony' in which she placed a leather, spiked collar around my neck and then, rather than kissing me, she punched me in the face with her diamond studded wedding ring), steal a car only to crash it into a tree while arguing with the belly dancer about the lacerations on my face that she claimed not to have done, lose a horse, fall asleep and then wake up with both my collar and my true love gone, accidentally crush a mailman and pray for mercy from Hermes god of messengers and thieves, wonder how much time I had left on the earth, accidentally enter a ladies' restroom, fall in a hole, get the collar of a new jacket caught by a crane lifting me high up in the air, and escape a landslide. By the time I returned to my childhood home, it was Spring already. My loving parents were still there excited and shocked to see me. I was also greeted a by a rejection for my research proposal, as well as a pink slip from Wellesley for not showing up to teach Spring semester. There was the published obituary written by my parents (thus full of lies concerning my interests in nuclear war survival, neuroscience, Our Lord Jesus Christ, etc.) who had assumed I must be dead, as well as my dad's never-flinching resolve to not loan me a Toyota Camry (with the help of most of my life insurance money, he had done enough research on local used Camrys - straight shift only - to be only "three to four Camrys away" from the "singularity").

    "I suppose you'll have to take that tarot card reading job after all," my dad said.

"And how exactly am I supposed to make it out there with no car and not a single dime to my name?"

"Don't you have a friend who could give you a ride?"

"No. Haven't you ever read *the* book - *How to Win Friends and Influence People*?"

"Actually, no," responded my dad sheepishly.

"It's by this guy who pretended to have a lot of friends and be influential. He even changed his last name to Carnegie so folks would think he was related to the steel magnate. So, the first thing you need to make friends is money - or the illusion of it - neither of which I have."

"Well, there is some of your life insurance money still left over, but I'm saving that for the next used Camry..."

"Do you realize you're committing fraud by using that money?"

"It's only fraud if you're trying to deceive people son, and we really did think you were dead. Who knew you'd rise up from a cave like Jesus Christ himself?"

I was just about to burst into tears, when my father, with an act as simple as pulling a section of newspaper out of his jacket and handing it to me, restored my faith in him.

"I was going to use that paper to line one of the cats' litter boxes," my dad said, "but it says there's a carnival coming into town this weekend, and if there's one thing I know about carnivals, it's that they're like books, you can find anything you need in them."

"But carnivals travel too slowly dad, and they stop at every single town they think is far enough away not to have heard that the Wild Man of Borneo is really just a carnie who hasn't shaved in a while."

"Enough," my dad said. "I've dropped the egg inside

the milk bottle, and fed the chick until it is has filled up the entire bottle, but is too big to squeeze through the neck, and now you're asking me how to get it out of the bottle without shattering the glass and thereby killing the chicken. But it's already out I tell you. The chicken is already out. And now it's time for you to get out too."

I scheduled a phone interview with a local tarot parlor in San Jose the very next day...

Go West (1925, Buster Keaton Productions, Inc.)

Since I had already read plenty of books on tarot, I prepared for the interview that night by watching Keaton's great homage to Manifest Destiny, *Go West*. Friendless (that is Buster's name in the film), a dragger of his bed (and chest of drawers) from town to town, Buster finally heeds the advice of noted abolitionist and vegetarian Horace Greeley to "Go West, young man." Buster embarks on this journey by selling all his furnishings and buying a gigantic sausage to last him on his journey. To get West he stows away on a train car full of barrels which naturally roll off the train in the middle of almost nowhere. All the barrels, except for the one containing Keaton, are full of potatoes, and it is amazing to see them roll off the train, down a hill and explode into potato shrapnel.

But we should take this as a sign, because when Buster/Friendless runs into a cattle ranch, he finally does find a friend. Removing a rock from the hoof of a cow named "Brown Eyes," the two become inseparable.

That is, until the rancher decides to send all his cattle to Los Angeles to be slaughtered, including Buster's new friend. Smitten with "Brown Eyes," but in the most chaste way one could imagine being smitten with a cow, Buster sneaks onto the cattle car and, avoiding highwaymen and a self-created stampede in LA when he releases all the cattle upon learning they are headed for the slaughterhouse only to accidentally round them all back up again while running away from them in a devil suit stolen from a costume shop (he's been told that red attracts bulls, and he is trying to "steer" the steers away from passersby and women's clothing shops), Buster is met with the gratitude of the rancher, who tells him he can have anything he wants. "I want her," Buster says, and the rancher is quite relieved when he realizes Buster is not pointing to his daughter but to "Brown Eyes." It is safe to say that, given the symbolism of a film beginning with noted vegetarian Horace Greeley, the prominent scene of Buster eating his last sausage (though the eating is implied, never shown on screen, which is also noteworthy), finding his only friend in a beautiful cow, and assuming the identity of the devil when "rounding" up the cattle in LA, a city noted for its many vegetarian movie stars and other guru junkies, that a vegetarian (Horace Greeley) has been transformed into a vegetarian (Buster Keaton).

Related to Buster's vegetarianism, there is an absolutely wretched electro-hip hop duo from Denmark with a song called "Buster Keaton" which is about a hypocritical vegetarian woman, a "Full blood veggie dressed in fur." In Buster's case I think that his conversion to vegetarianism is without hypocrisy. When you see the love in Buster's eyes for "Brown Eyes," you just know that he'll never eat meat again. While hypocrisy does exist and I suppose should be called out, it is unfortunate that anyone should associate the concept with Buster Keaton, who, in transforming things into themselves, is the complete antithesis of the concept of hypocrisy, which is of course rooted in antithesis. The only redeeming thing about the song at all is a single lyric, "Saving the whales during the day / But at night, you're making them pay," because that is indeed a Keatonesque notion in that it defies imagination. Only Buster Keaton could somehow integrate such ideas into a film in a way that makes perfect sense.

But because Keaton never shot a film or sequence based upon such a phrase, one is left to wonder, "How does one 'make the whales pay?'" Is *Quadron* (the name of the duo), implying that this woman is working for Greenpeace for her day job and then secretly going out on the high seas at night to harpoon whales? That would not only be hypocritical, but require a vast range of skill sets. Perhaps "making the whales pay," coming by way of the duo's origin, from the land of Vikings, is an untranslatable idiom that makes sense in Danish. Anyway, and regardless of what anyone believes about the issue of vegetarianism, I'm just glad that Buster ends up with his cow.

The next morning, I was quite convincing about my ability to handle the cards, since I had written one third of my dissertation on them. "California" I told my prospective employers, "the land of Hollywood's magic, is full of unruly spiritual energies that need to be deciphered at any given moment." I sounded so authoritative, and apparently the need for tarot card readers in California is so great (recent developments in Silicon Valley having caused a "brain drain" of those who dabble in magick), they wanted me to start next week! Never let it be said that it was a stupid idea to become a tarot card reader in California. Since everything truthful lies in the cards, what else should one be? Plus I had to be closer to Hollywood and the energies of Keaton. I know it would have made more sense if I had applied for a tarot reading job in Hollywood itself, but I felt unworthy. San Jose was about as close to Hollywood as I felt I could safely get and not dishonor the specter of Buster with my presence.

But how was I going to make it across the country in only a week?

Let the Carnival Begin!

As forecasted, that weekend at the carnival, as I was walking around wondering "What would Buster do?" I found exactly what I was looking for - a hot air balloon. Carnivals had not changed all that much since Buster's day. All I had to do was find a way to steal the balloon between the trips it was taking up around the carnival and back again. I had actually considered stealing one of the Toyota Camrys, but my dad had let slip the amount of jail time for grand theft auto, which pretty much cured me of that desire even if I were able to figure out if he owned one which could make it across the country, which I was pretty sure he didn't. Plus, not actually knowing the jail time for stealing a hot air balloon gave me courage, as if not knowing actually erased the possibility that I would be caught. It felt that way, which was how I would need to feel if I was going to pull this off.

First, to blend in like Buster, I had to find a shirt with a lot of vertical stripes in it. I went home and borrowed one from my dad who had saved every shirt he had ever purchased or had been purchased for him on a bamboo rod stretching across the entire basement. Next I needed a round straw hat. This was no problem either. All I had to do was explain to my father that my days as a hobo had finally shown me the evils of the sun and that I now feared skin cancer as much as he did. Finally I needed a red ribbon to tie around the hat. This simply required a trip to my mother's bedroom where all the Christmas wrappings were stored for subsequent years. It did take several hours to make it from the basement to her room, given the newly installed animal doors and the ropes, crampons, and carabiners required to traverse my grandmother's antique furniture safely. For a while I was worried that I might be like the kid in the James Joyce story who arrives at Araby after it has already begun to close, but I was eventually outfitted in a carnie disguise and my father was kind enough to drive me in one of the Camrys to the carnival, hiding his emotions with the excuse that he could use the drive as a means to scout out safe places for Nikolai (the dog) to have her extremely large bowel movements.

From there, and with the blessing of my father who just happened to own a book on how to fly hot air balloons that I discreetly carried under my arm with the incriminating cover turned inward to my body so that it radiated its energy to me as intensely as if it were written by Walt Whitman himself (or maybe I was just excited), stealing the hot air balloon was no problem at all. With such matters, I find the trick is not to lurk about like your common house burglar but to simply walk right up to the thing you're trying to steal as if it belonged to you. You can achieve almost anything with this kind of sangfroid, with the right outfit (which I had) and a stone face. I even heard that on Easter Sunday in France once, some fellow donned priestly garments and walked right up to the pulpit of Notre Dame Cathedral and began lecturing on Nietzsche and the death of God. It was about twenty minutes before anyone realized something was amiss, but he had an escape plan, as did I - one which involved helium and a torch.

Now that I had a vehicle which could, if necessary, make it around the world in 80 days, I planned to take the scenic route to San Jose. I planned to fly over (and perhaps visit) all the places my family had travelled when I was young, my father sometimes running from the law, sometimes just running - the Rockies, the Grand Canyon, the haunted house where my mom punched a guy in the stomach for scaring me too much, the Great North Woods, the fishing boats right outside of Delacroix. But no sooner had I reached a safe altitude, the people in the carnival no longer visibly shaking angry fists at me transformed to abstractions and my socks frozen on a clothesline that I'd hung, when some blankets in the gondola of the balloon began to rustle and move. Suddenly, there was a stunningly beautiful woman pointing a gun at me. It turned out that she was trying to write a dissertation on Algerian refugees but had no idea what to say about them, and she too had heard that no matter what one needs, you can always find it at a carnival. I protested that I knew absolutely nothing about Algeria, or refugees for that matter, that she'd have about as much luck with me as she would trying to roast fish between two tennis rackets over an open fire.

"Ah hah!" she said. "That proves it! Only Buster Keaton would come up with such an absurd comparison!

And there is no one who is more of a refugee than you. Just look at you. You are in a hot air balloon you stole and which, from the looks of that book you're holding, you don't even know how to fly. I've been following you around all afternoon, dumbfounded by the lazy eyelids, the prominent nose, the questionable posture; I've even been noting the geometries of your movements. You moved just like him, crouching, then suddenly erect and confident, then furtive, wandering, but not really wandering, among the maze of tents and carnival games according to that most peculiar Keaton geometry, stopping suddenly, as if frozen, then just as suddenly striding quickly along an oblique angle that makes no sense to anyone but you, looking like you were being watched, then entering Madame Sosostris's tent as if completely oblivious to the world. This, I said to myself, is not only the doppelgänger of Buster Keaton, but the very person I came here to find today." Then she asked, "Where are we going anyway?"

"I got a job at a tarot card parlor in San Jose, and my dad wouldn't let me borrow one of his Toyota Camrys because he's hoping to one day achieve something he calls 'the singularity,' with all his Camrys that he has parked on his front yard, so I had to steal this balloon because I can't turn down a job like that when it comes along when I'm at such a distinct disadvantage when it comes to staying competitive in the global market. Now you are going to shoot me because I know absolutely nothing about Algeria and the knowledge of refugees you claim I have is purely experiential, you might as easily ask an Indian to write a dissertation about how he sews canoes together."

"I am not going to shoot you," she assured me, "From the looks of your shirt pocket, you bought a pack of tarot cards to practice with. And I have this stack of incomprehensible research notes that I've taken, and now you also have me. I'll worry about flying this thing. You just sit right down in the bottom of the gondola there and pretend to be my clairvoyant dissertation advisor."

So much for sightseeing, I thought.

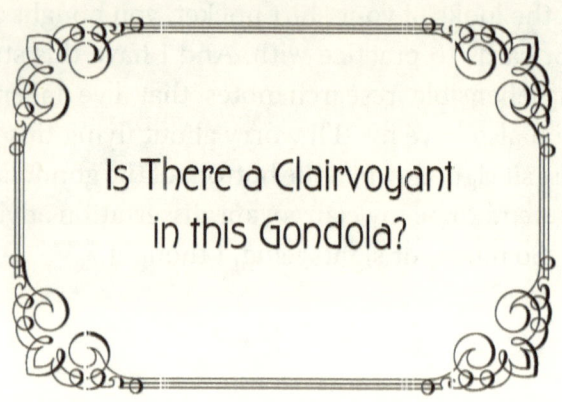

Is There a Clairvoyant in this Gondola?

After a brief but heartfelt marriage ceremony witnessed by a stray duck who later became dinner, I began reading the instructions accompanying the tarot deck. It wasn't long before I was able to lay out a fortune that would solve all of my bride's quandaries with respect to her dissertation.

"There are certain forces beyond your control which you'll have to be aware of in order to finish," I said. "The Queen of Wands is hostile to the Four of Cups or Luxury. These two will have to be mediated by the Aeon, who unfortunately has a habit of swallowing children's toys and sucking his thumb, even though he is well past adolescence. Most likely he will need therapy. I recommend a tall, icy blond hunk who will prescribe handfuls of Xanax and utilize lots of magnets of questionable origin. But for now, you will have to put up with his habit of sleepwalking through life, which is what you've done up until now anyways, never having done an honest day's work in your life and therefore completely unable to imagine the sort of creative energy required to complete your thesis on *The Post-Colonial Structural Inefficiencies of Algerian Refugee Repatriation in an Emerging Post-Marxist World* as represented by the Queen."

My lovely bride then admitted that in fact she had avoided honest work by having attended graduate school for the last ten years. An attendance fueled by a trust fund which was soon to run out. This knowledge allowed her dissertation topic to become the object of a personal feud between her committee members, who now no longer spoke to one another and thus were not in a state to advise her in any way. They had come to this state of silence debating whether she should adopt a post-Marxist or post-Lacanian definition of refugees. To her this was very odd since both parties had never met an actual refugee and, indeed, seemed unconcerned with their actual existence. In reality, both sides were mirror images of the other in terms of method, which meant that no matter what the subject, they each applied their respective philosophical backgrounds (what they had learned in graduate school) to the problem, even and especially when their philosophers of choice had nothing directly to say about the matter, which represented a chance to "break new ground in the field." Not only had this standstill left her own project orphaned, but the years of course work in which similar acts of analogical contortion were performed on everything from video games to mobile homes to bomb shelters had indeed, she felt, sapped most all of her finances and all of her creative energy. Astigmatically, she looked through a glass darkly, when she bothered to look, one eye trying to see beyond post-Marxism and the other through post-Lacanianism which was further complicated by the fact that she didn't, admittedly, adequately understand either theoretical model, which was further complicated by the fact that during her time of study post-Lacanianism had transmogrified into something that called itself materialist deconstructionism and had attempted to take on the post-Marxism as an object of deconstruction in its own right, which seemed like breaking some sort of rules concerning fair play, but who was she to say.

I had little (actually nothing) to say on these topics, whose very mention of Lacan made me feel like I was trying to read one of his seminars in a birch-sewn canoe while tumbling down a waterfall. The one where he invented a character named Antigone who loved her outlaw brother so much that she buried him despite Theban law which forbade the performance of burial rites for enemies of the state, thus leading to the great aporia of psychoanalysis, "have I been true to my desire?" Choosing to avoid such vertigo, I proceeded to the next set of cards, the psychological basis of the problem.

"Throughout your life, you have been pursued relentlessly by both the knight of wands and the knight of disks, the one full of pride and impetuousness, the other a dull farmer, both distracting you from the whirling force that you could invoke through the Ace of Swords," I explained.

To which she replied, "How in the world is a whirling force going to help me organize my dissertation? It is disorganized enough as it is. Look at all the different fonts and colors I've been using, intermixing. There used to be a code, a logic to such 'illuminations' of the manuscript, but that has long since been forgotten. Every day I work on this thing, weaving the different fonts and colors together, finally thinking I have got something perfect. And by something perfect, I mean a single perfect page of the dissertation. And then, just as I'm about to select all the type with a CTRL A and turn all the colors black and the fonts to New Times Roman, the Methedrine runs out and my head crashes onto the keyboard, scattering letters, unweaving what I've woven. When I wake up a couple of days later, I've completely forgotten what my dissertation was about, and the chaos on my computer is no help, so I have to start once again, completely from scratch. No wonder I haven't gotten married until now. I'm basically the digital Penelope," she surmised.

"Methedrine? You used Methedrine to write your dissertation?" I asked.

"If it was good enough for both the Allied *and* Axis forces in WWII, it's good enough for me," she replied.

"Maybe I've got the tarot reading backwards. That would explain the Methedrine. Let's say that while it gives you the juice to stay awake during the 'writing' of your dissertation, the speed also distracts you from the Knight of Wands and the dull farmer. Who could they be?"

After a moment of thought she said, "When my grandfather died, long before I was born, he left a car dealership to my dad and his brother. My uncle lives in Sausalito and grows pot, but he's definitely not dull. He studies Buddhism and travels the world on his half of the business (which he sold to my dad) while my dad slaves away maintaining the Toyota dealership. Luckily foreign cars sell themselves in the US of A, because he's the dullest guy I know. Even his commercials where he dresses up as various superheroes, both gay and straight, would put you to sleep. Regardless, my uncle *has* been pursuing me all my life, or at least his wisdom has. Now that we're ballooning to California I can seek his guidance. Considering the way I tangle my writings together in such a Gordian manner, maybe those energies can even affect the nature of my relationship to the cards, like maybe we'll have to, after drawing the group of cards, draw a new card that intertwines the major motifs of all three. And don't tell me you don't believe this is possible. You're not going to California just to read tarot cards. Admit it. You're trying to get closer to Keaton's creative energies, which have, over time, developed into a veritable geyser of ad hoc solutions to the problems we have made for ourselves."

She certainly had me there, so I went somewhere else, replying, "How is Buddhism going to help you write a dissertation on Algerian refugees?"

"I don't know," she said. "You're the clairvoyant here. Draw some more cards."

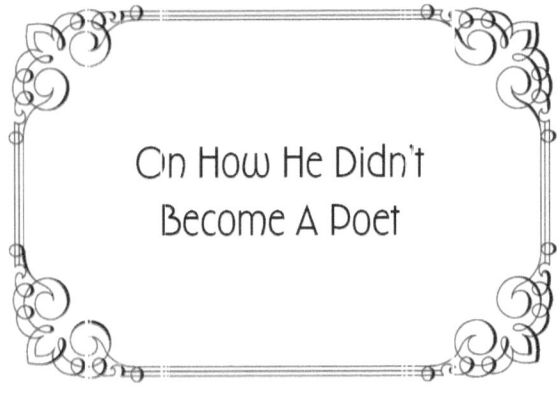

On How He Didn't
Become A Poet

Exhausted and crashing from Methedrine withdrawal, my beautiful bride then promptly fell asleep, giving me some time to navigate the balloon. I was finally able to do a bit of sightseeing, though not of the majestic type I had hoped for. We had drifted well south of Tennessee and were about to enter the Gulf of Mexico, which seemed like a bad idea until I remembered that Delacroix was straight ahead. I passed over an island that I had spent a week on during Junior High School learning about marine biology, but the only memories that I had were those of the gigantic dormitories where bullies lurked at every corner, practicing reverse roundhouse kicks on me and my roommate Gabriel. Old Gabe had brought a framed glossy photo of Humphrey Bogart - *Maltese Falcon* (1941,Warner Bros.) era - to act as his guardian angel. Judging by the bruises and scars we both left the island with, it would seem that prayers to gods sacred or profane were equally useless when it comes to suffering the "uneven development" of which the Marxist-Leninist, or is it the post-Marxist, endocrinologists speak. The teacher who had brought us on this trip, later named Bed Boltraw due to his affair with a precocious student (allegedly on the very lab tables where we dissected frogs) who was later named Pristine Nomore for obvious reasons, seemed completely unconcerned with the dangers that plagued us.

As class poet in high school I was commissioned by the principal, who had noted my narrative talents in other mediums such as defusing cold war fears by building a piñata in the shape of a mushroom cloud and filled with atomic fireball candies for Cinco de Mayo, and lessening the guilt of Catholic students with my photo essay on the Spanish Inquisition, which featured pictures of me in a thumbscrew, an iron maiden, on the rack, and being burned at the stake, my father patiently serving as both photographer (using a tripod and timed exposures) and executioner as I laughed hysterically through every single exposure, to write a piece that would help us all heal from the ethical uncertainties the teacher-student affair of Bed Boltraw and Pristine Nomore had produced amongst the student body. Knowing the gravity of the event, not only in terms of subject matter but because this was my first commission as class poet, I chose the form of a 4 part epic which the principal subsequently forbade from being published in the school newspaper, citing lack of space as his reason, but I knew better then, and even better now having experienced unfolding a newspaper so many times I was actually able to use it as a tent. I knew that he was a coward who couldn't face the truth. I was so humiliated that I immediately resigned my position as class poet and never wrote a poem again (excluding the unsuccessful 'love procuring devices' mentioned), but I carry that poem, and

its footnotes, in my heart even today:
Love on a Lonely Ridge
An Epick Rawga

I. Foreplay

Oh! the lonely burden of the Poet
Oh! Oh! Oh! Yes! Yes! Yeesss!
But please excuse me (I digress)
Oh! the lonely Burden of the poet
Actually there are two burdens I guess:
The first is to be one and not know it
The other, to probe, to thrust into the Strangenesse
Of Platonic love pierced with arrows of Eros
Until a once pure Desire look like St. Sebastian,
His mournful countenance and sixty-nine arrow wounds,
Each bleeding with a lustful Passion.
I play an Aeolian harp that is out of Tune,
But such Subject is too grave an undertaking
To be done Justice, even by Siegfried Sassoon
So I hereby invoke the holy Fuse
To aid me in this twisted Poetick Ruse,
The Fuse that drives the Green flower
The Fuse that opens the marriage Bower
The Fuse that raises the Ivory Tower
And moistens the walls of Love's Chamber
(or as King Richard might say, "The V! The V!"
as he raises his Hand triumphantly,
his noble fingers forging the sign of victory.)

You needn't be all that observant
To know by now whom I wish to Incant

I invite the Reader to break his Silence
And join in reading aloud this Chant:

"Go, Nad, Go
Oh Nad, that Divine Sexe hormone
Lead us in Thy mysterious Gonadal Way
Bless us with a great throbbing Bone,
For this is the End of Foreplay.

II. Plateau Phase

This tale takes place forthwith
On a cold and windswept Ridge
Where snowdrifts stand as Monoliths
Cover the Earth with milky Sludge.

Tis testimony to love's immortal Pow'r
That where by necessity the garb is puffy and modest
Cov'ring what would be flaunted in more sultry hour
In Desolate freeze love's Flames burn hottest.

The hero of this epic Rawga
Tis a ski Instructor of advancing Age
His parents christened him Bed Boltraw
(one was a Prophet, the other a Sage).

The ski Resort where he did play,
Twas called Gonadal Ridge[1]

---

1   For those students who have not yet taken AP Biology, the "gonadal ridge" is the first sex
organ formed in fetal development. It is neither a penis or a vagina, merely a setting (as in the
poem), where either may form, depending which way the "razor's edge" turns. The gonadal
ridge preceding gender differentiation would thus explain such "anomalies" as hermaphrodit-
ism, etc. that sometimes are discovered at birth. And yet, given the fact that the gonadal ridge is
neither one nor the other, I also look to it in the poem as an alchemical symbol of the "Chemical
Wedding" when feminine and masculine principles are united in anticipation of the magnum

And though his hair has turned to gray
His muscles do yet bulge.

Nowe Bed thought the Resort's proprietor
Was sick in Mind if wealthy
But that oft disputed truth the Future
Twould divide the Ille and healthy[2]

Nowe before the Reader twould deem this tale
The work of idle Shovenist
One who not Knowing the changing Times
Thinks Epicks have only Male protagonist
Be cheered this tale have heroine too
(may Criticks finde my Rend'ring true).
Her father's name was Nomore, who Christened her Pristine
Some claim she was a girl of Wilde ways
Though I knowe not what they mean.
They saye she Rode by Age fifteen
Could swab a matey's molars clean.

Oh me! Oh my! I lost my Head
Time for Me to get back to Bed.

He was a ski Instructor without Parallel
Twas Joye to watch him ride the mogul
Which he caressed and cleaved and Handled
As softly as a Maiden's nipple

---

opus or "great work."

2 This somewhat obvious allusion to biological evolution and "survival of the fittest" is, on another level, meant
to show that Bed worked at odds with himself, for while Darwinian evolution has no particular "goal" in mind, the
alchemist (from Al-Khem, Egyptian for "land of the black earth") has in mind a higher spiritual goal. The ambiguity of
the poem, at this point, lies in whether Bed will follow his more nihilistic or spiritual instincts.

Though Master of the feared Black Diamonde
his minde was also quite Fecunde.
Idle hours he dabbled in Biology
Genetics twas his specialty
And held firm to the Royal code
Only experiment twould prove one's Theorie
And lest you deem him Hypocrite
His cabin twas his Laboratory.

Pristine was a heart-broken, bitter Wench
Wrote dastardly poems about past lovers
What she needed was a strong yet jovial Mensch
To Warm her under the covers

She skied alone upon the mountain
On a black diamond she scraped her Bottom
Bed Boltraw appeared like a Vision
"May I be of Service to you Madam!"
And though Pristine was quite dazed from her tumble
Her eyes came to focus on Bed's bulging Scrotum

Did she seduce him, or he her?
Some say one, some the other
But I have Theorie I think hath more Pow'r
I think Nad, the holy Fuse[3]
Predestined their Snowy bower

They wrestled, writhed, tussled, and nestled
They heaved, they wheezed, he Farted, she sneezed

3   An alchemical reading of this poem would follow the magickal principal, "As Above, So Below" and thus while
"Nad" may be read as short for the biological gonad, it could also be "the holy Fuse" or philosopher's stone. Thus, even a
tawdry sexual encounter could have more spiritual aspects, and vice versa.

Never was seen such a love making session
Their bare burning Flesh melting Snow around them
Giving bones to Scarecrows, turning heads of snowmen
Oh, if only the lifeless had seen!
Twould have lit up their nerves like shadows on screen
Oh! Oh! Oh! Yes! Yes! Yeesss!
But please excuse me (I digress)

The Lust continued on and on
Til' our sun had Waned to history
And even for these Lovers' passion
The Night was a bit too hoary
But like Battling rams they were still horny
What to do? What to do?
"Let's go to my laboratory."

Bed had romanced the Chamber
One table arrayed for a candle lit dinner
Another was covered in satin sheets (for later)
When they had supped and regained their Strength
And Bed's Bolt had reached its proper length
They screamed and shouted, rooted and routed
In a fest far Greater than Don Juan[4] could have touted

III. Orgasmium

Muscle tone is gone, genital spasm!
Hold on to your seats, time for Orgasm!
<u>Don't worry if</u> you think these lines a bit short

4   In English verse, pronounced "Don Jew-un." Most think that Lord Byron changed the pronunciation because he was either anti- or pro- semitic, living in Southern climes where Jews were more prevalent. But anyone with a knowledge of meter would realize that Byron merely made the change to fit the iambic line.

Most people say that Tis the best Part!
When the Lab tables were Squeaking and creaking
And Pristine was giving her Orgasmic scream
And Bed was having a Lucid wet dream

Did Pristine yell Oh Bed! Oh Bed! Or Oh! Mr. Boltraw?
Alas we'll never deem, for only the Lab mice saw
And they were soon Silenced by a black Snake's jaw!

IV. Refactory Period

Sadly, Reader, we've reached the Refractory period
Interim after Love's Joy hath consummated
And that Ivory Tower (with purple penthouse)
Can no longer be Lifted
And sadly, as you will soon uncover
Bed's lasted longer than most Others

Somehow, the Regencies of Gonadal Ridge
Caught wind of their sensestuous Rage
(How else could you be reading this Page)
But how could this be if None saw
The Sexsational union of Pristine and Boltraw?
I have a Theorie, twas another Fuse
It's name is Prood, and she carries Ille news
She's the Arch enemie of our worthy Nad
And only when Luste hath been abolished
Nay polished, Roasted and fried
Will Prood be Satisfied
Shoulde Prood be Watching as Spirit unnoticed
And make sure the Regencies are notified
Such treach'ry twould leave Prood grinning Wide

So the Regencies confronted Pristine and Bed
Said she was too youthful to Ride the Black Diamonde
Bed twas blamed for All that occurred
They slapped then whipped his muscled behinde
Whipped and Slapped till he was nigh Blinde
Then issued a Decree in Red:
"Bed Boltraw hath disgraced Gonadal Ridge Resort
But instead of taking him to Courte
We banish him hence from this Mountain
And never shall he return again."

So Bed walked off dejectedly
His once proud organ hung Limply
So forlorn was he, it never Rose again
It merely hung, like a dead Flap of skin
But the damage had already been Dunne
For Pristine gave birth to a Sone
Who grew up to be a cut Cynic
With lively muscle, but heart and soul of Plastick
He'd pummel you down, and leave you in Shambles
If you told him a Reasone the wafer Crumbles

And thus, Refined readers, our tale has entered its Hole
But lest you thing this Rawga rigmarole
Let me Relate to you its Moral:
"Ye Lovers, before passion's Milke is tasted,
Remember ye that Sperme is cheape
But not to be Wasted."[5]

---

5   As my more astute readers will recognize from the inferiority of the lines' meter and rhyme in this "moral," it
is a direct quotation from our hero, Bed Boltraw, who may have been, as our tale relates, an amazing teacher and
practitioner of the "biological arts," but was much inferior to yours truly when it comes to poetickal endeavors.

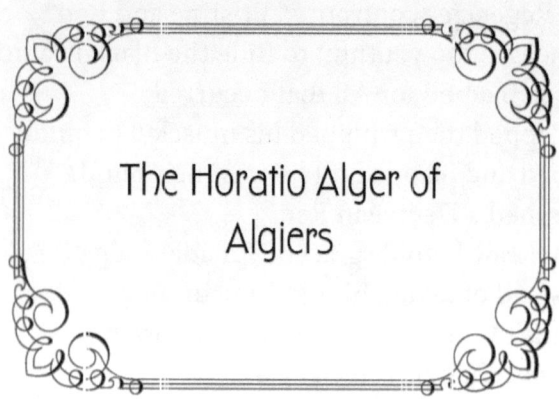

The Horatio Alger of Algiers

When my bride woke up again, we went back to the original division of labor, her steering the balloon and me reading the cards.

"The center of your reading," I continued, "applies to your actual dissertation as it now stands. At the center is the Four of Wands or Completion. The number Four signifies 'below the Abyss,' which doesn't bode well for our current situation given the fact that if anything, we are floating high above the abyss."

Pointing the gun that she had stashed in her makeshift bridal gown at me, she said, "Stop trying to get out of this. You know good and well that Lucretius's atomic theories of the coming into being of the universe do not differentiate between up and down, that indeed he uses as one of his primary examples of the swerving atoms 'the lightning path obliquely crossing the rainfall, now on this side, now on that.'"

To which I responded, "But it says here the Abyss is represented by Saturn, the planet of disintegration and explosion."

"Let me see," she said as she grabbed the Crowleyesque card from me. "At the top there's a female symbol, that's me, at the bottom a victory sign. That doesn't look like disintegration and explosion to me. Four staffs are in a wheel, and at the end of each it alternates between doves and some other animal I can't quite make out."

"They look like mules to me," I offered.

"I can't believe it! Now it all makes sense. The title of my dissertation must now be changed to *The Road is Long and the Mule Walks*," my bride exclaimed.

"*The Road is Long and the Mule Walks*? Are you kidding me," I countered.

"Believe it," she insisted.

"I mean, shouldn't there be a colon and something after it, like *The Road is Long and the Mule Walks: Algerian Refugees, Gender and Epistemology in Women's Language-Oriented Writing?*" I asked.

"What do the surrounding cards say?" she demanded.

"They say that completion is being surrounded by Futility and Debauch, two Sevens representing the perfect storm, for Sevens are 'doubly unbalanced; off the middle pillar. As for Debauch, 'its mode is poison, its goal madness.' It suggests that you take Methedrine not to stay awake and finish your dissertation, but to destroy its integrity, to never finish writing but instead wander in the endless labyrinths that your sentences produce. Futility is a card completely lacking in energy, like having a dream. That must be when your head crashes into the keyboard and your fontal and colorific weave gets destroyed. At the risk of falling into the same madness that has tempted you, I'm going to have to find out a little bit more about the dissertation itself. Why does it now demand such a strange name? How did you decide to write about Algerian refugees?"

And so she explained, "Well, it all started when I saw the Arabic language for the first time. It was so beautiful. The letters spoke to me like ukuleles. Every word looked like Buster Keaton being followed by a bear as he's following a squirrel. Every sentence was as powerful as an Amazon woman wrestling a bull to the ground. This latter feeling was most important to me, as I was a timid, shy girl who seldom went on dates, and when I did, my mother would follow us in her car with the headlights turned off. And to look at a whole page of Arabic, it filled me with the sort of exhilaration you would be feeling in this hot air balloon right now if I wasn't pointing a gun at you. The first time I saw a page of Arabic wrapped around a fish at the Arabic fish market, which I had wandered into by mistake while trying to hide from my evil stepmother, I knew I would have to learn the language and travel to the Middle East."

"So your evil stepmother followed you around in a car on dates with the headlights turned off?" I asked.

"No, that's my mother. She's not evil at all, she just loves me in that never let you go kind of love, kind of like the way I love you."

"What's it like to go on dates in high school?" I wondered out loud.

"Quit trying to distract me! So, I studied Arabic without ceasing, in the rain, while shuffling cards, while sitting in front of the heater, my knickers steaming, while basking in the sun and while shivering at the bus stop.

It wasn't long before reading the Koran to me was like reading 'Jabberwocky'. But as you may guess from my mother's driving habits, I was loathe to leave very far from home for any length of time."

"So you decided to go into academia instead?" I asked.

"Actually, not yet. Because I thought I was dying, I finally got the courage to travel to the Middle East. I wasn't actually dying, as you can see, but at the time everyone thought I was. I decided to go to Algeria first because its name reminded me of the great Horatio Alger, who wrote those amazing stories about young men who, through hard work and honesty, were able to climb up in the world. My favourite story being *Ragged Dick*. Because it shows that if you work hard as a bootblack and then save someone from drowning, you can rise to the middle. I wanted to be the Ragged Dick of Arabic, The Horatio Alger of Algiers."

"In my opinion, that book, as well as all the books of Alger, is nothing more than the puerile fantasy of the assimilation of the so-called dangerous classes to the bourgeois social order. In Alger's world vision the individual, of whatever class background, is superior to the objective social relations that he finds himself in."

"Oh yeah, and what exactly would Buster Keaton's world vision be," she countered.

"Despite the comedic reaction his movies may produce in the viewer, Keaton's world view is a much darker one where the individual is absolutely *inferior* to the social relations he finds himself in. Though one might become married at any moment, true love requires the construction of a love catapult for which the original instructions have been lost," I explained.

"Anyway, speaking of Arabic ragged dicks, I lost my virginity in a taxi upon my arrival in Algeria. To whom I'm not quite sure as in order to enter an Algerian taxi you have to jump into an open door with half a dozen other people and be willing to sit or be sat upon. Unfortunately, being new to the culture, I came in late and landed on top. Then, after having anonymous virgin-losing sex in the taxi I got appendicitis and had sex with the medic on the way to the hospital, and because of this the operation resulted in a uterine infection so dangerous I had to be flown immediately back to the United States. Ever since then, I've had a thing for Arab men but lacked the courage to return to the Middle East to be with them."

"So, having lost the chance to fulfil your dreams in any real way, you chose to sublimate them by entering the world of academia. Thanks to which, I'm stuck with you here in a hot air balloon at gunpoint," I concluded.

"You seem, suspiciously enough, to know quite a bit about academia, despite your protestations about not knowing a thing about deconstructionism or Marxist-Leninism."

"Guilty," I admitted, "I went to graduate school, but not on a trust fund like you. Penniless, I actually had to finish on time. Indeed, that was how I convinced my committee to let me defend *my* dissertation. I simply told them I was out of money and they had no other choice but to let me defend."

"What was your dissertation on?" my bride wondered, appearing to actually be interested.

"*Poetics, Tarotics and Magick*, which I had a great theoretical knowledge about but, as you can see here and true to the methodologies of the time, which appear to not have changed much since I graduated, I never encountered my actual object of study, which is why I'm having to read the directions while I do your tarot reading."

"If that's the case, why aren't you teaching at a university somewhere instead of flying a hot air balloon to some rinky-dink tarot parlor in San Jose?"

"I did teach at a university," I paused to think about how much to say, "but there were some accusations from my hermaphrodite butler, which I can't say are entirely false, and I lost my job. Once you have been branded a sexual harasser, well let's say, that's a hard label to shake."

"A what?"

"Okay, now it's your turn to stop interrupting me," I said brusquely as I got back to the tarot cards. "*The Road is Long and the Mule Walks*. There are two sets of cards related to this. The first analyzes the actual text, or in this case texts, related to your dissertation, and the second set of cards has to do with what *you'll* need to do in order to finish the thing."

And then, as if on cue, coming down from her latest round of Methedrine, my bride's head crashed into her computer again, which gave me time to consult the tarot cards and her pile of note cards, in what can only be described as an archive on Arab men, that had exploded on the gondola floor. We'd apparently already passed Delacroix during our last conversation at gunpoint and were headed straight into Texas. So as to avoid any encounters with Cowboys or Indians, neither of whom I trusted at this point, I set our course straight north to hopefully make the Rocky Mountains. I studied both the cards and the dissertation notes for what seemed like days, first employing the stamina the Germans refer to as *das Sitzfleisch*, or "Sit-flesh," a quality they value very highly. When that became too tiring, I lay on my back and simultaneously used the documents to keep the sun out of my eyes and obtain knowledge of them through astral projection. The Germans call this *das Schlaffleisch*, or "Sleep-flesh," which it is not very highly valued at all. But regardless of what the Germans thought, I proceeded with both techniques.

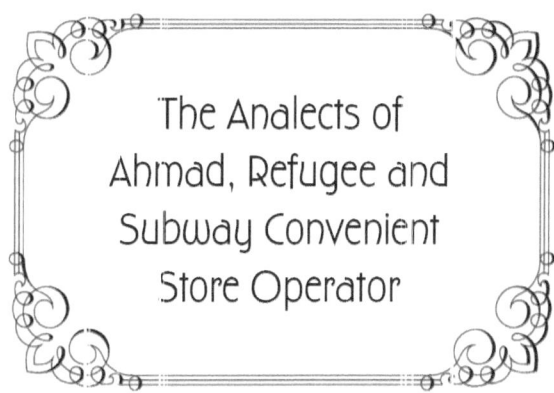

The Analects of
Ahmad, Refugee and
Subway Convenient
Store Operator

Without a gun in my face, I was able to employ both *das Sitzfleisch* and *das Schlaffleisch* in a more concentrated manner. First there was the Prince of Swords, who looked kind of like the Green Lantern if the Green Lantern had three miniature versions of himself he was holding on a leash. The Prince of Swords is a "young man, purely intellectual, full of ideas and designs, domineering, intensely clever but unstable of purpose, with an elusive and elastic mind supporting various and contradictory opinions." This obviously represented Ahmad, who though actually Moroccan and well into middle age, was the subject who inspired my bride's dissertation, which right now was more like an autobiography written through the lens of this individual. It was Ahmad, who my bride had met behind the counter of a convenient store located outside of a subway station, who said that "the road is long but the mule walks" when she complained about the difficulties she was having with her dissertation:

One day, I stopped by the shop [one day] and told Ahmad how I had injured my hand trying so hard to finish this my dissertation. I had known him for about five months by then, and he asked: "what IS this paper about?" I explained, "I still [actually] do not understand -- [some vague idea] called the 'Ways of Knowing'. . ." Of course, he knew all about it . . . . Immediately he drew a line and said,

"All right. You have to think of this mule . . ." He drew the line very slowly and told me: "Some Americans take a plane to L.A. in six hours and say, 'It was a beautiful day there!' . . . Or . . . you can take this mule on a road, and see a sunny day . . . then a rainy day. . . then a sunny day. . . and then a snowy day. . . See what I mean?"

I heard Ahmad's words and felt they were an inspiration -- and I felt that I agreed that I enjoyed taking the long road and seeing all the different phases and stops.

[Months later,] I typed until I hurt myself again. I stood in line at a drug store to buy a brace for my hand -- and I suddenly I realized that I am like an American on his plane, I want to avoid snowy phases of my journey, want to speed through gory details of that unpredictable physical illness known as life.

I cannot accept Ahmad's **view -- yet.**

Some call me a "stubborn mule;"

`His path is similar with his blindness.`

As I scoured my bride's multicolored and multifonted menagerie, I came across more of Ahmad's sayings. It became clear that the color system was an attempt to encode different inflections in Ahmad's voice and/or accent, as if my bride felt it was not only the content of what he said that mattered, but as with all magical incantations, the tone and pitch had to be exactly right. This was why she had tried to adopt a similar system in her own commentary. So that when her dissertation was read orally, as it was meant to be, something that Georges Bataille referred to as "the impossible" would happen. "The impossible," I now recognized, was an unwitting influence in my dad's attempt to achieve the Toyota Camry Singularity:

"Everyone runs here. And I sit here and watch the people running to the bus. I have been here twenty-two years and I am not used to it. . . Everyone **will get there eventually. And you get there in a Mercedes or a Pontiac.**"

" I don't know. . . . Guess!"

"**This is the land of opportunity, the land of free speech, democracy** - but the thing is you have to work your ass off here. I came here twenty-two years ago and I'm still not used to it. I am still not used to it - but this is the land of opportunity. I sit back and I watch people hurrying by, **but I'm still working eighteen hours a day. You don't know it.**"

"A piece of paper I can get my wife here with."

"They should help themselves."

"Don't be a quitter. **You'll make it.**"

"Americans and work."

The compositional process, as I now realized, was exactly the opposite of what my bride had described. Yes, she still took Methedrine and fell asleep a lot, but rather than the different colors and fonts representing things she was thinking of changing in certain ways, or deleting all together, they were in fact the finished product. But why had she lied to me? The irrefutable proof that she had lied was contained in the fact that Ahmad's more mysterious sayings had not yet been color coded, italicized, bolded or set in Comic Sans, and that instead my bride had conveyed the nature of his incantations with relatively simplistic attempts at esoteric punctuation:

"You know they call this country God, you know ... I'll tell you why – why people they want to come to this country. Because this country first of all shows the other world that they are the biggest, the toughest, you know, the strongest country on the earth, and sometimes I call this country God, which is not good in our religion, but I compare it. It's almost God."

" = used to be United States and Russia we don't know about Russia, you know, but mostly we know about United States is the most powerful country. And if I want a job and then because it's very hard get to the country here, you need the airline you need – there's a lot steps you can – you need visa, air – it's very hard, so that's why they – the Latinos you find them here very easy."

"Not easy to get in but it's easier to go."

"= I mean, like the labour. They used to have the

immigrants come to the country to build the country. And because – of those foreigners the country grew up. Like - like Great Bretagne, which is England, you know? = = And they get sick and tired of those foreigners. You know – because - they still – they - they had enough. They had enough. They cannot get anymore."

"= You know? And they couldn't stop them. The reason why – like for example I come to this country. I'm allowed to bring my family, which is I brought my wife, I brought my kid. I could've bring my little son, I could've bring my mother, I could've bring my father, even my brother, even my sister. And my brother can bring his wife, and his wife can bring his kid, her kid, and so on. And his wife can bring the mother, it's how it grew up, it's how it grows, you know? All of Morocco could enter God this way. So:: especially when they start doing those – ah – lottery, which is the ah:: diversity – d eh – eh – dv – or vdv - eh – I don't know what – dv visa, maybe, it's a diversity – or –like they go – like a lottery, and they can have these (   ) people (   ) the country, and it's still working till today."

"= Well, they – they do - uh - have this lottery, and randomly they- they - can pick people from different countries, /you know?/ And imagine – I know if they have fifty immigrants come to the United States:: they are not fifty."

"You tell your book I've been here for twenty-two years, and not following the both cultures:: nor the United States culture or the Moroccan culture. ="

"Ok, you know in the questions it's really hard – it's really hard to just ask me questions and you don't get interfere. There is no way you can ask – there is no one in the world that is not gonna interfere when you ask questions:: because psychologically I can get into your skin. You see, if I say it's not I didn't like this culture, and it's not like I like this culture:: I – I didn't in love with it."

"And I could knock on your door, and I met your father, and I say "hi, how you doin', Mr. Joe," and he says, "Yeah!" and he says, "Stephanie, your boyfriend is here," or you can go upstairs – she's there."

After finishing her dissertation there was one thing that was indisputable. All countries, including Morocco, are completely ignorant when it comes to the love catapult. Note that in the previous analects (that is what I am calling her notes, the *Analects of Ahmad*), the hypothetical boyfriend is able, simply by calling on Mr. Joe, to make it to his girlfriend upstairs, with utterly no explanation of how the boyfriend made it from downstairs to upstairs. Only "she's there." Or perhaps Ahmad *does* know, or Joe knows, the words, pronounced correctly, spin the wheel of a mandala, which in turn slices through a rope holding back the love catapult (which the boyfriend has in the meantime entered the gondola of) - but how did he know how to *build* the catapult? Perhaps, if we are to believe (and why should we not) that foreigners built Great Bretagne, which definitely contains some love catapults, we can also believe that many more people knew the secret of the love catapult. Maybe this is the secret of the refugees that my bride was seeking. Maybe only refugees know how to build love catapults and once a certain number had been built, the "host country" wouldn't want the refugees anymore because they would just keep building the love catapults in order to steal all of the local women and/or men, whether those refugees were pink-haired sadists, heroin addicts, 500 pounders with borderline personality disorder, policemen in bowel movement ceremonies, penguin pecked transsexual butlers who later accuse you of sexual harassment, countless Indians, or abusive belly dancers who force you to wear spiked dog collars. I needed to read the other two cards to find out.

Sure enough, the next card that I picked, Fortune, did have a mandala-like wheel onto which monkeys, sphinxes, and alligators were holding on for dear life. All these denizens of North Africa on the mandala suggested that middle-eastern refugees or immigrants had possession of this mandala which could cut the cord of the love catapult. Moreover, the mandala on the card of Fortune was cutting through bolts of lightning, which reminded me of Lucretius, the guy my bride seemed to know more about than me, which wasn't surprising. And him saying there is neither up nor down, just as there is neither up nor down with lightning bolts crossing the rain storm. Could it be that Lucretius fellow, way back in the times of the first Epicurean philosophers, knew the secret of the love catapult, sowing the seeds of its reinvention in the contemporary world? Because if, with a catapult, you begin down, are thrown up, and then fall down again, that is tantamount to there being no up or down when all is said and done, just as he said. Not only that, but 'down' being transformed into 'down', via the catapult's action, mimicked in mechanical terms the punceptual transformation of things into themselves present in all of Buster Keaton's films.

Furthermore, the tarot instructions said that the Fortune card corresponded to the letter Kaph, which I didn't know was a letter, but which evidently refers to the palm of the hand. Thinking of palms made me think of my bride standing in line at the drug store waiting to purchase a brace for her hand so she could type some more. It would be simple minded, the instructions said, to regard the Fortune card as representing simply *good* fortune. And it was true. The existence of a love catapult was the only way for a camel to enter the eye of a needle into heaven, but lord knows it never guaranteed a safe landing.

The Fool, the final card in the dissertation section, is undoubtedly the one launched by the catapult. He is assigned the number zero, which is what he becomes the moment he is launched into the wide blue nothingness, holding his arms and legs apart like the Vitruvian man, except where Da Vinci's man seems perfectly ensconced in a circle of perfection, the Fool is being thrown face first into the air, his fool shoes sticking their heels up in front of him as if those shoes could stop his forward momentum. My tarot instruction booklet confirmed this. The Fool represents "all which endeavors to transcend earth," or in other words the love catapult. Furthermore, the Fool revealed that all Ahmad's talk was meant to throw my bride off the track of his secret. I quote, "'You have to think of this mule . . .' He drew the line very slowly and told me: 'Some Americans take a plane to L.A. in six hours and say, "It was a beautiful day there!" . . . Or . . . you can take this mule on a road, and see a sunny day . . . then a rainy day. . . then a sunny day. . . and then a snowy day. . . See what I mean?" The mule my ass. Clearly Ahmad was toying with my bride, alluding in plain daylight to the catapult by telling her not to take the plane to L.A., when the plane to L.A. was obviously a coded reference to the catapult itself. And here she was trying to take the road of this mule, which was a mere red herring. Understanding this, the Four of Wands' reference to being "below the Abyss" made perfect sense, particularly in relation to Lucretius, because the key to the dissertation - and everything else - was obviously about learning how to construct a great love catapult, by deciphering the deliberately misleading and taunting *Analects of Ahmad*, that had placed my bride below the abyss of the sky. Despite the fact that I was so close to the answer, I couldn't proceed just then - I was too enraged by what Ahmad had done to her to even think. I felt like Ahmad had slipped her a *Sufi roofie* at our wedding and signed off with a chilly "cheers." Our gondola was nothing but a time-bomb of happiness that had just been set. My longest journeys to understand the nature of the relationship between Buster and myself were nothing but the reflex reactions of a quixotic porcupine, just as the fact that Ahmad was not Ahmad, but an evil sister-in-law who had intercepted all the prayer letters I'd sent Buster and told me, in a believable way, that they were an embarrassment to the family. An evil sister-in-law who then went on to mock my dad's theories of the Toyota Camry Singularity, even claiming that my dad's insistence on the veracity of the Singularity, though the theory was developed completely independently of any considerations of her existence, was a sign of disrespect to *her*. That my father had fed the dog too much, which resulted not only in morbid weight gain (how could such a happy looking dog know anything of the morbid?) but also in Nikolai's extremely large bowel movements, news of which could easily become known by the dog breeding community, the sexology industry, and the psychiatric wards in New York's Spanish Harlem, all of which had intimate ties with her Oxytocin conglomerate Public Image Ltd., thereby impeding her bottom line in distributing the "hormone of love" for ever higher and higher prices. I felt Ahmad must be my sister-in-law, but now she had turned her arguments away from my dad and toward me, in long conversations when, unable to leave a meal or jump out of a moving car being driven by my brother, she tried to convince me that both my parents were completely crazy and unloving and that they should have paid my sexual harassment debts instead of collecting Camrys or tithing to their church and that I should disown them, or using a combination of game theory and eugenics not only incessantly criticized me for getting married too often (they were mostly accidents) but also singled out individual wives as degenerates, narcissistic degenerates, or invalids in the process of degeneration. As this was going on, my brother turned the steering wheel from curve to curve on the way home from someone's 'legitimate' wedding (aka, a wedding in which numerous toasts were made to the pivotal role her sex books played in a couple's pre-matrimonial bonding), smiling blithely as if this is just normal conversation and not utter sophistry and that, combined with my heavy drinking done in preparation for such events, results in a lap full of purple glaze. The licensed professional "sanity-for-hire" specialists, that my brother and his wife were now dues paying members of, seemed to relish the inevitability of the event, including the admonition that I had brought chaos not only to their car, but their very home, and that I needed to exit the family-mobile immediately. They seemed to love this, driving slowly along as they watched my zombie-walk in vomit-pants a mile or two back to their house, especially the abject knock on their door an hour or two later, begging to stay in the basement of their Corbusierian mansion overnight whilst I washed and let my vomit-pants dry, them telling me that yes, I could stay in the basement this one night, but that at the Crack of Dawn I would have to leave and, if I knew what's good for me, I would march right in to the nearest sanity-for-hire office and ask why it was so unclear to me as to how my actions affected others, even giving me key phrases like, how they could "get me in a heap of trouble" or "stir up resentment in the ones who loved me the most." Knowing this to be true I felt like Ahmad had performed on me an ancient Moroccan wrestling move called a "Butt Drag," where, from behind, the wrestler locks one arm around the opponent's throat in a reverse choke and with the other hand penetrates the anus with a thumb, grabbing the penis and balls with the remaining fingers, just long enough for the wrestler to move his opponent where he wants him. But that rather than simply holding me down for the count and winning the match quickly and cleanly Ahmad just kept his thumb in there and kept spinning me around and around the mat just for fun and when, afterwards, I questioned him on it, he just looked at me casually and replied, "These things happen, they just happen." Anyway, those were the types of things going through my mind when I was too enraged to think.

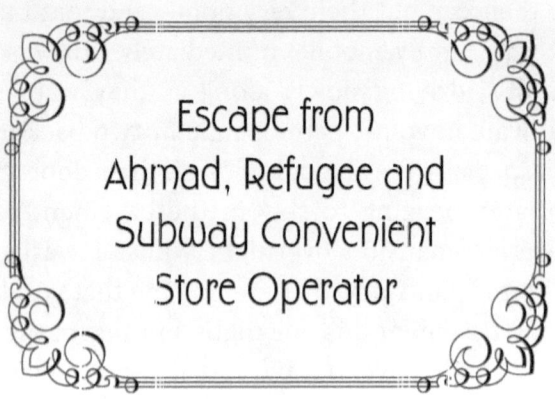

Escape from
Ahmad, Refugee and
Subway Convenient
Store Operator

And then, without warning, the snow-capped peaks of the Rockies rushed under me. It was so beautiful, the first true scenery I had encountered on the whole balloon trip. I felt like someone had knocked my hat off with a discus. And then just as suddenly, as if someone had knocked my hat off with a discus again, I remembered that I had to read the final triumvirate of tarot cards to figure out how to get my bride out of Ahmad's clutches.

The cards did not look promising. "Strength" and "Truth" cards on either side seemed like good things, but how could they compete with the madness and hysteria of "The Moon" and all its visions of wilting spiders and strange, dog-headed beings? So, I did the only thing I could do, I waited until the moon was rising over Longs Peak, made a 'milkshake' which I spiked with Methedrine, and shook my bride awake. After hearing my irrefutable explanation of how Ahmad had been misleading her all along, had in fact been doing nothing but using sophistry to hide the secret of the love catapult from her, holding each page of the dissertation close to her face so she could read the requisite passages by moonlight, a huge wind stream swept over the gondola and, given the fact that my nickname was "Steady Hands" in high school due to my inability to hold test tubes still enough for my lab partners to pour in the requisite chemicals, the entire dissertation flew into the sky. If we could have seen them, the pages would have looked like large square snowflakes falling into the mountains.

My bride let out a blood curdling scream and began grasping frantically at the windswept pages and I rushed to the far side of the gondola, both to try and grab any slow-to-fly pages of her dissertation, and to get away from her. Of course the far side of the gondola was not very far. Lucky for me I had the foresight to toss out her pistol during her last slumber, or I'm pretty sure that she would have shot me right then. Instead, she picked up the nearest heavy object she could find, which happened to be her computer, and tossed it right at my head. It hit me square on and, as I began to lose consciousness, I saw it ricochet off my skull and out of the gondola and meet a fate similar to the printed pages of her dissertation. If we could have seen it, the computer would have looked like the things falling off planes that we hear so often about. Sometime later I woke up and immediately my bride leaped upon me and with both hands around my neck made me pass out again, as she herself started to crash with the Methedrine milkshake wearing off.

At some point near the Canadian border my bride and I had both regained consciousness. She was completely drained, calm and lucid. "We don't need Ahmad to figure out how to construct a reliable love catapult," she said. "We are in a slow motion love catapult now, being launched from the east coast to the west. We can experience the nature of its motion, and when we get to San Jose, we'll be close enough to Keaton's energies to figure out how to build one that can catapult on command." And on that note, we decided to turn due West and finish our honeymoon over the Great North Woods. I had suspected, upon our nuptials, that a honeymoon in a gondola wasn't going to be that much fun and it turned out I was right. In addition to such close quarters being a definite exacerbating if not causal factor in any quarrel, from our high altitude the Great North Woods was just a bunch of tiny trees pointing their needled tops up at us. We sat and gazed for a spell, but pretty soon the axe just fell so we turned south down the other side of the Sierras towards San Jose where I was lucky, after all, to be employed.

Escape From Broncho Billy, Sheriff of Niles, CA

As our balloon descended lower into the Silicon Valley, my bride spotted an old town which the balloon's telescope, which we only recently discovered, not thinking to look for one in its "Supply Basket," revealed to be Niles, California, one-time home to Essanay studios who produced the Broncho Billy Westerns in Niles Canyon and such classics as *A Box of Matches* (1915), *Versus Sledge Hammers* (1915), and Charlie Chaplin's *The Tramp* (1915). It wasn't the perfect place for a honeymoon (Keaton hadn't shot any films there), but it was pretty cool nevertheless. People who think about it tend to see Chaplin and Buster as the two greats of early cinema, but Keaton is by far the greater because he understood what cinema was all about, what Marcel Duchamp calls the "amusing physics" (in reference to his masterpiece *The Bride Stripped Bare by her Bachelors, Even*) of the world. Whereas Chaplin saw cinema as a means for using that "amusing physics" to tell stories, Buster knew that stories were nothing but a pretense for moving amusingly through the world, experiencing its "uncontrollable weight" and "oscillating density" (Duchamp again).

We did a brief flyover across the rooftops of Niles, which seemed strangely deserted, and landed our balloon near a river bank just outside of town. Walking down Main Street, I tell you it was unbelievable, it looked just like 1915, like I could have been the sheriff marching through town in a Broncho Billy film, except instead of my hand at my holster, I was holding my bride's hand. And that made me feel slightly queasy, because I realized that if I were in a movie, I wouldn't be the sheriff at all but the hapless groom parading his beautiful bride through town - just before the moustachioed bandits rushed in and kidnapped her. Whenever I start to feel this way, and don't have any mind altering substances at hand, I find the only cure is to take my mind off things by looking for the largest tree in town. This is harder than it sounds, because most trees look about the same size, and you have to be careful not to be fooled by height alone. To locate the largest living organism in town (which is always a tree), you have to consider total volume, which involves considering not only height, but also average circumference, and number of branches. Over the years I have become quite the expert at it, and I had further honed my skills wandering through the woods to flee my sizeable sexual harassment debts. In fact, it's the only thing I can think of that I'm really good at. Unfortunately it is not a skill that makes one good marriage material or competitive in the global marketplace. So it wasn't too long before I had located *the* tree. You see once I've located the largest living organism in any town I mark it as the largest living organism by urinating on it. Now, like most men, I've put out camp fires with my urine, taken target practice at aluminum cans, engaged in competitions with other pissers for distance and height, written messages to both lost loves and new loves in the snow, and experienced what the Romantic poets call "the sublime" while pissing from the top of abandoned fire towers. But none of this compares with urinating on the largest living organism in any given town, because once your stream makes contact with that tree (it's always a tree, and indeed the largest living organism in the world, in fact, is "The General Sherman" in Sequoia National Park, which I hoped to visit late one evening now that I was in California), the entire world begins to spin around you, and your penis oscillates between seeming extremely large and extremely small, and then extremely large and extremely small at the exact same time. I'm certain that ancient peoples must have done this in places like Tenochtitlan.

Then, just as my post-piss rushing head began to regain its equilibrium and I was zipping up my pants, I gazed down Main Street and saw the actual sheriff of Niles staring right at me. He was a portly individual, and made the portly choice of getting into his police car in order chase me and my bride. This gave us just enough of a head start to make it to our balloon, cut the ropes from the gondola, and push it off into the river, thereby following in Buster's ontological footsteps and effectively converting the gondola into, well, a gondola.

Frantically at first, we paddled down the waterway of Niles, along Alameda Creek, past the Coyote Hills and all the way to the San Francisco Bay, which took quite a while. As my bride and I had very little in common, and she had lost both the paper and electronic copies of her dissertation, it left me a lot of time for personal reflection, which in effect means reflection on Buster.

I thought once again about all the bottoms (false and real) in *Sherlock Jr.* realizing that I have only enumerated a very small portion of the bottoms, which would require a closer analysis of the film than I could produce from memory while paddling my sleeping bride across San Francisco Bay in the gondola detached from our hot air balloon we stole from a carnival in Tennessee to make it all the way to Niles, CA, whose sheriff we were technically still in flight from, though I doubt he believed I would have the fortitude to keep paddling this long or that our gondola would be so seaworthy. Plus he's probably gone back and, examining the evidence, realized that I was not urinating in public for urination's sake, but that I had in fact chosen the largest living organism in Niles and had some compulsion (which I do) about urinating on the largest living organism in every new town I enter and that even if he were to arrest me, I would most likely be exonerated for reasons of insanity (and this would be the correct verdict). Anyway, a closer analysis of the film than can be produced from memory I believe would turn up even more bottoms both false and true, but due to Keaton's desire to show us adepts the true way and demonstrate that Karl Abel's *On the Antithetical Meaning of Primal Words* is itself a false bottom in the form of a book, I'm confident that a strict accounting, along with the help of cultural theorists and other cloacal philosophers who could help decide cases of bottoms whose falseness and trueness was somewhat ambiguous, yes I'm quite sure that such an analysis would, in the end, turn up many more false bottoms than true bottoms in *Sherlock Jr.* and that, all things being equal, the net result would be, numerically speaking, a case of a film in which false bottoms are transformed into false bottoms.

Here I was in California, with nothing but a crazy wife whose *Analects of Ahmad*, now strewn like mad pamphlets throughout the Rockies, seemed to only tease us about Arab knowledge of the love catapult. In point of fact, the *Analects* were nothing but a meaningless sign taunting you with what lies behind, which is nothing, Wizard of Oz style, or like the sign in Buster's dorm reading, "WHAT, NO BEANS." Nothing but her and a job reading tarot cards in San Jose which, if I didn't paddle our gondola more quickly rather than spend my time thinking about all the refutations of Karl Abel in Keaton's films, would probably have already been given to someone else by the time I got there. Although, if I did make it there in time, reading tarot cards would be no doubt a more useful and rewarding form of employment than teaching 18 year olds how to construct logical arguments in a world where logic has about as much respect as Buster's valedictorian speech on "The Curse of Athletics" in *College* (1927, Joseph M. Schenck Productions).

I was thinking these thoughts when my bride woke back up again, irritable and bored now that her dissertation and computer were gone. So I said, "Here, you take the paddle," and proceeded to reveal my innermost secrets - that would be those of *The Refutation*. And since we were both on some level longing for our days in academia, back when we were students struggling through our respective mental pursuits, I demonstrated Keaton's theories by talking about his film *College*.

"Anyway," I said, "Buster's points about 'The Curse

of Athletics' were right on, that 'jumping the discuss' and 'hurdling the javelin' would not advance society in the least, that 'Ty Ruth' and 'Babe Cobb' had not made one significant discovery in science, but he cleared the room with that speech. At least reading tarot cards, as opposed to teaching uninterested thumb-jockeys at Wellesley, I might be able to give people a little guidance about their next move in life.

"Anyway, we know that Buster wants us to think about 'higher learning' in alchemical terms due to the utter proliferation of proto-catapults in this film where, in order to impress his beloved, he attempts to become a perfect student-athlete, no matter where it leads. And it leads from catapult to catapult to catapult: 1) bullies using a makeshift trampoline (catapult) to toss him into the air, eventually in full view of a woman in her 'skivvies'; 2) track practice where the shot put's weight throws him backwards (catapult), and he practices to no avail the high jump and pole vault (both catapults); 3) the power of love allowing him to take a mere stick used to hold up laundry to pole vault (catapult) into the dorm room of his beloved, who has been locked inside by the local jock.

"I know it's hard to think about this film without feeling sad. But in reality, what is worse, being all alone in the desert or alone in a crowded room? To watch this film, with all its catapults that are really para-catapults, is to experience the latter. I did learn one practical thing from the film, however, and that is if you are an inexperienced coxswain, it is easiest to tie the rudder to your own body and use the more grounded sense of orientation contained within one's ass (as opposed to the brain, which must be constantly vigilant to the counterintuitive motions required to operate a rudder with one's hands.)"

As soon as I recalled this part of the film, I immediately cut out some of the upper part of the hot air balloon's gondola, which due to its circular structure, had caused us to drift all over the Bay despite my best attempts to remember the Indian stroke or the Canadian "J" stroke taught me in scouts - a stroke that works better with an oblong boat and something better than the river sticks we had salvaged for paddles anyway - and, taking the last 'paddle' back from my bride, I let my ass guide us to our destination.

I believe that having my ass guiding us is why our gondola ended up crashed against a beach near Palo Alto, California. Even though her computer and all her dissertation materials had been lost somewhere over the Rocky Mountains, my soon to be ex-bride decided with the remaining funds in her trust to enroll at Stanford rather than come live with me on my meager tarot card salary. At least that's what she said. My suspicion was that she had been so utterly bored by my analysis of Keaton's *College*, she had gone the way my Wellesley students could not (even a W on their transcript preventing them from attending Harvard Law). Nevertheless we parted ways both agreeing that it was best. She only had a short stroll to her new home while I, Buster-style, made it to my final destination pretty easy as well. All I had to do was jump out of a tree onto a train called Cal, though it just looked like any other train to me, and ride the rails right into San Jose.

Mystery Houses

The first thing I had to do upon my arrival was to find accommodations, and though my credit had been ruined by sexual harassment lawyers, with my as yet unexpired Wellesley faculty card I was able to secure a small 2nd story apartment, without air-conditioning, on the Western side of the building. This meant that I was going to have some pretty warm afternoons. After getting my keys and sleeping on the floor for a night, the next morning I went across the street to a yard sale and immediately began getting good vibes. A lady was bending over a homemade garden in the apartment's courtyard. She tore up some herbs and then turned to look at me, and with her gnarled fingers she waved them under my nose. "Smell these?" she asked. They smelled horrific. "These are good for opening up your channels, which is what I really need right now since over the years I've been writing about all my psychic experiences and have twelve notebooks full - I'm trying to type them up on this computer I found for cheap at Goodwill. Do you know how floppy disks work? I may be a clairvoyant, but

I'm no whiz when it comes to new technologies."

We sat down with some herbal tea and I began with Charles Babbage, moving on to Alan Turing's 'discrete machine' and his role in breaking the German ENIGMA code, his untimely death via cyanide poisoning after being convicted of homosexuality (his work for the Allies being so secret he could not play his "but I'm a hero" card at the trial, which I thought was unfortunate, citing the Michael Jackson defense that never was but should have been used). The defense is somewhat Aztec in nature, suggesting that if someone has made a significant enough contribution to culture or society, they should be granted a couple of 'virgin sacrifices' or their equivalent, according to taste. From there I told the Horatio Alger stories of Bill Gates and Steve Jobs, who went from homeless Great North Woods residents to the men more or less responsible for the very machine she had at her disposal. When I was able to convince the clairvoyant that what she typed on the screen could be magically transformed to the floppy disk, she said I was "a Frankenstein who skipped the birth canal," which I, absent of any context for such a statement, decided to take as a compliment. But there was one final test. She took a stone off her neck and 'dowsed' me. Fortunately I passed.

"We will be kindred spirits from here on out," she proclaimed, "but you may not see too much of me in the near future because I am in a somewhat fragile state, spiritually speaking, at the moment. And I need to be careful of absorbing too much energy like yours."

After I kindly rejected her offer to purchase a 'ghost trap' she had personally made according to Native

American methods she had intuited in the desert, I went to the rest of the yard sale and was able to pick up some minimal furniture. Everyone seemed to know the clairvoyant but recommended that, if I was into that kind of thing, I should just go up Winchester Avenue to the Winchester Mystery House. It was sort of fortuitous that I should be caught between Janet Devore, clairvoyant and ghost trap peddler, and the Winchester Mystery House, especially given the fact that, being in the barrio as I was, my topless tenancy was immediately looked upon as suspect by all the other tenants. I was topless, of course, due to the fact that I was in my own apartment and it got really hot in there in the afternoons. I was suspect because I did not own a car, was white, topless and over thirty and therefore either gay or a pedophile or both, and perhaps even rich since I was occupying an entire studio apartment by myself, sans wife and several kids.

The second night I was there, toplessness and suspicion collided with each other like a fence and a motorcycle without handlebars. It was around eight pm and I had my shades open and was eating from one of those eight pound cans of black beans because I like black beans and I also wanted to advertise to the neighbors that I wasn't rich by eating the beans - I had been tempted to buy baked beans which I like even better but thought that even in bean form, something sweet might be interpreted as a thing I would use to lure kids inside my spacious studio apartment where I was surely hiding a sex dungeon. In an attempt to project my poverty and with respect to cultural sensitivity, I was careful to advertise how much I was *enjoying* eating beans straight from this huge can, which wasn't hard because, though cold, they did taste good, and figured that my "neighbors" would most likely assume that gay people tended to eat things like sushi and edamame (immature green soybeans served in their inedible pods). I was topless, tis true, but it was so hot I had no choice. I figured they might cut me some slack on that part.

Suddenly there was a knock on the door and I knew it was Betty the apartment manager, and I normally out of principal don't answer the door when apartment managers come knocking but in this case I had no choice given the fact that my attempt at rebranding my tarnished barrio image sort of made it obvious that I was there. Now, to give some cultural context let's just say that Betty is from the Deep South and while I'm no geologist, she was also as old as dirt. So, I'm doing the old stand in the doorway routine to suggest to someone that there is no way in hell someone's getting inside my apartment, but Betty is standing there with two glasses of iced tea and asks if she can come in for a bit. Whatever. We sip on our tea for a bit and then Betty lays out the situation.

"You see," young man, "I received a complaint from two female tenants, who go to work around 2 or 2:30 in the morning, and they were complaining that...whoa, it's like a furnace in here, you should get another fan or two. Anyway, they were complaining that, since you leave your shades open at night, it is very easy to see inside your bedroom."

"You came here to tell me that two tenants complained that it is easy, if they so choose, to look at me in my bedroom."

"I was just suggesting maybe," Betty continued, "for your own privacy you might want to shut your shades at night."

I sat there and took a "Southern moment" or two to contemplate what I was being told, and upon which planet I might be living, what dimension even.

"Well Betty," I said, "correct me if I'm wrong, but I don't think it's your place as 'manager' of the apartment complex to tell me what to do inside my unit that is legal and decent. If anyone stares inside my window when the shades are 'open at night,' as you put it, they won't see anything they wouldn't see if I were sunbathing in our pool."

"Now that you put it that way," Betty commiserated, "I see your point. But it is my job to make sure all our tenants are comfortable. Indeed, I just hope I haven't embarrassed or upset you."

"I don't get embarrassed," I lied. "Those ladies, whomever they may be, can look inside my window anytime they want, they just shouldn't complain about what they see. But I am annoyed that you as apartment manager would attempt to recommend how I conduct myself in my own apartment. No one is requiring these women to stare in my window. It's like a peeping Tom complaining to the police about the 'indecency' he has seen in the victim's window. It would be like me staring down at the Irish chicks when they sunbathe and complaining to you that I can't concentrate because I am choosing to watch them sunbathe and therefore they shouldn't be there when I'm around to look at them and be aroused."

I proceed, "Why don't I go over there with you right now and I can inform the women of peeping tom laws and then dare them to get a photo of me in my bedroom naked and take that to the police. First, they would never get such a photo, and even if they did, what would a judge have to say about the means and effort they took to look inside and photograph me naked in my bed asleep?"

After leading Betty down many Socratic paths to this same point, she insisted on "a hug" and "some sugar" and invited me to have a beer with her on the weekend. As she walked away, I had the strange suspicion that she made the whole thing up just to come and chat with me.

Not packing my things, I proceed to vacate my hotbed of licentiousness and move instead up the street to the Winchester Mystery House. And though the place was closed for the night, apparently folks were so freaked out by the place, or simply because of the number of doors, they didn't even bother to lock it, so I was able to walk right in. Regardless of its ghostly legends, the house seemed to me like the perfect place to stay since the many extra doors made it feel just like my childhood home. To stay for any length of time, I would have to sneak in every evening and sneak out each morning, but if that wouldn't be a problem for Buster, it wouldn't be for me. According to various placards, the house was constructed for ghosts, the ghosts of those who had been killed by Winchester rifles in fact. And assuming the placards to be correct, it would seem that ghosts have very unusual taste in architecture. Filled with stairways into walls and doors to nowhere, I felt less self-conscious about the maladroit behavior which had earned me the title, even if only in jest, "The World's Most Inept Man." Plus, since they apparently only cleaned out the popcorn machine in the mornings, I would also have all the stale popcorn I could eat – not that this was very nutritious, but it definitely promised to be filling.

Reverse Casino

Before I could begin my job at the tarot parlor, which was, strangely enough, located in an old Catholic mission a couple of miles up the road, I had to take a computerized sexual harassment test. It was pretty stressful but probably a good idea since, from the moment I arrived there, I noticed that the clients were very fit and attractive, nothing like the Cheetos eating divas of the Deep South I grew up with. The fact that the exam was designed so that I was a "character" encountering various "situations" on a simulation of the mission itself did not help things, as I had only really encountered environments like this in first-person shooter games, so I had to shake off the aggressor mentality which made me want to "shoot" or in this case "fuck" everything I saw, as if by fucking all my opponents and reaching the bell tower, I would reach some sort of prize, most likely the hottest nun on the mission. In fact, however, the interface was meant to help people with short attention spans (I learned later) imagine the situations in real time. This was not good for me either because not only did I not know California law when it came to sexual practices at tarot parlors or elsewhere (for all I knew, every McDonalds had a casting couch), but in matters of the heart I have always been a bit slow on the draw. If it were a true or false test, a "fuck" or "don't fuck" decision, I might have been able to handle it better. But instead there were issues like whether or not I should "report" something, what sort of "report form" I should use, and which level of the tarot parlor hierarchy should I report to. There was this one question that asked whether it was okay to hug my "clients" (those receiving the readings) and I thought, "Surely not!" Wrong. Apparently, I could attempt to hug each of my clients once and if they did not object, I could hug them as often as I wanted! I thought about that for a bit, could barely believe it and thought maybe it was a glitch in the system, or worse, a trick of some kind. I hadn't seen much hugging going on as I strolled down tarot parlor row that morning, and it seemed a little strange to me that with the beauties they were dealing with, the other readers wouldn't be all over that exemption. Or maybe I misread it; maybe it said something like I wouldn't *necessarily* be subject to a lawsuit or dismissal. I wanted to be sure, but it's not like you can just say, "Hey, can I take that online sexual harassment seminar again?" Because no one in their right mind would want to do it *more* often than they were legally required to except people looking to see how much they could get away with. And even if it was okay for me to hug my clients once, would I have the nerve to do it? I mean, they were, as far as I could tell, largely tall, bronzed and godlike. I just don't know if I could. "It's probably best to just assume it's a trick," I told myself, "because if it wasn't, every single day would be nothing but the sheer torture of lurking about, hoping to find a client crying, or excited enough to jump towards me with open arms, and feeling like the hunchback of Notre Dame or something, the town monster who lurked about as I searched for that hug."

Fortunately the tarot card reading business was booming, so no one seemed to mind that it took me five tries (each try prolonged by fantasizing about various of the scenarios I was presented with) to get a "pass." It also helped me deal with the guru junkies whom I had only read about in some of my dad's books, and though I had developed a distaste for them on that level, I was not prepared for the combination that beauty and sheer bodily proximity could add to a purely literary experience. On my first day, chatting with my clients hair salon style, it quickly became apparent that guru junkies are very easy and very annoying to talk to. They are very easy to talk to because they only talk about themselves, but that is also what makes them so annoying. Plus, you know that they are going to talk about their latest gurus, who change quite often, so there are no surprises or awkward moments conversation-wise, which can be very nice. On the other hand, they either preface or postface their commentary with the suggestion that you could really benefit from following their latest guru. This is annoying because you have to say, "That's a good idea," or at the very least "Interesting," no matter how dumb the idea or how much effort it would take to carry out. Plus, there is the overriding implication that because they all have these gurus working to improve them they are somehow superior to you. And just like sitting in church, week in and week out, listening about how you're going to go to hell, if you hear something enough times, no matter how stupid it is, you inevitably start to believe it. And since, as a professional tarot card reader, I was pretty much awash in guru junkies, being guruless (silent comedy stars like Buster apparently didn't qualify, as far as I could tell), I now not only felt like "The World's Most Inept Man" in a physical sense, but in a spiritual sense as well.

After having studied the booklet that went with my tarot deck (I had billed myself as an Aleister Crowley man, to create a niche), I got the impression that tarot dealers were supposed to behave ethically, that is, rely upon the random shuffle of the cards to answer the questions of guru junkies and like-minded "querents." No matter what cards came up I felt it was my solemn duty to let my junkies know what was coming down the pike regardless of what their gurus had promised them. Even though a seven day a week junkie habit does not allow for any sort of serious romantic interaction, except, as we shall see, brief and superficial flirtations with humility swimmers, gurus, and cinematically dong covered nudes, as I suspected, guru junkies were no different than Buster, or myself, which is that all we were really interested in was love - whether we admitted this to ourselves or not. So without fail, every single junkie who came to my booth asked me what their love life was going to be in the future. Of course, given their quasi-corporate mindset, they spoke in coded terms I soon learned to identify, phrases like "future partnerships" and "deal breakers" meant love and its vicissitudes. Now, if I were to be analytical about their daily schedules of self-improvement and repressed lifestyles of fake egolessness a.k.a. fake self-expression, I would say that things are looking pretty grim. Or, if I were not working a volume business, and thought the junkies were there for anything but the cards, I would have ventured to interest them in Buster Keaton's theory of the love catapult. But, I had to do my job, and I *thought* that meant shuffling the cards and truthfully telling the junkies what they said.

Since I had proven to my initial supervisor that I was deft with the cards and knew their meanings, I was surprised on my first day at work to see that there were as many supervisors as there were tarot readers. I mean, it seemed a pretty simple endeavor to me, and a waste of manpower to have so many people walking around with microphones they pulled out of their shirt and curly cords dangling out of their ears. After a couple weeks I was still nonplussed at their presence, but as I was pulling a steady paycheck and living "rent-free" at the Winchester mystery house, I soon was able feel their presence as almost natural, like the ghosts wandering about the mystery house, there and not there, which was fine with me. Until that one fateful day...

I came to work and was just ready to set up my booth when one of the supervisors grabbed me by the shoulders and said, "Come with me." I was sort of nervous as I was escorted to the bell tower of the mission, where instead of a bell, there were all kinds of video screens - all with pictures of me reading tarot cards! "Sit down," I was told. "Look at this screen here. This is video was taken yesterday. Do you notice anything wrong with it?" I stared at the reading for a while and said, "No, I really don't. I dealt the cards when the client asked me about her prospective partnerships, and gave her the reading the divine Thoth had assigned her."

"Listen, we don't know anything about this divine Thoth you speak of."

"He's the Egyptian god of writing," I explained, "the namesake of the deck I use."

"Shut up and listen. You gave her the standard three card reading and - "

"It was midday," I protested, "and she still had several places to find in the Bermuda triangle of organic farms so she could eat that week, so I couldn't give her a longer one."

"The Bermuda what?" bellowed the supervisor impatiently, "Listen, if you want to keep your job you'll shut up and listen."

"So here you are, right there on the screen," he continued, "and you drew the following three cards. The Prince of Wands, the Ten of Swords or Ruin, and The Chariot. And what did you say?"

"I told her the truth." I said.

"You said that due to the fact that her reason was divorced from reality she had been following too many 'gurus' who claimed to have spiritual powers. You said that she was always changing them when one disappointed her, that she had been in the Bay Area for much too long and that she needed to escape in some kind of Chariot, which you said might uncannily resemble a catapult, and just see where it led, or as you phrased it, 'be launched from the catapult to wherever you land, as long as it was not in the Bay area.'"

"Yes, like I said, that's what the cards said."

"What the cards said. What the freakin' cards said," eyes rolling, "Just look at the expression on her face.

Don't you know to always draw two cards at a time, which statistically gives you a much better chance at a good reading? Why do you think we keep the lights dim, to hide your ugly mug? Right under Ruin, or the Ten of Swords, was Happiness, the Nine of Cups. And if you had laid that one out instead, it would have told her what every guru junkie needs to hear when she comes to our establishment, which is that the two horse riding cards surrounding happiness indicated travel, that the next guru would be beautiful, funny, yet deep enough to have obtained a financially stable position in the global marketplace, and would fall for her hard enough to take her with him to Carmel or Monterey or even Marin, where it was much easier to find your crazy child without releasing your *enfant terrible* and that together they would find their crazy child by having crazy children together, except they wouldn't be crazy in a clinical sense, only a Berkeley sense. They would be blonde, blue eyed, smart and beautiful and they would grow up to be famous, though well-educated, models and actors. And in the process of being together with her guru, she would find out that she herself had always been a guru, and with the two of them working together (along with his earnings at Chase International where people earn their six figures without having to answer questions), would have enough discretionary funds to send the kids off to wonderful private schools and colleges, so that the gurus would be able to rekindle their romance indefinitely."

It was then that the truth hit me like a sandbag falling from the rafters of a Vaudeville show. I was not working for a real tarot parlor, but for a reverse casino, a dream machine. All the "supervisors" were walking around to make sure that, rather than everyone eventually losing, everyone would eventually believe that they too could "win" the game of wealth, fame and fortune. This was the guru junkie version of that old saw of false consciousness, the Horatio Alger story where everyone rises above the circumstances to which they are superior, not Buster's revelation that we are all absolutely inferior to our environments.

"Do you understand what we're getting at?"

"Yes, I think so sir."

"Then get back to your booth."

But when I got back to my booth, I was still reeling from the fact that my job out here on the West Coast, where I had nary a friend but Mrs. Winchester's ghosts, was not about giving actual spiritual advice, but lying to people about the nature of Buster's most sacred alchemical designs, designs of love he had spent his life researching and encrypting on celluloid. I grabbed the tarot cards, but when I did, it started raining again but not for everyone else, just for me, and the cards were getting wet, really wet, and since the cards were wet, the tarot cards look as if Salvador Dali had painted them. Unnerved, I asked to take the day off so I could go to the nearest Salvador Dali museum and purchase the tarot deck that he actually painted so I could compare them, getting wetter all the time, with the ones that had been wet for even longer.

That night, mulling over Salvador Dali's tarot cards and munching on stale popcorn while Mrs. Winchester's ghosts performed their nightly Cowboy and Indian routines in the rafters, I thought about what I should do. If I had actual skills which could make me competitive in the global marketplace, there would be no question of remaining at the reverse casino (a.k.a. fake tarot parlor), but I was the world's most inept man, and I had no friends. How long could I keep lying to people just for a paycheck?

What were the chances a carnival would come along and have another hot air balloon to abscond with? To get me out of here? Indeed, what were the chances?

Back to Vaudeville

The next day was even worse. While I was able to use all the tricks my supervisor had taught me, my heart was just not in it. Indeed, I could only give the readings with the solemn, stone face of Keaton, which the junkies did not seem to appreciate that much. I knew I'd be sacked by the end of the day. My supervisor came and gave me the news, but did say that I had actually received a fan letter that day, from someone named "S." He handed me the letter and, in a rare moment of camaraderie, pat me on the back and said, "Maybe this will get you through this rough patch, which is all it really is." He continued, "For me, running a reverse casino is no problem, but I have no soul, and you do. That's why if I were you I'd follow the advice in the letter."

The letter seemed to be from a repeat customer, but there was so much in it that I never remembered talking about that it was clear that it was a typical case of the guru junkie's projection of her own ideas onto whatever I had said. There was only one lead at the end, and I planned on following it, having no other recourse. The letter read, "Another enchanted exchange...humbled once again by your radiographic readings into nous, or, at least, the pictures you have created of it (I qualify this statement with the understanding that Seeing of a Thing Itself, As It Is, is rare, indeed). Hafiz states this rare practice as: 'Oh God, it may be that I have just poured a toast that would wash love clean of all its images!' Hooray for telekinesis! Plotinus, Hermes Trismegistus, Plato and subsequent neo-Platonists and Hermeticists, look to the secondary causes of the Nous-demiurge as the ontological field emitting energeia, soul, acting upon or *actualizing* its own thoughts creating 'a separate, material cosmos that is the living image of the spiritual or noetic cosmos contained as a unified thought within the Intelligence.' The Demiurge is second to God, The Monad, as the nous or thought of intelligibles and sensibles. Energeia is that aspect of Mind believed to act upon and form matter telepathically and that resonant somatic response experienced as wing and warmth. Wow, had no idea this poem (or any aspect of this being I refer to as 'myself') could elicit such an affect/effect! Amazing! Must look more deeply into Magick . . . what rare fortune to live next to Sarah Winchester and Janet the clairvoyant who is afraid of you. . .looking forward to understanding the interplay of numerology and poetics... yesterday, gorgeous........danced contact improv with old dudes....like to invite you to share some of your magick at the Triptych, Oakland's Vaudeville Coven, just near where San Leandro St. meets High St. Meet you there around 7:30. Your loving S."

Well, it was obvious that this was my equivalent

of Buster Keaton's James Agee, someone who admired my depth and stone face so much that she had dropped all kinds of terminology she figured I must have known, assuming that, like her, I too had hit all the guru junkie spots around town. Regardless, despite the fact that I was slightly intimidated by this S. character and the fact that I had never done vaudeville, I figured if it was a good enough way for Buster to begin, it was a fine way for me to continue.

The Oakland vaudeville joint did not begin with sexual harassment training, though in retrospect I wish it had. I was greeted not by S., whoever she was, but by the owner of the establishment and thrown right on stage. There were lots of spectators, but apparently no one scheduled to perform that night. I would have to be their guru. So I began with some love letters I'd written to women over the past several weeks while holed up in the Winchester House in the middle of the night:

Dear Lilmissincredible,

I was considering at some point getting some plastic surgery. Actually I've considered it for many years but have never gotten around to it, or have resisted it. Or perhaps I have taken too much to heart conceptual artist Naim Jun Paik's dictum: "Work hard. Be lazy." Or at least I've taken too much to heart the latter part of his statement.

Or maybe it's because I lacked sufficient inspiration. I really like your nose and mouth Lilmissinc, and I guess I was wondering if perhaps you wouldn't mind if I used you as a model if I do indeed go through with this decision. I fully realize that often a woman's features don't translate to those of a man, for instance Angelina Jolie's bee stung lips look quite scary on her father John Voight, which is probably why they are now estranged, but in this case I think it just might work.

Perhaps we could work out some sort of fee for the indignation of your nose and mouth existing in more than one place at a time.

Anyway, let me know.

Sincerely yours

--

Dear LoudItalian,

Okay, so here I am writing a model, which is what one does in this fantasy world. But you do love animals, so perhaps I have a shot. Those cows? Do you know them? They seem nice. So do you.

Intriguingly yours,

--

Dear Gallerylover1913,

I guess the ultimate goal would be to find something which utterly disgusts you. But after all the upside down urinals, all the religious icons soaked in urine, all the black and white photography of somdomites, what is there left to do? Nevertheless, I think if you gave me the chance, and it might require several months of satisfying my every sexual whim, I would be up to the task.

Adoringly yours,

--

Dear Mimi,

I get the feeling that the turtle in your back yard, no matter how much lettuce you feed it, gets lonely sometimes. In fact, I received a psychic message just last night from your pet turtle, and this is exactly what he told me, and I could tell that he'd been feeling this for some time as he dictated his feelings to me in the form of a sonnet he had composed and memorized. Perhaps if I tell you the sonnet you will realize how amazing turtles really are and you will pay more attention to him. By the way, your turtle doesn't mind the fact that you're divorced at all, and is glad that you've retained custody of him instead of you know who.

Sonnet (from your turtle)

Responses, thoughts, acts of lexpionage,
Greek philosophers, defined, accounted,
Poets lived in and out of le menagre.
Vain eclipse announced, we turtles mounted

embarked upon acts of green espionage
our eyes, unknown to us, moved to the side
our brains, camera obscura, collage
machines leading always to the green-eyed

creatures who love eyes, traveling, on the hajj
precocious beings who know our eyes are odd
move backwards, forwards, leave the guns of Dodge,
random because the world itself is god

Who could fulfil that French writer's desire
divorce be sacrament, who could not care?

Deeply yours,

--

Dear LeftCoast,

How's Zizek going? I personally am always wavering
between bodies without organs and organs without
bodies. Man it's a tough choice. Oh, and by the way,

I too have a soft spot in my heart for the special victims unit!

Quizzically yours,

--

Dear Livtillyoudie1118,

I noticed you have a lot of pictures of yourself skydiving, but that you also like to curl up on the weekends with a good book. Personally, I don't believe that you ever do "curl up," as you put it. Well, they say you haven't lived until you've skydived. Hence, a tragedy. I will die before ever having lived. That said, those cobble stone streets look pretty interesting.

Already Fallen for you,

--

Dear Porcelina,

I'm not especially professional or attentive, except when mesmerized, but I do love puppies and wandering. . .

Mesmerizingly yours,

--

Dear AudreyWilde43,

So much meteorology out there! Show me some of that public affection!

Or not.

Anticipatingly yours,

--

Dear Sweet SFGrrrl,

I'm not within 20 miles of San Francisco, but your hair, upon reflection, totally makes sense.

Thoughtfully yours,

--

Dear Luvnomatterwhat2087,

I noticed that most of our conversation centered around your dislike of drugs and those who take drugs. In that way you are very similar to the governor of Florida who spent 180 million dollars drug testing all the welfare recipients in his state at testing facilities that he owned no less. Personally, I feel like we should all have the right to drugs, rich or poor! But I'm wondering if, for instance, I never do drugs in your presence, if you might reconsider your stand, at least for one date. Even though I do drugs on occasion, I'm really quite a charming lad.

Soberly yours,

--

Dear WakeupMaggie,

Regarding your question about my taste in fashion, I must say I find it quite refreshing that you have asked me this rather than about my taste in music. Personally I believe there is no difference between high rises and trees or between cinema and life, except where there are differences. Right now, I'm wearing a sweater a girlfriend asked me to buy, a pair of Ecco's I bought myself, and a pair of pants that a heroin addict roommate left behind when I kicked him out of our apartment for stealing from me. It's sad, I think of him whenever I wear the pants. . .

Fashionably yours,

--

Dear AlliMcKitt,

Hey, I'm really good at finding things, because all my past girlfriends have been really big losers (of things). This may not be the biggest issue in your life, but you did mention it, and it happens to be one of my talents. See, when they lose things, I ask all the right questions and look in all the right places (with their permission of course). I'm just very thorough that way, it makes up for my lack of introspection because it's like a search (but not of myself). So, if you ever lose anything, keys, your mind, whatever, give me a call.

Sincerely yours,

--

Dear AlliMcKitt,

It's me again, the losers' finder. So, after 22 hours, it's pretty obvious that you're not going to give me a call. That's okay. But surely you will lose things in the future. But just to show you what kind of guy I am, I'll tell you where I learned how to find things. It took *100 Years Of Solitude* (the book, not the act). There's a passage in it about how things get lost because they fall just outside a fairly narrow route-ine (I made that word up) which we don't realize we follow. Like, something could be in the pocket you don't normally put stuff in, between your legs because you stuck it there while stuffing on your gloves before going outside. The latter two examples show how "outside the route-ine" is not normally how we think of it. The lost object could actually be very close to you. It's possible that it could be farther away though. Like, imagine that you had your credit card in your hand while you were coming home and then you checked the mail, and you grabbed a bunch of mail as the card, which happened to be silver, got tossed back into the mailbox. It would be virtually invisible. But you see, those are the kinds of things that occur to you once you learn to see outside of your route-ine. They occur to me all the time. I don't remember what page exactly of *100 Years Of Solitude* discusses this method, but I think I've given a fairly succinct and accurate paraphrase of the method. Besides, it's a good book and you should read the whole thing anyway, because a 100 years of solitude is what you've got in store, you fucking bitch, because you can't see a good thing when it's right there in front of you!

Screw you; I was just trying to help,

--

Dear AlliMckitt,

Please please please read this because in the midst of apologizing for calling you a fucking bitch I forgot to mention that the other day that I felt, myself, like a lost object. Which reminded me to tell you that, no matter how closely you follow the

100 Years Of Solitude method, there will be things you undoubtedly lose for good. And then what? Well, you could call me and I could explain to you in detail about Jacques Lacan's theories of how we are all born prematurely and thus, we don't start out with everything found, and then start losing stuff. We've already lost from the get-go and start trying to accumulate more and more images and objects to complete ourselves, and it's never ending. You spend your whole life doing this! And if that's the case, you've just got to imagine that even if you're a big loser (of things) you probably aren't that far behind people who don't lose that much, at least in psychoanalytic terms.

Sincerely yours,

--

Judging from the reactions of the crowd, who kept calling me a "total freak," a "creepy guy," and a "sexist pig," my act was not well received. Nevertheless, it seemed like Oakland was full of vaudeville junkies but few actual performers, so I was invited back the next night to do something a little more serious, something like an "advice night," as the manager put it. I told him I'd see what I could come up with.

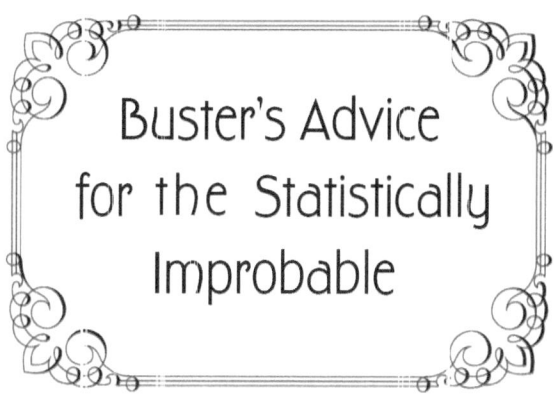

Buster's Advice
for the Statistically
Improbable

The next night I came back in full Keaton regalia, porkpie hat and all, with what I thought was some pretty helpful advice for things that don't happen that often, but most likely will happen at one point in your life or another. Still no one approached identifying themselves as S. After explaining to the audience the significance of my outfit and the purpose of that night's performance, I began with situation number one.

"Situation number one. You are at a karaoke bar and a prostitute sits next to you, and you want to ditch her."

"What kind of karaoke bar is this," I was heckled.

"It is a Platonic karaoke bar, one that doesn't exist but could, a hypothetical bar, or actually, the bar does exist but I have not found it yet."

"This is complete bullshit. There is no such bar, and this concatenation of events would never occur."

I was impressed by that word, "concatenation," and felt my audience deserved a measured response. "Did you not read the sign on the door to the show tonight?! It said STATISTICALLY IMPROBABLE YET INEVITABLE SITUATIONS. It's like getting struck by lightning, it won't happen to a good number of you in your entire life, and for others it might happen several times - what I call the Buster Keaton exception - while for most of you it will happen just once and once only, and for this one night I am giving you advice for when it does, so I'm going to ask you to shut the heck up now or leave. But beware, should these things happen to you, and you left, you will be completely unprepared!"

The absolute silence at my hissy fit let me know that I would be allowed to proceed.

"Nota Bene: This method of having a prostitute sit next to you at a karaoke bar and wanting to ditch her only works, as you will soon see, on female prostitutes seeking perceived heterosexual males. It will not work for transvestites or other homosexual situations in most cases."

As if my differentiation of different types of prostitutional situations were some sort of Aristotelian ethos, the crowd immediately moved to the edge of their seats, demanding that I get on with it. I knew that I needed to up the ante.

"First, realize that there are, as Plato observed, two worlds, the world of illusions and the real world. Second, realize that most of the time you live in the world of illusions, and only at this karaoke bar do you encounter the real world."

A gasp of recognition moved through the audience like wind through the forest.

"In the real world, everything costs money except karaoke, which is free. So, inevitably, in the real world, when you are trying to sing karaoke but instead find yourself sitting at the bar most of the time as other people sing, inevitably a prostitute will come up to you.

"The difference between prostitutes and women of the illusory world is that prostitutes sit next to you and start touching you immediately, even though you don't know them.

"In the real world, you don't want to have sex with the prostitute, but since she wants to have sex with you, she has marked you, accurately, as sitting alone and available for sex.

"In the real world, prostitutes are like everyone else, which means that they must make a living but are lazy and afraid of crazy people.

"Also, in the real world you are polite to everyone and don't want to endanger the prostitute's chosen profession and you don't even want to reject her, as she is a), a human being with feelings and b), being chosen out of a crowd full of men, even by a prostitute, is something of compliment.

"In this real world, the situation is, not easily, but definitively solved by being on the karaoke song list and being called up to sing.

"When this happens, be sure to change your chosen song to NIN's 'Closer' at the last minute. Make sure to walk around the room as you sing, occasionally glancing at the prostitute. Sing the song well and, like Trent Reznor, emphasize the words 'I want to fuck you like an animal' and 'You can have my isolation / you can have the hate that it brings, etc.'

"Having delivered the song convincingly, hand over the mike and glance over at where you were sitting, then gaze across the landscape of the bar and you will notice something amazing, you will be amazed at the powers within you.

"The prostitute who, like everyone else, is both lazy and afraid of crazy people, will not just have moved on to another customer, but will have left the bar entirely, knowing that you rule that domain where prostitutes are held to higher standards than prostitutes of the illusory world, that in your world they must work hard, they must 'fuck like an animal,' and not only that, but must fuck someone as insane as Trent Reznor or, in this case, you pretending to be Trent Reznor. Not wanting to do this, the prostitute will have left Plato's cave, the karaoke bar, which is the real world, and departed for the illusory world in which we dwell most of our lives.

"Now," I concluded, "this may sound like a rather involved process for ditching a prostitute who sits next to you at a karaoke bar, but it is worth it as it allows *you* to be the rejectee, and you don't mind because you knew in advance that your plan would result in the prostitute rejecting you and the real world entirely, so everyone leaves the situation with their feelings relatively intact."

I was greeted by a standing ovation. Perhaps even, people were lying about how often they were approached by prostitutes at karaoke bars and really appreciated the advice on a practical level. Whatever the reason, I've never been one for leaving well enough alone and, addicted to approval, I moved on to situation number two.

"The first situationist installment of the evening," I continued.

"Installment? Is this an installation?" some hipster asked excitedly.

"It is whatever you want it to be," I resumed in a mysterious tone, "since we are now living in the illusory world, preparing ourselves for another entry into the real world of statistically unlikely but inevitable situations." Silence.

"So the first situationist installment of this installation was on how to get rid of prostitutes at karaoke bars without offending them, because they too are people just trying to get by, while this next situation deals with the fear of spiders. I will be open about the fact that I once sank a canoe trying to avoid the least of all spiders, a daddy longlegs. Then I read about the Surrealist painter Tanguy.

"It *is* an installation, I knew it, a Surrealist installation," interjected that villain of all vaudevillians, the heckler of the obvious.

"So this Tanguy dude used to like scaring children - back when you could do that sort of thing without being arrested - by eating spiders in their presence. I thought about that for a while, the thought of eating what you fear, when I was at an outdoor dinner party last summer with a spider climbing up the edge of my empty wine glass.

"So this one actually happened to you," the villain continued.

"Yes, as I pointed out, these situations will inevitably happen to you, no matter how statistically unlikely. Indeed, one could say that life itself *is* the sum of so many statistically unlikely yet inevitable situations, most of which we do not notice as such."

I thought about explaining this in my dad's terms, asking to people to imagine the state of California covered six feet deep in electrons, but reminded myself that this evening was dedicated not to theoria, but praxis.

"So, this fact, this spider on my empty wine glass, was pointed out to me by my male and female companions at the table. On a whim, I said, 'Well, that obviously means I was meant to drink this spider.' I must have looked like Dracula to them from the looks on their faces. I did not eat the spider, mind you, but simply picked up the empty wine glass and drank the spider so that it could live for a while as it went down my throat, experiencing what it was like, as a solid thing, to be treated as if it were a liquid."

"Are you crazy! That thing could have been a brown recluse," someone in the audience screamed.

"Perhaps," I replied, "but you must remember that I was at a dinner party and brown recluses are, well, fairly reclusive. Some might even go so far as to diagnose them as agoraphobic. So the chances of it being a brown recluse were pretty slim. Besides, in theater, whether it is agit-prop or a night at the Metropolitan Opera House, one must take chances or fail miserably. As Lada Gaga once said, 'All the world is a stage, and we are merely players strutting on it in stiletto heels.'"

Then some vegetarian got all up in arms, calling me a murderer and a torturer and even worse things. I was quite taken aback, given that it was just a freaking spider, but not unprepared.

"Do you not know how many insects of various kinds even the most Hinduistic of us consume every year, nay every day, inadvertently? There are tiny mites that live on your face, and every time you take a shower, you are like the Count Dracul of mites. You might as well have a field of bobby pins in your bathroom upon which you impale them from anus to mouth. That's right, when it comes to mites, you are Vlad the Impaler. Nay, you are the Gilles de Rais of pubescent mites, and they are your catamites!"

The vegetarian bent over and began sobbing, so I raised my voice for the death blow.

"Besides, what if that spider were suicidal. After all, it was climbing up the precipice of my glass, which to a spider would be something akin to a tall building. Maybe it wanted to leap to its death but, knowing that its hardy arthropodic anatomy would not permit this, picked me out of the group of cowards I was dining with. Indeed, I think that spider wanted to know what it was like to be drunk as if it were a fine wine, and I provided that spider with the opportunity it desired. Why else would it be crawling up my wine glass, of all the wine glasses available to it on that beautiful patio? And to this day, I have felt that all of god's creatures should be regarded as a fine wine, not necessarily to be consumed - but something just as valuable, as valuable as an obsession, a castle taken brick by brick from Europe and reconstructed somewhere in Northern California, by a man who really knows how to love something, and to support that love by also bringing back a torture device or two from the same time to attract those of us in love with torture (love is torture, but some of us have to start from the torture end to understand this). So, the next time you encounter something you fear, I recommend, with its permission (or implied permission) ingesting it. Then it is a part of you and no longer subject to external fear. Internal fear is another matter, perhaps to be addressed in another way, with an exorcism or enema perhaps. But, in summation, I have to say on my end that ingesting external fears makes you feel much less vulnerable to internal fears, since once something enters your system, you are the thing to be feared, or loved, or at least appreciated, depending on the spiritual development of those you encounter. It doesn't really matter. What was it that the Apostle said about places that don't accept your prophecies. Just leave them, and wipe the dust off your shoes."

Upon hearing this, that lentil eating scum began writhing on the floor and screaming in pain, so I had him escorted out of the building. I was starting to feel like I owned the place.

"Situation number three." Who was going to stop me now that they had seen the way I had dispatched of the vegetarian.

"You are at a karaoke bar and, forgetting that singing David Bowie songs from the 1970s is code for switch-hitters, you are accosted by a beautiful transvestite in the audience, to whom you have been singing because she has been cheering so loudly for your bitching vocals and you like trannies but you are not really into dudes, at least not that month."

"Is this the same 'hypothetical' or 'Platonic' karaoke bar?" someone heckled me.

"Most likely," I recovered, "because weird bars are like batteries with alternating and direct currents. Certain bars, especially ones not designated as such, are 'queer' in the sense of odd, repelling 'direct' customers and attracting those customers who, in one form or another, could be classified as 'alternators.' If some stranger can walk into a bar you're in and exclaim, 'Dude, you can just smell the stench of vagina in here,' you are in a direct bar. If that kind of statement horrifies you on some deep, autochthonic level, and you find yourself not horrified but rather constantly freaked out at a different bar, that bar possesses an alternating current. There is no good bar, and there is not even a good coffee shop, do not be fooled by various television series I will not name here that suggest otherwise. Any place where people go to hang out for hours at a time to fill some void inside themselves is a place that will either horrify you or constantly freak you out. If you are lucky, you'll find a place where people wander in trying to sell you poems with lots of exclamation marks in them, or you have to occasionally deal with the escalating levels of transvestite intimacy. The places with alternating currents are the ones you want to be in, but nevertheless they do tend to produce a higher frequency of statistically unlikely yet inevitable situations and, when one happens to you, it is your duty, in whatever format, to pass that knowledge on to others."

"What about the Trent Reznor idea, aren't tranvestites lazy too?" asked some patchouli-wearing slob.

"Not at all. Try, if you are able, to imagine the amount of time you spend bathing and putting on clothes per day, and multiply by 30. How long does it take you to get ready?"

"Dude? I have no idea," the slob responded.

"Will someone get this guy a calculator?" I asked. "Is there anyone in this place who is decent at math?"

I wasn't confident. It's like asking if there's a doctor in the house when some poor schlub has a heart attack at a greasy spoon, not a likely occurrence. But luck won the evening and there was a calculator in the audience. After some average time calculations from the crowd we came up with a number of hours, let's just say it was more than one but less than two.

"Okay," I said, "that figure we just came up with regarding your monthly grooming and dressing? Imagine doing that every single evening before you go out, with makeup, crotch taping, size 13 high heels, and tights. So no, transvestites are not lazy, and thus cannot be dispatched by threatening them with extended, void-filling animalistic sex. May I please proceed?"

After what I considered a long enough period of silence, I continued, "So this transvestite, and like I said, when you meet your first you'll be totally into her, especially if she's been cheering for your Bowie tunes like some creepy dad at a Miley Cyrus twerkathon. So, you have to decide upon the levels of intimacy you're going to allow your latest fan."

"What was her name man?"

I sensed my cover was being blown, but the show must go on.

"Let's say, for argument's sake," I proposed, "her name is something clever, alluding to her double status such as Bridget. Get it?"

Silence.

"Bridge-It, like between the genders, creating a 'bridge.'"

"Oh yeah, of course," the crowd exclaimed collectively, seeming to no longer be so interested in the autobiographical versus hypothetical nature of my story.

"So if Bridget has been properly devoted to you on this karaoke evening, you will want to complement her on her clothing, just like you were taking her out to the prom.

This will precipitate an invitation to 'feel her boobs', which are indeed gigantic and beautiful looking. Remember, if she's a transvestite they will not be real boobs, so it's more like two truckers discussing mud flaps or something of that nature. Shop talk. Nevertheless, those boobs will feel magnificent, no matter what your persuasion, fake boob technology being where it is at the moment. But, like the proud owner of a Harley, Bridget will have not only purchased top of the line fake boobs, but 'tricked them out' with some additions of her own. Those rock hard nipples? Furniture stoppers glued inside out."

"Are you doing all this in the bar itself?" someone asked.

"Yes," I answered confidently. "Since they are fake boobs, it is within the realm of proper etiquette to inspect the boobs in the overhead lamp of day, so to speak. Indeed, the threshold of the bar itself is your best friend, and your greatest obstacle, for once you step outside, I guarantee you that Bridget will go into overdrive."

"So what do you do, how do you get out of the situation," straight karaoke fans asked, looking at me with pleading eyes.

"There's nothing you can do," I said. "I billed tonight as advice for statistically unlikely yet inevitable situations, not how you can always get out of these situations. Sometimes you just have to endure them. And in this case, you must endure."

"You mean you have to have sex with the guy?" asked the straight ones with their pleading eyes, some excited, some truly fearful.

"Well, I suppose you could. But since I began the situation assuming you were not into dudes, that will not happen. But you will have to endure some shit," I warned.

"Like what?"

"Like, you're going to have to behave like a gentleman and see some shit you don't want to see, hear some shit you don't want to hear. But you won't have to suck Bridget's dick, or let her suck yours, that is unless you want to."

I scanned the crowd to see if I thought they were ready. They were as ready as they were ever going to be.

"Having spent so much time dressing up for the evening, there is no way Bridget will allow you to slip out of the bar on the sly. She will be there until you leave or until last call, most likely those times will be one and the same. She'll be taking her pisses in an alley that gives her full view of the bar's entrance, so don't even think about avoiding the inevitable.

"As you exit the bar together, Bridget, wearing a tight skirt and size 13 fuck-me heels, will turn to you and say, 'Could you walk me to my car. There are so many homophobes.' Not wanting to feel homophobic yourself, you will agree. It is a long way to her car, which is not a car, but a truck. One that seems parked unnecessarily far from the establishment you have just left together. When you finally get to the truck, it will have its sun visor unfolded across the windshield in the middle of the night. Ask why she has a sun visor on her truck at nighttime and she'll give you a sufficiently ambiguous answer."

"Bridget will then mention the need to urinate, and the mere mention of the word will trigger the same need in you. Not wanting to appear homophobic, you will piss in the same general area, upon which you will be complimented on your penis, no matter how large or small it may be. If you are uncircumcised, Bridget will talk about how she loves uncircumcised men. If you're circumcised, you'll receive the reverse comment."

"Then things will start to happen very quickly. Bridget will pull up her skirt, revealing a thong and completely shaved ass-cheeks. You will parry off a request to receive a blowjob, to which Bridget will respond how good her blow jobs are, talking about how cum will be flying everywhere and how you won't believe what she'll be able to do with your balls and shaft - this part is a mere summary since it is impossible to do justice to the way Bridget, or transvestites more generally, speak 'dirty talk' with shamanistic prowess, able to produce in less than 60 seconds the amount of verbal filth you'd hear in an extended play gonzo-porn DVD. Having now sufficiently shown how un-homophobic you are, you'll politely decline her balls and shaft invitation. 'Okay, but next time we're totally going to have the nastiest sex,' Bridget will say, and you will say 'Yeah, we'll see about that,' in a half-flirtatious tone as you walk away from this statistically unlikely yet inevitable situation."

"And that's it, and it's over?" the crowd asked in almost perfect unison.

"Yes, that is it," I said, feeling like a sage, "except for the final statistically unlikely yet inevitable situation."

"The final topic I would like to address this evening is receiving a box in the mail, most likely UPS, and finding a penis quilt inside."

"A what?"

"A penis quilt is much like any other quilt, except, rather than more traditional Home and Garden type designs, it is covered with penises."

"This is never going to happen, can we just go home

now?" someone said.

"You have always been free to go," I answered, "but before you do, you might consider just how possible, if unlikely, such an event might be. Men, think about the bathroom stalls at the high schools and colleges you attended. Sure, there were some vaginas up there, but penises are much easier to draw and, for someone of average talent, the result is much more striking. Indeed, the artist Yayoi Kusama, the only individual we are sure 'got it on' with that reclusive maker of surrealist boxes Joseph Cornell, once constructed an entire sofa made out of penises. And we need not limit ourselves to contemporary or even profane art, for as Jewish art historian Leo Steinberg pointed out in *The Sexuality of Christ and Modern Oblivion*, despite many differences among artists and art schools when it came to depicting the baby Jesus in the Renaissance, one thing united them all, the *ostentatio genitalium* or prominent display of Christ's genitals, often to the visual and tactile delight of the Virgin herself or the Magi, who could thusly contemplate the mysteries of the incarnation. So if all of this can happen, someone might become inspired to construct a penis quilt and then send it to another person as a gift, most likely a male."

"Okay, but what's the big deal about a penis quilt. I suppose you could proudly display it or hide it or some of both, or get rid of it all together," said someone from the crowd smartly.

"It does seem like a fairly easy thing to deal with, at first glance, but once you have received a penis quilt in the mail and you lay your hands on it, it's like Midas touching gold. It's half curse and half blessing. Of all things a penis quilt might be, it is never simply benign or neutral."

"So what is 'good' about a penis quilt?"

"The same thing that is good about any quilt. Well for one thing, it's a big deal to give someone a quilt you have sewn by hand. A penis quilt is constructed in the same way that any other quilt is constructed - which means it is an art form that is also functional, like a 'real' penis - and was made with loving care. And you don't just have to dwell on the penises themselves either. Also look at the 'background' as opposed to the 'foreground' and realize that there is a bigger picture here, that substance/substrate etc. is as important as 'form'. Women, even if only ironically, are interested in flowers and plaid and other 'superficial designs' which, while superficial, make the penis quilt worthy of an extended meditation, as you recognize the penis quilt is an allegory of the relations between men and women.

"And, let me assure you, someone who quilts a penis quilt is not just going to send it to a stranger. So, when you do receive one, and you will, recognize how lucky you are to have the friends that you have, but especially the one who sends you a penis quilt. Most likely, you are a total freak who has some quality which matches some 'sensibility' of the freak who, despite all your abrasive freakiness, has stuck with you through 'thick' and 'thin'. The mystery of the penis quilt is the mystery of friendship itself."

"You freaking sentimentalist," someone screamed, "I thought this was a vaudeville show, not a romantic comedy."

"Philistines! Lovers of the boot in the face, those who cannot exist without a fascist oppressing them. You simultaneously rail against poverty *and* wealth, not being able to handle either. So I give them both to you wrapped up in a penis quilt!"

Wanting to drift back over from the Klaus Kinsky side of things, the actor Werner Herzog called "My best fiend," and cross the line back to Buster's way, I walked offstage momentarily and counted to ten, then came back on.

"Don't you see," I exclaimed, "how double-edged the penis quilt can be? For upon first viewing, and then caressing, the penis quilt that has been sent to you in the mail, your first instinct will be to compare your own member to those which are lovingly stitched upon the quilt. This instinct is one that, no matter how cool with your penis size you think you may be, you will not be able to overcome. So I implore you ladies in the audience who may have already caught the penis quilt bug to consider the ramifications of constructing and mailing such as that of which I speak."

"Does the same apply to penis quilts made with photo-shop?" asked a tech-savvy woman who had already caught the bug, and was now looking for a loophole.

"No," I countered forcefully, "a penis quilt sent over electronic mail will immediately be dismissed as a joke, like James Franco's nude paintings, in the style of Rubens and Matisse, of Seth Rogen. So if you are truly serious about sending a penis quilt, you must take the time to make them in the old-fashioned, 'meaty way,' or whatever they call the few non-digital artifacts still in existence. Now, back to the receivers of the quilt," I continued.

"Once 'the comparison' has begun, and it will be the comparison of all comparisons, it will send your 'head,' so to speak, spinning. You'll go to libraries, electronic or meat, and consider the history of philosophy's obsession with the question of 'reality' vs. 'representation' and all the competing views on how close or distant these two categories are. And, it should go without saying, only when your penis is fully erect should you indulge in the instinct to compare your own penis to that of the penises represented, more or less realistically, on the quilt. For it is a truism that, with the exception of Michelangelo in his *David* or Sistine Chapel, all artistic representations of penises throughout history have been performed as if the penis were in an engorged, or at the very least, a semi-engorged state."

"What else should we do?" all the men in the audience, who were suddenly interested, gasped.

"There is another, psychoanalytic, category," I responded, "known as fantasy, which you should begin studying as soon as you get home tonight and heavily believe in when comparing your unit to the penis quilt."

"Forget psychoanalysis, give us more art history!" they implored.

"Fully believe," I crowed. Though personally, I was uncertain as to what I should say as my talk was becoming increasingly Greek strophe and antistrophe in nature. I felt like Mark Antony explaining why I had castrated Caesar, and I was pulling dick knowledge out of my ass, to save my own. I had opened up a real bag of worms.

"Fully believe, despite what you have been told, that the producer of the quilt has in fact chosen the size of her penises to match the size of the square of the quilt, and for no other reason. For unlike, say, Japanese painting which uses blank space to full advantage, and more like, as Aristotle in his debates with Epicurus and Lucretius concerning atomism insisted, both nature and quilts, like a husband on his day off, abhor nothing in this universe more than a vacuum."

"What about contemporary physics," some thick rimmed nerd in the audience challenged.

"Are you more concerned with contemporary physics or maintaining some dignity with respect to the size of your penis," I advised. "Forget Heisenberg's 'Uncertainty Principle' when placing your penis in relation to the representations on the quilt, believe that you have 'empirically verified' that your penis is the same size as those sewn upon the quilt. *If* you know what is good for you."

"Some of us are more interested in truth than anything else, even if it means a diminishment in our penis size," the nerd replied, thrusting his finger in the air. What a dick. He must have been pretty well hung to continue this discourse after seeing what I had done to the vegetarian.

"I am not talking about a diminishment," I said, "I'm talking about nothing less than the smoking gun that will become a mushroom cloud completely obliterating your penis, or what Steinberg, mentioned earlier, described as 'modern oblivion.' And not only that. If you do not heed my words, not only will *your* penis be gone, but all others will remain intact. Indeed, they will multiply. You'll start to see penises everywhere - on the sidewalk, in ambiguous tattoos on people's arms, in bark patterns, stucco walls, you will even see snails that look like penises affixed to the stamps which ensure safe delivery of our snail mail."

"I thought snails represented vaginas," said a woman, obviously a psychology student, in the crowd.

"Nice try, Carla Jung," I sneered, "but you are wrong. The penis quilt, and not that prissy mandala twirler, determines all genital symbolism. As you yourself have proven, women are not *that* interested in penises. Because even on the penis quilt, at least half of the squares are devoted to things a 'devoted representationalist' might recognize as hourglasses - the woman's equivalent to the man's 'size of his penis' obsession, which would be the 'desired' hour-glass figure for which we can blame many things - the corset, or perhaps Jayne Mansfield, God rest her pretty head. Nevertheless, women, unlike men, have discovered many coping mechanisms to deal with this obsession which, ironically, usually turn the obsession into a real problem."

"But what about us," how can we cope, asked an emo twig-man.

"Well, there *are* two paths." I answered. "The first is the path of *Samsara*, which involves things such as penis exercises, pills, lying classes, 'self-help' books, and other such things."

A perceptive Buddhist in the audience replied, "But that is the unenlightened path. Surely there is another way."

"You are correct sir," I answered respectfully, "the only true way to avoid the double-edged sword of the penis quilt is to become completely detached from your own penis. Realize that all penises, whether made of flesh or cloth, are illusions, and therefore of no importance except inasmuch as all penises, and for that matter, all vaginas, are constantly expounding the *Dharma*."

"And how do we achieve such enlightenment?" everyone begged.

"BE MINDFUL!" I shouted, and walked offstage for effect.

Although I felt like I had placed the audience in a state of awe and wonder, before I could leave the backstage area, the manager of the vaudeville joint grabbed me by the shoulder and said, "Dude, that was a little heavy for vaudeville don't you think. Listen, you're always welcome to come back on open-mic night and do a short set, but I'm afraid I'm going to have to terminate your status as a member of my vaudeville retainer squad."

"But you're the one who encouraged me to do an 'advice-based' night!" I stage-whispered in exasperation.

"That is true. But you gave every single person out there a case of castration anxiety! Including me, and I'm pretty freaking hung," he insisted, thus proving he wasn't.

"*I* gave them a case of castration anxiety. Have you read a single word of Freud? I may have opened the Pandora's box on that situation, but I definitely did not dole out that slice."

The blank look on the proprietor's face let me know he was a fool, and I did not pity him. I just walked off into the night. I felt completely vindicated, except for one tiny nagging thought. Now that I had 'invented' this idea of giving advice to people on subjects that are 'statistically unlikely yet inevitable,' I wondered if it was a sort of self-fulfilling prophecy or, even worse, some sort of curse. Maybe I had created the Joseph Cornell box, or the Buster Keaton electric house, on such a 'category of experience,' opened it, and unleashed many more such situations, many if not all of which would happen to me.

"Performance" Art

Still I had not yet met the mysterious S. So I attended a few more open mic nights, but my experiences were dismal, as it was clear that the Oakland vaudeville scene was not ready for what I had to offer. Strangely, though they claimed to be vaudevillians, they wanted me to hold a mirror up to life, whereas what I wanted to do was more or less construct, in real time, a fun-house mirror that was blown and twisted and beaten and tilted this way and that. However, not having told the public (or myself) when or where the mirrors were one way or the other, I decided giving the crowd a short statement of poetics.

"I now 'declare' myself a fun-house mirror operator, one way or the other without 'justifying' myself," I intoned. "Everyone else lives in a world of self-justification and I too feel that world as closely as anyone else but I would have to say that I have, since a very young age, felt driven to the calling of fun-house mirror operator, which is no more or no less estimable than is any other calling. When you've heard the call, whether it be to preach the word of Jesus Christ or to murder others more or less systematically, it is not something you are able to analyze."

Apparently my audience had not felt the call, as they watched my brief acts with little or no interest or comprehension. I thought the act of telling "inside jokes" to people, like the one about my dad and the frijole hold, and then laughing hysterically as I explained why they were funny if you knew the right context, was a brilliant deconstruction of hipsterism. Plus, I got to relive a lot of jokes like going into my friends' dorm in college and, thanks to my own roommate's expertise in carving, switch their bar of soap with one carved into a penis with scrotum attached. "It was funny," I explained as I cackled, "because we left it there so that next time a person from the dorm washed their hands and absent-mindedly grabbed for the soap, they would discover that they were actually lathering up with a penis." I was always careful to never cross the line into pure self-indulgence, instead using confessional techniques as a means to aesthetic insight. Nevertheless the heckles still came, and I probably set myself up with the 'soap carved as a penis' bit when I was told, in no uncertain terms, "Get off the stage you self-absorbed prick!"

With impressions, I was quite Brechtian in nature at first with my "Russian doll" impressions, showing the audience how an impression could be broken down into content, target, context, syntax, tone of voice, gesture, and tick. I started small, doing an impression of the great German director Werner Herzog (target) narrating a documentary of *The Empire Strikes Back* (1980, Lucasfilm) as if it really happened (context). Now,

obviously in any impression, there will be syntax, tone
of voice, and gesture, but usually impressions collapse
these so that we have what I refer to as a "two-doll"
impression, so that in this case Herzog is not only the
target but also gets syntax, tone of voice, and tick – his
penchant for engaging in philosophical meditations at
unlikely times – with gesture being less important for
someone narrating a documentary scene. Then, voila!

"I wondered," Herzog would narrate over some
found footage of Luke and Yoda in the Dagobah System,
"if Luke Skywalker knew placing the blindfold over his
eyes would not lead him to inner sight, whether he
recognized it as an old Jedi trick, poised somewhere,
existentially speaking, between sensitivity to one's other
senses and something one might be forced to endure at a
carnival show? And if Luke knew this, would he find an
even deeper respect for Yoda, who brings a charlatan's
inventiveness to moments that seem like the ends of
dead branches, and if the trick which simulates the force
might indeed be the essence of the force itself?"

Now the six doll impression, of course, makes
separate use of each of the six elements, one inside the
other, and you must declare the impression in the order
in which Russian dolls themselves are unveiled: gesture,
tone of voice, syntax, target, context, and tick. So, for
instance, I once declared and performed - not that it was
appreciated - a rapper from the 1980s (arms and fingers
twisted inward, as if a victim of some unnamed palsy), in
the tone of voice of Joel Osteen (my favorite television
preacher, who speaks in a quiet soprano pianissimo as if
he's always gasping for air, as if breathing both the spirit
of Texas and the Lord Jesus Christ, via microphone, into

your ear), in the syntax of Yoda (as you can imagine, when juggling all six dolls at once, you want to cut yourself some slack in one or two of them, and Yoda is an obvious syntactical 'go-to'), with a target of Billy Bob Thornton, the context when he (in character as Karl Childers) is about to kill Dwight Yoakum in *Slingblade* (1996, Miramax Pictures). The tick will be Seth Rogen, who has a habit of narrating things that are happening to him or others as if he himself is watching the movie he is in, as in the famous quote from *Pineapple Express* (2008, Sony Pictures), "Oh shit!, your leg is sticking out through a hole in our front windshield."

Now, tone and gesture one must picture in the mind's eye and ear respectively, unless you are witnessing it. The rest, I will provide to you, dear reader: "Shit! This lawnmower blade through Dwight Yoakum's head, I have put. Hello, operator, an ambulance or hearse to the Wheatley place, I need."

There was one set of impressions which seemed quite successful, my "motionless impressions," which combined the inside joke with, well, lack of motion. Of course, to get them started, I began with a simple one, my legs flat on the floor, my torso raised forty-five degrees, my arms reaching straight out.

"Frankenstein doing a sit-up!" someone shouted excitedly.

So I adjusted to expose my canines, and they guessed Dracula correctly. But this made me realize that they wanted a context to go with the target of the impression. So, they were delighted to no end when I merely stood in front of a doorway for several minutes, and I told them I was Billy Bob Thornton from *Slingblade* forgetting to knock. Holding my hands up, like a begging dog, except with my fingers clawed out like someone with arthritis, my lips smashed backwards as if I had just sucked on a lemon. Impossible to guess. But when I said I was doing an impression of Harrison Ford, as frozen Han Solo, people were delighted. Sitting in a chair, my head turned backward and my mouth wide open - I was Meg Ryan faking an orgasm in *When Harry Met Sally* (1989, Columbia). I'm certain the popularity of these motionless impressions was akin to the "gondola into a gondola" puns in Keaton's films. For, when you are not moving, you are yourself and not yourself. Lord knows I look nothing like Meg Ryan, but I *was* Meg Ryan faking an orgasm. To people in the audience, however, I was just some dude sitting in a chair with his head back and his eyes wide open. I could have been any number of dudes trying to catch a grape in his mouth. It was the reveal that astounded people - an unrecognizable Meg Ryan suddenly transformed into Meg Ryan.

So I was finally getting some laughs, and though I couldn't tell if the audience was laughing with me or at me, it didn't really matter. Now that I had finally achieved some success at vaudeville, and doing so literally by not moving, I was reminded that I literally had achieved a stasis in my life - one in which S. would never reveal herself.

Reading back over her note, which I kept folded inside a locket around my neck, it was apparent, from the tone and content, that perhaps S. had moved on to another scene. But which one? There were so many. From the letter, it was obvious that she thought and wrote in poetic terms, and then it struck me that the name of the vaudeville club, Triptych, was eerily similar to the three card draw used at the tarot parlor I was fired from. She'd moved from those three cards to Triptych, and a triptych is a term from the art world. But there were so many art shows in the Bay Area, meeting S. on any given night would be like finding a needle in the right haystack from Monet's prodigious haystack series. It was obvious what I needed to do.

Cracks from the Crack

The next several days I felt right at home in the San Francisco Main Library with all the homeless folks trying to sleep with their eyes open and surf the internet for a maximum of 15 minutes if someone was waiting. The bathrooms were kind of disgusting, as they often doubled as shower rooms where my homeless brothers performed their monthly ablutions, plus the shit everywhere in various stalls from the crazy ones who flipped out during a bowel movement flashback. But I was used to that kind of thing from living with the 500 pounder who suffered borderline personality disorder, and I was also on a mission.

After several days of reading, I was pleasantly surprised to find that not only were bodily excretions of all kinds accepted on the contemporary art scene, they were, as they say in art, *de rigueur*. Before that, abstract expressionism had been *de rigueur* and I had read about this guy named John Cage who had once gone to an art show and complemented it by saying that it reminded him how interesting the cracks in sidewalk were. What if I reversed Cage's logic and combined it with my newfound art knowledge and a certain bodily excretion I had learned a lot about in my brief stint as a plumber?

So I bought a couple of wedding-sized disposable cameras and, taking a cue from the 500 pounder, proceeded to eat some spoiled meat so that I would be completely cleansed, unable, after the cleansing, to take a bowel movement (assuming I survived, which I did) for 6-8 days. On the fourth day, I began an all meat and baked bean diet and began planning my installation. For the next several weeks, all I did was take bowel movements in various locations and settings, creating what would eventually become *Cracks from the Crack: A Visual Narrative Allegory.*

Once I had enough pieces, I had no problem obtaining a solo exhibition in the SOMA Gallery District, given the timeliness of my topic. I went to the opening in disguise by shaving and bathing, which I hadn't done for a while, so that for the first half I could witness the mastery of my opus, framed and behind glass like real art, unmolested by my adoring fans. It began mysteriously, with a picture of a cat walking down an alley as if it had been startled from sleep, double exposed as if its soul was lingering just above the body. Then, viewers were confronted by the first bowel movement I had taken after the cleansing. That is, if they even recognized it as such. For it could have been several things, a catfish, a manatee - at any rate, some creature that lurks near the surface of questionable waters. Just as suddenly, you are transported to the desert, and depending on the perspective you assume (it being one of those duck/rabbit images), you are either staring down at the burnt carcass of a bird that has flown too close to the sun, or you are a tiny being confronted by an impassable mountain range with deadly crevasses on the left and impassably steep crags on the right. Overhead there is a dark cloud, signaling the only storm to come to the desert that year. A shoe-horn looms over the mountains, indicating in Brechtian fashion that you are confronting a shit storm. Just when you think you are about to be smothered, you find yourself flying above the top of the mountain range, like one of those old testament prophets who, rather than dying, was carried straight up into heaven. A foot, which is much smaller than the mountain range, is a Magritte-like pun reminding you not to "step in it." The orientalist diorama is swept away, revealing the artist's inspiration, a bathroom rug purchased in a flea market, because someone decided that when people are in a bathroom, some of them might want to imagine an Indian elephant bejeweled enough to seat the Buddha himself. It is an overhead shot, centered on an oval object called "Universal Rundle," something that had always fascinated me as a child because I was amazed that something I had never heard of, a "rundle," could be, in point of fact, universal. The phrase was tattooed upon every single domestic toilet I had ever encountered, and was my first clue that there may be more things on heaven and earth than Southern Baptist preachers discussed on Sundays. The shoe-horn was back, perspective revealing it to be more of a boot-horn, perhaps three-feet long, for I had taken it from the karaoke transvestite in payment for allowing her to give me a blow-job, which seemed to be her thing. Sometimes those kinky boots don't come off very easily. It was wedged under a gigantic mound of feces, as if some handyman at his wit's end were trying to pry it loose from the toilet. Indeed, it was a triptych with the shoe horn in the center, representing three approaches to abjection. The shoe-horn stood in for the "disenchanted, modern view" of the sacred, which is to pry it out of contemporary life as an impediment to utilitarianism. From my readings of Georges Bataille I had discovered the sacred could just as easily refer to blood, genitals, and excrement as it could the host in the Catholic mass. It was a controversial theory but one which, the instant I had come across it, made sense to me. I felt an *affinity* for the claims of this French librarian with the mug of a serial killer. The sacred, apparently, was unrelated to content, but was solely based upon proximity. Those things which were normally kept on the edge of town, a slaughterhouse for instance, or locked away in bathrooms, or hidden behind an iron church rail, all were candidates for 'the sacred.' The one thing they all had in common was an ability to provoke a simultaneous feeling of awe, revulsion, and fear in those who were not trained to deal with such objects. The utilitarian view was flanked on the left by the 'savage' view, symbolized by two runners on a trophy for a father-son road race, another product of those prodigious, almost magically prodigious, flea markets that seem to cling to coastal metropolises like barnacles to a ship. On the right was balanced the 'enlightened' view, a life sized head of the Buddha gazing tranquilly over the water, knowing that feces too expounded the dharma, where I had also placed a flower resembling the famed lotus. The interpretation of this triptych would seem obvious, but I had also read that even when dealing with the abject, when it comes to art, obviousness was not how to win the day. So the next frame erased all perspectives and brought the camera eye so close to the feces as to erase all those things attempting to frame it. And from that close, each wet curve seemed like a brown eyeball waiting to explode if you gazed for too long. Which, if any, of the three major approaches to the abject, could win the day under those circumstances?

To calm things down, I had a series of pastoral scenes in which the feces had folded in such a way as to look flower-like, an effect that was reinforced by long grasses and long waits for various animals, including a duck, to pass within the frame. Then, just as the mind grasps for meaning, I had a close-up of the hand reaching toward the 'flower' of literature leading to a photo series of allegorically-titled paperbacks. *The Last and Future World*, by James Montgomery Boice, is the sun on the cover setting or rising - it is hard to tell when it comes to the resonances of biblical prophecy, in which time is as spherical as the cover itself. *Through the Gates of Splendor*, by Elisabeth Elliot, chosen more for the resonance of its title even if the martyrdom of missionaries in Ecuador, for those in the know, created an air of gravitas that resonated throughout the installation. A National Geographic book, *Restless Oceans*, stands in stark contrast to the still waters of a perfectly cleaned toilet bowl. The book is opened to reveal a giant oil ship plowing through oceans as if it were diving in headfirst, dangerous white spray shooting up into the air - the sort of double-page, 17" by 11" photo which made National Geographic the gold standard when it comes to photography! A photograph of a photograph, an allegorical *mise en abyme*! Another National Geographic book, *Continents in Collision*, strides the toilet bowl in its entire pre-Internet splendor, completely covering everything but the Universal Rundle stamp, its cover photo of the swirling brown earth resonating with the next photo, as if in revelation, of a log that has, upon exit, stayed intact yet coiled around like a giant brown snake. Then another log, mostly intact, but splitting apart along various fault lines. Gazing into the photo you are struck with the instinctual fear of falling into the mouth of the earth itself, being swallowed in its brown, noxious depths. Another National Geographic book devoted solely to earthquakes, placed at an angle over part of the previous movement suggests, along with the cover of cobblestone streets torn to shreds, that you have barely survived a cataclysmic event.

Now, we are left with the question, is this world dominated by one or the other side of the Cartesian split. For a close-up of this same movement, which if any deserved artistic preservation, reveals that on one end, the mysteries of viscosity, the physics of flow, and gravity itself have produced an almost perfect model of the left and right hemispheres of the brain. For the *Battlefield of the Mind,* as Joyce Meyer puts it, can soon become a *Prescription for Disaster* as pharmaceutical and parent hating Thomas Moore writes in an attempt to distance himself from his namesake Thomas More. The next photo, another of the floral series, only wilted, suggests that we would be better served by discussing the Cartesian shit.

Oops! Wrong Party! Operation World Affliction! The American flag rises above it all - planted in a gigantic shit, Iwo Jima style. The dead bodies of plastic army men litter the sides of the mountain. Self-portrait, reason for disguise, scratching my head as if wondering what to do about the phantasmagoria I have created. A hand holding a blank tarot card, as mentioned in T.S. Eliot's *The Waste Land*. Red eyes and red face paint. Sacerdotal images. A bamboo spear raised in fury. Log demolished into a sea of brown liquid.

Calming down, a mixture of abstract expressionism and pop art. Logs covered in chili powder, squirts of mustard as if giant yellow slugs (in homage to the university in Santa Cruz whose mascot is the banana slug) were feeding. Topped with ranch dressing. Making the mustard look like little yellow ghosts running in terror. Another cat, the tidiest of animal shitters, looking at a remote control as if wishing he could turn it all off.

As I passed the last frame of this photo-essay stretching in a clockwise fashion around all four walls of the modest gallery, I found myself staring into the face of the most beautiful woman I had ever seen – short black hair with French-style bangs, a glittering silver and black dress revealing a dancer's body, cobwebbed stockings, an onyx pendant hanging between her breasts. She looked vaguely familiar though, and I hoped we weren't related.

"Hello," she said, "I'm S., and I think your shit is the bomb. Do you want to get out of here?"

I stepped into her ten year old Pontiac, revealing her elegant garb to be the production of a thrift-store magician, which made the butterflies I felt for her flap with the intensity of flying monkeys.

"Where are we going," I asked, and she replied "North Beach." I didn't ask any questions, but merely gazed at her in awe as she wove in and out of traffic like Buster fleeing from the cops, not missing a beat to refresh her lipstick, pull her Fast Trac pass from the pocket of the car and fiddle with an IPod she had plugged into the cigarette lighter. Once the music started playing, S. began spraying her neck and then her wrist with perfume. She stuck her arm towards me and I bent down to kiss her hand, which is what it seemed this goddess was, somehow, for some reason only known to gods and goddesses, allowing me to do.

I grabbed her wrist and, with my freshly shaven mouth, touched my lips to the palm of her hand which, while an ivory slice of divinity unto itself, harbored lines which were the only clue that she might be (other than perhaps her original letter to me, so full of a lifetime's erudition), slightly more mature in years than a ballerina first taking the lead role at some Wagnerian opera house in Berlin. In retrospect, I did think it odd that she didn't offer me the back of her hand, but I figured it was either a goddess move or a West Coast thing. S. slapped me playfully and said "No silly, I want you to smell my wrist." Ah, the perfume.

"What do you think," S. queried.

Somewhat lacking in perfumic vocabulary, like someone struck almost dumb I replied, "Uh, it smells good?"

I've always been somewhat immune to all but the strongest smells. Extreme sense of smell was always more my dad's God-given specialty, fortunate given his need to survive in the wilderness and all. And, up until this point I had always considered my olfactory disability a "no harm, no foul" sort of thing. On the one hand, it occasionally caused awkward social situations, as it seemed that others were able to detect the bacteria that cause body odor more readily than myself. I often had to cross that mysterious, often snake-like line known as "Western personal space" in order to figure out whether or not I was beginning to smell. I could often tell from people's facial expressions that they viewed me as a "space invader" and, frankly, as someone who smelled bad, but how else was I supposed to know when to hit the local fountain, watering hole, or public library restroom. On the other hand, whenever something did inevitably cross the threshold of my nasal myopia, which I found out in a Junior High encyclopedia was actually called "rhino-myelitis," it was inevitably something *incredibly* foul, along the lines of one of Nikolai's (my father's dog) prodigious and multi-daily fecal downloads. So I figured, then, and now, that all smells, including ones 'below the threshold,' were nothing but potential assaults upon my thankfully myelitic nose. It was probably a false extrapolation, but speaking of dogs, I had always sort of wished that I was one, at least nasally speaking. For, constantly musing upon my own rhino-baggage, I had observed these canine Lothario's for whom the desirability of a smell seemed completely unrelated to whether it was good or bad, but was solely based upon its intensity. Yeah, dogs would smell anything, but if it was something relatively uninteresting like a bush, they'd just lift their leg (if they were male) and piss on it. I'd always admired this leg lifting move, as combined with the pissing it seemed like a double-insult, something like an Italian mobster pissing on your dead body and giving it the old "non mi frega" or "chin-flick" at the same time.

Now if a dog found a rotting squirrel carcass on the road, he or she would piss on that too, but not until a gonzo-porn worthy 'roll in the gravel' with it.

"It's spikenard," S. said, awaking me from my nasal flashback, "the same oil Mary Magdalene used to anoint the feet of the prophet Jesus in your Christian faith. She performed the ritual with her long flowing hair." I was glad that this gave S. a chance to caress her short flowing hair.

"My Christian faith? I don't really have a faith any more, at least not in the traditional sense. If you had to put things in those terms, I guess you could say my 'prophet' would be Buster Keaton."

"Oh, please forgive my stereotypy," S. apologized, "I just assumed from your accent and skin tone, the fact that you live in the United States."

"Don't you live in the United States," I countered.

"Oh, yes, but I escaped its chauvinism long ago through a series of fortunate encounters, beginning with my time living on a commune in Alaska."

"Seems like a pretty tough place to commune," I replied, "at least for 8-10 months of the year."

"So this spikenard," S. continued, "this is the real deal, extracted straight from the petioles of dried lavender when I was visiting the Middle East on a spiritual journey."

"So, you're Jewish," I queried.

"No, I follow the Sufi path."

Before I had the chance to ask her how one could follow a path that was, I assumed, nowhere near the Bay Area, S. demanded, "What do you think of this music?"

I was about as knowledgeable about music as I was about smells in the ultra-violet range of rhino-myelitis. I wasn't tone deaf, at least as far as the opinions of transvestites at karaoke bars were concerned, had even sung in a band in college called "Cult of Bacchus" which helped me open up my scream registers. But I knew nothing about categorizing or analyzing the quality of music. Word and image. Word and image. Us cultural studies types were fairly helpless when it came to analyzing sounds, precisely because they didn't lend themselves to words and images, to the production of tenure winning essays and books. I remember as a young boy, with my mother trying to acculturate me via piano lessons. When it came to that part of learning the piano where the hands themselves had to play different things, as if hands had brains, I was through. An hour before my next lesson, I snuck over to my piano teacher's house (which was just around the corner) and raided her rock garden, writing "I QUIT" in giant letters made of pebbles arranged in a manner to be visible from space, filling up her entire driveway. It was my silent rejoinder to the cruel demand for sound.

Still, I didn't want to commit a second faux pas with my Sufi beauty, so I gave it my best shot. "Interesting approach," I began hesitantly, "I think that if a couple on their honeymoon were trying to cook a lavish dinner on the yacht purchased for them as a wedding present, and then suddenly a Nor'easter blew in and the pots and pans starting flying everywhere, and knives and forks started colliding with plates which consequently shattered against the floors and walls, and water starting spewing backwards out of the sink and toilet – if you tweaked those sounds slightly, arrange a pot-clang here and dish smash there at opportune moments, and turned the volume down about fifty times, it sounds kind of like that."

"This is the soundtrack to one of my favorite genre of movies," S. explained, "where someone, either via plane crash or an expedition gone awry, gets lost in the jungle, or a mountain range in either South America or Asia, is rescued by a shaman from a nearby indigenous tribe, and then comes to love that tribe. You like those movies?"

I was totally out of my element. As specific as S. was with respect to her definition of the genre, I couldn't be sure whether I had actually seen one of its representatives. It was almost as if the genre was too specific, and ornate as well, for me to keep all the elements in my mind at once. Sure, I'd seen some movies with some of those things. No doubt. But a film with all of them? It was like being asked to play the piano with both hands at once. I had certainly never heard a score like the one S. was playing, one which definitely put the *sound* in "soundtrack."

After thinking about it, I asked, "What if there was this butterfly hunter, and he was very dedicated to his craft, so much so that he chased this one butterfly so far he found himself captured by Indians."

"Native Americans," I was corrected.

"Native what? Oh right," jumping out of the 1920s long enough to regain my identity as a former Cultural Studies professor. "So yeah, I get captured by these Native Americans, and they think that *I* must be a shaman, and that there is magic in the butterfly, because the only other option would be that I was insane to expend so much effort trying to capture an animal with such negligible caloric value. Then some truly crazy white people come along and try to steal the Native Americans' land for oil, and I help scare those white people off by making them think I have the power to make Indians, can I just say Indians for now, I'm running out of breath. Anyway, I make the white people think I can 'direct' the tribe in a deadly dance with a mere tomahawk waved back and forth, Top of the Pops style. And I do this because not only do I try to right injustices when I deduce, usually incorrectly, that I'm not in too much danger of bodily harm, but also because I'm sort of sweet on a particular squaw from the tribe."

"I've never seen that one," S. conceded, "but I suppose it might qualify. What's it called?"

"Well," I admitted, "it doesn't exist as such. It's based on a real film called *The Paleface*, directed by Buster Keaton. But I changed a couple of details, made some psychological assumptions, left out some nonessential plotlines, to see if that's the sort of movie genre you were talking about. So I guess you could say it's partly Buster, and partly me."

"Here we are!" S. exclaimed, parallel parking in a space that seemed barely large enough for a clown car, much less a ten year old Pontiac. But with S. being a goddess and, me being a clown, perhaps we changed the time-space continuum just long enough to make it in with only twenty or thirty turns of the wheel.

When we got out of the car, S. said "Follow me!" as she strode down the street, making a couple of phone calls and texts as I tried to keep up with her vicious pace. I was able to stick on her though, and soon enough we were standing in front of a coffee shop called *La bohème*, me gasping for air and S. shuffling through her purse for the poem she wanted to read at their open mike night.

There were several types of poems read that night,

very few resembling the fare I had cut my teeth on in the *Norton Anthology of Postmodern Poetry*. Most of the poems just seemed like stories about what might happen to someone (not me of course) when walking around the city or through nature – only with slightly more flowery language. Then there were all these 'cocks and balls' spouting dude poets, and then a bunch of clitoral, labian lesbians. I figured the boys versus girls segregation when it came to genital mentionings must have been a West Coast thing. And then there was this guy who was pretty good at citing passages from Shakespeare. Why he felt the need to do so dressed as a swashbuckling, sword and cap gun shooting pirate was lost on me though.

The only poem that really mattered to me though was the one by S., called "S.", which she said was about "looking in a mirror," though not necessarily a literal one. That made me wonder if S. actually was in the audience, maybe in disguise, when I gave my statement of poetics at the Oakland Vaudeville coven, declaring myself not a realist but a "fun-house mirror operator." It was impossible to say, of course, and if S. had chosen not to reveal her presence to me then, she probably had a good reason not to reveal it now. At any rate, the mirror that "S." looked into, the hard copy of which S. refused to let me see, was phantasmagoric to say the least, if beautiful. She read slowly, right into the mike, emphasizing each line, like some strange mix of someone trained as both a rock singer and an old-school orator. But it was her eyes that spoke, eyes I thought were dark and endless but according to the poem were made of glass and floated on foam. Her eyes spoke of terrifying summers and unopened envelopes. Her dancers' arms gestured right through the wall of *La bohème* and straight through the titty bar next door, all the way from North Beach to North Africa and its "annihilated crevices" and rivers that somehow talked to boats, upside down obelisks, and exotic fruits I had heard of but could not, if I witnessed one committing a crime, positively identify for the police. It ended with the line, "How do you hurt me so perfectly," and I thought of the many times Buster's family was prosecuted for child abuse back in their Vaudeville heyday, since their act was widely known as the most 'violent' one in New York. I knew S. was referring to something else, but it seemed to contain a similar magic, the magic of the revelation—a young Buster, after an extended testimony from the prosecution about broken chairs and an 'innocent' child being thrown across the stage and used as a "human mop," would roll up his shirt sleeves and pants legs revealing, in fact, nothing at all. Not a single bruise.

On our way back to the car S. and I passed a Greek Orthodox Church. It looked sort of haunted, cracking paint and weeds climbing up the black metal fencing like the place hadn't been whacked in years. Nevertheless, apropos of nothing and despite the fact that it was 11 o'clock at night, S., still on a poetry high, said, "Let's go see if it's open!" Knowing that beautiful women, unlike me, are pretty good at talking their way out of trespassing situations, I let S. hop the two-footer herself and pull on the door which, of course, was locked. This didn't keep her from knocking on the door, however, as if there might be some priestly version of Mrs. Havisham waiting inside to lay down some Greek orthodoxy on us before breaking our hearts. On her way back, S. grabbed some of those unwhacked weeds and stuck them in my face, much like the clairvoyant Janet Devore had when I first moved to the barrio. "Eat the seeds on top," S. demanded, "as she took a handful herself." Like Adam to her Eve, I entrusted my gastronomy to her.

"I can't believe there is wild anise, which is native to the Mediterranean, growing in a Greek Orthodox churchyard. It's almost spooky," S. exclaimed, "What do you think?"

Trying not to giggle at the sound of the term 'wild anise,' I attempted to comprehend the flavor. But I couldn't come up with a word for what it tasted like. I flashed back to my head spinning as I urinated on the largest living organism in Niles, CA, then flashed to my theory of dogs enjoying smells not in terms of good or bad, but solely in terms of their intensity. And I realized I was having that dog experience I'd always fantasized about.

"It's the most intense 'wild edible' (my dad's shorthand) I've ever tasted."

"No, *this* is the most intense one you've ever tasted," and S. grabbed my face, kissing me fully and deeply on the lips, another experience so intense I can only describe it in Harlequin Romance terms. I felt completely ravaged, but in a good way.

Now, I know that, in describing the lead up to this kiss, I have stretched the reader's credibility a little bit, if not a lot, precisely because it seems the sort of lead up that only happens in movies. But as Buster prophesied in the projector's booth scene in *Sherlock Jr.*, we learn almost all of our behaviors – especially the important ones like making love to a man or woman – from the movies. Indeed, if *most* of your life doesn't, in retrospect, resemble a biologic film, I suggest you search the couch for whatever money you can scrounge and hit the cinema. When I was studying for my one man art show, I ran across a statement from the Surrealist poet Robert Desnos who said, "Admitted by cinema into an anxious and precipitate life, we shall no longer be satisfied with banal reality. During the intermission we will seek out the man or woman who will sweep us along in an adventure equal to cinema's twilight dream."

"Wow S., after touching your lips how could I ever forget the delicious mysteries of North Beach, of you."

S. gazed into my eyes and said, "You're such a darling, you tarot reading, feces photographing lug."

As we walked hand in hand to her Pontiac and clown-carred it out of the parking space, S. very matter of factly said, "I usually don't sleep with guys on the first date, and I think I'm going to stick to it. But I definitely want to see you again."

"Me too," I replied.

S. drove me to the nearest Caltrain station and said, "Listen, I'm attending what I think will be a seminal seminar tomorrow. It's only 300 dollars, and it's about how to balance your spiritual life and your work life. I think you'd get a lot out of it, given your budding art career. Would you like to go Dutch with me?"

"I'd love to," I responded without thinking where I would obtain 300 dollars. "Can I ask you something though?"

"Anything darling, we can and must be totally connected to one another, and that can only occur through complete sincerity."

"Don't get me wrong S., but 'S.' is more of an initial than a name. It is definitely one of the most beautiful letters of the alphabet, top twenty by anyone's ranking on any day of the week, but isn't it short for something else?"

"I used to have another name," S. replied mysteriously, "but I changed it to merely S., after Lacan's symbol for the ego in the state of constant becoming. Unlike Lacan, however, I do think the process has an end, but I have chosen to only rename myself when I have attained my spiritual goals."

Junkie Love

Fortunately, a nascent technology millionaire who dabbled in art collecting had bought the entire series of photographs anticipating their marked increase in valuation, which made me immensely happy as I felt that the eighty framed photographs only made sense as a series, and only desperation had ever made me even consider selling them piecemeal. S. had actually used her charms to help broker the deal without my knowledge. I could have felt betrayed by her pretending to be my agent, if that sort of thing bothered me, but I just felt lucky to have the most beautiful art agent in the Bay Area. Plus, I had one less aesthetic/ moral quandary to deal with and was more than able to go Dutch with S. to the seminal seminar. As we drove to Marin, she demanded silence. She said she wanted to get to know me first via my reactions to the seminar. I didn't mind, as cruising in her Pontiac sure beat jumping out of trees to ride the Caltrain, and the scenery to both my left and right was exquisite.

Dr. Svengali, who met my criteria for an expert by hailing from at least fifty miles away, began by insisting that it was only in the 18th-century, when the dissociation of sensibility occurred, that it ever occurred to people to separate "the spiritual" and "the career" into separate categories. In reality, they are inextricably intertwined, and this artificial separation, contrary to Karl Marx's theories of underpaid labor, was at the root of people's feeling of alienation in the workplace. "Indeed," Dr. Svengali proceeded, "you can be fulfilled in whatever job you happen to have landed in, if you incorporate certain daily breathing and stretching exercises and 'meditation moments' I will introduce to you briefly today, but which are complex enough that you will have to buy my book, which I will personally sign at the end of today's seminar, to understand them in full."

As we performed several of these exercises, I wondered how practical they would be for those who, for instance, did not have jobs. Or, what about those people who worked on jobs that involved "overseers," aka foremen, etc. Perhaps Svengali, rightly or wrongly, supposed that if you paid 300 dollars for his seminar, you were most likely yourself the overseer or at least had the luxury of repairing to a 'private office' in order to perform your exercises and meditations. Indeed, his comments did seem to be directed mostly to the need for these exercises and "positive thoughts" in relation to dealing with "underlings," whose laziness and lack of productivity can be really galling both personally and in the global marketplace.

I raised my quandaries not with Dr. Svengali, but with S. when we stopped in at a local Japanese tea shop afterwards.

She replied by citing a Persian poet from the 11th century, "Man does not have it in him / to desire things the like of which / have been prepared for him."

"That's a nice poem," I said, "Are you trying to suggest that today's situation was prepared for me, and that therefore I was bored because I do not have it in me to desire it? Because if that's what you're implying, then I'm sort of left off the balance sheet of wisdom."

"Yes," she replied somewhat over exuberantly, "so much for algorithms! Poo poo on the mathematical reductionists who, instead of accepting life's 'sloppy' uncertainty, improbability and unpredictability, set out to try to crack cosmological codes in order to control or pattern The Mystery! Yes to 'There is no solution because there is no problem.' And also to self-loathing Jews! No mercy for the cynics!"

S. drove me to her apartment across the Bay and, upon hearing that I actually lived in the Sarah Winchester Mystery house on a diet of whatever meat I could get my hands on, baked beans, and popcorn, had been transporting myself around by riding, not in, but on the tops of Caltrains and Bart cars, she insisted that I stay with her in her apartment in Burlingame for the night. The place looked like a dojo for meditation, with no furnishings in the living room for actually sitting down on. As part of the process of my aura dispersing peacefully throughout the apartment, I was to sleep in the meditation dojo under a ceremonial afghan (after learning how to use the water filter on her shower, which she had to show me how to use because the thought of having to filter the water that cleanses one in the shower had never occurred to me, who showered as seldom as possible, though I sensed this was about to change drastically). The dojo consisted of a gigantic prayer rug stretched across the entire floor of the room, but with the rug being so large (probably imported from a place where the rents were cheaper), she had to allow it to run up the sides of the walls several feet on each side. Other than that, there were all kinds of elaborately framed mirrors on the walls, orientalist pillows of various sizes, shapes and colors strewn about, and dressers with photos of Swamis on them, about half of whom sported Ghandi-style spectacles. I can't say that it put me in an especially meditative mood, but I was so tired from preparing my photography exhibition and the work-place meditation exercises from earlier that day that I fell right to sleep.

I was awakened unceremoniously - or perhaps I should say ceremoniously - to a cymbal crash and a subsequent "breakfast mantra" that sounded like people yodeling in middle-eastern accents.

"Rise and shine! as they say in your American South," said S. in a deep if playful tone, "it is time for us to do our weekly shopping and it is already 5:30."

"A.M." I queried?

"Of course, silly."

After a breakfast of pickled rutabagas and another filtered shower for each of us, S. determined that we had enough time for one of the lesser, 17 minute "physical sutras," and I was even more amazed by this new level of intimacy than by our Hollywood kiss. I had to keep my eyes closed but was able to feel, with her hands guiding mine, what I would guess was most of her body. I was even more amazed that I was able to last the whole 17 minutes, which was a new personal best for me. I attributed this to the carnal skills of S. as well as to the fact that she guided my every move. This no doubt prevented me from committing all the sexual 'miscues' I had in the past, which, however delightful my sensual dalliances were at the moment, I tended to pore over – always in vain - in subsequent days. After yet another filtered shower, we piled into her car and began what I can only refer to as the guru junkie's Bermuda Triangle. Of course, as a beautiful, unmarried white woman in her mid-30s living in the Bay Area, statistically S. would most likely *have* to be a guru junkie, and nothing that had occurred thus far had dissuaded my suspicions, even if I felt perhaps I had misjudged the type. Or maybe I didn't account for the fact that some guru junkies didn't fall so neatly into the descriptions my dad had read about in the book he was using to help me survive in California. For it is a truism that, when you write about people as 'types' rather than as individuals, there is almost always a certain xenophobia involved. Even, and especially, Cultural Studies falls into this trap, or springs it for itself, despite its claims about promoting 'difference.' Cultural Studies scholars often cite Roland Barthes as their patron saint. But how thin is the line between Barthes' great work *Mythologies*, written in the 1950s, where he could claim that the face of Greta Garbo – a real person albeit one seen more on film than in real life – was "a sort of Platonic Idea of the human creature" and the French *physiologies* of the 19th-century, those illustrated, pop-psychology books 'educating' newcomers to the city on such 'types' as "the Englishman in Paris," "the drinker," the "dockworker," the "prostitute," etc. Some of these people may have been recognizable at home, as individuals, but in urban life they became types, or needed to become types in order to calm people's nerves about the anonymous quality of urban/ contemporary life. Perhaps Alfred Lord Tennyson, the great English poet, recognized this tendency when he has Ulysses say in his eponymous poem, upon returning home from his travels, "I am become a [mere] name." But S. was not a name, but an initial leading, where?

So S. both was and was not a guru junkie, and beautiful enough to me that all I wanted to do was keep my head together and try to adapt, or at least "ride this train" for a while. And what else was I going to do, walk away from the situation, sleeping on the eternally chilly Burlingame bench whilst I waited the two hours for the first weekend Caltrain to arrive? I remembered what the artist Marcel Duchamp had observed in one of the library books I'd read in anticipation of my art show, "I always say yes to people when they ask me to do something because I find this the easiest way to get through life. If you say yes and do what they ask of you, the slate is clean. But if you say no, it actually places you in an uncomfortable state of debt to the person you said 'no' to." As with my encounters with Georges Bataille, I felt an *affinity* for his logic, even if I would not call it impeccable. So I fastened my seatbelt and readied myself for what was to come.

Little did I know that the guru Bermuda triangle (the original, though it connects three points - Miami, Bermuda, and Puerto Rico - has come to be known more as a metaphor for the mysterious waters, or any mysterious space, roughly 'inside' the triangle rather than the overly simplistic geometric name) would, first, be an actual triangle and second, take from sun-up to sundown to complete. Even at my most destitute, I had never spent so much effort obtaining food. Whole Foods (which was the worst I could imagine, given its prices) was out of the question. After all, with the many corporate cover-ups going on these days, you'd be better off, hormone and pesticide-wise, shopping at Safeway, even The Grocery Outlet. And don't even get her started on Trader Joes. In any event, S. showed me a printed map of our itinerary, which would begin in downtown San Francisco, where the microfarms were that emptied out pretty quickly. Getting there was fairly easy, about a 20 minute drive, but parking was prohibitive as usual and by the middle of the day (I would estimate 2-3 hours of 'finding parking' time – apparently the Sunday morning microfarms were far more overrun than Saturday night poetry readings occurring in roughly the same area), all we had were the beginnings of a simple salad. Given the pickled rutabaga breakfast, this did not at all please me, and I had to drop some serious deuces whilst S. was distracted, mostly in abandoned, construction site porta-potties.

Most of the time at the microfarms was spent discussing parking logistics and me agreeing with S. that, no matter how many greenhouses gases we put into the air - be it my methane or her old clunker - it was worth it to have, entering our own bodies, food that was completely free of toxins.

The microfarms in San Francisco were merely the Masonic eye in the middle of the gigantic dollar bill of California, whilst the Bermuda triangle was actually the Masonic pyramid on the back of that dollar connecting Santa Cruz, Sacramento, and Santa Rosa. This itinerary was necessary given the fact that, in our contemporary global economy, even organic farms are subject to economies of scale, meaning each farm usually specializes in only one or two products.

Since it was our first grocery date, we decided to go down to Santa Cruz via Highway 1 and not the 101, since it followed the coastline. With redwoods on the left, and the ocean on the right, we spent the two-hour drive talking about trees and water. That meant that, after hearing I had grown up as a Southern Baptist, S. felt the need to school me on the gnostic gospels, which were not located in the Bible (or "propagandistic suppression of maternal forces in the scriptures" as she called it) I grew up with.

S. intoned, "Jesus warns that the Kingdom of God is not a location outside of ourselves or a place one may dwell for eternity, after physical death, if one has lived according to the dictates of a stone tablet of writ - it is a psycho-spiritual state one experiences within oneself as part of creation: *The Kingdom is a state of self discovery. The Kingdom is inside of you and outside of you. When you come to know yourself, you will know that YOU are the Son of God . . . but if you do not learn this, you will live in poverty.'* How impoverished we truly are if we do not undertake the true knowledge and seek out where God is a living reality, each breath, each moment, in each and every interaction, in harmony with all creation, thus, the Creator: *'Split wood and I am there. Lift up the stone and you will find me there.'"*

I admitted to S. that this was indeed a new take on Christianity as I was raised to understand it.

Then she asked me, "How many spiritual paths

have you followed?"

That stumped me for a bit, but I figured she was asking me how many times I had been saved. The first time was when I was seven, which I did because all my friends started doing it and I felt like I was being left behind, spiritually speaking. I explained to her that according to my faith, one need only pray a single prayer to ask Jesus into your heart to be saved. She was amazed, like a mathematician, at the simplicity of the formula.

"But it's a two-edged sword," I continued. "Since we had been told, 'We believe that if you said that prayer in earnest, Jesus has entered your heart and saved you,' I wasn't certain if I was truly in earnest when I went up and got saved, since I was only seven, plus I was wondering if I had only done it because I was one of the last of my friends to do it. That quandary bothered me for a long time. I wanted to be saved, because hell sounded pretty bad from what I'd heard in sermons and on certain heavy metal albums I had snuck from my non-church friends, but I also did not want to embarrass myself by admitting to my parents that I had gone down the aisle in front of all the church and said those words without being completely sincere about it. So the next couple of times I got saved on television, thanks to the many televangelists who were thriving in those days. I figured that if I prayed the prayer with them, secretly, then I would still be saved, just at a later date than most people thought. But then I began learning about hypocrisy, and 'not hiding your candle under a bush,' and once again began to doubt my earnestness. Luckily, our church held several revivals in which preachers from out of town would come and offer us the opportunity to 'rededicate our lives' to Jesus and this seemed like a nice way of hedging my bets. Indeed, usually about half of the congregation would come to the altar to do this at the end of the revival, so I didn't stick out like a sore thumb. Looking back on it, I sort of realized this 'rededication' stuff was probably the Southern Baptist equivalent of a standing ovation, except they were kneeling at the altar so I guess you would call it a kneeling ovation. As I entered my early teens, I finally got around to reading the book upon which my beliefs were based, and there was this passage that said 'Faith without works is dead.' Since I was a kid, I wasn't really doing any works, at least none of the kind that were described in the Bible. I wasn't 'sharing my faith' or 'getting people to join the church.' It always struck me with a twinge of envy and doubt, noting that the kids who were popular in school seemed to have no problem getting people to come to church with them, usually their boyfriends or girlfriends. Lacking those skills and those items, I was forced to go hard-core and 'witness' door to door with my parents. That too was a psychic disaster, because at the same time I was going door to door to sell overpriced candles for the Junior High choral team we were in so that we could travel to Nashville and, wearing striped pants and bright red shirts, compete in a singing competition. I knew that no one who bought my candles (and they were in the minority) actually wanted them. That parallelism with 'selling Jesus' threw me into a sort of mental tailspin. Then, we read *The Importance of Being Earnest* in high school English class, and the entire basis of these years of self-doubt (including one perceived demon possession, which I was able to ward off using words I had learned in church and which most likely predisposed me to the suggestion of demon possession in the first place), earnestness, was itself called into question. By that time, I was done with all the self-torture and said several prayers of 'unsalvation' and 'blasphemy' which I had in turn learned from the Bible and the secret heavy metal records. The only problem was, our church had a 'once-saved always saved' doctrine and cited the story of the prodigal son as evidence, so I could never be sure if I had at one point, during those seven salvations, been sufficiently earnest to enter that 'safe-zone.' For all I know, I may still be saved, but even if there were a place I could go to check on this, I would be about as excited as going online to check my credit score. Some things you would just rather not know - you'd rather operate pretending they do not even exist."

"Sounds like someone needs to attend Sufi meditation with me tomorrow night," S. offered, patting me on the shoulder.

"That might be a good idea," I agreed.

By the time we got to Santa Cruz I was famished, and was able to sneak off for a quick hotdog on the boardwalk under the pretence of needing to "drop a deuce." In retrospect, I have changed my ways when it comes to breakfast before a date - now I eat pickled rutabagas like other guys horde condoms. Because if you drop your deuce early and in secret, you can always use it as an excuse to leave a date temporarily (whether it be for a hot dog or a shot of whiskey) in order to recoup yourself.

After S. had obtained some Pak Choi, Kale Slaw, and Orange Squash Blossoms, we were off to the next point of the triangle, Sacramento, a mere three hour drive if traffic held. This part of the trip was a bit less scenic, so I questioned S. on Sufism for a bit, which she discussed somewhat cryptically while munching on slaw and Choi with one hand and driving with the other.

For one thing, whenever she mentioned the word "love," which she did quite a bit, it seemed to mean either divine or earthly love, or some combination, but there was never any contextual clue for me to determine which love she was referring to at any given moment, no matter how clear the context may have seemed at first.

When I pointed this out to her, she said that her guru - at last she was using the actual term, though it seemed strangely out of place given the fact that it was a Hindi word, whereas Sufism came from what is now modern-day Iran, but I suppose it doesn't matter since we were in the Bermuda triangle. Anyway her guru said that we all have an unconscious spirit that allows love to move this way and that, on its own terms, that love itself was not something we produced but was more like the weather, something that passed through or over our bodies and minds (though such categories had no bearing when discussing something like love). Not only that, but there is a "structural unconscious" in language itself which makes the word "love" no more than a superstition compared to the higher reality to which it feebly points, and thus redundant to place in quotation marks, such as "love." This "structural unconscious," furthermore, is designed to polish the ego's rust and break our hearts because the love we want so badly is subject, in our world, to a "possibility of being severed from its referent or signified (and therefore from communication and its context) which makes of every mark of love, even if oral, a grapheme in general, that is, as we have seen, the nonpresent remaining of a differential mark cut off from its alleged 'production' or origin." Adding insult to injury, at least from my Busterian point of view, this law of love "will extend even to all 'experience' in general, if it is granted that there is no experience of pure presence, but only chains of differential love."

When I confessed to S. that, even though I had a Ph.D. in Cultural Studies I was having trouble understanding what she was talking about, she said with a smirk that there is no Ph.D. in love.

"Once," she began in more parabolic fashion, "wandering around North Beach at dawn, I found a yellow heart on the sidewalk, signed on the back by someone named, of course, 'Marc.' Marc had become nothing but a mark, and on the other side of the yellow heart he had remarked '#116 (not sure if that's right) . . . Let me not to the . . .' It turns out that Marc was indeed right, it is Shakespeare's sonnet 116 that reads, 'Let me not to the marriage of true minds / admit impediments.' So either Marc made a lucky guess, was being falsely modest about his literary abilities, is not good with numbers, or is not sure if it's right to believe in such things as 'the marriage of true minds.'

"Now you are wondering if that yellow heart, which like every letter can always not arrive at its destination, was dropped by Marc, perhaps from his trembling hand (the heart was yellow, after all, the color of friendship, not red, and cited the 'marriage of true minds' sonnet, although bodies in decay are discussed later on) on the way to his beloved, or if he tossed it to the ground in a gesture of futility, or if it made it to his love and she accidentally or, even worse, shamelessly dropped it to the ground.

"At the end of the sonnet, after affirming his love in all the ways that twelve lines can affirm it (though we must note that up until now Shakespeare has been speaking of love in the abstract, not about a particular love), the final two lines read: 'If this be error and upon me proved, / I never writ, nor no man ever loved.' So Shakespeare, like Marc, was not absolutely sure if he was right. But the great Sufi poets, unlike Marc and Shakespeare, do not see this condition as a state of confusion out of which one arises but as the very nature of love itself - and this is the type of love that they celebrate."

As we traveled along the outskirts of Sacramento, gleaning its "Soil Born" farms for Kiwi, Quince, and Sunflower Sprouts, I hoped that perhaps the Sufi guru would be a bit less cryptic about the tenets of their beliefs, but I wasn't counting on it.

The two hour trip from Sacramento to Santa Rosa was more memorable for its smells than its sights and sounds, especially around the aptly named Vacaville, but I must say the Bermuda triangle was completed in a fashion much more to my liking. For there was one aspect of Sufism that S. interpreted completely literally, that would be Rumi's references to wine, one of which she quoted me:

O incomparable Giver of life, cut reason loose at last!

Let it wander grey-eyed from vanity to vanity.

Shatter open my skull, pour in it the wine of madness!

And shatter our skulls we did. I'd never seen anything like S. after a couple of bottles of Santa Rosa's finest. We tore the place up, what little of it there is, eventually breaking into a local artist's collective, taking pictures of wire sculptures (their preferred medium) in every shape imaginable - though much to my cutting-edge pride I noticed a significant dearth of fecal sculptures. We fell asleep in each other's arms, nesting in a wire bird that was approximately five feet long. Not exactly the sort of nest suitable for a physical sutra, but that night her skin did make me dream that we had come together in a forest, embraced without a word, and melted together into a tree.

The next 'day' S. woke me up at four A.M. so that we could make the two hour drive to Burlingame before rush hour. As soon as we got there, she showed me her bicycle and gave me some traveling money and several instructions before she had to go to work at some data processing outfit and, most likely, practice some of Dr. Svengali's work/spirit combination exercises.

The first thing I had to do was get rid of her cat Pandora. Apparently she had recently learned that in the Nimatullahi order of Sufism cats were considered unclean. She felt kind of bad about it, and I had personally enjoyed having it curl up next to my head that first night, but S. insisted that if I took the cat far enough up the mountainside, where the really rich Burlingamers lived, dropped it off, rode my bike in a zig-zag pattern to prevent the cat from chasing me, then it would no doubt be picked up by some bleeding heart, millionaire suburbanites. I can't vouch for the latter part of the plan, but everything else went off without a hitch. Then I had to go to the local Goodwill and find some flowing white robes my size, as that is the only thing you are allowed to address the guru in. The only thing that seemed to fit the bill was a karate gi. Unfortunately whomever had donated it owned a black belt, so I also had to buy an entire Storm Trooper costume from *Star Wars* (1977, Lucasfilm) just to have the white utility belt that was standard issue. Then I had to get a haircut. Riding back and forth across lower Burlingame, I had noticed plenty of salons but no barber shops, so I just picked one next to the laundry mat where I needed to bleach the blood-stained gi. The guy seemed nice enough, and as it turns out, he was even a Buster Keaton fan, so I was feeling good when he went through the whole Houdini-esque backward and sideward mirror checks for me and I said, "How much do I owe you." The answer came back as 55 dollars. Now I've done plenty of dine and dashes in my day, always leaving a tip for the waitress if she's pretty as the owner chases me down the street, but this was my first ever haircut and dash, which was pretty harrowing given the salon's close quarters and stockpile of cutting instruments. I had to hide in the bushes for about an hour behind the next-door laundry mat before I felt safe enough to sneak back in for my improvised Nimatullahi outfit.

The Sufi "service," like the ditching of S.'s cat, also went off pretty much without a hitch. The only thing I would say was that I wish they had gone a little more mega-church style - I'd always loved watching those frustrated rock musicians and their praise music, with lyrics for everyone printed up on screens like a universal karaoke get together. Whenever I went to one with my parents I managed to embarrass them and everyone else nearby with my castrati-style rock and roll vocals. Unfortunately, this service merely opened with a prayer in either Arabic or Farsi, an hour of meditation, and then waiting in line to "consult" the guru. When it finally came time for my turn, the guru turned to me and asked, "Do you have any questions for me, my son?"

"Well," I paused, "do you think S. and I are compatible on a, um, spiritual level?"

"Who is this S. you speak of?" he queried.

"You know, the white chick with the bewitching eyes and dancer's body?"

The guru looked slowly up and down my karate gi and Storm Trooper utility belt, then said, "Ah, you mean Afshan, 'The Sprinkler.' Although I am obliged to verbally give hospitality to all questions brought by someone in earnest, in, er, proper Nimatuhalli garb, this I cannot answer. Guru/client privilege you understand. Because to answer your question, I would have to speak of her. So, my son, polish your ego's rust and come back next week with a question that shows you have no self-interest."

I spent the next day trying to destroy my ego, which wasn't too hard. Basically I just had to go over the details of my life. Over a dinner of Kiwi, Kale Slaw, and a Quince, Sunflower Sprout, Pak Choi, and Orange Squash Blossom stew (the second night in a row!), I told S. about how I had rode the rails to the local prison, gotten some rocks to break, failed miserably, and in doing so attempted to destroy my ego. She accused me of being a self-hating Sufi and said, "We'd better go to the Shaolin center tonight." Luckily, I still had my gi and utility belt.

The Shaolin center, where holism has been chopped up into whatever delectable bits fit one's guru junkie schedule. Thus, it was much more too my liking, as it had far less down time. Sure, there was meditation, both

Shaolin and Zen. But there were also fist forms, animal and drunken forms, the famous 18 Shaolin weapons, 8 pieces of brocade, change of sinews, soft fist bone marrow cleansing, etc. Oh, what was a poor Orientalist like myself to do! A little bit of everything was the answer. I went nuts at that place, like a kid in a violent candy store. Everything went fine until I accidentally chopped a couple of those round glowing piñatas they had hanging around all over the place. I guess flying Nine Section Whip was not something they appreciated newcomers trying out. Even though the fires were easily put out, I was also given the bum's rush and had to wait outside in the Mission District until S. had finished her sinew change, which wasn't too bad in retrospect because it allowed me to sneak some real food.

Concluding that I was, based upon the last two days, suffering from a not irreparable split between body and mind, S. decided that I needed to practice an improvisational interaction between the two, which is exactly what we did the next evening at an event called "Humility Swim." I asked S. if I should try to purchase some swim trunks at the local Goodwill but she said that my karate gi would work just fine. That's because "Humility Swim" is actually a form of dancing - or what they referred to as the art of Contact Improvisation. While I had gone too far in terms of humility of mind (trying to destroy my own ego), the Shaolin episode proved that I had absolutely no humility of body. Allegedly, totally letting yourself go and rolling over other people requires egolessness a.k.a humility of the body, plus it feels like swimming if you're doing it properly. But, for something improvisational, it sure seemed like there were a lot of unwritten rules. I wish they had a sexual harassment seminar beforehand, as it would have saved me some embarrassment. I was sure that people would be copping feels left and right, but apparently the traditional erogenous zones were totally off limits. I was told that I had sex organs all over my body, which was news to me, and that I should focus on those. Also, I was completely unprepared for the sorts of improvisation they were looking for. Like Buster, I've always considered improvisation something you do when you are in an extremely precarious situation usually involving life or death, so the thought of "choosing to improvise" with nothing to improvise against, didn't make any sense at all to me. Nevertheless I gave it my best shot, which was difficult as S. already had someone she "had good body chemistry" with, which made me kind of jealous, more Buster Keaton frame of improvisational mind than Humiliation Swim state. It wasn't too hard to find a partner though, as all the beautiful people, as usually happens at dances, seemed to pair up naturally. That just left a few of us. Still, I just wasn't good at it at all. The people I attempted to improvise with kept complaining about my Storm Trooper utility belt and how I was hitting the wrong pressure points and chakras. As a Humility Swimmer I was all washed up even before I had a chance to start a career.

"After all that egolessness and improvisation," S. said the next day at a Kurdish restaurant, "we really need to express ourselves. Let's go learn how to write! By the way, I wonder if I could get a job waitressing here, and get free food."

"But you already have a job that pays you sixty

thousand a year," I noted.

"Ah, that's barely enough to live on - do you want to know how much I've spent on food, gas, rent, and classes this week alone? It would definitely be a weekend job. I could make plenty of tips *and* get free food."

"I got a 55 dollar haircut this week, but was out of dough so I had to do a haircut and dash," I commiserated.

Not hearing the latter part of my sentence, S. exclaimed, "That's a pretty amazing deal. Is it somewhere here in town?"

I was not excited about attending our creative writing class, given the fact I had given up literary writing since the epic humiliation of my Epic Rawga's censorship way back in high school and the 'court assigned community service' number of hours I had spent writing the five hundred pages of *Unsuccessful Love Poems*, but S. assured me that she knew the perfect writing guru (she used the term so liberally) who could help us get our crazy children outside of ourselves.

S. pulled out her cell phone and showed me his resume, which looked pretty impressive if you don't know what a vanity press is, and S. did not. He'd even known a couple of people who had known some of the Beat poets. Plus, who was I to refuse the woman I was falling – no doubt there was a catapult lurking somewhere near us - in love with?

Having dealt with "satellite" instructors at Wellesley, I sort of knew what we were in for. Luckily it was not a poetry night but one reserved for "free writing." I could live with that.

The first half of the class was not unexpected, consisting of pitches for the many exotic locations (from Monterey Beach to the Bahamas) where the guru organized trips for the upwardly mobile convinced that, like in the movies, real writers went to cabins in the woods, or in this case hotels on the beach, to find real inspiration.

Then there was a short exposition of his methodology: "I am here to teach you that craft is pointless, and the only thing that matters when it comes to writing is accessing this thing inside all of us which I have come to know as the 'Crazy Child,' pictured here by my daughter as a geode with eyes on the cover of my book *Let the Crazy Child Write!*. If your penis size has ever been questioned, if you've ever been unceremoniously dumped by a used car salesman who seemed 'ripe for spiritual attainment,' your crazy child knows all about it, but you know nothing about your crazy child. That's what I'm here for, to 'guide you,' much like shamans guided their communities (and white plane crash victims or lost explorers who stumbled upon them) in jungles all over the world, in allowing your crazy child to write. But I'm also here to make sure that your crazy child does not get too out of hand. No one wants that. After all, your crazy child *is* crazy."

Then we got down to businesses, which was actually quite exhausting as he kept asking us questions we had to write down the answers to, constantly, for five minutes, elaborating on whatever first entered our head without lifting pen off of paper. And they were hard, bizarre questions, such as: 1) What animal do you most resemble? 2) What are the most contradictory elements of your personality? 3) What place you've never been most represents your psyche? 4) What work of literature do you exist in? 5) What song best describes your mood or state at this moment?

After this exhausting thirty minute exercise (like athletes, we got one minute of rest between writing sprints), the dude went around the room asking us to read our answers to various questions. When he finally got to me, he asked the worst (or best) question possible, "And what animal do *you* most resemble?"

"The animal I most resemble," I began hesitantly, "besides myself, as humans are animals too, is a possum. Most of the time you won't see me, but I look and am demonic, I'll be running across a ledge and we'll encounter each other, make eye contact, my eyes are beady and my snout definitely looks like the devil. I'll look mesmerized by you but you'll be the one who is mesmerized, as my interest is solely penetrating souls, for I am legion and do their bidding. You will want to run away, but can't, because you're in a real dream, running up that hill but not running. You'll be filled with unspeakable desires, to eat me, to fuck me, watch me freeze. If you see me dying in the street in the snow on the way to church, and I'm dead when you've returned home from church and it has been below freezing the whole time, you will pick me up, skin me and eat me, then tan my hide and make a possum skin hat just to prove to your family that it can be done."

After a few moments of silence, the satellite teacher said, "I'm afraid your crazy child has become an *enfant terrible*, and there is nothing I can do for you, the reasons for which I discuss in the appendix in my book. Please leave the class now and do not darken this threshold again."

I gravely, yet with joy in my heart, walked out the door, and as I did the satellite man actually had the gall to ask if I wanted to purchase a copy of his book.

"No thank you," I said politely, "for it provides me with no hope."

"But you might have some friends who might like it," he pleaded.

"I have no friends," I fired back.

Even though I had to wait for S. to finish the class, I was satisfied to walk the Berkeley campus unmolested. As open-minded as gurus are, or claim to be, they abhor *enfants terribles* like nature, and husbands on their day off, abhors a vacuum. If you let your *enfant terrible* loose, you will be out of that guru's class and on your ass quicker than a Shaolin master's oscillations between internal and external systems of expression. Of course S. would not let me hear the end of it as we drove home, asking me whether or not I considered her a friend, if I really felt demonic forces inside me. I said that I didn't, but she of course replied, "Your denial proves that you do."

"Well," she said, "if you want to live inside a Hieronymous Bosch painting, I can make that happen."

All's Well That Ends Poorly

At the Foundry, in a warehouse somewhere in deep Oakland (S. insisted I wear a blindfold as we drove there), it turns out that Bosch painting did exist. We entered a place where the sign above was slightly more encouraging than Auschwitz's "Work Will Set You Free." Tonight's three dimensional garden of earthly delights was entitled "Grind, Press, Burn: An Evening with Café Nëgrø."

It turned out to be an evening dedicated to all things black for the context-deprived tweaker crowd. Black coffee, black metal, and soul food were the night's offerings. Not being a fan of racism, but a raging fan of Swedish black metal, I was instantly offended. Not surprisingly, they had managed to throw a performance art party in Oakland without a single black person in attendance. I instantly wished I weren't there, in this self-described place that had all the comforts of Burningman's most brutal black metal camp, brought to us without the dust or the epic journey to the desert! And what can I say about the food? Chicken and Waffle Tacos? Homemade Dognuts? - doughnut wrapped hot dogs - a supersecret recipe, described as 'the best thing on the playa' by many a fan) - and what, no watermelon? All this for just a $10-$20 donation at the door.

A wretched band called The Cosmonaughties had obviously spent about a week trying to master the Wagnerian riffs at machine-gun speed of Mercyful Fate, Mayhem, Babylon Whores, and others. And then there were their outfits, which were straight out of a minstrel show, blackface and all. A "mulatto wench" slapped the bass guitar with the fury of someone whose mother had been raped by a plantation owner. On rhythm guitar was the old darky. A slave, complete with chains, pounded away at the drum kit. On lead guitar and vocals, of course, was mammy. This is saying quite a bit, but I truly could not tell if I was more offended by the antebellum outfits or the butchering of music meant to be played by the descendants of Vikings, not the irony-infused bastards of Vaudeville's heyday.

At the end of the first (the first!) set, the mammy screamed out triumphantly: "Thank you, thank you kind sirs and madams! We are The Cosmonaughties! We degauss your spirit with heavy metal and serve cold-brew coffee to the starveling, demyelinated, aporetic wretches of Burning Man. Shouldering our way onto the playa amidst drunken dubmongers and spendthrift sparkleponies, we hold our head up and do justice!"

The lights hit black for about a minute, only to reveal S., completely nude, doing a solo humility swim with Shaolin accents. I had not yet seen her naked (during our seventeen minute physical sutra, as you'll recall, I was asked to keep my eyes closed, and I actually did out of respect!) No, I was not allowed to see her naked, that is until she was "rescued" as avant-garde by having Kenneth Anger dong films all over her body. That didn't bother me so much as the fact that it was the masturbator of ceremonies doing all of the projection work, as if he were slapping her with the cinema in some mixture of gonzo-porn and real life. It made me think about him slapping her with his own semi-erect dong, which I was now certain he had done at least once, if not many times. How could she allow herself to be debased so? Not only by dancing in an event with such a racist and technically-disastrous rendition of 'black' metal, but in this particular act, this humiliation swim? I barely recognized her even as I started to develop a chubby myself.

In the corners of the stage I saw several dudes, lurkers, pads out, sketching furiously what they saw like the closing seconds of a circle-jerk. I recalled the art books I'd read in preparation for *Cracks from the Crack: A Visual Narrative Allegory*: "the human form [always female], especially in an artistic sense, is inherently intricate and beautiful." Then, in the midst of everything, I remembered as a kid taking an art class at the top of a mountain and we were asked to crumble up a piece of paper and then draw that piece of crumpled paper instead of drawing, for instance, the mountains we lived amongst. Of course, I would not want to marry or even go out on a date with a crumpled up piece of paper unless something cryptic were written on it, or a vagina was drawn on it - then I could drive around divining its meaning or nonmeaning. After, of course, appreciating its surface, much like we do with people.

On the way home I kept hounding S. as to why, although she was so willing to display her naked body to all-comers was nevertheless so reticent about showing it to me in private. She demurely replied that she did not have to explain her art to me, as its meaning was completely transparent, and promised me a leisurely day tomorrow, Saturday, exactly eight days after our relationship had begun.

In my dreams that night, under the sacred afghan sans Pandora, I imagined our leisurely Saturday. First, no earlier than 10 AM, she would come and take me on her dojo prayer rug, eyes open. Then we'd go out for breakfast at a greasy spoon that could serve up enough pancakes for a marathoner who was carbo-loading. Returning to her house, she'd ask me into her room, ask me to treat her like a slut, a beautiful angelic slut but nevertheless. After a couple of rounds, both exhausted, we'd watch some Buster Keaton movies which she had no idea I was so in love with but which she should have guessed given the way I'd conducted myself that week.

Imagine my surprise - not really - when a leisurely Saturday for S. involved waking up at 6 AM rather than 5:30, so that we could make the hour drive for a "half-day sitting" at the Green Gulch Zen Meditation Center. It was a beautiful drive, I'll admit, curvy as it was. I didn't even mind parking a mile away from the center and walking past the fields of cabbage and other things being grown. There were some speckled horses too, which S. showed me how to feed without getting my fingers bitten off. After the sitting, we walked over the top of the headlands toward Muir Beach, and S. asked to walk ahead of me for a while so she could think. All the horrific images of the previous night seemed to vanish as she got far enough away to become an exquisite silhouette.

When S. finally returned to me she held me by the hands and said, "Listen, I don't think we're on the same spiritual pathways. I think it's time for us to go our separate ways and look back on this week for what it was."

I wrenched my hands out of hers and turned around for a second. At first I felt like I wanted to vomit. Then, on an intellectual level if not an emotional one, I realized how lucky I was. S. was indeed that crumbled piece of paper I had drawn on the mountaintop, only she was smooth and beautiful on the surface. Below the surface she was a guru junkie, but one as labyrinthine and complex as a crumbled piece of paper with secret traces of poems inside.

I think S. wanted me to cry, but I turned around and instead presented her with my stone face, my tragic mask, whatever you want to call it, and just nodded. As we headed back to the car, I told her to go on without me, that I'd read this thing on one of the bulletin boards where you could work in the cabbage and sunflower fields in exchange for room and board. This time it was her turn to nod, and that was the last time I ever saw S.

I had figured that some good hard labor would help me get my mind off of her, and that was definitely true, especially with the monks interrupting me constantly to show how I was plowing incorrectly, scattering seeds with seeming disregard for what I had plowed, and overfeeding the horses apples with my newfound horse-feeding skills. Meals were wonderful too, and I learned much about Zen philosophy. But the meditation was killer, as that was when thoughts of S. kept returning. This blankness of mind they talked about, I just couldn't achieve it. Plus I hadn't taken a solid shit since I'd met her, and the Buddhist diet was no help in that matter either. After a week I walked up to the curvy road and hitched a ride back to town. "Where you headed," the couple asked. "North Beach," I said, "or thereabouts."

I stopped by several used book stores, and found a copy of Buster's *My Wonderful World of Slapstick*. I scoped out an alley to urinate in, and then wandered down into the mists of North Beach to read and meditate. After an hour or so I came across a passage which I had first read as purely bodily advice, but it seemed to resonate so much more broadly now: "If I never broke a bone it is because I always avoided taking the impact of a fall on the back of my head, the base of my spine, on my elbows or knees. That's how bones are broken. You also bruise only if you do not know as I do which muscles to tighten, which ones to relax." Now that, my friends, is some advice for the ages.

Epilogue: Steamboat Coda

Steamboat Bill, Jr. (1928 Joseph M. Schenck)

The Stonewall Jackson, a decrepit boat owned by his father, is used by Buster during a tornado to ram a prison that has slid into the river, a prison which just happens to contain Buster's dad, who has wrongly been jailed by the Donald Trump of the town. Thus, a Stonewall has been transformed into a stone wall. This single instance of a thing transforming into itself while splitting in half is Keaton's homage to the fact that he is leaving the world of independent productions and taking up contract work with MGM, thus ending Keaton's filmic odyssey, a *tour de force* in philosophical refutation (of Karl Abel), one that took a mere 9 years to complete. As for the love catapult, as I have said in various ways, even Keaton's films can only gesture in the direction of building a working love catapult.

ALSO FROM **ALAN RAMON CLINTON**

Poetry from Alan

Horatio Alger's Keys
Blaze Vox

Horatio Alger's Keys is set in Boston as well as in the private dream and nightmare worlds of its protagonists, all of whom have a relation to a ghostly Horatio Alger who takes on personae variously of a schizophrenic jailor handing out keys with the whim of a Greek god, a fragile cat swinging an empty purse, a woman with multiple sclerosis, and a disintegrating trail of pills and voices that want nothing more than the erasure of memory. The work finds unity if not solace in the thought that each of the poem's entities, wittingly or unwittingly, is a devoted seeker of lunar presences.

Criticism from Alan

Mechanical Occult
Peter Lang International Academic Publishers

Parabilities
Palgrave MacMillan

ALSO FROM **ALAN RAMON CLINTON**

Necropsy in E Minor
Open Books Publishing

Necropsy in E Minor, *shortlisted for the Dundee International Book Prize, is the tale of a young college professor who sits down to write what he calls a "memoir," but which really only records the past six months of his life (with numerous digressions), and ends, with the last line, after a richly devastating encounter, at the moment of writing.*

Curtain Call:
A Metaphorical Memoir
Open Books Publishing

Stalking academia, re-ordering double prints and maniacally rewriting biographies of various personae, Clinton's hapless, sophomoric, yet highly intellectual narrator offers his poignant and very, very funny insights on modern-day culture in a series of literary misadventures.

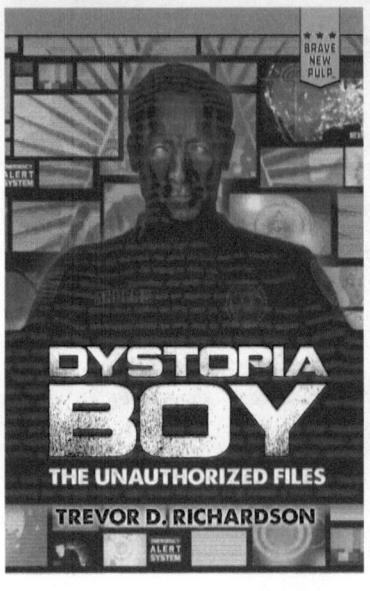